"Urban fantasy with a w... uinely fun book with a fresh take on the idea of paranormal police. I'm looking forward to seeing what Strout does next."
—Kelly McCullough, author of *WebMage* and *Cybermancy*

Drop-Dead Gorgeous

Although Connor didn't show any signs of psychometric power himself, he was the perfect instructor for someone like me who already possessed it.

"You never get even the tiniest of visions like these?" I asked. "No flashes, glimpses, maybe something you might have labeled as déjà vu?"

Connor shook his head. "Nothing. I guess it's not in my area of expertise."

"So you've only got the one, then?"

"One what?" Connor said, confused.

"Area of expertise," I said.

Connor nodded. "That I'm aware of. In fact, you're sitting across from it."

"Huh?"

Connor leaned in and whispered, "Across from you. The brunette." He gestured toward the woman sitting on the couch next to his chair.

I tried to appear casual as I glanced her way and found myself staring at the fetching woman I had made eye contact with earlier.

Outside of her natural beauty, I saw nothing particularly out of the ordinary. Great skin, smartly dressed. I judged her to be in her late twenties. I leaned across the table toward Connor.

"Women are your expertise?" I whispered. "What about her?"

"Oh," Connor said matter-of-factly, picking up his iced coffee and taking a lengthy sip, "she's dead."

DEAD TO ME

Anton Strout

ACE BOOKS, NEW YORK

THE BERKLEY PUBLISHING GROUP
Published by the Penguin Group
Penguin Group (USA) Inc.
375 Hudson Street, New York, New York 10014, USA
Penguin Group (Canada), 90 Eglinton Avenue East, Suite 700, Toronto, Ontario M4P 2Y3, Canada
(a division of Pearson Penguin Canada Inc.)
Penguin Books Ltd., 80 Strand, London WC2R 0RL, England
Penguin Group Ireland, 25 St. Stephen's Green, Dublin 2, Ireland (a division of Penguin Books Ltd.)
Penguin Group (Australia), 250 Camberwell Road, Camberwell, Victoria 3124, Australia
(a division of Pearson Australia Group Pty. Ltd.)
Penguin Books India Pvt. Ltd., 11 Community Centre, Panchsheel Park, New Delhi—110 017, India
Penguin Group (NZ), 67 Apollo Drive, Rosedale, North Shore 0632, New Zealand
(a division of Pearson New Zealand Ltd.)
Penguin Books (South Africa) (Pty.) Ltd., 24 Sturdee Avenue, Rosebank, Johannesburg 2196,
South Africa

Penguin Books Ltd., Registered Offices: 80 Strand, London WC2R 0RL, England

This is a work of fiction. Names, characters, places, and incidents either are the product of the author's imagination or are used fictitiously, and any resemblance to actual persons, living or dead, business establishments, events, or locales is entirely coincidental. The publisher does not have any control over and does not assume any responsibility for author or third-party websites or their content.

DEAD TO ME

An Ace Book / published by arrangement with the author

PRINTING HISTORY
Ace mass-market edition / March 2008

Copyright © 2008 by Anton Strout.
Cover art by Don Sipley.
Cover design by Annette Fiore.
Interior text design by Laura K. Corless.

ISBN: 978-0-441-01578-8

ACE
Ace Books are published by The Berkley Publishing Group,
a division of Penguin Group (USA) Inc.,
375 Hudson Street, New York, New York 10014.
ACE and the "A" design are trademarks belonging to Penguin Group (USA) Inc.

PRINTED IN THE UNITED STATES OF AMERICA

10 9 8 7 6 5 4 3 2 1

To the mystical and elusive Orlycorn,
a rare creature that possesses the power
to make all things possible

ACKNOWLEDGMENTS

Nature abhors a vacuum, and apparently so does an acknowledgments page.

First and foremost, I must thank the other Dorks of the Round Table, authors Jeanine Cummins and Carolyn Turgeon, without whom I never would have written much of anything; my editor, Jessica Wade—your red pen is swift but just; copyeditor Joan Matthews, for making my words seem all the more polished; Montana Wojczuk, Daniel Schermele, and my agent, Kristine Dahl, over at ICM; author Jennifer Belle, queen bee of the "world's worst" workshop, and the rest of my fellow workshoppers.

I may write the words, but that is only one of many integral steps. To every department at Penguin Group (USA) Inc., for every last thing you do to make a book like this happen, but especially Norman Lidofsky and the paperback sales force.

To all my friends, family, and colleagues for their support: Susan Allison, Bonnie, Dustin, and Elyse Clark, Ginjer Buchanan, Hank Cochrane, Christine Cody, Laura Corless, Sharon Gamboa, Leslie Gelbman, Michelle Kasper, Patrick Nolan, Don Redpath, Don Rieck, Lisa Pannek, Gary and Jean Strout, Jeremy Tescher, Clan Trieber, Edna and Raymond Van Valkenburg, Trish Weyenberg, Michael Yarmark, and finally Annette Fiore, Judith Murello, and artist Don Sipley, for an amazing cover that I couldn't be happier with. If I've forgotten any of you, don't worry . . . I need to save some thanks for the sequel anyway.

And last but not least, to you, the reader. Without your bloodshot eyes poring over these words, this book would only exist in my mind. Writing it was only half the journey; sharing it is the other.

There is no question
that there is an unseen world.
The problem is how far is it from midtown
and how late is it open?

—Woody Allen

1

I managed to get out a quick "Tamara, wait . . ." before I felt the interior doorknob of my SoHo apartment jab into the small of my back. Tamara ground against me like she was trying to make her body occupy the same space as mine—and I certainly wasn't complaining. Our mouths locked, the sweet taste of whatever umbrellaed concoction she'd been drinking mixing with the Corona flavor of mine. It was a surprisingly good combination.

"Simon, shhh . . ." she whispered, pushing me even farther into the apartment. She fell toward me with a sudden "Ow!" It was dark, but I could still see her hopping about on one leg. She had been trying to strip off my brown suede coat and the GABBA GABBA HEY Ramones T-shirt I was wearing, but now she clutched her knee.

"You okay?" I asked, finding the switch from horn-dog to concerned a difficult one to make.

"Yeah," she said, and hissed out a long, slow sigh of pain. "What did I hit?"

"Just a packing crate," I said, reaching out and steadying

her. I contemplated turning on the lights to check on her, but hesitated, debating whether or not the other two dozen packing crates around my living room might scare her off. It wasn't that I was a slob, but given my workload at the Department of Extraordinary Affairs, my personal antiques acquisitions had become backlogged. They were spread out across my dangerously darkened living room like little landmines from the Ghost of Bruises Yet to Come.

Luckily, a little knee pain wasn't enough to stop Tamara. We resumed our lip lock while I weaved us safely past the labyrinth of crates and down the hall to my bedroom. If she was still hurt, she hid it well. I guessed that the promise of sexual healing was helping her tough through any damage to her knee.

Thankfully the last part of the journey toward my bedroom went without incident. The edge of the bed hit the backs of my calves, bending me at the knees, and I fell back onto it as Tamara threw herself on top of me.

Ever since I'd accidentally knocked over her drink at Eccentric Circles three weeks ago, our encounters had consisted of one sexually charged (but unfulfilled) moment after another. But not tonight. Tamara straddled me, her hotness lit only by the moonlight coming in through the window. The smell of cinnamon rose off her, swirling around in my head, and under her jacket her tight little black dress— the one that every other woman in New York City seemed to own—clung to her like a second skin. I was in heaven.

Not that things stayed heavenly for long. Around me, things rarely did. As Tamara finished struggling out of her coat, she threw it to the side. Her cell phone slipped free from it, hit the mattress, and rolled to rest against my arm. No big deal for most people, but with my preternatural powers, that was all it took to ruin things.

It's called psychometry—the ability to divine information about people or events solely by touching personal objects.

As Wonder-Twin-powers cool as that might sound, it wasn't. I tended to end up knowing more than I should about a person . . . or wanted to.

I started thrashing around underneath Tamara, desperate to avoid what I knew was coming. She seemed oblivious to my escape attempts, and when I tried to sit up, she pushed me playfully back down. With an evil grin, she pinned my shoulders to the bed before attacking me with a barrage of kisses. My last thought as the electric pulse of my power kicked in was *Oh shit*.

Once under the influence of a rush of psychometric power, I had very little control, especially when it took me by surprise. Without my emotions in check, the power latched on to the sexual energy between the two of us and buffeted me with a flood of details from Tamara's past.

It was full Technicolor glory in my mind as I was struck by the psychic vision of Tamara's firm, naked form. It stung all the more since I'd been mere seconds away from experiencing the real thing for myself. Instead I was forced to watch her getting it on with another guy—a goatee-sporting, muscle-bound blond who was, of course, infinitely more attractive than me. Tamara wore nothing but enough red, gold, and green beads around her neck to make Mr. T jealous.

Mardi Gras. It *had* to be.

The beads swayed hypnotically, rhythmically—*shink shink shink*—as the two of them pawed at each other like cats in heat. I wanted to turn away, but in the vision I was incapable of doing so. One moment I was watching the guy's well-muscled chest as he thrust his body against hers. The next brought Tamara's face into focus, her eyes shut tight and her curly brown hair loose around her shoulders as this stranger enjoyed things I had hoped to be doing myself this very evening. And the beads *shinked* on . . .

What the vision showed me was something deeply private from Tamara's life. I was someplace I shouldn't be, feeling every touch, hearing every sound of her and some guy from her past bumping uglies . . . it was enough to drive me mad. With every Mardi Gras–fueled gyration, gouging my eyes out started to seem like a better idea. Not that it would have blocked the visions.

Flashes of reality slowly began to slip back to me. Tamara was still oblivious to the private mental hell I was experiencing while pinned underneath her. Her lips were now clamped down on my neck like a vacuum hose and her hands were busy tugging up my shirt. All of these were things I would ordinarily have been thrilled to experience— but I couldn't enjoy them. The images of Tamara's own private *Girls Gone Wild* moment had become a permanent scar in my brain. Parts of me withered in response. The troops retreated, as it were.

When the psychometric flash finally faded, the usual hypoglycemic side effects kicked in and my entire body felt drained of energy. Using the last of my will, I somehow found the strength to push Tamara off me. She fell back onto the mattress, and I rolled weakly off the bed and onto the floor.

"What the hell was *that* all about?" she asked as she righted herself on the bed. I could hear the surprise in her voice, but I ignored the question and started crawling for the door. Between my psychic disorientation, physical weakness, and the occasional Mardi Gras flashes echoing in my head, I felt like I might pass out. The images had almost faded for good, but then one last vivid burst of wild thrusting brutalized my poor brain. Tamara's voice moaning his name echoed wildly in my head: *Fergus! Fergus! Fergus!* With that, my body gave out and I fell over, unable to move. The refreshingly cool wood of the floor pressed against my face.

"Fergus . . . ?" I muttered weakly before I could stop myself. I still felt half in the vision, unable to control myself. I stared up at Tamara, her eyes now wide.

She leaned over and lowered her face until I could see the sheer shock on it.

"What the hell did you just say?" There was genuine surprise in her voice now.

All I could feel was intense sadness over the way things were rapidly unfolding—the way they always unfolded when I started to get close to anyone. For three weeks, I had been able to enjoy the myriad little things about the tease leading up to tonight. The way she walked across a floor, the way her eyes drew me in, the way I had become envious simply of her clothes because they had the pleasure of moving over her body. And now, it was all coming down around me.

Tamara jumped up from the bed and paced toward me. She looked embarrassed and shook her head like she couldn't believe what she was hearing. "How do you know about Fergus?" she said, confused.

Her words swam around in my head, but I couldn't force myself to say anything more. My struggle to stand back up took all my focus and energy. I pressed my back firmly against one side of the doorway and began inching myself up. My legs shook beneath me with the effort, but shortly I found myself standing with the arch of the door stabilizing me. As I steadied myself, Tamara adjusted her dress and moved closer, getting in my face.

"How could you know about that?" she asked, but didn't wait for an answer. Instead she became defensive. "It was New Orleans . . . just us girls away from our boyfriends. I . . . I got caught up in how much attention was being paid to me, but I *never* told *anyone*. I didn't tell the girls later that night, I didn't tell my boyfriend when I got back . . . *nobody* knows about Fergus."

All I could do was take it. Hell, I had to. I could barely stand, let alone tell her the truth. Besides, Tamara's sense of normalcy had been pushed over the edge and she was desperately trying to make connections that might make sense.

"Have you been stalking me?" she said, still puzzled. She paused before discounting the idea completely. Then a new idea struck her and her eyes opened wide.

"Have you been reading my diary?" she asked with venom.

My first thought was *When the hell would I have done something like that?* I had never even *been* to her place—and for good reason. The last thing I wanted with my abilities was to surround myself with an apartment full of another person's belongings. To Tamara, though, my snooping through her diary made a lot more sense than any explanation I could possibly share with her.

"Answer me!" she shouted suddenly, alarming me. Tears started running down her face, but I stayed silent. And woozy.

Without warning, Tamara swung at me, surprisingly making contact with my shoulder. It wasn't terribly painful, but it was enough to unbalance me and send my weakened body falling back to the floor. My head bounced off the floorboards, and my vision flashed white with the searing pain of impact. I lay there, waiting for the disorientation to pass, watching helplessly as Tamara gathered her coat, her shoes, and lastly the cell phone that had triggered all of this.

She wiped at the tears running down her cheeks. "Find someone else who'll put up with that, Simon. Someone who likes having their privacy violated. I hear a lot of women are really turned on by guys going through their stuff. Yeah, good luck finding someone like *that*."

Tamara ran down my darkened hall, tripped over something, and swore. On her way out, she slammed the door fiercely. My strength slowly returned as I lay on the floor. I could have gone after her, but then I thought of my track record with women and didn't bother. It was best to just let her go.

I understood where she was coming from well enough. I *had* violated her, albeit unintentionally. Fergus was a private shame from her past, and I had just thrown him out there on the table. But what could I have told her that would have made sense? There was no reasonable explanation I could have given. And even if I'd been able to explain it away and smooth things over with Tamara, I would still have to live with those images burned into my mind.

For now I would have to deal with the sad turn of events that the evening had taken, but maybe over time my work at Other Division at the Department of Extraordinary Affairs would teach me to cope better. It was easier this way, I told myself. Chalk up another loss in the relationship column. Alone was my natural state. It was better this way.

Saying it over and over in my head, the words started sounding convincing. But the dull thumping feeling in my chest said otherwise. Tamara was gone. I was alone. Again.

2

I was so shaken from such an intense psychometric reading that I hurried to the kitchen and grabbed my keys from the counter. I ran back up my hall to the door next to the bathroom, unlocking its three locks. I flicked on the light and was instantly blinded by the absence of color.

Every last object in the room was exactly the same shade of white. There was an unused desk, two empty bookshelves, and a block of large, square storage cubes. A single cushioned chair—also white—sat alone in the center of the room.

The White Room was my inner sanctum, a room I had put together to be as psychically neutral a place as possible. I needed a place that was clean of any potential triggers to my power, since everything else in my apartment was potentially chock full of other people's pasts. I came there whenever I needed to calm myself after a particularly bad psychometric incident, and tonight's Mardi Gras Slamfest definitely made that list.

I sat down in the chair before I collapsed. When my

panic finally settled down after several minutes, I realized that sitting here doing nothing wasn't the solution.

I just had to get out of my apartment for now. I got up from the chair, turned off the light, and relocked the three locks on the door. On the way out of the apartment, I chugged a glass of OJ to fight the hypoglycemic aftereffect of using my power. I slipped my black gloves on, heading for the elevator. I rarely went anywhere without my gloves these days. They were old and worn and the one thing that muffled my powers. It just made life easier to wear them, but second skin or not, they always made me feel a bit like the Bubble Boy.

As I walked from my digs in SoHo up toward Union Square, I stopped at my trusty coffee guy and caught word that some real vintage Antiques Roadshow action was happening under the West Side Highway at Seventy-Ninth Street. I jumped straight into a cab. When the taxi approached the turnoff, the driver spooked out on me, refusing to take his cab any farther west. After a minute of pointless arguing, I got out and slammed the door.

Prick. Did he think antiquarians really posed such a threat to society that he couldn't take me a few streets closer?

I walked the last few blocks west toward the address my coffee guy had given me. Makeshift lights flooded an impromptu night market that had taken root directly beneath an underpass of the West Side Highway, its tables and booths looking hastily thrown up and capable of disappearing in a flash if need be. The first time I had heard of these quirky shopping markets was through a friend of mine who had visited Taiwan. They were a life-form all their own, he told me—spur-of-the-moment shanty towns that sprang up and broke down in a single night, only to reappear like a magician's assistant in a completely different location the next. Last year, I noticed that the phenomenon had quietly made its way stateside, mutating into a scattering of caravan flea markets that popped up occasionally throughout Manhattan. I looked forward to the times when I was lucky enough to come across them.

It was only a few years since I'd given up a life of thievery and running with a criminal crowd. That meant that these days I was always on the lookout for my next big *legitimate* score, because the only true luxury I had established for myself was my apartment. Keeping up with my outrageous SoHo maintenance fees was hard, but now that I worked for the Department of Extraordinary Affairs, I was determined to do it somewhat honestly.

I had worked hard to put my unscrupulous use of my powers behind me. Long before finding the D.E.A., I had been an impressionable, confused kid with burgeoning powers, working part time for any antique shop that would have me. Cutthroats swarmed that business like sharks being chummed, and there were plenty of sketchy opportunists more than willing to drag me into the world of big scores, petty cons, and fast money. I started stealing from the legitimate stores I worked for, lying to them as I found hidden treasures I psychometrically discovered were worth a lot. All my less-than-honest role models just thought I had a knack for it, never guessing that I had some strange power, and I was happy to keep them thinking that. By the time I turned twenty, we were going for the big cash scores—priceless pieces of artwork—but we were sloppy and worse, greedy. After one too many close calls and the constant betrayal and backstabbing that you encounter with bottom-feeding miscreants, I was lucky enough to barely escape a stint in jail. Others weren't so lucky. I took the whole misadventure as a serious wakeup call to get my act together and disappeared off their radar.

My life of crime had started gradually, but it ended the second that fear pushed me to see who I'd really become.

I wasn't a clever kid using his powers to pull the wool over a couple of too-rich dealers anymore. I was a thief. A criminal. I was a bottom feeder, too.

I sold off the last of my stolen goods to finance a new apartment and start fresh. After all, I knew it would be easier to turn over a new leaf in style.

At these midnight markets, I still found it impossible to resist going for a score—that feeling of finding something only I could tell was valuable. The call of life's secret treasures waiting to be reclaimed was too great, and as long as I was paying for the goods, it was all on the up and up.

These markets fueled a deeper need in me, an emotional one that appealed to the same part of my secret heart that loved design-on-a-dime TV shows. I was as excited as a club kid finding out about a late-night rave. Plus if I could discover the right hidden treasure, it meant I would finally be able to fill my fridge with something more edible than its current contents of baking soda, packets of mustard sauce, and a month-old chicken marinara that was on the verge of growing its own legs and leaving on its own accord.

For 4 a.m., the aisles were crowded with an interesting assortment of people. Euro trash, insomniacs, and a few better dressed New Yorkers like me. I recognized a few familiar faces working behind the tables at their crude little stands. Over the years, I'd grown to know some of these wandering salesmen well. Some, I might count as friends, but even those I knew best were probably mostly after my greenbacks. All of them, though, had told me how much they admired my impeccable taste. Little did they know.

I wandered for twenty minutes before coming to a table that I thought was abandoned until a chipped-tooth Native American forced his bulk out through the trailer door behind the table. I nodded politely and then put on my poker face to look through his merchandise, pretty sure that Chippy wouldn't be hard to outnegotiate if I found something worthwhile. I needed my poker face. Some of these vendors were con artists, and I refused to get ripped off by over-paying for a Snoopy Sno-Cone Machine or a warped LP of *Sing Along with Mitch!*

Chip-tooth had two long tables sitting under his watchful eye. They were full of eclectic junk spread out cleverly with-out price tags. He wanted haggling room, which was fine by me. The smug look on the big guy's face showed that he thought he had the art of the haggle down to a science, which was also fine by me. There was no way he was going to outhaggle a psychometric. As long as I could downplay any real finds, I'd get a bargain and he'd be none the wiser.

I picked one end of the table to start with, took off my gloves, and began to run my hands across everything he had on display. A pair of wedding flutes. Nothing. A Legion of Doom lunchbox. Cute, but nothing either. A hideous collec-tion of early eighties fast-food glassware. They didn't trig-ger my power, but I knew they were valuable because the paint on them had turned out to be toxic. Still nothing. My confidence started to waver. Had I picked the wrong table? It had felt so promising.

Chip-tooth watched me closely as if I might try to steal something. Clearly he hadn't heard of my reputation from the other vendors. I didn't blame him. Still, I found it frus-trating. I was about to give up on his merchandise and go check out some of the Victorian furniture I had noticed two tables back, when my fingers touched a rectangular video game unit. The name Intellivision was printed across the top of it and the majority of the unit was plastered with *Star Wars* stickers. Two keypad controllers with circular push pads dangled lifelessly from tightly wound cords. Next to it was a pile of game boxes—twenty in all.

Instantly the electric snap of connection flowed up my arm and I fought to keep my poker face in place. I picked up the gaming console, and held it in front of my face as I pretended to examine it, but what I really hoped was that it hid my sudden look of interest. I closed my eyes and the market around me fell away.

In the vision, I was a young male, eleven or twelve years old. I focused quickly for clues to his name or location because if I didn't figure out who he was or where he lived, it would be impossible to sell this long-lost property back to its original owner, a gambit of mine that's proved incredibly lucrative over the years, especially with childhood memorabilia like this.

I was in a bedroom and the décor clearly indicated the late seventies or early eighties. From a hook on the back of the bedroom door hung bell-bottomed corduroys and a plaid cowboy shirt complete with pearl white snaps. It was the Farrah Fawcett poster, however, the one every boy in my middle-school class had drooled over, that convinced me of the time period. The Intellivision console was pristine back then and the boy was cutting up bubble gum stickers with *Star Wars* characters on them. He proceeded to tape the assembled clippings across the face of the console, carefully avoiding the controllers. May the Dork be with you. He then proceeded to add color-coded stickers to the corner of each game box, but I couldn't make rhyme or reason as to what they meant.

The world of the vision shifted and fell out of focus. When it surged again, what I saw made me feel real sorry for the kid.

Time had passed in the room and now the kid's mother was there. She had discovered the console and the stickered boxes, and with the ferocity of a feral cat, she tore a *Star Wars* sticker from the unit. Thankfully for me, she did what mothers who were pissed at their kids always did—she called the teen by his full name. Kevin Arnold Matthews. I had what I needed to try and find him, but I couldn't escape the vision. Kevin begged for her to leave them alone, but the mother just ignored him.

The vision went blurry again. I knew time had passed because Kevin's toys had all shifted place. He was standing there, watching and crying as his mother packed up the unit and games and, this time, threw them away. I felt the burn of his tears, his nose thick with snot.

Whatever caused this hateful display in this boy's mother, I didn't know. It was beyond my power. Only select glimpses were imprinted on items like the game console. I had to do a great deal of interpretation to figure out the whole story behind an item, and I constantly had to remind myself that I was human and therefore wrong sometimes.

But my interpretation of this vision so far was that the woman was a stone-hearted bitch for throwing the games out in front of Kevin. I felt compelled to return them to him, though, and I hoped they would help the guy reclaim a bit of his youthful idealism or happiness. If I was able to find him via the Internet. Sometimes I simply couldn't track someone down if his name didn't come to me in the vision and I'd end up selling the item back to another antiques dealer who simply thought I had a good eye. When everything fell in line, it felt great. It was those little victories that kept me going. Well, that and being able to pay my maintenance with the finder's fee they hopefully felt compelled to cough up. Kevin Arnold Matthews, I repeated to myself over and over.

I heard a voice that called from outside the scene in my mind's eye.

"You like George Plimpton, huh?"

I felt my concentration snap back to the real world. Being torn out of a vision prematurely was always disorienting. Like clockwork, my low blood sugar kicked in and I felt a little weak in the knees. I set the console back on the table gingerly and fished in my coat pocket for my Life Savers. They were the most portable and convenient source of quick sugar short of carrying a syringe full of pure glucose. Less pointy, too.

The chipped-tooth Indian was smiling. I knew I had blown my poker face. Damn.

"I'm sorry?" I said, trying to focus on the immediate world around me.

"George Plimpton," Chip-tooth repeated, this time with a phlegmy chuckle. I could see the dollar signs light up in his eyes.

"The actor?" I said, trying to sound as nonchalant as I could. Next to the console was a Mickey Mouse phone, and hoping to draw attention away from the Intellivision, I picked the plastic rodent up and tested its ancient rotary dial. "What about him?"

Chip-tooth's attitude shifted and he put his pudgy thumbs through his belt loops. "He did a series of commercials for Intellivision. Now you wanna make me an offer on that or you gonna fondle my stuff all goddamn night?"

I didn't appreciate his impatience or the attitude. I continued examining the phone for a few seconds more before I slowly put it down and took up the console again. "It's not in the best shape. There's some wear and tear to it. How much you asking for that and the pile of games?"

"A king's ransom," Chip-tooth said and proceeded to laugh with such force that he started to cough. His body shook with the violence of it. I thought the big guy might keel over right in front of me.

"Seriously," I said when he finally recovered. "How much?"

He scratched his sizable gut with one hand. With the other he rubbed his chin in thought. For a moment, he looked as if he was mulling it over sincerely, but I was sure he already had a set price in mind.

"Well," he said, drawing his words out, "seeing as how it's got a little damage to it, I suppose I could let it all go for two hundred dollars."

I stifled a knee-jerk urge to laugh in his face.

Two hundred dollars? He was insulting my mad phat antiquing skills! To anyone but the guy I was going to return it to, the console was worthless because of the stickers all over it. I cursed myself for blowing my poker face. I also cursed Chip-tooth for his greed.

"Three dollars," I counteroffered, totally deadpan.

"Don't waste my time, son," Chip-tooth fired back.

"Three dollars," I repeated with even more conviction.

Chip-tooth sighed and shook his head.

"Listen, son," he said, poking one of his pudgy fingers at my chest. "That console is a gen-u-ine piece of history—of rock and roll history, in fact. I purchased it at great expense from none other than Yoko Ono herself. She and John Lennon bought it in seventy-five and they used it until the day he got shot right here in New York City. That makes it worth two hundred dollars and not a dime less."

He was so full of shit that I felt real anger building inside me, but I simply kept calm and looked him straight in the eye.

"First of all," I said, pushing his finger away from my chest, "even if this console had ever been within forty miles of John Lennon, you're still as full of shit as the Hudson River. Lennon died in 1980. That gaming console didn't release until later in the year, *after* his death. Now I'm gonna give you twenty dollars for this, tops, and you're going to take it. You know why? Because I know my shit."

Chip-tooth snorted and rolled his eyes.

"You don't believe me?" I said, grabbing the Mickey Mouse phone and dashing it to the ground. "Ask anyone here."

He stared at me, angry and dumbfounded, and then turned to look around. The sound of laughter rose from several of the nearby booths and I almost felt sorry for the guy. I pulled out my wallet, and held a twenty out toward him.

His face dropped in defeat. Without argument, Chip-tooth took the twenty and began to wrap the console and games in silence.

My cell phone vibrated to life in the pocket of my brown suede coat and I nearly jumped out of my skin. The last thing I expected in the predawn hours was a phone call on my private line. I pulled it out and checked the display. CONNOR CALLING.

Connor Christos was my Other Division mentor. He specialized in working with ghosts, but was surprisingly not a part of the Department's Haunts-General Division. They took more of a ghost-busting approach to their work, while Connor was more of a spirit spotter and ad-hoc psychologist to the lingering undead, when his lack of patience didn't get in the way. Why he was calling me this time of night, I had no idea.

I flipped my phone open and was greeted by an earful of static.

"Hello?" I said. Another wave of static crashed into my ear and I pulled the phone away as fast as I could. "Connor?"

"Simon!" Connor called out through the choppy signal. "Did . . . wake . . . ou, kid?"

"Don't worry," I said. "I was already up."

There was desperation in Connor's voice.

The signal on my cell phone continued to break up. It sounded like listening to an old-time radio as it was being flipped through a variety of stations.

"Still hav . . . trouble . . . sleeping?" Connor asked. In the background, I heard a loud crash from his end of the phone line. "Dammit!"

"Never mind my nocturnal problems," I said, dismissive. "Is everything okay?"

Another wave of static crackled in my ear and I pulled it even farther away.

"Need . . . help. Can you meet . . . University . . . Seventh?"

Maybe it was the bad connection, but I thought I could hear nervousness in his voice and I didn't like it. Usually he was the calm and collected one.

"University and Seventh?" I repeated. "Yeah, I'm up on Seventy-Ninth, but I can be down there in about ten minutes. Traffic should be light."

"Thanks, kid," he said, "and hurry." The static rose once more and the line fell dead.

Something strange was brewing and a horrible feeling began building in the pit of my stomach. I needed to get moving, but Chip-tooth was still taking his sweet time finishing his packing job.

"Can you bubble wrap it?" I asked. "And hurry up. I'm packing for battle."

3

After I hung up with Connor, I jumped a cab and headed downtown. Thirteen minutes later, the cab dropped me off at West Eighth and University and I headed toward Washington Square Park. I looked for signs of Connor, but didn't see him. When I came across a small crowd of drunken late-night tourists fleeing toward Union Square, however, I figured I was on the right track. They jostled their way past me, and I lifted my shopping bag over my head and out of harm's way. A clamor of footsteps and the crash of metal came from the alley between Sixth and Seventh, and I ran toward it while the last of the tourists snapped a few quick pictures.

The alley was filled with a weak yellow light from high overhead and I slowed as I followed the sound, partly out of caution but also because the last few blocks had winded me. I followed the alley along another fifty feet before it turned right. I rounded the corner and found Connor standing a few feet away with his back to me. Something stirring farther along in the darkness had caught his eye.

At my approach, he turned and held a single finger to his lips. His muss of sandy brown hair looked more unkempt than usual and there was a strange white streak an inch wide in it that hadn't been there the last time I'd seen him.

"What happened to your hair?" I whispered. Then realization dawned. "You've been skunked!"

"You're kidding," Connor said with an almost schoolboyish glee in his voice. He tugged at his hair, trying to pull it far enough forward to see for himself. "Really?"

"You're excited about it?" I asked. "Makes you look older."

"Course I am," he whispered back, beaming with pride. "You know it's something special to be skunked, kid. A mark of prestige in the Department. It means you looked the devil in the eye and lived to tell about it."

"That's comforting," I said, feeling for the retractable bat hanging from my belt. "So now you're in their elite little *Hair Club for Men*?"

"They *prefer* to be called the White Stripes, thank you," Connor shot back.

"I know that, but they're sooo not hip enough to pull that off," I said, adamant.

Connor shushed me and sighed before changing the subject.

"You're late, kid," he whispered. There was a bit of venom to his tone. "And thanks for saying I look older. You're all heart."

I ignored his attitude. "What's the sitch?"

Connor turned back to the dark and unexplored section of the alley.

"I was minding my own goddamn business walking up University," he said, "when I heard a scream. It was hideous—like someone getting their back waxed. Then, out of nowhere, this spectral phantasm appears, streaking up and down the alley and scaring the souvenirs right out of a group of tourists."

I looked at the ground. Shot glasses with the Statue of Liberty on them, "I Heart NY" T-shirts, bootleg copies of cheap Asian porn videos, and postcards showing the New York skyline were scattered all around. There was also an odd assortment of broken clay pieces mixed in with everything, but they didn't look like any kind of tourist chatchke I knew of. I stepped carefully over the mess and moved closer to Connor.

"What's with all the broken pottery?" I asked. "Did someone drop their kiln?"

Connor shrugged. He looked distracted and there was a shortness when he spoke. "That was already here before the tourists dropped all their stuff. Maybe it has something to do with the ghost. I dunno. I'm too busy trying not to die right now."

"Sorry," I said, "but isn't this a job for Haunts-General? Ghosts aren't really my thing. They give me the stone cold heebie-jeebies. I'm not trained for this."

I eyed Connor's streak again and ran my hand through my own jet-black mop of hair, hoping it wouldn't meet the same fate.

"Don't fall apart on me now, kid," Connor said. "You had all the training sessions."

"Training sessions?" I said. I threw my hands up. "The Enchancellors haven't even covered apparitions with me yet. When I asked one of them about ghosts, they handed me a pamphlet entitled *Ten Simple Ways Your Job Will Disfigure You*! Nothing I've learned at the Department has trained me to tangle with anything like that. If it gets ahold of me as well, the other investigators will be calling us the Skunk Twins."

"Look," Connor said. "No one from Haunts responded and I was nearby . . ."

A clatter that sounded like overturning garbage cans interrupted him. I stared into the darkness, but in the pitch black of the alley there might as well have been an entire army of zombies riding in giant zombie tanks. Still, if it *was* zombies, I had at least read a pamphlet on them.

Connor spoke again, this time his voice dropping to an exasperated whisper. "I just happened to be at the wrong place at the right time, okay, kid? There were all these people standing around, snapping pictures of the damn thing like it's some goddamn movie star, so I start moving in on it. It must have sensed I wasn't afraid of it, because it hauled ass down this alley in the opposite direction, which is what I expected. At that point, I figured it could do one of two things: If it was aware it's a ghost, it'd just pass through an alley wall and I'd have lost it, but if it thinks it's still alive, it would feel cornered when the alley dead-ended. It wouldn't have anywhere to go and I could keep it at bay until Haunts-General showed up."

Something in the shadows moved closer, but I still couldn't make out what it was or even where it was. I felt pretty close to useless.

Connor signaled for me to move farther along the right side of the alley. Since he outranked me in the Department and had a hell of a lot more experience, I complied. Connor crept down the other side of the alley, but kept whispering.

"I didn't expect this phantasm to make a break back up the alley *toward* me, though. Before I could react, it phased right into me, but I resisted its energy. This spirit isn't acting like anything I've ever encountered before. Something weird is up. Now it's cornered somewhere back here."

Keeping a noncorporeal being from passing through an agent hadn't been covered in any of the assigned reading, handouts, or company e-mails.

"It actually *phased* through you?" I asked. "What did it feel like?"

The thunderous sound of another trashcan overturning rang out. I jumped, hating myself for reacting like such a noob in front of my mentor. Connor didn't even flinch. He tugged at the white streak in his hair again.

"You don't ever wanna feel it, kid. It felt like someone running electrical current straight through me. It was like a billion fist-sized rocks pummeling my body all at once."

He tugged harder at the strand so he could just barely see the ends of it.

"Nice souvenir of a standard op." He sighed. "As if I didn't feel old enough! Well, as least I'm a White Stripe now . . ."

Saying he felt old was ridiculous. Connor was only ten years older than me, although I don't know how I would have reacted if I'd been striped. Hell, there was still a chance it might happen before the night was through.

"We wrap this up soon," I said, mustering the little bravado I could, "and I'm buying the drinks, 'kay? Maybe it'll cheer you up . . . old man."

Connor winced at my words and I started to laugh—but quickly slapped a hand over my mouth. Luckily, Other Division had started me out with a pamphlet entitled *Witty Banter to Ease Any Paranormal Situation*. In unpredictable and potentially life-threatening circumstances like this, levity really helped an agent concentrate.

"Kid, this job is going to make me old before my time," Connor said.

"Oh, who are you kidding?" I said. "You'll be dead long before you get old! Now, c'mon!"

I took the lead and crept down the alley toward the weird crashing sound. Connor groaned and played catch-up along the opposite wall.

Something very close to me rustled—much closer than I thought it would be.

"Incoming!" I shouted.

Something closer to living fog than human flew out of the darkness toward us, and it was only my foolish vanity that saved me. *My hair*, I thought, and back-peddled up the alleyway, narrowly escaping the phantasm's touch as a crackle of electricity from its clawlike hands passed inches from my face. The smell of burning ozone filled the air, and I shuffled farther away.

The barest hint of facial features—deep hollow eyes and a gaping mouth that hung low—floated where the creature's head should have been. Its dead eye sockets bordered on hypnotic. This creature craved the life emanating from me—I could feel it—and it surged with great power toward me. No longer concerned about their breakability, I threw my shopping bag full of the console and games at the creature, and pulled the retractable bat from my belt. With a click of a button, I extended it and swung wildly, but it did no good.

All I could do was stare. Through the ghostly form, I could see Connor standing directly behind it. He was fumbling something out of his pocket, but I had no idea what it was. I was too busy backing away to care.

As I continued, my foot hit something solid, and my arms pinwheeled as I fell. My ass hit the ground hard, and my palms scraped against the pavement. The wetness of the puddle beneath me soaked through my clothes and the clamminess chilled my skin. I crab-crawled backward as fast as possible but it was no use. This monstrosity was going to overtake me.

I waited for its chilling touch, but instead the overwhelming smell of patchouli oil washed over the area . . . and the phantasm's smoky form turned from spectral white to reddish brown. It stopped moving and froze in place inches from my face and I wasted no time scuttering out from underneath it. Connor still stood on the other side of it with an empty vial in his right hand. Tendrils of smoke were drifting like a net around the now-still spirit.

He shook the last of the vial over the creature. It wasn't moving, but that didn't make it any less intimidating. Connor stepped closer to examine it.

"I don't get it," he said, stepping back. "It's gone totally feral. Usually when a spirit lingers, the humanity in it begins to stretch, become almost cartoonish. I can barely make out the humanity here. I don't know what would do this to a spirit, what would cause that much degradation. Unless it has something to do with all those broken clay pieces . . ."

I grabbed one off the ground and handed it to him. He gave it a cursory once-over and slipped it into his pocket.

"Thanks," he said, circling carefully around the phantasm.

"Thanks?!?" I asked. "For what? I should be thanking you!"

"These things feed on fear, kid. And frankly, I'm too seasoned to go all weak in the knees, so I really couldn't get the drop on it all on my own, you know?"

I dusted the filth of the alley off me as I stood and moved to recover my now dirty bag of collectibles from a nearby pile of debris. The bag looked like crap from the outside but I hoped everything in it would look better once I was home. I was soaked through and pissed.

"So what does that make me in all this, exactly?" I

shouted at Connor. "Bait? That's it, isn't it? You knew it would scare the crap out of me, feed off that, and totally forget about you, right?"

Connor shrugged and stoppered the empty vial before slipping it back into his pocket. "That's one way of looking at it."

"And what's another?" I fired back.

Connor slapped me on the shoulder, turning all smiles.

"Calm down, kid. You've been an integral part of this operation. It'll look good on your performance record with the Department. Think of it—the Inspectre might even grant you some sort of commendation."

"I'm not here to be your personal worm on the hook," I said, pulling away.

"I'm sorry, kid," Connor said with a hint of sincerity. "Really."

Connor leaned toward me and brushed his hair over his forehead. The new streak of white was even more pronounced now. "Look, I don't like how this went down, kid, or the fact that we're doing Haunts-General's work, but what are we gonna do? With all the budget cuts, Other Division picks up the slack. It's what puts the Extra in the Department of Extraordinary Affairs."

Connor was right and it really wasn't his fault. We were overworked and caught up in the red tape of New York City bureaucracy. I let go of my anger. After all, my hair had been spared. Who was I to complain?

By the time Haunts-General finally showed up and decided it was time for them to do their goddamn job, Connor looked ready to pass out. He pointed out the mist-shrouded spirit in the alley to them, along with the strange broken pieces of clay scattered everywhere. I looked like an Olympic medalist comparatively, even covered in a mix of something both sticky *and* pungent from the puddle. The nappy brown suede of my knee-length trench was a mess, not to mention that it also reeked of the patchouli-scented concoction that Connor had used to trap the ghost. I wasn't sure which was worse—smelling like a dirty hippie or smelling like garbage. Either way, I was in dire need of a shower.

The pains and aches of my overexerted muscles set in during the ten-block stumble back to my apartment. By the time I hit my elevator, I felt like the Tin Man right before Dorothy used the oil can on him. As I worked my way through the door and across my crate-laden living room, I hesitantly opened the shopping bag. I expected to find shattered circuit boards and soggy cardboard boxes covered in street sludge, but somehow they had survived intact. I slipped the console and games onto the shelf with the rest of my collectibles. Figuring out how to find Kevin Matthews would have to wait until morning. For tonight, I decided to stick with the basics in order of importance: (1) a shower, and (2) sleep.

The night's events had proven a perfect remedy for the insomnia I had been suffering from earlier. I was exhausted.

I struggled out of my jacket—my arms stuck helplessly to the wet sleeves—as I stumbled toward the bathroom. I was so tired, I felt drunk. My apartment phone rang. A call at this hour meant one of three things: someone I knew was dead, someone from my past wanted money, or worst case, Tamara was calling to talk things through. The first two possibilities were ones I could contend with. Death, for instance, while often unpleasant, was a universal inevitability (except for those rare creatures that we came upon in my role with Other Division). And dealing with the people from my past—seedy though they were—was usually cake. A couple of bucks thrown at their problems (not that

I had much these days) could solve most things on a short-term basis for that lot. But talking out my issues with my brand-new ex? That was something I was ill prepared for. I didn't even know where to begin.

By the fourth ring, I had freed only one arm, but it was enough to reach for the phone. As my hand grabbed the receiver, I noticed the answering machine flashing the number sixteen over and over looking like two beady red eyes. Did I really have sixteen messages after being out for only a few hours? As I hesitated with the receiver in my hand, the machine picked up.

"Just what the hell have you been doing when you come over here?" Tamara spat into the phone. "That's the only explanation that makes any sense, that you've been going through my stuff, you psycho . . ."

Sixteen messages, I thought. *And* I'm *the psycho?*

I turned the volume on the answering machine down as low as it would go, and her voice became a faint hum. I picked up the phone, flipped it over, and shut off the ringer before setting it back down. I'd go through all the messages later, but right now I didn't think my soul could take it. I knew I'd listen to them all—the yelling, the crying, the pleading—I wouldn't be able to help myself. I owed it to her to at least listen, but not right now.

I peeled off the filthy remains of my T-shirt. The large white letters across the front were mostly still there with the exception of a missing Y, torn off in battle and reducing the Ramones's catchy rock anthem to GABBA GABBA HE.

The faint sound of Tamara's voice was still loud enough that I threw the unit into a drawer and buried it under a pile of shirts until I could no longer hear her.

A lot of people would be troubled by an ex ringing them late at night, but I willingly put up with it. How could I get mad at Tamara over her bad reaction to what was essentially my own freak show of a problem? Many of the women I had dated over the years wanted to label me as commitment-phobic or just plain weird, citing an utter lack of character on my part. But my failure, like any other construction in life, was something built over time, creeping like roots and vines into the very bricks and mortar of my relationships. My power of psychometry was the richest fertilizer for that on the market.

Tamara wanted answers.

I couldn't give them, but the hope of controlling my power grew every day given my past four months with the Department. As I headed for the shower, I thought about how much I had already changed in such a short time.

After I'd abruptly left the criminal world, I'd been stuck in a long depression as I'd shed my less-than-ethical past, and especially the more criminal element I used to associate myself with. They were real scum-of-the-earth folk that I should have been happy to be rid of, but strangely, cutting myself off from such miscreants left me feeling alone. Turning to legitimate work was a last resort for a criminal like me—anything to keep my mind occupied and my hands busy in a less preternatural way. But I needed a job, a new start. As I flipped through the seemingly endless *New York Times* classified listings one night four months ago, I'd circled several options, mindfully skipping an all-too-tempting post at Christie's auction house, but nothing really excited me. There were a million dead-end jobs in the city and few that I qualified for. I started to worry that the only road for me was the one that ended in a ten-by-ten cell. That's when I saw a light at the end of the job tunnel wedged quietly between RECEPTIONIST and SYSTEMS ANALYST.

It read:

SCRYER

We're looking for unique individuals
for unique growth opportunities!!!

Wanted for detail-oriented, interpersonal casework
in a busy office environment. Some travel.

Knowledge of Excel, Front Page, Clairaudience,
Clairvoyance, PowerPoint, and Word a must.

Special in-house training program for motivated
self-starters. Familiarity with basic armaments a plus.

About our company—Misunderstood but special.
About you—Special but misunderstood.

NO Scientologists or actors!
Respond Box D3P7-07H3R

I was intrigued. What type of organization would post such a bizarre message—part business, part Amazing Kreskin—that wholly peaked the interest of someone like myself? Clairaudience and Clairvoyance might have turned out to be computer programs, but my gut told me they weren't. My gut told me reply to the ad.

I left a message the next day, and within a week, I found myself pulled into a world beyond my own personal pains, a world that promised control of what I was and what I could do.

A world, I noted through the crusting liquid film solidifying on my watch, that with only two hours 'til sunrise, was rapidly approaching. I would gladly have traded my powers of psychometry for the ability to turn back time—maybe fly around the world like Superman—all for an extra five hours of blissful sleep.

I mournfully threw my ruined jacket into a basket in the bathroom marked TO BURN. The coat was beyond hope, but maybe I could salvage my dear Ramones tee. I threw it into the bathroom sink to let it soak overnight. Maybe I'd become a trendsetter and soon bootleg GABBA GABBA HE T-shirts would be all the rage.

A shower never felt so good, but it was slow going as my body popped and cracked like that of a ninety-year-old. It took forever to free myself from the street ick I had rolled around in, but eventually time and several shampoos won out. I got out of the shower and toweled off as I ignored a volley of fresh new aches and pains. I gimped myself across the room and collapsed on the lonely expanse of my bed. The Bed That Sex Forgot.

As I drifted off to sleep, I tried with little success to hold back a montage of psychometric flashes of all my old girlfriends having much better and sweatier times in bed with men other than me. Tamara was now part of that list. Some people counted sheep. I counted orgiastic, writhing bodies. I was up to forty-six when calm, dreamless sleep finally engulfed me, and the discomforting sound of Mardi Gras beads rhythmically going *shink shink shink* faded from my brain.

4

I wrestled myself awake a few hours later feeling low on sleep and short on caffeine, but reminding myself that I needed to get back to the office. Although my mind was still on the fiasco with Tamara and last night's close call in the alley, it was the mountain of paperwork back at the Department of Extraordinary Affairs I was worried about most.

I dressed in minutes and pulled a fresh coat from my closet, this one black leather and knee length. I guess watching all five seasons of *Angel* in one sitting had influenced me more than I thought. Thank God New York hadn't had a vampire sighting in well over two years.

I walked the short distance up Second Avenue toward East Eleventh to my home away from home, the Lovecraft Café. The fall weather was being exceedingly generous about not giving way to the chill so I took my time. I walked past the hurrying crowds of NYU students and white-collar drones on their respective ways to classes or skyscrapers. I strolled slowly through Greenwich Village while they fought their way past me like cars passing a granny on the highway. I was too busy marveling, as I always did, at the quirky little shops and old-school architecture of a world gone by. Sadly, I noted that a plague of Gaps, Baby Gaps, and Subways had recently infested the Village, as history gave way to commerce, but I could still find the beauty if I looked hard enough.

When I saw the familiar red-framed windows and enormous oak doors that marked the Lovecraft, I stepped in. The strong, pleasant smell of coffee was mixed with the buttery cinnamon swirl of baked goods and my stomach nearly leapt out of my body in Pavlovian response.

I put my stomach in check and surveyed the main room. Movie posters ran along both exposed brick walls. The dark wooden floors probably hadn't been touched since the 1800s, creating a cozy, lived-in atmosphere that I loved. The usual mismatch of furniture reflected the mismatch of people that the Lovecraft Café attracted. I looked for a seat up front by the television and found one across from a very attractive woman with shoulder-length dark hair seated on a hideous mauve couch. A few scattered patrons filled a plaid couch here and a lemon yellow chair there, but my mentor was nowhere to be seen.

"Connor around?" I called over to the counter. The espresso jockey, a rainbow-mohawked punk whose name escaped me, stopped polishing the wooden counter along the right side of the room and looked up. I wanted to call out his name, but I couldn't remember it. *Was he a Jared or a Jason?* I knew he was one of the many Department employees who didn't actually possess any powers, but that was about it. As far as I recalled, he just served coffee for the Lovecraft's front operation. The counterman shrugged his shoulders noncommittally and moved off to rearrange a stack of muffins that had gone terribly awry.

"Thanks loads," I muttered to no one in particular, and sat back in my chair. On the television, David Davidson—the

Department's liaison at the Mayor's Office—was fending off verbal assaults concerning allegations of paranormal activity in Manhattan. I shook my head with amusement.

"Mr. Davidson! Mr. Davidson!" various members of the crowd shouted. The sunny New York City weather had made it possible for the latest of these press conferences to take place on the steps of City Hall.

Dave Davidson stood before the crowd of reporters and took a moment to smooth his tie into position. He looked out over the sea of people beyond the forest of microphones on the podium and pointed at random.

"Yes? You!" he said. The camera cut to a reporter who scanned his notebook anxiously for the right question to throw out. The camera cut back to Davidson as he waited with a look of serenity.

Cool as a cucumber, I thought.

Finally, the reporter found what he was searching for and looked up.

"Mr. Davidson," he said. "Can you confirm rumors concerning the use of psychics by the Mayor's Office to help investigative crime units? Specifically, I'm talking about events that occurred just north of Washington Square at University Place last night."

David fixed his face with the practiced smile he was famous for. Disarming, jovial, and mixed with a touch of "you must be kidding." It was his best tool, and I was sure it had helped expedite Davidson's meteoric rise at the Mayor's Office of Plausible Deniability.

"First," he said, holding up one finger, "I'd like to clarify exactly what happened last night. I know several calls came into emergency services as well as to the news stations concerning the report of a ghostly encounter. Apparently, several drivers passing by said they saw something in the area that caused a traffic pile-up. Thankfully, no one was hurt."

"Does this have anything to do with the legendary spectre

that people have been reporting for decades in that area?" the reporter persisted.

I watched Davidson closely and could see he was resisting the urge to laugh. The reporter was more on the money than he could possibly know, but Davidson simply shook his head in response. "No, I'm afraid I can't give any credence to rumors of *that* type. However, I personally talked with the head of Con Edison this morning and I'm told that this particular 'ghost' that people thought they saw was nothing more than wisps of steam coming from a series of pipes that run under that area. Con Ed assured me that they will be fixing those leaks today."

Again, Davidson pointed randomly into the sea of media. "Yes?"

This time the camera settled on a young woman with glasses. "What about the eyewitnesses on the sidewalk who claim they actually saw this apparition pass right through another person?"

The camera quickly cut back to Davidson and the practiced smile was already back in place. *Cool as a cucumber,* I thought again. *Ice water in your veins, buddy.*

"Look, the Village and the people who live there are some of the most . . . colorful in the City. I'm not surprised to hear an eyewitness account like that. It is New York City, after all! I recently had someone stop me in Washington Square Park to tell me how the squirrels were plotting a coup d'état against the Department of Parks."

The crowd rippled with laughter. The camera switched back to the female reporter as she dug into a large bag hanging off her shoulder and pulled free a stack of photos.

"What about these photos a tourist took of the incident? They clearly show something distinctly spectral—"

Davidson cut her off. "Double-exposed film or merely a trick whipped up on the computer."

I watched uncomfortably as the camera stayed with the

reporter. She tucked the photos under her arm and began rummaging through the bag once more. This time she produced a small clay pot filled with a jellylike substance, just like the ones we had found last night. "What about this? Some sort of residue left by the manifestation?"

I knew the stuff well. I had rolled around in it last night. *Damn,* I thought, *physical evidence.* Surely that would throw Davidson, but when the camera switched back, I was relieved to see his unfazed smile.

"Miss," he said, "I just have to say . . . you're a brave young woman for scraping anything up off the streets of Manhattan."

The crowd roared with laughter and I was pretty sure that he was in the clear. Davidson held his smile for a few moments before the camera pulled close in on his face.

"Look. We've been over this type of situation before and my answers are still the same. Time and time again, the Mayor's Office would like to state for the record that there is no government body that handles any sort of 'paranormal' investigations. His Honor is a practicing Catholic, and as such, he refuses to give credence to rumors of endorsement for any program that encourages a belief in life after death or the supernatural, unless it is in an appropriately monotheistic manner."

"Simon," croaked an elderly voice from the back of the coffee shop. It was Mrs. Teasley and her voice sounded roughly like the creaking of well-worn leather. "Is that nice young man Davidson helping us out again?"

"Yes, Mrs. T, I suspect he is."

I rarely entered the café without finding the plump, pleasant woman with her kind face and always-present tabby cat seated somewhere at the back of the Lovecraft's main room. Mrs. Teasley supposedly possessed the gift of telling the future by reading leftover coffee grounds from the morning brew at the Lovecraft. I had seen her powers at work only once, but it had taken a great deal of interpretation on my part to make any sort of sense of her vision. The old mystic had told Connor that he would "soon come into money." When he left the café later that day, an armored car on Eleventh Street almost ran him down.

I turned to see Connor walking through the door among a crowd of the White Stripes, of which he was now a proud member. They were patting him on the back mercilessly, and although Connor looked a little bit rough around the edges from last night, I could tell how proud he was to be sporting the new shock of white in his hair. A female White Stripe went to tease Connor's hair, but he brushed her away good-naturedly and waved to them as the rest headed off to the hidden offices out back.

He spotted me by the television, and headed over as he tried to wipe the out-of-place goofy grin from his face. He took a seat across from me in a ghastly purple chair covered in a paisley print that I bet even the seventies had rejected. He gave a nod to the punker behind the counter, who began whipping up Connor's usual.

"Hey, kid," Connor said, settling back.

"Morning," I said. "I see the Stripes noticed your badge of honor."

He tugged the streak of white in his hair. "If I had known how many free drinks this thing was gonna get me, I woulda worked harder to do it years ago. Maybe you should have jumped through that ghost while you had the chance."

I smiled at that but remained silent. Maybe it was vanity, but I hadn't quite made up my mind where I stood on the hazinglike esteem that was part of the White Stripes clique. It smacked of elitism, and I didn't see how it fit here on Team Good.

Hoping to change the subject, I motioned toward the television. "Davidson was just talking about how last night's event *didn't* happen."

"Tell my stripe that," Connor said, still playing with his hair.

"At least we made the news," I said with an optimistic shrug.

The counter jockey arrived and handed an iced coffee to Connor. Before Connor could reach for his wallet, I slipped the guy a ten. "Keep the change."

Connor looked surprised.

"I promised you a beverage if we survived last night," I said. "Remember?"

Connor raised his glass in salute to the distinguished Davidson on the television. I raised my own, joining his gesture.

"Davidson was just on TV. One of the reporters held up one of those clay pots we found. I guess Haunts-General didn't do that great a job cleaning up the scene."

"Not our concern, kid," Connor said. "That's their problem."

As I took a hearty swig of my coffee, my eyes caught those of the attractive brunette across from me and the two of us stared at each other. A notable awkward silence stretched out and it was only when Connor rustled around in one of his coat pockets that I was able to pull my attention away from her.

"Whatcha got for me, boss?"

Connor's mood shifted. In his hand was a reddish blue object about the size of a cigarette lighter and he tossed it to me. I caught it and gave it a cursory examination. It was a common enough item from my own childhood, three simple letters running down the worn rectangular body of the object, ending any possible doubt as to its identity.

"It's a PEZ dispenser," I said matter-of-factly.

"Case solved then, isn't it, Poirot?" he said, brushing his hands together as if wiping them clean. He pointed to the television, where Dave Davidson was still press-conferencing away. "Let's just close up shop and put him out of a job denying that the Department of Extraordinary Affairs even exists, shall we, kid?"

"Forgive me for pointing out the obvious," I said with retaliatory testiness. I flicked the marred and unidentifiable head of the dispenser back, the empty candy clip mocking me with its lack of PEZy goodness. At one time the dispenser might have had a cartoon character or the mask of a superhero for its hinged top, but with age, the identity had been worn away. Just another mystery on top of Connor's little test. "Is this honestly from a case?"

"You tell me," Connor said, refusing to give anything away.

I knew this was just another little challenge meant to help me channel my powers more effectively, but after the night I had been through, I really didn't feel like jumping through anyone's hoops.

I thought about refusing, just getting up and heading off to my backlog of paperwork and mountain of forms back at my desk. Deep down, though, I knew that random exercises like this were good for my training.

I wrapped my hand around the object and focused the entirety of my concentration. I felt it wash over the tiny plastic toy as my eyes glazed over. I opened up a closed-off section of my mind.

Mrs. Teasley cleared her throat at the back of the coffeehouse and my concentration broke. I had come to know that sound all too well during the past few months. One of her half-baked visions was coming through, and since there was no getting around Mrs. Teasley having her say, I simply waited. She kept her eyes focused intently on the pile of soggy coffee grounds spread out on the table before her, not once looking up. "Simon, dear, I think you ought to know . . ."

She paused to shuffle the pile around with her stained fingers. I raised my eyebrows at Connor, who simply looked pissed off. He was, after all, in the middle of trying to instruct me.

"Yes, Mrs. T?" I asked. "What *is* it?"

I tried to hide my annoyance, but as soon as the words were out of my mouth, I knew they were too harsh. Did I really want to be the kind of guy who shouted at well-meaning old ladies? I looked around the room to see if there were any babies I could steal candy from.

As Mrs. Teasley sifted her fingers further through the coffee grounds, I felt a slow, curious energy building in her corner of the café. Everything around her—except the cat on her lap—seemed to course with the mounting power. Magazines on an unbussed coffee table shuffled around of their own volition as if unseen hands were haphazardly flipping through them. Nearby coffee mugs clattered on saucers, adding their own cacophonous soundtrack. Through it all, Mrs. Teasley maintained her focus on the coffee grounds. I looked around to see if any of the norms had taken notice, but none of them were paying the old woman or the energy dispersal any attention.

Mrs. Teasley moved her face closer to the table and sniffed deeply before raising her eyes to meet mine. She looked at me with total seriousness, as if she had just been given a sign direct from the Almighty him (or her) self. Even though I generally thought her precognitive powers came from a secret pact as a Psychic Friend of Dionne Warwick, for once I took her seriously.

"Simon," she sputtered. "You need to know this . . . there's going to be some turmoil in your near future. Oh yes, great turmoil, indeed!" She pressed her eyes firmly shut as if she were going off to a distant land in her mind. Her lips trembled as if she was in great pain, and her breathing became irregular. She looked on the verge of passing out and I started to rise, fearing for her safety, but she spoke before I could get fully out of my chair. "You're going . . . you're going to be surprised by an unexpected guest."

"That's it?" I muttered. "Jesus, could you be any vaguer?"

Connor scolded me with a look, but I really couldn't see what worth she had to the Department. I secretly thought they *must* keep Mrs. Teasley around simply as a way to teach other staffers tolerance and patience. I made a mental note to grab the pamphlet from the Training Department called *Your COworkers & You: COoperate!*

"That sounds right on the money, Mrs. T," I said by way of apology. "Just great. Thanks for the heads-up."

Quietly, I turned to Connor. "Honestly, why do they keep the old woman on? I've seen better guessing at a carnival sideshow."

"And certainly better-looking women, too," Connor replied. Then, lowering his voice, he said, "Truth be told, Simon, I think she's got some pull with the Enchancellors. I know most of her predictions and precogs are limited to only a few minutes into the future and the accuracy of them is shaky at best, but someone higher up than either of us clearly feels different about it."

I sighed.

Connor turned away from her entirely. "Never mind her. Just take a stab at the PEZ dispenser."

"Right," I said sheepishly. "Sorry."

Settling back into the task at hand, I pushed away the surrounding chatter and smells of the coffeehouse. As I raised the PEZ dispenser once more, my eyes glazed over. A stir of energy much like the one Mrs. Teasley had generated began to form around me. It crackled like electricity and was charged with such intensity that it blew a wash of static through my hair. The last thing I saw as I fell into the vision was that Connor's skunkish mop had gone all Einstein as well.

My mind's eye kicked in and I was blinded by the brightness of the sun and the salty sting of the air. There was a light breeze carrying the pleasant smell of sand and sea. I concentrated on other surrounding details, hoping for clues. In the window of a car parked nearby (one of those midseventies fishbowly cars like a Pacer or a Gremlin), I caught the momentary flash of my reflection. A sandy-haired boy of about ten years old with a somewhat dull expression on his face stared back at me.

He (and I) ran across a parking lot toward a rise of grass-covered dunes, arm in arm with a slightly older boy who looked a lot like him. The two of them were laughing and half out of breath, skipping foolishly along. Thanks to his smaller size, he was barely managing to keep up with the older one.

My brain kicked into a lucid dreaming TiVo-like mode as I sensed the inevitable about to happen and I was able to slip the entire vision into slow-motion. The boy's shorter legs were no match for the older kid, and down he went, the older boy dragging him along. Because I sometimes experienced all the tactile senses of my host body, I felt the full pain of his knee scraping across the blistering, gravelly pavement. A sizable patch of skin peeled off before he shook free from the other kid and bounced to a stop.

Immediately, the older boy broke away from him, not out of concern, but because he knew he would be the first one blamed. His face was full of panic. As the younger kid began to cry, the older immediately started denying any involvement to the gathering of looky-loos forming around them. The younger one tried to stand up, but with a queasy look at his raw, pebble-embedded knee, he plopped weakly back to the pavement. An even saltier sting filled his eyes, and I could taste the bitter tears as they rolled down his face and into the corners of his mouth. He sat there crying until the comforting hands of an older woman scooped under his arms and lovingly lifted him up.

Through the blur of tears, her sympathetic face and frosted blond stack of hair came into focus. Lucidity kicked in again and I compressed time, speeding it up until I found the boy standing at the counter of a penny-candy store. The older woman tended to the one thing that she knew would soothe his pain and stop his crying—sweets. She paid the clerk and handed him a small bag full of waxy bottles filled with juicy bursts of liquid, caramel bull's eyes, and Atomic Fireballs. At the top of the bag, playing king of the hill, was the best of all, a brand new PEZ dispenser. As he beamed from ear to ear, I could already feel the pain in his scraped knee fading. Ah, the healing powers of sugary goodness.

I pulled out of the vision. Connor stared at me expectantly, his hair no longer static ridden. As reality took hold, I began to feel shaky from the toll my power had taken on my blood sugar. I snatched Connor's sugary iced coffee out of his hand and drank it with all the table manners of Cookie Monster.

"Juice! And an iced coffee with five sugars!" Connor shouted over to the counter. When it arrived, I chugged half of it down in one gulp. Mainlining such quick sugar replenishers helped and my disorientation passed. "Easy, kid," Connor said, patting me on the back.

"God, I hate this feeling," I said. "Does this shit ever end?"

"You're not the first noob I've instructed on this," Connor said. "There's always a price to be paid, kid, but with practice, it will lessen."

"That's a juicy little carrot to dangle before me," I said. My hands were still shaking as I set the dispenser down. "I'm so sick of this hypoglycemia."

Downing the rest of the juice, I attempted to further

shake off some of the weariness and felt slightly better for my effort.

"Well?" Connor asked with a certain amount of boyish hopefulness. Connor was back to business. He wanted something personal from this test, but what?

"Well, it's not part of any case we're working on," I said. I raised my eyes. "This is something specifically from *your* past, Connor."

He kept his face poker-straight and returned the dispenser to his pocket.

"Why do you say that?"

I scrunched up my face as I tried to find the words. I explained what I had just experienced in full detail right down to the dull look on Connor's youthful face.

When I was done, Connor chuckled. "So the dopey-looking kid is me, huh?"

"Hey," I said defensively, "it was your mop of sandy brown hair that gave you away more than your Stepford expression. Besides, you should be thrilled these days. You've really outgrown that Cro-Magnon look!"

I knew that seeing the world through another's eyes was a particularly invasive procedure and I left out how hard young Connor had cried, mostly out of kindness but also because I didn't want to risk breaking the trust we were developing as partners. This was the first time he had ever let me use my powers on anything personal of his and it meant a lot to me.

"What about everyone else in the vision, kid?" he asked. "Tell me who they were. I need to see how accurate your power is."

I thought for a second. "It seems obvious that the older kid must be your brother. And I'll take a stab that the woman was your granny."

"Why do you say that?" Connor asked.

"She did exactly what my grandmother would have done," I said, laughing. "I was hella-accident prone."

"All right. Good so far," Connor said, nodding. He pulled the unidentifiable PEZ dispenser back out. "One last piece. The PEZ dispenser?"

"Easy," I said. "Spider-man."

He sat there looking both saddened and amazed. "Astounding," he said. "I know we deal with these kinds of minor miracles on a regular basis, but I tell you . . . being on the receiving end of it, when it's actually *your* life being told back to you . . . well, that's a horse of a different color, kid."

I nodded. "But I'm curious," he continued. "You sounded unsure that we were at the Cape? Why couldn't you tell? I mean, yes, we were, but you couldn't tell that?"

"Not for sure," I said, shaking my head. "I'm a passive passenger in these visions, not a driver. I'm only able to take in details of what the younger version of you specifically saw. I can't force him to focus on any signs that might tell me where I am, but I do pay attention. Nothing screamed out 'Cape Cod' directly, but I remember the town of Amity from *Jaws*, so it seemed like a fair assumption. The way my visions happen, I can kind of fast forward and rewind them a bit, but they don't let me be in control of what I'm allowed to see."

"Maybe we can change that," Connor said with encouragement.

I smiled with the tiniest hint of pride and sipped at my coffee. Feeling triumphant, I asked, "That older kid *was* your brother, right?"

He nodded in response but his face grew dark. Gone was the amazement of the last few minutes, replaced by the more familiar look he used when distancing himself from a case.

"I'm sorry," I said, breaking the silence. "Is there bad blood between you two? Do you not keep in touch?"

He stared at the floor for several moments, just long enough for me to feel truly uncomfortable.

"Not really," he said softly. "My brother and I *haven't*

talked in years, as a matter of fact, but it's not what you think. It's not like we had a falling-out or anything. He went missing about two years after that summer. It was another one of our yearly trips to the Cape, like the one you saw, and he just disappeared one day while we were all at the beach. Busy day, lots of people, and he was just gone in a heartbeat. That was the last any of us saw him. Big police investigation and everything."

"Jesus," I said. "I'm sorry. I had no idea . . ."

Connor clapped me on the shoulder, reached back into his pocket, and pulled out the dispenser with a nostalgic look.

"How could you, kid? I had totally forgotten why I had kept this thing anyway. Came across it while searching for some old hex dolls. Hadn't thought of it in years. Everything got kinda cloudy when he disappeared, you know? I'm just glad you were able to catch a glimpse of him in your vision, kid. I'd give anything to see those days again. That's gotta be something."

Connor had hinted at learning more about my kind of power, and now it made a bit more sense. Through teaching me, he hoped to awaken some dormant psychometric power of his own to track down his missing brother.

"Maybe I could help you manifest the power," I said hopefully. "I even picked up one of the departmental pamphlets about recognizing the signs of psychometry in others."

"*Clairvoyance or Clair-annoyance: You Either Got It or You Don't?*" he asked. I nodded, but he shook his head. "Been there, read that, kid. It has surprisingly little to offer on whether it's even possible for me to be taught or if it's simply something a person is born with."

Seeing the melancholy look on his face, I was more determined than ever.

"You never get even the tiniest of visions like these?" I asked. "No flashes, glimpses, maybe something you might have labeled as déjà vu?"

Connor shook his head. "Nothing. I guess it's not in my area of expertise."

"We'll see about that," I said. "I'll be damned if I can't teach it to you somehow." I paused. "So you've only got the one, then?"

"One what?" Connor said, confused.

"Area of expertise," I said.

Connor nodded. "That I'm aware of. In fact, you're sitting across from it."

"Huh?"

Connor leaned in and whispered, "Across from you. The brunette." He gestured toward the woman sitting on the couch next to his chair.

I tried to appear casual as I glanced her way, pretending to check out the *Maltese Falcon* poster on the wall behind her, and found myself staring once more at the fetching woman I had made eye contact with earlier.

Outside of her natural beauty, I saw nothing particularly out of the ordinary. Great skin, smartly dressed in black pants and a dark brown leather blazer. I judged her to be in her late twenties with an elegance that radiated from porcelain-like features perfectly framed by a river of wavy brown hair. Luckily, she wasn't looking directly at me this time. I congratulated myself for stealthily sneaking a peek at her and avoiding any awkwardness. I leaned across the table toward Connor.

"Women are your expertise?" I whispered. "What about her?"

"Oh," Connor said matter-of-factly, picking up his iced coffee and taking a lengthy sip, "she's dead."

5

I often imagined how cool my life would be if I were in a movie. I would say all the right things and have all the right reactions in any given situation. Most importantly, I would no doubt be as cool as I have always imagined myself, but at that moment in the Lovecraft Café, I found that reality was having no part of my delusions. As soon as Connor mentioned that the brunette was dead, I felt a chill run up my spine and I literally jumped straight out of my chair. Apparently, I had taken the remedial *Deadside Manner: Staying Cool in Troubled Times* seminar for nothing. I helplessly watched myself with the same type of slow-motion detail that I used in my visions.

My foot caught the edge of the coffee table, causing an alarming clatter of cups as it began to flip over (−1 to me for causing a commotion). I started to fall, but not before my replacement coat billowed out around me like bat wings while I spun out of control (−2 for appearing spastic). As I fell back, I accidentally kicked Connor's coffee right out of his hand (−3 for punting my partner's drink).

That's when things got weird.

The delicious beverage flew through the air, sailing toward the woman on the sofa, but instead of splashing all over her (regularly a −4 offense), it passed straight *through* her (with no previous scale to judge it on, I'd have to give it a −8 million at least). Oddly enough, she didn't seem to notice, but suddenly I could see what was wrong with her. Now that I was looking at her closely, she was semitransparent. I could see the plastic cup resting inside her form against the back of the sofa, its contents sloshed all over. The woman seemed to become slowly aware that something was going on, but the look of confusion on her face told me she wasn't quite sure what exactly had happened. She glanced back and forth between Connor and me, searching our faces in silence. Connor broke the tension in a way I was getting used to—he yelled at me.

"Simon!" he shouted. He grabbed a napkin from the table and beginning dabbing the area around the woman without actually reaching through her.

She stared at me and I shrugged sheepishly, and then we both looked to Connor.

"I'm sorry about what the kid did there," Connor said, continuing to clean around her. "I know this must all come as quite a shock to you, the way things tend to phase through your semicorporeal form. Being dead and all . . ."

A look of absolute confusion spread across her face.

"Dead and all . . . ?" she repeated. Her voice was quiet but refined.

She looked around quickly to see if perhaps Connor was talking to someone else. Finding no one there, she turned to me. "Who's dead?"

"Oh crap," I said. I felt like a deer caught in the headlights. "Connor, you want to field this one?"

I looked to Connor for help, but he was too busy scooping ice cubes off the mauve sofa back into his glass. I felt absolutely useless in the situation. I had enough trouble talking to *living* women. All I could do was smile and stare. Here was this beautiful—but clearly deceased—woman sitting across from me, and she was seemingly unaware of her situation. How could she not realize she was dead, especially after a coffee cup had passed straight through her?

I had to say something, though. "Who's dead?" I repeated. "Well . . . you are."

The woman's face scrunched up in immediate disbelief. She laughed.

"Oh, I don't think so!" she said. Then, with total conviction, "No, absolutely not."

"Hrmh," Connor said. He stopped cleaning up the spill and finally turned his full attention on us. "I think we may have a problem here."

"What sort of problem?" the woman asked, nervousness creeping into her voice. "The spill? It's nothing, really. I'm sure a good dry cleaner will be able to get the stain out. If you'd be kind enough to pick up the dry cleaning bill, I'm sure everything will be—"

"Look at your clothes," Connor said abruptly.

The woman looked as if she had been slapped in the face.

"Excuse me?" she said.

I found myself taken aback by his interruption, surprised by the gruffness of it. He certainly could have handled it with a gentler tone, but remembering that the deceased were his bailiwick, I held my tongue and let him work.

"Just . . ." Connor said, exasperated, "just take a look, okay? Humor me."

The woman looked down at her outfit, and her eyes widened as she finally noticed what Connor was talking about. Her body was even more transparent than before and I could see the entire couch through her now. The area on the couch where Connor courteously hadn't reached through her to wipe was still covered with ice, coffee, and whipped cream. Her outfit, however, was spotless, untouched by even a drop of the drink. She grabbed for the pile of ice sitting inside her but her ghostly hand phased straight through the mess. "Oh . . . my . . ."

Connor and I waited in silence as we watched the realization set in. Connor's mood had changed from moments before. His early morning tedium—another day of pencil-pushing at the office—had just gotten interesting. This mysterious apparition wasn't acting according to the book, whatever arcane text that might be . . . probably *50 Haunt-ful Tips for the Helpless*.

Connor turned to Mrs. Teasley nearby and chuckled. "You see, Mrs. T? Here's the 'unexpected visitor' you mentioned." He turned to me and whispered, "The old broad may not see too far in the future, kid, but at least she still keeps the ball in the park. Even a broken clock is right twice a day, huh?"

I worried that the people around us might have noticed the cup go flying through the woman and I checked the rest of the coffee shop. Normal customers who had simply stopped in for a cup of coffee, a stale muffin, and nothing paranormal had momentarily turned their attention toward us, but only because of the noise from kicking over the table. Everyone had quickly turned back to their conversations. Had I remembered my training better, it made perfect sense. The Department's orientation pamphlet, *D.E.A. or DOA: Your Choice*, stated that most regular folk were ill equipped for dealing with this sort of supernatural situation. Yes, they sensed something out of the ordinary, but their minds were protective of their sanity and made them happily oblivious to things such as this woman's unliving-ness. If I polled them about what was wrong, they simply wouldn't be able to put their finger on it. Instead, they would grumble about how crumbly the muffins were or that their coffee needed freshening up. Nothing out of the ordinary for them, thanks.

"Maybe we better take this out back?" I suggested. Connor nodded.

"Miss?" Connor asked. The woman was flustered and paid him no attention. Despite the oddness of her circumstance, she was desperately trying to keep her composure.

Admittedly, I was, too. The only thing that made sense right now was taking this situation out of the front room of the Lovecraft Café. It was perhaps the best idea I had come up with during the entire encounter. Things would be better once we were out back in the Department's offices.

Being the well-meaning gentleman that I am these days, I tried to help the woman up from the couch by taking her arm. My hand passed effortlessly through it and a shock tingled through my fingers, startling her. Connor shot me a look.

"Please don't do that," he warned.

"Why not?"

"Because you might force me to say 'please don't do that' again," he said, agitated.

"Oh."

I had never experienced such a sensation before. My fingers continued to tingle as if they were charged with electricity. In the reflection of the glass covering a Bogart poster on the wall, I checked my hair to make sure that I hadn't suddenly become a member of the White Stripes. Luckily, I was fine.

I turned my attention back to the situation. Connor finally caught the woman's eye. He smiled purse-lipped at her. "Yes, hello? Hi, could you tell me your name, please?"

My heart softened as she attempted to smile back despite the obvious stress this situation caused her.

"It's Irene . . . I think."

Connor looked at me and lowered his voice. "Not good.

Memory displacement's already set in." He turned back to her. "Hello, Irene. My name is Connor Christos and my young colleague here is Simon Canderous."

"I'm not *that* young," I mumbled. Connor shot me another glare and I fell silent. Now was not the time to be glib, apparently.

"If you'd just follow us back to our offices," he said, "I think that I or one of our other 'guidance' counselors can help make sense out of everything you're experiencing."

Irene cocked her head, distrustful. She looked far from convinced, and I didn't blame her. How would I react to being told that I was dead? Probably far worse than she was.

"We're here to help," Connor said with a smile. "Honest."

He reached into his right pocket and pulled out a small vial like the one from the other night, and twisted its stopper free with a well-practiced motion. I watched as the same smoky haze rose from the vial and twisted dreamily around Irene's head. The familiar smell of patchouli and cloves hit my nostrils, and the woman's face went slack. She rose from the couch like smoke rising from a fire. Just like that, Connor took control of her.

Connor's approach bordered on wrangling her like cattle, and I wanted to speak up—but what was I really prepared to say? None of the departmental seminars or brochures had covered this, and my own training had yet to cover the shaky legal gray area of spirits' rights. Wasn't Connor somehow violating those, coercing Irene by magical means? Before I could give it another thought, Connor turned away and led our brown-haired beauty toward the back of the coffee shop. I stumbled my way over the upturned coffee table and followed. The counter jockey scowled at me for leaving the mess, but I pointed to Connor and the ghost, shrugging as if to say, *Whatcha gonna do?*

Irene floated along with an unnatural, ghostly grace. But she took care to avoid tables, chairs, and other people as if she were still alive. We moved like a procession of geriatric zombies. I smirked at the image it conjured in my head. If she *had* been a zombie, at least she'd be something I had read up on in the departmental pamphlet *Shufflers & Shamblers*.

Her body flickered as if she had a loose bulb inside her.

"You okay, Irene?" I asked.

"I think so," she said. Her voice came out as if she were off in a faraway dream. "Just troubled a bit. I want to follow your friend here, but . . . I'm not sure why. Strange." She tried to move her head to look at me, but her eyes couldn't turn away from Connor. "It's that intoxicating scent, isn't it?"

I stopped. Surely this was coercion at it basest level. "Connor . . ."

My partner stopped and turned.

"Kid, it's okay," Connor said in an effort to soothe both of us. "Nothing's going to happen to her."

As we passed through the black velvet curtains at the back of the shop, Irene gasped. The ordinary confines of the coffeehouse gave way to a majestic, old movie theater that embodied days of glory gone by. In the soft glow of the movie's projector, I could make out the muted gold leaf fleur-de-lis hidden on the wall amid the decorative architecture. I was especially taken with the ornate chandelier that glittered in the darkness high overhead. What stories it would tell if I ever got my psychometric mitts on it.

We headed down the right-hand aisle. The theater was enchanting, but not in a paranormal way. It always gave me the impression that something magical would happen if only I were to fall back into one of the red velvety cushions of the Lovecraft's hundred seats. But that was the point of old theaters—to weave a spell, preparing a journey beyond these four walls. Up on the screen, Clark Gable was noisily chomping a carrot as he sat on a fence talking to Claudette Colbert.

Irene craned her head about the theater. She was taken in by the majesty of it all. At the end of the aisle, Connor stopped opposite a large wooden door marked H.P. and produced a ring of keys. He sorted out a plastic keycard and waved it in front of an electronic plate to the door's left. The latch clicked softly and Connor pushed the door open, gesturing for Irene to enter.

"Welcome to the world of weird," Connor said.

6

Holding the door for a woman who could just as easily walk through it was a nice touch on Connor's part. With five years on the job, Connor did have many of the finer points down when it came to helping the deceased cross over. Keeping me alive on a daily basis? That was a different matter.

He waited for Irene to pass through the doorway before he spoke.

"The dead have heap-big issues," he told me in the worst Native American accent he could muster. He was a movie buff and always doing accents or impressions. Almost all of them were impossible to figure out. In his regular voice, he continued, "Sometimes the simple gestures we associate with being human can get an investigator through even the most difficult of spirit-handling situations. Think of the soul as shell-shocked when it's torn from the world of the living. Spirits who can't get past that tend to linger with the confusion of it all. That's when it can grow restless and a haunting might commence. I'll get reports from family members who say that they've started seeing dead ole'

Uncle Lou sitting on the can in the upstairs bathroom. Stuff like that."

Although I had hoped to catch up on the paperwork threatening to take over my desk, Irene had suddenly become our "heap-big" issue du jour—which meant that I would have to table two zombie infestations and an investigation of a Shambler sighting. The Department of Extraordinary Affairs was probably going to be a big shock to Irene, and that would pretty much fill up a good part of our workday.

Irene looked overwhelmed by the change of pace from the mesmerizing tranquility of the theater to the red-tape office environment that spread out before her. Dozens of desks, cubicles, and a throng of pencil pushers cluttered the busy aisles of our unlikeliest of office spaces. The stucco walls gave the lengthy main room a warm, golden glow, reminiscent of California's grand hotels from the early days of Hollywood. Irene spotted the only significant difference between those hotels and our main office at the D.E.A.—an assortment of arcane symbols carved deeply into a vast portion of the wall.

"What on earth are those?" Irene asked. Her eyes were wide with wonder, everything remaining of her humanity exaggerated to cartoonish proportions.

"Standard ritualistic markings, ma'am," Connor said politely as he led her down the main aisle. " 'All operations involving the use or potential use of supernatural powers must be properly warded, glyphed, and otherwise protected by our Division of Greater & Lesser Arcana.' "

"I'm afraid I don't know what that means," she muttered absently, too busy drinking in the flurry of activity around her.

"Allow me," I said. I wasn't sure how much I was allowed to tell her, but I figured Connor would stop me if I overstepped my bounds.

"This," I continued, "is the heart of our organization, the Department of Extraordinary Affairs. We're mostly a hush-hush offshoot of the Mayor's Office that deals with paranormal matters in the Tri-State Area." I pointed to an endless row of doors along the far wall. "See those? We're divided up into several divisions . . ."

"Too many divisions if you ask me," Connor added. "Greater and Lesser Arcana, Haunts-General, Things That Go Bump in the Night . . . the list goes on and on."

"And which are you?" Irene asked, turning to me.

"Connor and I work for Other Division," I said, "which basically means we pick up cases that don't pigeonhole neatly into the rest of the divisions, or that we pick up their slack when the casework builds up. I only know a handful of the divisions by name, but the Enchancellors seem to come up with two or three new ones every time I turn around."

"What's an Enchancellor?" Irene asked. She reminded me of a little kid with all her questions, but I realized to an outsider, it must all seem overwhelming.

"They're like an overseeing committee for the D.E.A. They monitor the whole of what's going on, assigning new divisions at will while overseeing the rest."

"Sounds confusing," she said. I nodded. "So you're a part of the government then?"

"Yes and no," I said. "We're official, but they don't really acknowledge us."

"Really?"

I nodded. "Look around you. Are most government offices hidden behind a hipster coffee shop–slash–movie house? Remember that guy on the television before?"

It was Irene's turn to nod.

"David Davidson. He's our liaison to the Mayor's Office. The fact is that the bulk of citizens in Manhattan—and more importantly to him, the registered voters—are simply not ready to cope with the notion that The Big Apple's government deals in the supernatural. 'Living Voters are Happy Voters!' is his motto. Besides, most residents turn a blind eye to it anyway. It's New York City. Weird shit happens."

"And people just ignore it?" she said, fascinated.

"Mostly," I said. "Even though it's right under their noses. Most occurrences end up being reported in the daily New York rags. Urban Bigfoot in Central Park, alien abductions on the Great Lawn . . ."

Before I could finish my diatribe on the finer points of half-assed journalism, I sensed watchful eyes upon me. I scanned the room only to find Thaddeus Wesker—Matrixy sunglasses forever hiding his eyes—looking in our general direction while he verbally bitchslapped a team of people from his division.

"So Wesker's in charge of both Greater *and* Lesser Arcana now?" I asked.

I knew little about the man except that he was very, very scary. I had heard that he had impressed the Enchancellors by carving the latest batch of arcane runes into the walls by himself. I also knew that he seemed perpetually pissed off. Somehow, he still looked like slickness personified as he yelled at the elite squad—black hair slicked perfectly straight back and sporting just the right amount of five o'clock shadow at all times.

Irene gave him a quick glance and just as quickly turned away.

"Are you all right?" I asked.

"It makes me uncomfortable to look at him," she said, her voice trembling with weakness.

"Relax," Connor said. "It's not you, Irene. Everyone gets the same spooky vibe from him."

"Makes me wonder exactly how Mr. I-Wear-My-Sunglasses-at-Night got involved with us men in white hats in the first place," I said.

Connor continued along the main aisle of the cubicle farm, and lowered his voice. "He volunteered to head up the Witchcraft backlog around here, kid, and when they merged departments with Greater Arcana during the City Hall budget crunch last week, he simply stared the other directors down for leadership. And he pulled that trick again over the newly formed Greater and Lesser Arcana that rose from the ashes."

"Authority through intimidation," I said. "Nice."

Irene looked terrified.

"Don't worry," Connor offered with reassurance. "I don't think you'll have to deal with him."

I smiled at Irene and stepped closer as we continued walking.

"When I was first training, the big threat for us newbies was that if I didn't keep on my toes, the teachers would assign me to one of Wesker's seminars over at Witchcraft."

"Well, I don't care for him," Irene said. "He gives me the heebie-jeebies."

"I said the exact same thing!" I exclaimed.

Connor looked at me with eyebrows raised, but said nothing. He turned and walked on.

The back part of the office was hidden from the front by a ceiling-length dark red curtain that ran from wall to wall. It deadened the sounds of the hectic world of the filers and cube dwellers for the rest of us working behind it. Connor pulled it aside and the three of us passed through the narrow gap into the back office. The atmosphere was more casual back here, but still too waiting-room for my tastes. We headed toward a quiet corner, where several leather couches were surrounded by a glass table that was cluttered with file folders and old coffee mugs. We waited for Irene to take a seat before the two of us sat.

The luck of the draw put Irene directly opposite me again. Now that we were a bit more familiar by a whole ten minutes of talking, I was able to look her in the eyes without shying away like a teen at a high school dance. Strangely, the life that emanated from her had woven its own little spell over me. My eyes fell into hers . . . for how long, I wasn't sure. Connor cleared his throat loudly, pulling me out of it. Irene was still looking at me, smiling.

I blushed like a fool in reaction, feeling a strange mix of pride and embarrassment at being the focus of her attention. I looked to Connor for guidance, but he merely shrugged in response. *Thanks, pal.*

"Irene," Connor said, clearing his throat once again. "I've got some good news and some bad news. Which would you prefer to hear first?"

She turned nervously back to me, seeking some kind of guidance, but I remained silent. The debriefing part of dealing with spirits was Connor's territory and I wasn't going to overstep my bounds here. In my first four months I had already stepped on enough toes while scrabbling to learn the intricate ropes of paranormal investigation.

"I think I'd like the good news first, please," Irene said after a brief hesitation. One of her hands moved to cover her mouth as she braced herself. Even the good news might be dreadful.

Connor put on his most chipper voice and said, "The good news that the kid and I have to share with you is this: You have *not* been relegated to a flaming, fiery hell, complete with pitchforks, demons . . . the whole works."

I was sure he hoped his tone would lighten the situation but the panicked look in Irene's eyes told me that Connor had failed completely. What remaining color there was in Irene's face drained away. Her body flickered in and out. "If that's the good news, I don't know if I'm prepared to hear the bad."

Connor scratched his temple, searching for the right words. I couldn't imagine there would ever be a right choice of words in a case like this.

"Well," he said, opting for unadorned bluntness this time, "let's put it this way. You've recently become less . . . earthly."

"Meaning what, exactly?" she asked.

"Meaning . . ." Connor said, drawing the word out like a sigh. He was buying time, hoping for inspiration to strike. It didn't. Connor was off his game around her, for reasons I couldn't quite figure out just yet. "Meaning . . . you're dead. You're what we call 'the recently living,' which is the PC term to use these days according to the Mayor's Office."

Irene slumped back against the couch, attempting to take in Connor's sudden, life-changing (or was it death-changing?) statement about her entire worldly existence. I could only imagine what the poor woman was going through. I knew that I wouldn't take it well if someone walked up to me and cheerily said, "Hello! Sorry to piss in your cornflakes, but you're dead. Have a nice afterlife."

Irene sat statue still for the next five minutes. Only the muffled sounds of the office indicated that the world continued on around us. Finally, she leaned across the cluttered table, and beckoned for us to lean in as well.

"I don't buy it," she said.

"Don't buy it?" Connor scoffed. "You don't *have* to buy it, Irene! It's a *fact*. You 'buying it' doesn't change anything! As a matter of fact, you've already 'bought it,' if you follow my meaning. Look!"

Connor picked up the folders on the table and, one by one, threw them at her. Well, through her. They vanished into the space her semitransparent body occupied, but I heard them hit the fabric of the couch behind her. Gone was the sensitive Connor who opened doors for the undead—he obviously felt shock tactics were in order to get Irene through her "denial" phase. But it was too much for Irene and her eyes brimmed with tears as she attempted to brush the protruding folders away from her body.

"How is this even possible?" she said as she turned to me.

I looked away, ashamed at Connor's approach. Maybe I missed the memo declaring Tough Love for all walk-in cases. I brought my eyes back to hers. "I don't know. But I'm afraid it's true, Irene. Death comes to all of us."

"Then why am I here?" she demanded, her voice rising with anger. "Why aren't I in heaven or hell or whatever there is out there? Why am I sitting in the back of a Village café talking to two strangers about the fact that I'm *dead* while one of them obnoxiously throws things *into* me? Shouldn't that be all she wrote, gentlemen? I mean, I've reached the proverbial end of the line, haven't I? *What am I still doing here?*"

"I wish there was an easy explanation I could give you," Connor said, the frustration melting from his face. "There's . . . just . . . a lot we don't know yet."

"Why don't you tell me what you *do* know?" she asked with open bitterness.

Connor was trying to keep his own hostility from kicking back in and I hoped he remembered just how traumatic these events were for Irene. But there was still sarcasm in his voice when he spoke. "Well, I *can* say for certain that you are definitely deceased."

"Connor," I pleaded, hoping to soften him. "Come on."

Why was he being like this? Too many years on the job? Maybe as with all service-oriented jobs, it was easy to lose sight of the fact that we dealt with other humans, touching their lives. Day in and day out, it took an extreme amount of effort to remember how to treat people.

"I apologize," Connor said, backing down, "but like I said, you're definitely passed on. I'm not sure how you died, but the kid and I can look into that. Don't worry if you can't remember anything right now. It'll probably come back to you. As far as why you're still here, well . . . usually when a spirit lingers, there's something binding them to the material plane. Unfinished business of some sort. Nothing mundane, mind you. Nothing like 'I forgot to turn the stove off.' More of a vengeance thingie . . . or perhaps you have an important message to pass on to a loved one. It must be something that your soul found very disquieting when it was forced from your body so unexpectedly."

"Do you *have* any loved ones?" I had to ask, even if it sounded like I was suddenly playing *The Dating Game*. But Irene was too caught up in what Connor was saying.

"And if I figure out why I'm here, then what?" she asked as she flickered in and out with increasing nervousness. One moment she was there, the next she looked like she was being energized by the transporter beam on *Star Trek*. "Where do I go from here?"

"That's where it gets a bit sticky," Connor said. "We're not quite sure. Clearly the soul is meant to go somewhere, but we earthbound aren't privy to that. We get stuck with the burden of determining just how these supernatural occurrences happen in the first place and what sort of impact it has on the living. Obviously there's no known way to explore what lies on the other side without, you know, dying. It could be the soul gets recycled, reincarnated, and you'll find yourself as a furry lemming headed off the cliffs of Dover in the next life. Conversely, you *may* go to a heaven of some sort, but whose version of heaven? Is there a pantheon or are we talking monotheistic? In the end, though, there's no simple way to give you a solid answer."

"Can't you research it?" she asked. "Or do something? This is my life here!"

I shook my head.

"There's way too much paperwork to even set that in motion," I said. "Our secretly sanctioned agency wouldn't even know what forms to fill out to investigate what happens in the afterlife. We're not budgeted for it, either."

Irene had gone from angered to shocked. "So you're

telling me there's too much bureaucracy, red tape, and too little funding to give me a definitive answer on my fate?"

"In a sense," Connor said. "That's merely the very tip of an enormous investigative iceberg, Irene. Let me see if I can explain this a bit further, because at this point, you really don't have a lot of avenues. You're dealing with an autonomous agency that deals in the paranormal, but we're still under all the constraints of an office. Half our investigative results contradict what they're finding in at least two of the other divisions! On any given case, we've got monotheistic proof, polytheistic proof, and no proof whatsoever—all at the same time! It's mind-boggling, even to me. I can't even address some of the seemingly simple questions."

"Such as?" Irene asked.

"Well," Connor said as he pointed to Irene, "here's a good one. I can't tell you why your hand can pass through most solid objects, yet somehow you're material enough to sit on that sofa without falling through it."

Irene looked nervously at the sofa below her. "What exactly *is* your function here, Mr. Christos?"

Connor smiled. "I see dead people . . . for a living."

"Meaning what?" Irene asked with persistence.

"Look around the room, Irene," Connor said. "Most of the people in this room are trained specialists in some bizarre field or another. Most of them can't even see you sitting here with us. Not everyone does what I do. Not everyone can see what I see. Hell, the kid didn't even notice you were dead until I pointed it out to him."

"Well, I noticed you," I added. "But I didn't notice that you were . . . recently deceased . . ."

Connor continued, "People like you, Irene, are one of my purposes for being here. I need to figure out why you're still with us."

"Maybe we all become like this?" she offered. "Maybe

this is as good as it gets. What if all we have to look forward to is hanging around after death, being ignored by the living and occasionally spotted by some crackpot on the street!"

"Well, then, you're in luck," I said cheerfully, "because we're just those types of crackpots!"

Connor ignored us, shook his head again, and continued.

"That's extremely doubtful," he said. "And I'll tell you why. Manhattan is a city of over eight million residents, not to mention tourists and commuters. The amount of death that occurs daily in an energy center like this is astounding, but the documented occurrences of souls walking around are negligible in comparison. If what you're proposing were the case—if all spirits hung around after dying—I wouldn't be able to go two feet in any direction without tripping over someone's soul. It's just not the case."

There was a moment's silence as Irene thought it over. I watched her, looking for signs of comprehension, but only noticed the cute crinkle of her nose. She looked to Connor and quietly asked, "Why do *you* think I'm here?"

"Honestly, I haven't a clue, Irene. But I need you to think. Think hard. Are there any words, any thoughts that spring randomly to mind? Anything at all? I want to see if you're capable of free-associating any information that might be useful to us. Names . . . faces . . . an address, perhaps?"

Her brow furrowed with the effort of recollection, her nose scrunching up again.

After several moments of trying, she said, "Nothing."

"Damn," Connor said.

"Well, now what?" I asked.

"Wait a minute!" Irene said with a sudden burst of excitement. "That word. *Now*."

"I think we'd need something a lot more specific there, Irene," he said.

"Quiet," she said, waving him away. "It triggered something, I'm not sure what. I have an image of that word floating in my head. I've seen it somewhere recently. I think it was on one of the movie posters out in the café."

I leaned across the table wanting to reach out to her, but refraining. God only knows what part of her I'd accidentally put my hand through this time.

"Can you tell us which one?" I asked.

Her hands shook excitedly as she tried to recall. "It's that one with Martin Sheen. Where he goes up a river . . . ? And there's this tribe of men dedicated to Marlon Brando!"

"*Apocalypse Now*!" I shouted, bouncing on my seat as if I had just won a prize on a game show.

Irene nodded. "Yes! That's it. That's the image I have in my head. That's really not very helpful, is it?" Her face sank. "God, I feel so useless."

"It's all right," I said. "It'll come to you. Give it time. Right, Connor?"

When Connor didn't respond, I turned to look at him. His eyes had narrowed considerably.

"What is it, boss?"

"I know that front room like the back of my hand," he said. "There *is* no movie poster for *Apocalypse Now*."

That put things in a different light. I rose from my chair. I didn't want to leave Irene alone, but things were getting frighteningly interesting.

"I'll tell the Inspectre," I said. I leapt over my chair and raced for the curtains.

Connor's voice faded as I climb the stairs two at a time, but I heard him telling Irene, "It may simply be a coincidence that you had an apocalyptic memory, or possibly . . . something more than coincidence."

7

I sprinted up the stairs to the Inspectre's office, eager to de-
liver the news of what was happening down below and I
had butterflies. I had never had a reason to report directly
to such a revered figure as the head of Other Division. I ran
for his office door, where I found the following memoran-
dum posted on it:

The Three Commandments of D.E.A. Public Relations:

1) Say Nothing.
2) Acknowledge Nothing.
3) Deny Everything.

If you have any questions, please refer them to your
Divisional Manager.*

*All members of Things That Go Bump in the Night are exempt
from this last statement.

That memo could have easily applied to the way I had handled Tamara last night, but now was not the time for those thoughts. I could deal with our breakup later.

I burst through the Inspectre's door without so much as a knock. The blustery Argyle Quimbley sat behind a large oak desk sipping tea and he jerked to attention at my unexpected entrance, sloshing his tea in the process. His handlebar mustache absorbed most of it, but he winced in pain and slammed the cup down.

"Damn and blast!" he barked. The sound of his voice froze me in the doorway, panting and out of breath. His look softened to concern once he got a better look at me, though. "What's the matter with you, my boy? Did the Devil chase you up the stairs?"

I nodded in response, still unable to speak, and wondered which of us would win the prize for most ridiculous in appearance—me, looking a fool for being so winded from a mere flight of stairs, or the Inspectre for his bookish tweed suit from the seventies, complete right down to the elbow pads. Our head of Other Division looked out of place in modern-day Manhattan. He would have looked more at home with Hemingway, toting some archaic blunderbuss while big-game hunting in the wilds of Africa.

His stuffy English accent had the odd habit of occasionally disappearing if the old man seemed to be distracted by something important. But as Inspectre, he not only headed Other Division but answered directly to the Enchancellors—so his eccentricities were forgivable.

When the fire in my lungs faded, I spoke. "We have a potential situation downstairs, sir."

The Inspectre was now wringing his mustache out as if it were a miniature towel. "Something worth scalding my palate over, I hope."

"Possibly," I said. "Maybe . . . I'm not sure. It's just . . ."

Clearly exasperated by my inability to articulate, Quimbley shouted, "Out with it, boy! What exactly *is* going on?"

Eccentric though he might be, Argyle Quimbley could be intensely intimidating at the same time. Caught like a deer in the headlights, I paused for a moment and gathered my thoughts. "We've got someone downstairs who's had a vision."

As he stared at me across the vast expanse of his paper-strewn desk, the Inspectre narrowed his eyes. "Well, visions are something we trade in, lad. What sort are we talking about?"

"Oh," I said. "She's the pretty sort. Long brown hair, sparkling eyes you could fall into . . ."

"Not what sort of person, blast it!" Quimbley slammed his fist down on the desk. A cloud of papers flew off it and onto the floor. "What sort of *vision*?"

I was amazed how quickly I could feel like an utter ass in the Inspectre's presence. He had been with the Department forever and commanded respect through all the divisions, even ones that didn't answer to him.

Two weeks after I'd started, Connor had taken me aside and explained that Quimbley was also a member of the Fraternal Order of Goodness. F.O.G. was a secret society far older than the D.E.A. Though the D.E.A. had officially assumed many of the duties and investigations that the F.O.G.ies, as they called themselves, had traditionally undertaken, the Fraternal Order still existed. They worked both inside and outside the confines of the government, in that many F.O.G.ies were D.E.A. employees, but when a case was dire enough, they acted under F.O.G. directives, ignoring little trifles like filing forms in triplicate and liaising with David Davidson's office.

The F.O.G.ies were secretive like the Freemasons, but unlike the White Stripes, F.O.G. was elitist in a way I actually approved of. They stood for Good. Being a part of them proved that the Inspectre was a man at the top of his field. In his youth, he had been a legend. He had stared The Un-Nameable down until it had been subdued. The Geismann Guard had fallen single-handedly at his hands. I thought about all those achievements . . . and here he was, stuck talking to a petty ex-con like me. It was no wonder I got nervous.

I pulled myself together. "It could be nothing," I said apologetically, "but it could also be apocalyptically huge. Then again, it might just be sheer coincidence. I don't know. We've got someone downstairs who's having some form of Armageddon-based premonition."

"Oh ho!" Quimbley exclaimed. "Well, *that* type of judgment call isn't for you to make, my boy."

"Who is it?" the Inspectre demanded. "Is it Mrs. Teasley and her damned cat again? The old bat! You know, she came in here last week babbling on about some half-baked notion that a glacial mass was about to descend over North America, destroying life as we know it. After a little investigation, it turned out that it was simply her freezer needed defrosting."

"It's not a staffer," I said. "It's a *dead woman*. She was a walk-in and she seems so . . . alive still. Seems convinced of it, too. She keeps refusing to acknowledge the fact that she's dead."

Quimbley nodded knowingly as he folded his arms and raised one hand to stroke his mustache. It seemed to comfort him. "Yes, sometimes the recently living have trouble believing that they've passed away. Surprised you didn't pick that up in the *Dealing with the Dearly Departed* seminar, my boy."

"It was booked solid by the time I joined the Department, sir, and I haven't had a chance to fit it in my schedule since taking on a full caseload." He looked at me disapprovingly. "She wasn't just having trouble believing she was dead, sir. To me, she still looks very much *alive*. I didn't even notice she was a ghost until I spilled a drink through her."

"You what . . . ?" he said, not sure he had heard me correctly.

"That's not really important right now," I said, hoping we could gloss over my mishaps. "I mean, she was dead all right. All spirit. Pure soul through and through, but whatever her soul is projecting to give her a corporeal presence is stronger than anything Connor or I have encountered."

The Inspectre moved to one of his bookshelves, pulled down a small leather volume, and began to thumb through it. It was full of scratchy, frantic handwriting. "My best guess, without talking to her, my dear boy, would be that she's still on earth because something of great importance is keeping her bound to the material plane."

"That's what Connor said. And the thing is, we found her down in the café . . . having apocalyptic images," I added. "Throw in her determination to still be among the living . . ."

"And we'd be fools to ignore it," Quimbley finished. He walked around his cluttered desk. "Let's check her out. Then I'll see if we need to bring the Fraternal Order of Goodness in on this." I swelled with pride. The inspector thought my case might be important enough to bring the F.O.G.ies in on, and he trusted me enough to tell me that.

Quimbley paused as we headed for the door and looked back at the now cold cup of tea he left behind. "Bollocks!" he shouted. "Another teatime shot to hell."

I heard a shuffle in the hallway and looked up to see Thaddeus Wesker trying to linger inconspicuously by the Inspectre's door.

"Hello, Thaddeus," the Inspectre said, narrowing his eyes. "Did you need to see me?"

"Just passing by," the Arcana director said. The smile on his face looked forced, yet diabolical. I made myself disappear against the wall as the two men locked eyes in a struggle for dominance.

"I see," the Inspectre said. He motioned toward the floor and pretended to scatter something with his foot. "Well, make sure you pick up these eaves you seemed to have dropped on your way, won't you?"

Wesker's smile fell away and he clenched his fists at his side.

"Come along, Simon," the Inspectre said. Wesker looked at me with sheer disdain, but I was already moving away toward the stairs. "Let's get moving before he corners you into hearing his woeful story of injustice for the millionth time. He's still angry," the Inspectre said conspiratorially, "because he's been denied entry to F.O.G. again."

Wesker stormed off toward his office as the Inspectre and I headed downstairs. Once downstairs, I was pleased to see that the Inspectre had a gentle touch with Irene. He fired off rapid questions at her, but without a hint of the irritation he had shown with Wesker moments before. Irene recounted much of what she had told us. When Quimbley pressed her about her death, she said all she remembered was a yellow blur. Then she began asking questions of her own. Her frustration over being dead, something she still didn't seem to be buying into, crept out and her questions began to get more belligerent and sarcastic.

To the Inspectre's credit, he took them well. Quimbley had seen a world of wonders over the years, and I doubted if this one woman's sarcasm would be his breaking point. As it turned out, Irene was not the Inspectre's breaking point. I was.

"Dammit, man!" he barked at me. "Stop cringing every time the woman asks me a question! You're trifling with my concentration. Now sit quietly and listen . . . or better yet, why don't the two of you do something useful . . . like figuring out how the devil she died and who she is!

"Unless you want Haunts-General to take care of this?" the Inspectre asked us quietly.

Connor shook his head. "This isn't just a simple ghost bust. I need to figure out why she's so . . . lively. Something peculiar is going on in the spirit world. There was that peculiar ghost we came across last night and all those broken jars. Maybe there's a connection."

The Inspectre nodded.

"Then you two had better get on with it," he whispered to us. "I want you to find out as much as you can regarding this dear soul here."

Connor looked frustrated, but nodded. "I guess we can backburner the Shambler," he said. "The zombies can wait also."

"This is wrath of God apocalypse stuff she brought up here," I said. "Surely that takes priority."

Connor turned on me, and I could see annoyance in his eyes.

"Kid," he said, "you realize how many Four Horsemen scenarios we get every *day*?"

I shook my head.

"How many of the supposed Seven Seals do you think Greater and Lesser Arcana break weekly?"

This time I shrugged.

Connor snorted.

"This is just another apocalypse," he said, "lowercase 'a,' as far as I'm concerned. It's no big. Probably is just a harbinger that something really bad happened to keep Irene's spirit sticking around instead of crossing over."

"Nonetheless," the Inspectre said, moving our little powwow farther away from Irene. "I'm concerned that we're getting this class of vision from a ghost, and a ghost so clearly full of life. I'll have the Fraternal Order check her out, but my initial assessment is that, given Irene's strong presence, you chaps make this a top priority."

Connor swallowed whatever words were on his lips. "Yes, sir. We'll figure out who she is and then check out her home, and get back to you."

The Inspectre stood there waiting for us to leave. The final word had been his, and it was clear that, for now, any further discussion was over. As we walked away, I heard the Inspectre ask, "You don't perchance recall if you were married, love?"

I turned to look and felt a wave of relief as Irene shook her head.

"I'm sorry," she said and nervously tucked a lock of her dark brown hair behind one ear. "I wish I knew."

Connor shook his head at me. I smiled guiltily. We stepped back through the curtain and stopped at our desks. I winced at the towering stack of files and reports sitting untouched in my in-box. I ignored my pile and looked over at Connors. His was just as tall and, like mine, getting taller. We divided up the most basic of tasks at hand. Connor called around to all the metropolitan area hospitals while I checked Google and the newswires for anything involving the disappearance of a woman named Irene. After a half hour, Connor hung up the phone.

"Anything, kid?"

I shook my head.

"Looks like we're going to have to get off our asses . . ." he said and stood up.

"Too bad," I said. "I was kinda looking forward to doing all this paperwork."

I wondered if I had lighter fluid and matches somewhere in my desk.

"That can wait," Connor said. "We need to figure out who this Irene is before her ghost starts degrading on us to the point she's like that rogue spirit last night. I can think of only one place that might give us the answers we're looking for. There's this book—"

"Tome, Sweet Tome?" I offered.

Connor nodded.

I grabbed my retractable bat off my desk and slipped the handle of it into the loop on my belt. You never knew when you might need a good blunt instrument in a bookstore.

8

The Department of Extraordinary Affairs had its own stock of books regarding the paranormal, but there were plenty of dark and evil tomes that even we refused to keep on the premises. That meant that sometimes we were stuck having to go elsewhere for our supernatural information needs. Thus, Connor and I found a visit to Tome, Sweet Tome on the Upper West Side in order. It was Tamara's neighborhood, and I dreaded running into her accidentally, but we had to hit Tome. Almost anything you could ever want on the subject on the dark arts, the gray arts, and even the off-white arts could be found somewhere on the dusty shelves of the nefarious bookstore. The two of us rode silently uptown in a cab. I thought about asking more questions about this missing brother of Connor's to break the silence, but he was busy getting into character for our visit.

Tome, Sweet Tome was famous in the heavy-duty, no-holds-barred world of serious arcane research, but surprisingly its collection of knowledge did not make the store itself a dangerous place. Its owner, Cyrus Mandalay, had never been robbed, mugged, harassed, or otherwise mistreated in all the years that the D.E.A. had dealt with the bookstore. At nearly six feet four inches and sporting a tribal tattoo down the entire left side of his face, Cyrus was an imposing-looking fellow. His pale skin was drawn tight over his angular features and he sported long black hair done up in dreads. Cyrus was definitely not the type of shopkeeper the average criminal would think of messing with, and he definitely didn't fit the bookish stereotype one would normally be buying literature from, either.

Connor and I pushed through the front door. A red-lettered sign hung just inside it that read:

* *Please check all extra dimensional objects at the counter.*
* *All undead are subject to a $10.00 cleaning fee following use of the Reference Room.*
* *Shoplifters will be dispelled.*

Cyrus was busy ringing up a pretty young Goth and her grandmother, who were purchasing a deck of Tarot cards. He looked over at us from behind the counter, recognized Connor, and gave us a toothy smile than ran from ear to ear. Even a grin from Cyrus was enough to make me feel uncomfortable and I looked away. Connor, veteran that he was, looked at him unfazed.

"Gentlemen!" Cyrus said with a pleasant ring. He looked around nervously before thanking the two customers. As he sent the girl, her new Tarot deck, and her grandmother on their way, he reached behind him and pulled a loop that hung from the ceiling. The door swung open for the two exiting customers, and the elderly woman gave a startled looked back at him. She hurried the young girl out the door.

"Crone," Cyrus said, the smile falling from his face.

Everyone knew that Cyrus ran a bizarre shop, but something that garnered him favor in the Department was that, surprisingly, he was a great supporter of literacy. While his appearance tended to frighten off many timid book buyers, he worked hard to make the store accessible. He'd even added a "newbie" section for young people who might be interested in all types of arcane matter. An inviting little area just to the right of the entrance had been set aside for it—a room filled with happy pictures of cartoon witches generating rainbows. Zoo animal warlocks were painted there as well, producing flowers and bunnies from top hats. There was even a little wizard-robed turtle sporting a Dali-esque mustache melting a watch with his magic wand.

Cyrus flashed his toothy grin again—which simply made him look like he was guilty of *something*. God only knew what it was. *"Que pasa?"* he said. He placed his enormous hands on the counter and leaned forward, towering over us not only because of his natural height, but from the built-in rise behind the cash wrap. He laughed when he saw the white stripe in Connor's hair. "Got skunked, eh?"

Connor ignored the question and stepped forward, his confidence not wavering in the face of Cyrus's imposing figure. "How's it goin', Cyrus?"

I could hear a hint of *I know something you don't know* behind it. I knew the routine, something so simple that even I could handle it given my limited amount of fieldwork at Connor's side. It was time for a bit of the gently applied good cop/bad cop. They were roles that fit both of us surprisingly well—Connor, his seasoned badass attitude with the field experience to back it up, and my own role as, well . . . the gentle new kid on the block. Real acting stretch there, I know.

Connor raised one eyebrow, looked slowly around the front of the shop, and said, "You keepin' your nose clean?"

"Cleaner than an elephant's trunk, guys," Cyrus answered, flashing his grin once again. This time I caught the full effect he had evidently been going for. His entire set of teeth was filed to finely sharpened points that reminded me of a shark. "I run a solid enterprise here. You gents know that."

What this massive wall of a man said rang of the truth, but Cyrus was also high on the creepy scale—maybe not as bad as Wesker, but definitely first runner-up. He made it hard to believe that whatever went on at Tome, Sweet Tome was on the up and up.

"I hope so," Connor said. He peered back into the darkened Stacks of the cavernous bookshop. I followed his lead, but from where we stood, it was near impossible to make out anyone or anything who might be lurking somewhere deep in the aisles . . . which was the whole idea behind the shop's design, if I thought about it. This eclectic collection of grimoires dealt with everything—mysticism, shamanism, witchcraft, spellcraft, glamours, and other arcane matters. Those interested in such subjects probably fancied a little privacy, and the store's layout reflected that sentiment. It was a maze of towering shelves and wild piles of books that stretched to the ceiling.

"Thought we'd throw some business your way," Connor continued. "We need some time in the Black Stacks, okay?"

Cyrus gave a chuckle—jovial, but just evil sounding enough to send a shiver up my spine. "Don't ask me if it's okay, Connor. Ask the Black Stacks yourself. I am merely their proprietor. Don't hold me responsible for what they will and won't do."

Connor strode boldly up to the counter. He leaned in close to Cyrus, craning his neck upward to meet his eyes. "Well, then," Connor said. There was piss and vinegar in his tone already. "*As* proprietor, you might want to consider exerting a little control over your merchandise. You start letting the Stacks run things, you might find yourself cleaning up a lot more than dust around this place."

"Whatever," Cyrus said dismissively.

Cyrus's attitude toward wrongdoing reminded me of the people who'd led me down the wrong paths. He was imposing, but Connor's lack of fear had bolstered something deep inside me, and whatever bullying charm Cyrus held over me broke with his flippant response. "Those books represent a hell of a lot of chaotic malevolence if left to their own devices," I said, spurred on by my newfound bravado. "You think it's simply a matter of magicians coming in here and taking advantage of the Stacks? It's the other way around. Most of the poor saps who get wrapped up in the whole evil game are there because they were too stupid or too malleable, easily controlled by what's contained in those very books! They were too stupid *not* to get used by the Stacks."

Our good cop/bad cop act had skipped straight ahead to bad cop/bad cop. That was what happened when one was new to fieldwork. I had tons of book knowledge with the occult, which made for great speeches, but I had little experience in dealing with it face to face. Still, verbally smacking down an occult book dealer alongside Connor was something I could check off my résumé of thrilling fieldwork. I wished Irene were here to hear how daring I sounded.

"Relax," Cyrus said, too calmly for my liking. "Everything is under control here." His eyes darted back and forth between the two of us. Suddenly, I did feel an overwhelming desire to relax—and I knew he was up to something supernatural. There had been power in his words. Connor's grip tightened on my arm until the pain caused me to snap out of it. He forcefully pulled me out of Cyrus's direct line of sight and stepped forward.

"Good," Connor said. "I don't want—"

"But understand *this*, gentlemen," Cyrus interrupted. He seemed miffed that his little trick hadn't held us in his sway.

"You know and I know that a lot of the hoodoo-voodoo we deal with is even beyond our comprehension. Our mortal lives are nothing in the face of the unseen world, and what comprises the Black Stacks has a life all its own. Things are only as under control or out of control as *they* allow them to be. If you want to know the truth, or the truth as I believe it, I don't think anyone can control what is in those books. And like I said, I am merely . . . a gatekeeper."

Gatekeeper. I noticed the pride in his voice as the word rolled off the tattooed man's tongue. Anyone, not just a paranormal investigator, could see the man took his dangerous dealings seriously. He'd had his say.

He reached beneath the counter and pulled out a ledger, picking up a pen at the same time.

"Will that be cash or charge?" Cyrus purred out, slick as a cat.

I couldn't let my last few moments of righteous anger slip by as if they hadn't happened. I was petty like that. I lashed out in the only way left to me.

"Just put it on our tab . . . before we close your ass down," I said. I wasn't sure if we even had the power to do so, but even if it was an empty threat, it felt immensely satisfying.

The path winding back to the sectioned-off area known as the Black Stacks wove throughout a lengthy portion of Tome, Sweet Tome's main floor. Connor and I followed Cyrus carefully through the labyrinthlike twists and turns that were mostly made up of musty stacks of ancient— possibly rotting—books. They were piled everywhere and threatened to tumble over at the slightest touch. I pulled up closer to Connor and whispered, "You ever knock over one of these precariously balanced piles?"

"I don't think so, no," he said. "Come to think of it, I

can't recall a single stack of books falling over ever in Tome, Sweet Tome."

I stopped for a moment and placed both my hands against one of the more dangerous-looking towers of books, tempted to see what would happen if I gave it a little nudge, but Connor pulled my hands away.

"I really don't want to do the paperwork when you get buried in an avalanche of literature," he said, pushing me in front of him.

We quickened our pace to keep up with Cyrus, who had already reached the back of the store. The Black Stacks themselves were caged off from the main stock by tarnished copper bars that ran from floor to ceiling. Connor and I stood back as Cyrus made a few arcane gestures and spoke in a tongue I wasn't familiar with.

Cyrus moved aside and gestured for us to enter. "Good luck, gentlemen."

"Don't wait around on our account, Cy," Connor said and elbowed his way past him. "We'll call if we need anything."

Cyrus chuckled at that. "I've got a first aid kit up front should anything . . . unfortunate happen," he said as he wandered back to the front of the shop. "It's at your disposal. For a nominal fee, of course."

"Of course," I said and pushed my way past him also, but with less force than Connor.

As I passed the threshold, the familiar smell of brimstone hit my nostrils. It was a tried-and-true stereotype, like cops in a donut shop, but brimstone always seemed to permeate the air anywhere the dark arts hung around in any great concentration. And let's face it—the dark arts didn't get more concentrated than here. The smell was still hard on the nose, though. "Well, that was unpleasant," I muttered as I turned to Connor, who was already nose deep in a book. It didn't surprise me one bit that he wasn't wasting any time.

We were on the clock back here in the Stacks, and ever since the Mayor's Office had further cut funding to our already suffering Other Division, Connor had been paying strict attention to all our expenses. I, however, was wasting the departmental budget just standing there.

"Is there anyplace specific I should be looking?" I asked, feeling guilty.

Connor pulled down a sizable leather-bound book. I was surprised to realize it was one of the few I *had* heard of, the *Dread Tome* (also known among the arcane literati as *Literaris Deus ex Negres*) and he began flipping through it. "Just checking something here, kid. Go get me the *Directory of the Dearly Departed*. That's the book we want. It's about six rows back, four shelves in. Hopefully your little crush from back at the Lovecraft will be listed there."

"Don't call her that," I snipped back, surprised at my own reaction. "She's . . ."

Connor took his attention away from the book for a second to give me a look of amusement. "Well, that was a little defensive," he said. "Got a little thing for Irene, kid?"

I didn't know what I felt for our newest case, but I wasn't about to let Connor put me on the spot for it. "No . . . it's just . . ."

Connor slapped the tome shut. "It's just what?" Connor demanded sternly, keeping his voice low enough so as not to attract Cyrus. "She's *dead*, kid. She's not like us anymore. Twenty-four hours ago, yes, she was just fine. Doing whatever a woman like her did. Having tea, perhaps hostilely taking over another company, doing the last few entries in a crossword puzzle . . . whatever her life entailed. But all that changed when she died, Simon. She's gone now. If you have feelings for her, I'm sorry but you're being naïve. You should have paid more attention during the *Desensitizing Difficult Deaths* seminar."

"They don't teach that anymore," I said peevishly. "All

you get now is a pamphlet on it in your welcome kit." I felt like some sort of necrophiliac pervert just thinking about Irene, ashamed that Connor had struck so close to a nerve I didn't even realize I had.

"Oh," said Connor. "Look, let's just focus on solving our first problem then: Who is she? You want to help her, you figure that out first, okay?"

I nodded. I started walking farther back into the Stacks.

"But I meant what I said, kid. Forget any foolish notions you're entertaining. You'll only hurt yourself."

Connor could save his warnings. My love life sucked enough as it stood. I had enough to contend with just deleting Tamara's calls of rage off my answering machine. I still had no idea what I was going to do about her.

When I found the *Directory of the Dearly Departed*, I pulled it from the shelf. It weighed a ton.

"You'd better watch out down there," Connor started. "Don't forget to . . ."

His words were drowned out by a sudden resounding roar that sprang up all around me. One second I was looking at what I thought was an ordinary bookcase—tall, ornate, carved from a thick, dark, polished wood. The next I was running from what was actually one pissed-off, bounding-with-great-agile-strides-toward-me kind of bookcase. I backed frantically down the row toward the junction and caught a glimpse of Connor running toward me, his face filled with panic and—I could have sworn—amusement.

"Wrong way, kid!" he shouted. "Don't stop, though!"

The bookcase tore after me down the cramped aisles, spilling books to the floor as it went. Occasionally, I caught a glimpse of Connor chasing it as it chased me. He struggled with the bag over his shoulder as he followed the renegade bookcase.

The aisle before me came to an abrupt end so I juked left down another. The stomping bookcase followed suit, but now I had lost sight of Connor. I hoped he had a plan, because running didn't seem to be doing much except tiring me out. I doubted, however, that the bookcase would get tired.

"What the *hell* is that thing?" I shouted, nearly breathless. I hoped hearing my voice would help Connor get an idea where I was. I was lost in row after row of books.

"Just keep moving!" Connor shouted back. I dashed by shelf after shelf. When I rounded the next corner, the tail end of my jacket snagged and I risked a glance back while I paused to tear myself free. The vicious-looking bookcase was hot in pursuit, its sides expanding and contracting as if panting while it closed the distance. My coat came free with a panicked tug, and I returned to fleeing.

"What *is* that thing?" I demanded again. My legs ached and I feared they would cramp up.

"Explain . . . later," Connor huffed, sounding closer. "Keep . . . running . . ."

At the next intersection, I threw myself down an aisle on my right, but with horror, I realized that it continued on only a little farther before coming to a dead end. No side aisles, no turnoffs. Just ceiling-high shelves on all sides, not to mention the living, breathing one closing in fast behind me. Giving in to total panic, I found a burst of speed that only marathon runners and career criminals could dig deep for and sprinted forward until there was nowhere left to run. Winded, I staggered around in a circle to fully take in the oncoming bookcase. The books that miraculously remained on its shelves formed a menacing gap-toothed smile.

This is not going to be pretty, I thought. In a last-ditch effort to save myself, I threw open my coat and pulled the retractable bat from its loop on my belt. It extended with a satisfying *shhhhkkt,* and I raised it into classic batter's stance, prepared to swing. I might die a stupid death—death by library—but I was determined to go down swinging.

As the bookcase thundered toward me, I spied a single arm popping over the top of it and then Connor's head came into view. His face was contorted with the struggle of clambering up the backside of the unit. From atop the bookcase, he caught sight of me poised with my bat and smiled.

Bless us, I thought, *we're going to Butch and Sundance this one. We're both going to be terribly crushed by this bookcase, but we're going out in a blaze of ridiculous glory.*

Connor reached into his bag, producing book after book as he slammed them onto the shelves from atop the charging bookcase. As each book hit the shelves, the case stumbled a little more unsteadily. With a great lurch to the left, the bookcase bounced off one side of the aisle like a pinball off a bumper and gave one final smash into the opposite side. It spun on one corner from sheer momentum and flipped over, pinning Connor underneath it as it crashed to the floor.

I rushed forward to Connor's aide. He was completely buried under the still squirming piece of furniture.

"Are you all right?" I shouted into the mass of books and limbs.

"Of course I'm not all right," Connor wheezed out testily from somewhere underneath the bookcase. "I'm stuck under an enchantedly pissed-off bookcase! Does that sound all right to you?"

"Right," I said apologetically. I tentatively grabbed hold of one end of the bookcase and lifted it up the few inches that I could. "Sorry."

The damn thing weighed a ton and was still thrashing around. Connor quickly slid himself out from underneath it and helped me lower it back to the ground.

"It's okay, kid. It's my fault," Connor said, catching his breath and checking to make sure his ribs were intact. "I wasn't thinking. I tried to warn you. I should have done it sooner."

"What the hell is it?" I asked as I nudged it with my foot. It gave a sudden helpless thrash and I raised my bat again.

"The Department's still not quite sure," said Connor. He brushed himself off. "All I know is that we're supposed to be extremely polite when asking for books from it. Since you didn't know that, it attacked . . ."

"Because I didn't ask nicely?!" I said. "How did . . . How did you . . . ?"

"How did I stop it?" Connor stooped and picked up one of the books he had shelved on it. He flipped through it. "Anytime I come in here, I carry a ready supply of really dangerous material. Dangerous to these shelves anyway. Self-published poetry anthologies, vanity press publications, local writing contest winners. Some chick lit for good measure. Really God-awful stuff. The bookshelves can't stomach them."

It had stopped moving by this point, and I leaned closer. "Is it . . . dead?"

"Oh, heavens, no," Connor said lightly as he gathered up his books. "We can't put a dent in something like this, not really. We've tried before. Or the D.E.A. has. Long before my time. Best we can do is render it harmless for a little while. I imagine what it'll experience is akin to a hangover more than anything."

I looked around.

"The place is a mess!" I said. "Should we go tell Cyrus?"

"And run the risk of him charging us for damages?" Connor said. "I don't think so. Besides, it'll get up in a little while and make its way back into place, books and all. Cyrus will be none the wiser."

Connor flipped over one of the books, scooped it up, and handed it to me. "Here you go."

"What's this?"

"It's the book I sent you to look for," Connor snapped. "Remember, kid? Geesh, maybe I *should* have let it crush you."

"That's not very nice," I said, kicking the bookcase once before stepping past it.

"It's better than being crushed to death," Connor said dismissively.

I opened the *Directory of the Dearly Departed* and flipped to the back, following Connor toward the door as I read. Beautifully cross-indexed, the directory provided a wealth of options that concerned hunting down sketchy information on the recently deceased. I could search by last name (I had no idea what Irene's was), religious affiliation (no crosses or other indicative jewelry so a blank there as well), location of death (I assumed Manhattan but nothing more specific), known demonic forces responsible for possible demises (I ignored this as there were mostly corporations and politicians listed), and lastly the means of demise.

Without hesitation, I flipped to a section entitled "Death by Bookcase" to see what other unfortunates had met my (almost) fate. There was page after page of entries; the most recent listing read "Simon Canderous" and gave my address in SoHo below it. Before I could even call out to Connor, the words faded from the page. Now I knew how Ebenezer felt in that graveyard with the Ghost of Christmas Yet to Come.

Thanks to Inspectre Quimbley's questioning earlier, we had a possible lead from Irene—a flash of yellow. Not much to go on, but this being Manhattan, I immediately flipped to "Death by Taxi." It looked like half the book was dedicated to such instances and the most recent page was filling up with new names and addresses at the speed of a stock ticker. I flipped through eleven pages of listings just from this morning until I came across the first listing for an Irene—a Manhattan address on the Upper West Side. As I wrote it down, I noticed her full name.

Irene *Blatt.*

Her name left a little to be desired. She had been so striking when I met her, so full of life and class, that I was sure that her name would be something exotic. I felt both relief and disappointment as I stared at the page.

Irene Blatt.

I rolled it around my mind, seeing if it would fall into place, and realized that it wouldn't. I double-checked the listing. There was a brief description of her, right down to the clothes she wore and the deep blue eyes of hers that I had fallen into. There was no doubt that this Central Park West resident was indeed our Irene.

"Irene . . . Blatt," I said out loud.

Connor turned and looked up from his book.

"I'm sorry, did you just burp? Blatt?" Connor said, his face curling up with distaste. "You must be joking."

"Does Irene *Blatt* seem like something I'd joke about?" I asked.

"Actually," Connor said with a chuckle, "joking would seem like the *only* way to bring up the word 'Blatt.'" He snapped *The Dread Tome* shut and slipped it back onto one of the inanimate shelves. "Is the address listed?"

I nodded. A heavy, clattering thump came from far back in the Stacks and I jumped at the sound. I caught the slightest twitch from Connor as well.

"Someone's waking up," I said.

"Yep," Connor said. He took the book from my hands and reshelved it as well. "Let's not stick around here for Round Two, shall we?"

Another volley of noise came from behind us, and I looked up the aisle toward the gate. There was a lot of space for us to cover and a whole lot of side aisles for something to charge us. "Do you think it's safe to leave?"

"I suppose," answered Connor, sounding quite unsure. "But just in case, you might want to get your bat out again."

9

I desperately wanted to head straight to Irene's address, but Connor wouldn't hear of it.

"Look, kid," he said. "I don't know what to expect when we get to her place, but I'm pretty sure we're gonna need your psychometry in top form. I don't want you walking in there unprepared or unable to deal with any surprises we might encounter. I don't want you flopping around on the floor like a fish out of water from low blood sugar because you couldn't control your powers. All right?"

I nodded. Even though I hated him for his clearheadedness, Connor was right.

We cabbed it from Tome, Sweet Tome down to the Twenties and over to Sixth Avenue before Connor got out and led us into a donut shop.

"Sugar yourself up, kid. We've got some tests to run."

If I was going to expend my powers during some field training, I was going to need as much sugar as I could take, and after scarfing down three Boston kremes in a row, I felt bouncy. Connor had never been around someone who went hypoglycemic from using their powers, but he seemed to be getting a kick out of watching me all sugared up.

"You gonna be all right, kid?" he asked. "Do you need a special helmet or something so you don't hurt yourself?"

I shook my head. We continued across the street, paid the two-dollar admission, and entered the ramshackle warehouse that played host to the Annex Antiques Fair. It was exceptionally warm outside for fall, but inside the market they were thankfully churning the air conditioning. It was a smart thing to do, really. Without controlling the climate inside, a lot of the antiques—especially the older furniture—would be at risk. I typically shied away from furniture when I wasn't buying for myself. I liked to snag the more portable discoveries when I was trolling for antique finds.

Bare bulb fluorescents hung high overhead, their unflattering light washing everything a little too brightly. The floor of the open warehouse space divided into row after row of sheetrock stalls that each vendor had stuffed full of their wares.

"It's like that warehouse at the end of *Raiders*," I said as I looked down one of the never-ending aisles. "Think they have the Ark of the Covenant here?"

Connor ignored me, but I didn't care. I was too busy taking it all in. This was the air that filled my lungs. Like the night market, this was its own type of holy ground—an enchanted place that whirled and swirled with rich fabrics and the light of a thousand lands reflected in almost every stall. It was living, always shifting, and sometimes dangerous. The world of secondhand goods was a dog-eat-dog world, gypsies and nomads fighting for every last sale.

I stopped to check the wares at one booth and noticed a young Asian woman approaching Connor. He had taken off his coat and was walking the aisles in tourist mode, and her "sucker radar" had picked up on his naiveté immediately. She swooped in, coming to rest on his arm like a falcon.

"Right this way," she said with a flourish of Mandarin in her voice. It rang out like the soft tinkling of wind chimes. Connor smiled and turned to follow her as she kept talking. "I show you something nice. Something you give your girl-friend. She like earrings? We got many beautiful earrings here for her."

I hurried over, waving at the woman. I grabbed her hands from Connor's arm politely but firmly, and said, "No, thank you. He's not interested."

"Ohhh," she said, with a knowing wink and a coy smile. "I see how it is. We have something nice he buy for *you* then!"

"What?" I said and then it dawned on me—she thought we were a couple. I had to give her credit as a salesperson, though. Without any judgment call or even skipping a beat, she continued her sales pitch unfazed.

"No, it's not like that," I said.

She nodded and winked again.

"Connor," I pleaded. "Tell her."

Connor turned to me and put his hands on his hips "Honestly! No need to be such a *bitch* about things, Simon. I swear! It's like you're embarrassed to be seen in public with me!"

He stormed off down the aisle like a faux drama queen before I could get a word in. I chased after him, thankfully ending my conversation with the woman. Connor had ended up in a quiet section full of Indian fabrics, throws, and pil-lows in rich shades of purple, orange, and deep red. Thank God no one was paying attention to us. When I caught up with him, tears of laughter were running down his face. I just stared at Connor and shook my head.

"What's wrong?" he said when he saw I wasn't laughing.

"Can you please not make a scene?" I said, angry. "Do I have to remind you that I'm recognizable in these circles? I've worked very hard to be taken seriously here."

"Sorry," Connor offered, sobering. "Fine. Let's get started. Just grab anything. I need to see how you compare to some of the other psychometry experts in Other Division."

"*What* other psychometry experts?" I said. "With the Mayor's budget cuts, there's only Mrs. Teasley and myself as the select few in the Department who exhibit any signs of psychic awareness. And truth be told, the jury's still out on Mrs. T."

But I was willing to play this game. I moved through the piles of decorative fabrics, watching them shimmer with dancing lights from the hundreds of tiny mirrors sewn into their patterns. I kept going until I came to a table piled high with books. Hardcovers, dog-eared yellowing paperbacks, and two full stacks of comics. I slipped my gloves off and passed my hand over the books one by one, looking for anything that might stir my power.

"In the past," I explained, "my visions have been somewhat sporadic when they come, but when they do . . . it's like I'm seeing a slice of the former owner's life. Some are clearer than others. Sometimes they don't come through at all."

"What's your best guess as to why it's so hit or miss?" Connor asked, flipping through one of the old paperbacks.

I paused my hand over a beat-up copy of *House of the Seven Gables*. Usually holding an old edition of a Hawthorne was good for something, but this time I didn't feel the slightest twinge of my power. I continued rummaging.

I shrugged at Connor. "I imagine that it all depends on the object and how long the owner has been out of contact with it, as well as whatever emotional significance the piece has."

I picked through more of the books, but it was hard to concentrate with Connor watching me.

"Anything?" he said with finality in his voice.

I shook my head. "None of this stuff is charged with anything I can read."

"Well, kid," he started, leaning against one of the support beams between the booths, "that's part of the problem."

"What do you mean?" I asked. My hands were dusty from touching all the books and I wiped them against my coat.

"If you want to help Irene and be part of this investigation, you need to think of what you do as something scientific, and in order for something to be labeled science, it's got to be repeatable. Some of the people who teach psi-science theorize that you should be able to pick up *any-thing* and get a reading off of it. *Every* object is supposed to have its own vibrations that reflect its entire history. So it follows that every object should resonate with that at all times."

I had never really treated my abilities as something scientific. They were simply an unexplainable phenomenon.

"If that's true," I asked, picking up another book, "then why aren't I getting a reading from this?"

"I don't know," Connor said. "Lazy? Unfocused, maybe? Let's try something—"

"Fine. What do you sugg—" I started, but didn't have a chance to finish my sentence.

Connor slapped me hard across the cheek with the back of his hand. I dropped the book I was holding. "What the fu—"

Connor picked the book up and shoved it back into my hands, and just like that, I psychometrically slipped into the life of someone else. I was the book's previous owner—a man—and I instantly knew the book was an il-lustrated copy of the Kama Sutra. A ton of the facts of this man's life flooded into my head. He taught philosophy at a small New England college, and at the moment of the vi-sion, he was sitting naked in his study at home. He was fit for a man in his midforties, with blond curly hair that was graying at the temples. Another eager-to-earn-an-A female student was just leaving his house. The Kama Sutra lay open before him on his desk. Without even bothering to dress, he started taking copious notes over his latest sexual conquest in the margins, detailing which techniques and positions he had experimented with tonight. The names of other students filled the rest of the margin, each with one, two, or three stars next to their names. Of particular note was the unforgettable Katie B., the only recipient to receive four stars *and* an exclamation point. The things she had done kneeling on his office desk, and all while a class was going on in the next room!

I jolted out of the vision with the fleeting memories of the randy professor's sexual encounters locked into my mind. My body's sugar dropped but the donuts I had scarfed helped make the aftereffects minimal. I swayed slightly as I attempted to shake off the disorientation. Connor grabbed my arm to steady me.

"Well?" Connor asked. "What did you see? Anything?"

"You don't want to know," I said. "Trust me." I felt my face flush from embarrassment. The stinging sensation in my cheek rose again and I rubbed it. "What the hell was with the slapping?"

Connor took the book from me and flipped through it. "That was part of the experiment, kid. Sometimes people have powers that activate under extreme circumstances. Anger, pain . . . you name it."

"Great! So I'm the psychic equivalent of the Incredible Hulk." I snatched the book back from him.

Connor laughed. "I wouldn't worry about it too much. It doesn't mean that you're going to become a raging psychometrist with no self-control. What it does show, though, is that you are able to use your powers on previously unreadable objects given the right emotional stimulus." He tapped one of the book stacks with his forefinger. "Try again, except I want you to do three or four as fast as you can."

I scooped up a tiny leather-bound copy of *Pride and Prejudice*. I flipped it open and was surprised to find delicate oilskin pages within, but the excitement of the moment flipped my mind's eye into yet another vision. It was always odd to be female, but that's who I was. Short reddish hair, "copper wire" her mother had called it years earlier, and tiny oval frames adorned her face. She was a writer, pigeonholed as a fantasist, but her true loves were the classics. As she discovered this volume of Austen, she could hardly believe it was only forty dollars! She adored its perfect little form, so compact yet so full of wonderful language that she could barely contain herself.

As I came out of the vision, the weakness hit again, harder this time, but Connor was waiting. He slammed a large floppy paperback into my arms and the only word I could make out on the book's spine was *Cookbook*. I braced myself, expecting some boring scene of a homemaker crockpotting soup or perhaps images of a family settling in for Thanksgiving dinner. I was not prepared to find myself in the back of a bookstore. I was a greasy-haired teen in a long black coat. I checked the book in my hands and saw that, upon closer examination, it wasn't a cookbook in the traditional sense. *The Anarchists Cookbook*, the cover read—a modern-day guide to urban survival, full of such fun stuff as growing your own weed or making a pipe bomb. The teenager checked to make sure that no one was nearby and quickly stuffed the book down the back of his pants, pulling his sweater down over it to hide the bulge. His heart raced as he walked past the cashier and toward the door, sure that he'd get caught . . .

When I pulled out of the vision, Connor was waiting with another book, but I waved it away weakly. "Enough. Are you trying to kill me?"

My heart raced and my palms were thick with sweat. I had depleted whatever reserve of sugar the donuts had built up in my bloodstream. I fished a roll of Life Savers from my pocket and consumed the whole roll in two sections.

"Just trying to toughen you up," he said.

I knew the drain was making me cranky, but I couldn't help snapping at him.

"Why don't *you* try it for a while then?"

"Hey!" Connor fired back. "Easy there. I'm just trying to get us ready to investigate your precious Ms. Blatt's apartment. If we're out in the field and your body craps out on me like this, it puts both of us in jeopardy. I'm trying to build you up. I want you at your peak."

I guess he felt that was apology enough and fell silent.

"Remind me why they've got you teaching me again?" Already I could feel my body processing the sugar, the dizziness fading.

Connor put the books back on the table. "It's simple," he said. "Those who can do, do. Those who can't do, teach. Those who can't teach? They get stuck teaching psi-science."

"*That's* comforting," I said.

"You want the truth?" he asked. He sounded pissed off so I nodded. "City Hall . . . again. Why else would they put a spook specialist in charge of you? The pay's not good enough to get more experts on psychometry in here even if we could find more people like you. There's no one left who's remotely qualified to teach you, not for the money we can offer, unless you'd rather apprentice to Mrs. Teasley?"

I shook my head.

"All our most promising parapsychologists have left either to film their own infomercials, become a Psychic Friend, or run a psychic retreat in the Bahamas on some cruise ship."

"Ooh! When do I get my own infomercial?" I asked. It

didn't sound like a bad deal. "I could stand a bit of the tropics."

"Look," Connor said soberly. I heard the Lecture Switch click over in his voice. "There's about a million better ways to make money with the abilities you have, and I can't stop you from choosing a route that's going to give you a big fat check, kid. But I guarantee you won't find any other use of your powers more gratifying. You're learning to do Good, with a capital 'G,' for Goodness' sake. Helping people like Irene. No amount of money beats that."

Usually, I only half listened when Connor went into this mode, but I was a captive audience while I regained my strength.

"We *are* poorly paid," I said, "and on top of that, the other more 'legitimate' arms of civil service and law enforcement hate us. They laugh at us behind our back and think we're all certifiable."

Connor nodded.

"Still, kid," he said, "when I think of the people we help in the face of all the red tape and bullshit, how many Irenes might fall through the cracks and get lost in the system otherwise? Well, without well-intentioned people like us around—"

I squirmed at the thought that my intentions with Irene might not be purely good, and cut him off.

"It's frustrating," I said, as I started back toward the exit. "I definitely had no idea what I was getting into when I joined the Department . . ."

Now it was Connor's turn to interrupt. "But you were surprised to find that you liked helping others, right? Doing Good *is* its own reward, kid."

I smiled. It was a very Hallmark moment.

"Besides," Connor continued, "you could always fall back on whoring out your powers to Dionne Warwick if you have to—once you do hone them, that is." Connor put his arm around me as a means of support. "C'mon. Let's go check out Ms. *Blatt's* address . . ."

Connor's phone rang, playing a digitized "As Time Goes By," and he pulled it out and flipped it open. "Yeah?" he said, then after listening for a few seconds. "Got it."

He looked at me. "Sorry, kid. Your dead lady friend is going to have to wait. We've got a Code Gray. Jesus, first all the increased lingering spirit activity and now this!"

"Code Gray . . ." I repeated, trying to remember what the hell it was, then it hit me. "Zombies?"

Connor nodded. "Whole nest of 'em. Bring your bat. Should be fun."

I wanted to get to Irene's, but I knew the rules. If another department called a code like this, everyone scrambled. Zombies were an insidious infection, and if you didn't cut them off quick, Manhattan was fucked. I felt surprisingly chipper as we headed out; I could use the batting practice.

10

By the time we finished helping out the Things That Go Bump in the Night Division exterminate the zombies, I was exhausted. I nearly fell asleep as I cabbed it back to the Lovecraft Café. It had been a long day of psychometric pop-quiz training, bookcase combat, and a grueling round of Whack-a-Shuffler. My bat reeked of rot from the Code Gray and I couldn't wait to clean it. Once again, the Department's "business as unusual" motto had held true.

I was too exhausted and repulsive to even contemplate investigating Irene's place tonight. But then, the thought of investigating Irene's home tonight or even things at my own—the clutter of packing crates in the living room, deleting Tamara's latest volley of berating messages from the answering machine—all these thoughts further exhausted me.

As I entered the offices, I was so distracted with thoughts of zombies going squish and sorting out the women in my head that I ran smack into Director Wesker. Unfortunately, I had just pulled off one of my gloves and my hand slammed into a Moleskine notebook that Wesker was carrying. I recognized it as one of the many that were kept down in the Gauntlet, the Department's ancient records archive. Before I had a chance to react or restrain my power, the electric charge of connection kicked in and images concerning the necromantic history of Benjamin Franklin started to fill my head. The images of a near-skeletal version of one of our nation's heroes filled my brain. The sudden shock of seeing it was too great, and with my exhaustion, I couldn't will myself out of it.

The vision snapped away suddenly and I came around to find Wesker holding the book protectively away from me. Having an object taken away from me was far more disorienting and draining than when I completed a vision myself, and all I could do was stare at him for a minute while I tried to steady myself. God, psychometry could be a bitch.

As usual, Wesker's eyes were hidden behind his mirrored frames, and even up close, I still couldn't see the hint of his eyes behind them. He shot me a smug smile.

"Out of my way," I said, hearing the waver of false bravado in my voice. Wesker just folded his arms defiantly across the expanse of his chest with the book now tucked neatly beneath them.

"I don't think so, newbie," he said, then sniffed. "What's the horrendous odor?"

"That would be me," I said, holding up my ichor-covered bat. He gave it the same dirty look he usually reserved for my face.

"Rumor has it that you caused a little ruckus over at Tome, Sweet Tome."

"Word travels fast around here," I said, attempting to push back most of the edge in my voice. I reminded myself that I should keep myself in check around the divisional directors. Thaddeus Wesker was, after all, still the head of not one but *two* divisions, and he aspired to even greater posts than that. Not to mention that although I was in the safety of our own office, I still thought he might hit me.

Wesker unfolded his arms and dug his fingers into my right shoulder. "When the owner of one of the premiere occult bookshops in the country calls my department to report an assault against some of his rare books and even rarer creatures, I do have a problem," he said. "One that I'll be bringing up with the Enchancellors, I assure you."

The mere thought of my name even being on the lips of our governing board worried me. I was happiest when I flew under the radar, learning my way through the ins and out of the D.E.A without the nervousness that came with constant attention. I had enough to worry myself over as it stood. Controlling my powers and reining them in were my priority, and that alone took up most of my concentration. I raised my slime-covered bat slowly and moved it toward the hand that was gripping me. Quickly Wesker released me.

"Do what you have to do, Director Wesker," I said wearily. "I don't care. Right now, as a member of Other Division, I answer to the Inspectre. I suppose he'll reprimand me if I've earned it. All I know is that we were paying customers in that store, renting time in the Stacks, when this . . . bookcase *thing* . . . tried to kill me. Seems I'm the only one who was wronged there, *sir*."

I couldn't see why anyone from the D.E.A., even Wesker, would side with a complaint filed by Cyrus Mandalay. Who really cared what an occult bookstore owner complained about? Wesker finally moved to one side. With a flourish, he gestured toward the rest of the office. He waved his hand in a shoo-ing motion.

"By all means then," he said bitterly, "don't let me keep you. I'm sure you have some paperwork to catch up on or office supplies to steal."

The reminder of my waiting paperwork stung hard, and as I walked past Wesker, I couldn't resist a parting shot.

"It's not my fault the F.O.G.ies won't accept you," I muttered.

"What was that?" he growled from behind me.

I picked up my pace now that I was past him.

"Nothing!" I shouted cheerfully. It was a small dig, but regardless of its size, it still tasted of victory.

At this time of evening, the offices were all but deserted. I washed my bat in the bathroom sink, collapsed it into its sheath, and then wound my way down the main aisle until I reached our desks. I sat down and wearily filled out the eight forms that an interdepartmental zombie exterminating excursion invariably generated, made three photocopies of each, and then dropped them in the right in-boxes. It was pointless not to do them right away—the director of Things That Go Bump in the Night was a real stickler for prompt paperwork, and he'd have his assistant harassing me at home if I wasn't careful. I returned to my desk. The tower of paper sitting in my in-box had doubled since earlier in the day, but I ignored it once again and started gathering reference material to go over at home that I thought might prove helpful to Irene's case. I grabbed a copy of *The Complete Riddles of the Sphinx* and a pamphlet entitled *Understanding the Fates* and stuffed them into my bag. That would count as my light reading for the evening. I was headed for the door, free and clear, when I caught something out of the corner of my eye and stopped. Irene was sitting in the chair next to my desk staring at me like a lost kitten. I don't know how I had missed her, except for being totally distracted in my hurry to get the hell out of there. Anxiety filled her deep, blue eyes.

"Hello," she said, hope spreading with a shy smile across her face. "Any luck today?"

"Some," I said, setting my bag back down. "We're pretty sure we found your last name . . . Ms. Blatt."

Irene scrunched her face up in exactly the same manner Connor had.

"Really?" She seemed disappointed. I couldn't blame her.

"Yeah. Sorry."

She sat there in silence, shifted in her chair, and crossed her legs. Not knowing what to say, I made busy with my paperwork again. But something struck me. I let the papers fall to the desk. "Irene . . . have you been sitting here all day?"

She nodded.

"Hasn't anyone talked to you . . . helped you out at all?"

"Other than Inspectre Quimbley?" she asked. "No."

Irene had fallen through the cracks, lost among the red tape and bureaucracy that passed as business here at the D.E.A. There was too big a caseload for most of the agents here, and no one picked up the slack on walk-ins like Irene. So just leave it for Other Division. It made me furious.

"Is there somewhere I can stay?" she asked. "If it's not too much trouble . . ."

I shook my head. "They're not really set up to deal with otherworldly accommodations of this sort, only for detaining troublesome spirits. The D.E.A. doesn't really function as a paranormal hostel."

Irene looked crestfallen. I made a note to talk to Inspectre Quimbley in the morning. We needed to have a policy in place for these exceptions. If I didn't put the wheels in motion, City Hall would delay us in setting it up for years to come with meetings and permits and permits to have meetings.

In the meantime, though, it made me feel terrible that Irene had been sitting here waiting patiently the whole day without another soul to talk to. I couldn't just leave her. Members of the graveyard shift were arriving through the movie house entrance, but I wasn't going to pass her off onto people she didn't know. There was only one course of action that felt right.

"Listen, Irene. I don't think you'll want to hang around my desk all night. Heck, it's my desk and I don't want to be stuck at it all that long. And since I haven't really made any headway other than finding out your name and address, I feel the least I could do is offer to put you up at my apartment tonight."

"That's really too kind of you to offer," Irene said. If moderately corporeal ghosts could be said to blush, her face reddened and she broke into a wicked smile. "Are you sure?"

I glanced away, feeling a bit self-conscious about having made the offer and stuffed a random handful of papers into my bag. I didn't know how the Inspectre or Connor would react to such a thing, but what other options did I have? "No, it's no trouble at all. Like I said, the Department isn't really equipped to host you for the evening."

"Really?" Irene asked as she rose. "I should think they'd be used to this sort of thing."

I couldn't stop futzing with papers or rummaging around inside my bag. Why was I feeling so uncomfortable? Hadn't I been told there would be situations stranger than this when I had signed on with the Department? If Connor had been around to consult, I would have felt more at ease, but he had left. That was a small part of my nervousness, but it also had to do with the fact that this would be the first woman in my apartment since the Tamara debacle. Well, ex-woman. I knew if Irene was to have any peace there, though, my answering machine would have to stay muffled in the drawer.

I smiled at her. "Yes, you would think the Department was used to this type of thing, wouldn't you? But . . . well, it's several things, really."

"Like what?"

I stopped futzing and turned to face her. She deserved my full attention. "You're different, Irene. The Department is used to all kinds of weirdness, but you don't really pigeonhole for them neatly. You seem too alive to be dead."

Irene's solid shape began to go semitransparent as she became agitated. I could make out one of the night shifters coming on duty straight through her.

"Well, I *am* dead," she said with a bit of angry sarcasm. "Doesn't that count for something with you people?"

"Please, let me explain," I said, and without thinking, I attempted to take her less-than-solid hand. My gesture made her more solid, and I felt that electric charge again when my hand passed through her. "The directors and agents here deal with the deceased in an almost entirely bureaucratic way, and nine times out of ten, most ghosts are far less . . . living than you. Far less interesting and far less alive."

"I see," Irene said.

"Dealing with you, as an apparition who is still clinging to human emotions and feelings, well . . . they're not up to it."

"And what about you?" she asked. "Why are you up for it?"

"Maybe because I'm still new here," I offered. "Maybe I'm too dumb to know any better yet."

I wanted to take it back as soon as I said it and say something more reassuring.

The silence grew between us as the sounds of the office coming to life with the arrival of the late shift rose up around us. As the silence began its journey into unbearable, I snapped out of it.

"Would you like to get out of here?" I asked and grabbed my bag.

She looked relieved and nodded. "Yes. I would like that very much."

I led the way out of the Department, past the oblivious moviegoers in the theater who were watching *The Thin Man*, and into the coffeehouse proper. Mrs. Teasley was still there, her cat softly purring on her lap and her fingers deep in a pile of still steaming coffee grounds. She smiled as we walked past, and then Irene and I were out on the street.

I wondered about how Irene would fare walking all the way to SoHo given her less-than-corporeal form. Would other people move out of the way for her, or was there a danger of them accidentally walking through her and setting off widespread panic in the streets?

"You'd better stay close," I said, and moved directly in front of her so she could follow me safely. But in fact, people naturally avoided her on the street, as if some untapped part of their minds knew something extraordinary was at hand, and wanted to get the hell away. Animals, however, noticed her. Before we hit the end of the block, four dogs had looked at us oddly and started barking. As we turned left onto Broadway heading downtown, the crowds thinned, and the rest of our trip went without incident.

I fumbled with the lock like a nervous teen bringing a new girlfriend home when his parents were out of town. I told myself to stop being ridiculous and finally managed to get the key in, then lead Irene down the main hall to the charming wrought iron elevator.

"It's beautiful," she said as she entered it. "So turn of the century."

"Yeah," I said. "I love it, too.

"I'm always reminded of a simpler age," I continued, "of times gone by."

Irene smiled. "That's a very romantic notion, Mr. Canderous."

As we rode the rest of the way up to the slow rhythmic clanking of the elevator, I couldn't help but check her out. The curve of her mouth was adorable. God, was my love life so messed up that I was finding any woman—even a dead one—attractive? Color me necro-curious.

Few people visited my home, and I had never knowingly had a ghost in my apartment before—certainly not one as intriguing as Irene. She possessed what my father had referred to as "carriage"—a special way of presenting herself that spoke of worldliness, a personal grace that seemed innate. I hadn't run across many women who pulled it off these days.

Irene caught me staring and smiled. My face flushed. "Sorry," I said. Few things in my experience were worse than being caught checking someone out. Thankfully, the elevator stopped and I quickly slid the accordion doors aside and gestured for Irene to step out.

"You'd think I'd never dealt with the dead before," I said apologetically.

She whirled around, looking upset—and once again I was able to see straight through her. I could make out my apartment door through her down the hall. "Please don't," she said.

"Don't what?"

"Please don't refer to me as *that*." She sighed. "The dead. I'm afraid I'm not quite used to the idea yet and I'd prefer it if you'd just call me Irene."

"I'm sorry, Irene."

Stupid, real stupid. I excused myself and headed down the hall toward my apartment door. I had to make a better effort tonight to think before I spoke. I opened the door and flicked on the light.

"You'll have to excuse the place," I said. "I haven't had a chance to clean."

Usually I was quite proud of my apartment, but not with the way I had left it. The main living space was still cluttered with crates, hiding the normally impressive Clue conservatory atmosphere I had been working so hard to cultivate.

"It's absolutely marvelous," she said.

"You think?" I asked, surprised by her reaction. "I've always wanted to live in a Nick and Nora film. I'm afraid my current look isn't quite doing it."

Irene walked across the living room, blithely passing through several unopened crates and boxes of every possible size. She stopped inside the middle of one of my brass-tacked leather sofas and looked around. I was surprised to realize that I desperately wanted her to be impressed. I watched as Irene crossed to the room's focal point—towering bookcases full of the finds I had recovered over the years. Last night's bag with the Intellevision and games was still there. I didn't know what she had expected, but as she marveled over the shelves, I could tell it wasn't this.

"You're certainly well-read," she said, looking at all my books and grinning.

"It's all lies," I said.

She turned, puzzled. "How so?"

"Well, none of this space is really me," I said. "I've developed a space for the type of guy I *hope* to be—a man who wants space to think, to be cultured, and to be able to do it in comfort and style. It still feels a little like a ruse to me, though. I never feel quite at ease with the finer things I surround myself with."

Still, I wanted Irene to appreciate it, and it looked like she did. I felt a rush of pride.

I cleared boxes from one of the leather Catalina sofas and stuffed handfuls of scattered packing materials into a tall wooden crate from which a Tiffany floor lamp poked out precariously.

"I've been meaning to get to all this," I said. I straightened the lamp and secured it with a few handfuls of the packing material. "Really. It's kind of gotten out of control lately with my caseload at the Department."

Irene laughed, covering her mouth with one hand as she did so. "I completely understand your appreciation."

"You do?" I asked. "How's that?" I muscled a painting-shaped crate to the floor and shoved it toward the row of bay windows that ran down the other side of the room.

Irene started to answer, but paused instead and sat down in the space I had cleared. "You know, I'm not quite sure *why* I said that."

I stopped what I was doing and sat down next to her on the sofa. "Maybe you remembered something . . . ?"

"It's possible," she said with a frown of concentration. "I'm really not sure."

She was agitated by her lack of memory. I couldn't imagine how I'd handle missing my entire memory. Hell, I got agitated when I couldn't remember where my keys were, and Irene's situation was worse to the nth degree.

"Just relax and think," I instructed. Maybe I could get something out of her with a little guidance. "You said it for a reason, Irene. Did something about my apartment trigger something for you?"

Her nose crinkled with even greater concentration as I watched, but I didn't smile in case it distracted her.

Finally, with a hesitant look of triumph, she said, "I . . . I think I may have been a lot like you, Simon. A collector. When you were talking about how you never could find the time to take care of all these things or get them put away, well, it struck a chord in me." She thought for a moment longer. "I think that's something that I may have been doing with my own life. Or if I wasn't, I think it's something I would have been very much interested in doing."

"Well, that's certainly a start," I said encouragingly.

My stomach rumbled loud enough for both of us to hear. "Are you hungry? I'm going to cook something."

She laughed and shook her head. "No, thank you. Given my . . . condition, I'm not exactly sure how I would manage that anyway."

"Right," I said, feeling the fool once again. "Sorry."

"Stop apologizing, Simon," she said sternly. "It's okay."

It was the first time she had said my name, and a smile crept upon my face.

"It's terribly sweet of you to offer, though," she continued. "For your sake, I could *try* to eat but I have a strong suspicion it would end up all over your couch, like Mr. Christos's drink back at the café."

There was an awkward moment before I took that as my cue to get up off the couch and made my way to the kitchen. I worried about leaving her alone, but I could still keep an eye on her over the counter that divided the two rooms.

I stripped off my gloves and pulled some questionable-looking chicken from the fridge. Living dangerously, I set it in a skillet over low heat while I chopped up a mix of garlic and portabella mushrooms. When I was done, I poured balsamic vinegar over the veggies and threw the mixture into the skillet as well. I started in on a zucchini as I noticed that Irene had moved herself to one of the stools on just the other side of the counter, where she seemed content to watch me work.

"No offense," she said, "but that seems like more of an effort than I'd expect from a typical bachelor."

"I used to eat take-out nearly every night. Enough MSG in my system for seven heart attacks, probably."

"So why did you learn how to cook?" she asked.

"The curse of my life," I said. "Women. I've never had luck with the ladies, but I thought I might keep them around a little longer if I at least learned to impress them with cooking. It didn't really work, but I did get used to eating well. Even though I'm alone, I don't feel like going back to my menu-collecting days."

"Well, I'm impressed," she said, clapping. "And just what do you call what you're making?"

I threw the zucchini into my countertop steamer and

leaned over the counter conspiratorially. "I call this meal *Third Date with Jessica.* Better known as *Last-Minute-Download Number Sixteen.* Not terribly romantic sounding, I'm afraid."

"I'm sure it worked like a charm," she said. "I know it would have worked with me."

I looked at her and her body flickered as she blushed. I suppressed a smile. As usual, I had made quite a mess in such a short time in my kitchen. I set about cleaning up the remnants of my handiwork as my food cooked. I hoped keeping busy would help me avoid any further dorkiness on my part.

"Do you miss it?" she asked, resting her chin on her open palms. "Cooking for two, I mean?"

I turned on the faucet and let the warm water run over my hands while I thought about her question.

"Do I miss having someone around is what you mean," I said. "I don't know. I've never gone long enough dating someone to really feel the ties of cohabitation. I've gotten pretty used to the hermit life. I like my space. It's set up the way I prefer it, except for all that packing clutter. I'm comfortable in it."

Irene waggled her finger at me. "That doesn't really answer my question, now does it, Simon? Shame on you!"

"Okay, okay!" I said with a grin. "I admit it. I like having someone around. I miss the company, the sound of another person's voice, someone to cook for. But what am I going to do, you know?"

"What do you mean?"

It had been a long time since I had confided the truth about my powers to anyone. I took a deep breath. I held up my soap-covered hands and flexed my fingers at her. "I mean, what am I going to do about these?"

"You mean, what you did with the PEZ dispenser back at the café?"

"You watched that?" I asked.

She grinned sheepishly. "I was eaves-watching."

I nodded. "Well, psychometry doesn't really make being with someone an option."

"I'm sorry," she said with a shake of her head, "but I'm afraid I still don't quite understand what that is really."

I washed my hands and slipped my gloves back on as I stepped to her on her side of the counter. I headed for a carton sitting behind the couch, grabbed it by its flaps, and rested it on my lap as I sat on the barstool next to hers.

"What is all that?"

"The remnants of girlfriends past," I said. I slanted the carton to show her the items within. Scarves, mix tapes, pictures, books, hairbrushes, and even a few pieces of sexy underwear from Victoria's Sock Drawer or wherever they had been purchased. I moved the box closer so she could see everything, making sure I didn't let either of my hands touch anything in it. I could feel the electric pull of my power stirring just holding the box, so I put it back down hastily. "Things they left behind or things they gave me. For most normal people? Pleasant memories of their time together. For me? They'll never be anything more than invasive doorways into other people's thoughts. Intimacy beyond intimacy. Everyone else's memories are stored in these, but for me they're pain in its purest form."

"Why do you keep them then?" she asked.

I shrugged. "I don't know. Look around, I'm a packrat, maybe that's it. Or maybe I have trouble letting go because in some sick way I see it as some sort of penance for being cursed with this power."

"But surely you must take some consolation in helping others with your gift!" she said.

Before I had a chance to answer, the smell of garlic overpowered me and I ran back around the counter to save my dinner from the brink of burning ruin.

"Yeah," I said once things were back in control. "For most of my life, my ability has been treated as nothing more than a magic act or something to laugh over. Now I'm finally able to use it to some good end other than my own selfish needs and I like it. I can deal with all that. What I *can't* deal with is how it affects my personal life, especially dating. I don't want to be in the head of someone I'm involved with. It's . . . it's devastating. Do you know what it's like to see someone you're dating having sex with another person?

"If that isn't some heavy strangely homoerotic shit to deal with, I'd like to know what is. And everything in that box is a trigger for visions like that. Just like anyone who gets close to me is."

To help the weakening sensation pass, I pushed past the disorientation and plated my food, setting the still sizzling skillet back on the stove. It felt exhausting to finally articulate out loud what had been rolling around in my head unspoken for months, but liberating, too.

"At least you can touch *something*," Irene said without a hint of sympathy.

There was awkward silence for a moment, but then we both burst out laughing. I felt a little embarrassed about how whiny I must have sounded. Still, it lightened the dark mood I was setting with my "poor me" ramblings. Suddenly I felt in better spirits. To tease her, I cut myself a nice, big juicy piece of chicken with several mushrooms piled high on top of it. I popped the whole thing in my mouth and chewed with slow, blissful satisfaction. "Too bad you can't taste. Delicious!"

Irene feigned pouting and stormed back to the couch. The whole act was so cute that I stole another discrete opportunity to check her out once again. She might be dead, but that didn't mean she wasn't hot. I felt no shame in thinking that this time. The nervousness of taking the wayward ghost into my home melted away. I strongly suspected that the reason I got along with her was because there was absolutely no chance of getting in Irene's pants or of setting off my powers by touching her. Touching was something we couldn't do, no matter what that pottery-spinning movie might have tried to convince me of.

While I finished eating dinner, Irene seemed content to poke through my collection of books. The shelves towered well above her normal reach, but she rose up in the air toward several books that caught her eye without even noticing she was floating.

The odd mix of my collection was not overly reflective of my own tastes, and I worried what she might think when she saw such eclectic combos as *Curious George* sitting next to *The Encyclopedia of Serial Killers*. Some were simply books that had caught my fancy and others I meant to redistribute to their original owners or antiquarian book dealers. I cleared my throat.

"I can show you where you'll be staying," I said, "if you like."

"I'd like that," she said with a nod, and drifted back down to the floor. I put my dishes in the sink as she headed toward the rear hallway.

"Irene . . ." I began, but panicked when I saw her phase through the first door on her left.

"Is this my ro—" She was cut off as she vanished through the door.

It was the one door I didn't want her or anyone to enter, the one door I kept locked. Shit. I ran for my jacket hanging over the back of the couch, fished out my keys, and dashed down the hall.

"Irene!" I yelled through the door. "Hold on."

I could hear her gasp on the other side as I fumbled my keys with nervously shaking hands. When I got the door open, Irene was standing stone still, giving off a soft luminescence that I hadn't noticed until I saw her in stark contrast to the darkness of the room. I flicked on the light and the blinding whiteness of the room sprang to life.

"What in heaven's name . . . ?" she gasped.

"Welcome to the White Room," I said. Compared to the rest of my apartment, the room looked completely out of place.

Irene turned to me apprehensively. "Would you care to elaborate on this?" she asked hesitantly. "It's all a bit . . . extreme, don't you think?"

"It's not as crazy as it looks," I said. I wished I could undo the past few minutes. If only I had been faster, if only I could have kept her away. I felt defensive, in panic mode. "No one is ever supposed to see this room! That's why I keep it *locked*. I didn't even think about you passing right through the door."

"For heaven's sake, Simon. Sit yourself down." Irene moved closer to me and there was compassion in those eyes. With a slightly clearer head, I shuffled to the chair in the center of the room before I collapsed.

"I'm sorry," I said. "It's just that no one's ever been in here. No one. Of all people, though, I suppose I'm lucky it was you. There's no danger of tainting the space since you can't really touch anything."

Irene kneeled before me. Her own concerns were forgotten if only for a moment. It was terribly ego-stroking and a little bit thrilling to be the center of her attention. But in the White Room, it was an uncomfortable sensation, and I fought the urge to leap out of my chair and run to the safety of another room.

"What is all this?" Irene asked again.

I took a deep breath and choked down my discomfort. "Superman has his Fortress of Solitude. Batman has his Bat Cave. I have this."

"Oh God," she said with a look of half-joking horror. "You think you're a superhero!"

I laughed and shook my head. "No, not at all. I'm not delusional, I swear. But those characters, fictional though they are, have one thing in common. A place to hang their cape, a secret place away from the outside world where they feel truly themselves . . . truly safe. This is it for me—or as close as it gets. This is my safety room. This is where I come when I fear my abilities."

The look on Irene's face only needed to have a light bulb coming to life over her head to complete it. "This is your inner sanctum. Your holy place."

I nodded. She actually got it and I could have kissed her.

"It's rather stark," she said. "Why does it look like it was designed after heaven's waiting room?"

"Everything else in this apartment is potentially loaded with other people's thoughts," I said. "That box by the front door was a prime example. I need a place that is clean of any potential triggers. A place I can retreat to, where I know I'm in control."

She had stopped staring and started checking out the contents of the room. "And all this furniture . . . ?"

"Straight from the manufacturer," I said. The slightest twinge of pride tugged at my heart. "I know it seems obsessive, but given the nature of my power, I really had to go out of my way to get items that were least likely to trigger an episode. Each piece of furniture is brand new, never touched except by the machines that crafted their basic components. I even picked them up direct from the warehouse myself because I didn't want deliverymen handling them. I assembled them and finished the job using the same coat of white on everything in the room. Fresh paint mixed up right in the store seems to dull the psychic impressions most."

Irene walked around the room. Her footsteps made no sound whatsoever.

"You know," she said with a grin, "psychologists would have a field day with your disorder."

"This chair," I continued, ignoring her comment. "It's from a store in the Bowery. It had been sitting among the back stock for years, but it was just what I had been looking for—something new, unused, and relatively untouched for a long period of time. You should have seen how absolutely hideous it was before I painted and recushioned it."

"Aren't you a regular albino Martha Stewart!" she said and attempted to touch my face with the palm of her hand. I felt a mild sensation, like the shock from shag carpeting. This time, however, the small burst of energy wasn't the same as before. This one felt mildly pleasurable and far less jarring. I let the moment stretch out as long as I could before I felt self-conscious. I stood and moved toward the door.

"I should probably show you your room now," I said. "Your right room, that is."

I laughed, hating how forced it sounded. I put on my best stern face and pointed my finger. "*You* follow *me* this time."

I felt like a total dork. Why was I rambling around her? *I am* not *falling for her,* I told myself. *Dead girl walking*.

As I debated the finer points of what branch of necro-eroticism this would fall under, I locked the door behind us. I pocketed the keys as I felt a crackle of electricity on my arm. Irene's hand was on it, sending another shiver through my body, one I was sure had nothing to do with the simple shock.

"Are you going to be all right, Simon?" she asked.

I nodded. "I will be. Thanks. But listen . . ."

She waited silently as I collected my thoughts.

"You can't tell anyone about the White Room," I continued. "Please. I hate even having to mention it, but it's extremely important to me."

"You don't have to worry," she said. Her voice sounded reassuring, but then she smirked. "Why would I tell anyone about that, my intrepid young gumshoe, when there are all those juicy homoerotic visions of yours to tell your fellow employees about?"

She floated off, laughing, and in that moment, I desperately wished that Irene were alive. Not because of my strange attraction to her, or that she was someone I could picture myself dating, but because it would be easier to strangle her smart ass that way.

11

Since I wasn't used to having guests in my loft, I spent the rest of my night staring at my ceiling, tossing, turning, and wondering if Irene was also lying awake off in my guest room. Exhaustion eventually washed over me, though, and before I knew it, I awoke to the shrill cry of the alarm going off. I crept to the open door of the guest room, where I could make out the curled-up shape of Irene. I wasn't sure what the cosmic rules were concerning the sleeping habits of ghosts, but Irene was resting peacefully on top of the sheets, hovering over them slightly. I didn't have the heart to wake her before I left. What was she going to do with herself if I did wake her anyway? Float around the office until I had figured out what exactly to do with her? She was better off hidden here in my apartment.

When I caught up with Connor over coffee at the Lovecraft, I purposefully neglected telling him that Irene had stayed at my apartment, even though the subject of Irene and *her* apartment were on the table.

We jumped a cab on Eleventh Street and rode uptown to

Columbus Circle. Although Irene's building was in the Seventies, we got out near Trump's latest eyesore and walked along the tree-lined length of Central Park West until we came across her building, which was a far better architectural wonder. The Westmore looked as if it were straight out of a Tim Burton movie. Gothic-era gargoyles with their mouths agape laughed at some sinister secret.

We entered the Westmore's red and gold lobby and were confronted with an elderly doorman whose dusty jacket looked like it had seen better days. A button was missing from the front of it, and judging by the size of his pot belly, I could imagine it had flown across the room whenever it had popped. We didn't have a game plan for getting past him, but Connor patted me on the back.

"All yours, kid," he said, and leaned against the wall with his arms folded.

I stepped forward to the tiny counter the man stood behind. His hand moved automatically for the house phone.

"Whose apartment may I ring for you, sir?"

"Irene Blatt, please," I said. It killed me just saying her last name.

A look crossed the old man's face and he lowered the phone back to its cradle. "I'm sorry, but I'm not sure if Ms. Blatt is in right now."

Since *we* knew that the lady of the house was dead, and *I* knew her spirit was holed up in my apartment, I was pretty sure that Irene wouldn't be answering her phone.

Connor stepped up to the doorman's desk and nudged me out of the way.

"Excuse us a moment, won't you, Simon?" he said. I moved away from the reception area, and Connor lowered his voice to the point where I could no longer hear. Whether he used some form of mind trick or simply slipped the codger a hundred, I didn't know, but suddenly the doorman was hurrying us into one of the mahogany-lined elevators.

He pressed the button, tipped his hat, and we were on our way.

"Sorry 'bout that, kid," Connor said. "I could already tell he was suspicious. We should be quick about this, though, just in case."

"What the hell did you do to him down there?" I asked.

"Sorry, kid. Classified."

I was hoping for more of a clue as to what had just transpired, but the look on his face told me it wasn't up for discussion.

After several silent floors, he changed the subject. "The view of Central Park must be spectacular."

"For what it probably costs to live here, the view better be," I said.

The elevator slowed and the doors slid open with a gentle *bing* onto an enormous hallway that could have easily held my whole apartment. There were only three doors. One was marked STAIRS, and the other two were set on either side of the elevator. When we stepped out, Connor walked to the one on our right. I reached for the doorbell, but he grabbed me by the wrist and shook his head.

"Let me handle this, kid," Connor said.

I pulled my arm away. I was pissed at him for taking charge again. How was I supposed to learn *anything* with him always taking the lead? I could have handled anyone who answered the door, dammit.

Connor put on his best game face as he prepared to greet whoever might answer. It was the one he put on to look as mundane as a door-to-door insurance salesman. He rang the bell and waited.

And waited.

And waited.

"Oh, for heaven's sake," I said after the first minute had passed, and pushed Connor out of the way. I dropped to my knees directly in front of the door, took off my gloves, and pulled several thin metal strips from the cuff of my jacket.

I slid two of the strips into the keyhole and flexed my fingers slightly as I felt around for the tumblers. Connor gave me a look of disapproval.

"What?" I said. "Clearly no one's home and I don't think Irene would mind if we had a look around."

"Did you requisition those from the supply room?" Connor asked, peeved.

"No," I said testily. "They're mine. Holdovers from my days as a petty thief."

"Did they get rid of the screening process in HR?"

"Can I help it that some of my criminal skills come in handy every so often? Besides, breaking and entering in the name of Good feels a whole lot better."

"May I remind you that it's still breaking and entering?"

"Not if we've got permission from the owner!" I fired back. "And we've got it."

"I'd love to see you explain it to the cops," Connor said. "It doesn't matter if she gave us her permission, kid, since she's dead."

There was no love lost between the Department of Extraordinary Affairs and the NYPD. The NYPD resented us because they had been told countless times by David Davidson at the Office of Plausible Deniability that we didn't even exist, and yet they were still supposed to cooperate with us.

"Irene's not totally dead," I reminded Connor.

I continued searching for the right combination of positions within the lock, but I was rusty with the whole lockpicking thing.

"She seems pretty dead to me, kid," he said, leaning against the wall as I worked. "We'll probably find pictures of her husband and kids in here, too. One big happy family.

One big happy family who'll come home in the middle of our breaking and entering, and demand an explanation as to why we're in their apartment."

"She's *not* married," I said, wishing I didn't sound so defensive.

"How do you know *that*?" Connor asked, but I met him with silence, under the pretense of being too busy working the lock. He wasn't falling for it. "I knew it! You *are* interested in her."

I tried to ignore him and threw all my concentration into picking the lock—and was rewarded when the tumblers finally clicked. I hadn't picked a lock in forever, wasn't even sure I'd be able to until it happened just now, but I felt a little swell of pride at the familiar sound of a door giving way.

"I'm shocked," Connor said with mock sincerity. He stepped back to allow room for me to stand up and swing the door fully open. "Does anyone at the Department know about your little transgressive skills?"

I nodded. "I think so. I bet the F.O.G.ies have already blacklisted me because of it."

"You've only been with the D.E.A. a few months," Connor replied. He pushed his way forward, crowding me. "Wait until you've been working there a couple of years. Even then, the F.O.G.ies are secretive and it's almost impossible to guess who they'll choose."

"Well," I said as I motioned for Connor to follow me through the door into the darkness of the apartment, "I doubt my criminal past would pass muster at the Fraternal Order of Goodness's membership drive."

"They took Inspectre Quimbley, kid, so I'm not so sure about that."

I rolled my eyes, but the effect was lost on Connor in the darkened room. The Inspectre a troublemaker? He had been my *How to Distinguish an East Villager from a Satanist* instructor during my initial three weeks of evening classes, and he didn't seem the badass type despite the legends of his past honors. The Inspectre, an old-school rapscallion? I couldn't imagine it.

"I don't think that our befuddled Inspectre has any dark secrets to hide, Connor."

As we moved farther into the apartment, the sounds of Connor fumbling in the dark came from off to my left somewhere, sounding not unlike a herd of elephants.

"Those old boys *all* have dark secrets to hide," he said. "That's probably half the reason F.O.G. exists, so they can have one collective burial ground for all their bad mojo."

I shook my head, another gesture wasted in the darkness.

My arm bumped into something tall, slender, and lamplike, and I groped around it until I found a switch. With the tiniest of clicks, a Tiffany floor lamp—much like the one sitting half unpacked back home—sprang to life, its stained glass dragonflies sparkling with color. Both of us gasped as the small pool of light lit up a section of the large room. We had expected spacious, which it was. I had expected elegant, which it was. Neither of us had expected for the place to be thoroughly and abusively trashed from floor to ceiling, which sadly, it was.

I felt like someone had sucker punched me in the stomach. The similarity to my place was so striking that it was like seeing my own apartment ransacked. Tasteful antiques littered the floor, many of them now broken or overturned. Irene's tastes definitely ran in the same circles as mine. Seeing a broken Venini bowl, a midcentury George III card table missing a leg, countless scattered books, and a shredded seat cushion on a late-eighteenth-century Highback— it all drove the pain home.

Irene Blatt might have been struck down by a cab yesterday morning, but someone had gone just as medieval on her apartment. It would be foolish to assume that the two were not connected. "My God . . ."

Connor whistled, and stepped carefully through the disarray as he looked around. "I know. D.E.A.'s not going to like the overtime on this one." We started poking through all the destruction. I was a bit confused about what I was supposed to be looking for, but when I asked Connor, he just said, "You'll know it when you find it, kid," so I didn't feel too bad.

"And remember, even though we got in a little practice with your powers at the Antiques Annex, use them sparingly if you have to, got it? This clutter could probably overwhelm you psychometrically."

I nodded, slipped my gloves back on, and started poring over the scattered books, smashed relics, and broken antiques in the living room before venturing farther back into the apartment. I slowly waded through the knee-deep clutter of books, papers, and boxes, looking for any kind of sign. Most of Irene's possessions, although broken, gave me greater insight into the living person she had been. I found myself liking her more and more, especially when I unearthed the worn-out box cover of an old board game. *Hungry Hungry Hippos.* A woman after my own juvenile heart.

I couldn't resist pushing my power into it. I took my gloves off and placed a tentative finger on the head of the yellow hippo. I tried to envision Irene as a child playing the game—or maybe I'd see that she had kids or a family that she played the game with. Either way, it might offer a clue to our case. Instead, my psychometry skipped all that and jumped straight to showing me the last person who had handled it.

In my mind's eye, the apartment was only partly trashed, but a figure in a dark robe opened the game box warily looking for something—but what? He tore the contents of the box out, smashing the plastic tray and sending the four rainbow-colored plastic hippos flying. The bottom of the box held nothing and the figure threw the whole game against the wall in frustration before heading farther down the hall, which was where I intended to go as well.

I pulled out of the vision—slightly weary—and helped myself to more of my Life Savers before wading down the hall to the first room on my left. I could probably read half the apartment with my power, but all I'd get was mental footage of that figure trashing it. I decided to conserve my power for now and entered the room on my left.

Irene had definitely been a packrat in life. The room was filled with overturned boxes, and every last article, book, or meticulously catalogued item she had ever come across was stored in them. There were other doors farther along the back hall of the massive apartment, and I imagined more of the same behind them. Whatever manner these items had originally been organized in was now lost to reckless vandalism.

A cracked frame showed a picture of Irene against a background of Italian architecture. In it, she wore a thick cable knit turtleneck sweater. The photo, at last, confirmed for us that my ghostly friend was indeed Irene Blatt, and that this trashed mess had once been her apartment. I slipped the picture from the frame and slid it into my jacket pocket, wondering who had snapped the shot. A boyfriend or maybe just a passerby. This didn't count as stealing, I told myself, but checked the door guiltily anyway.

I was relieved to find the next room empty, and I heard the sounds of Connor searching another room close by. I turned my focus back to my immediate surroundings. There were two closets at the far end of the room I had to check out. Simply moving was a distraction, so much so that when I finally reached the closets, I didn't even register the fact that the dark-robed figure from my vision was hiding in there—until he sprang out at me. He pushed me down in his effort to escape, and as I fell, I winced painfully as the pointy corner of a book jabbed into my lower back.

"Connor!" I shouted. "There's someone here!"

I floundered for several seconds in the sea of scattered books and crumpled papers. The dark-robed figure rushed nimbly across the top of the debris without sinking in before racing out of the room. I hoped Connor was having better luck navigating the apartment than I was.

Clumsily, I got back on my feet and waded as quickly as I could out into the main hall. The sound of a struggle came from the direction of the living room. As the hall opened up onto the main room, I saw Connor and his assailant grappling as the two of them toppled over onto an overturned couch. When they regained their footing, I noticed two things—one strange and one dangerous. The strange thing was a large, dark wooden fish that the intruder clutched close to his body. The dangerous thing was a heavy, curved dagger he held in his other hand. I had seen its kind before, unique in that its sharpened edge was along the inside of the weapon's curve.

A *kukri,* I thought. It was the calling card for someone prepared to perform ritualistic sacrifice. *That's a cultist if I ever saw one.*

"Knife!" I shouted to Connor, who looked down at the blade for the first time. He moved to pry the wooden fish from the cultist's hand. When the figure flicked the blade at Connor, he moved back to avoid its swinging arc. The blade ripped through the fabric of his shirt. Thanks to Connor's awkward positioning, he stumbled out of reach, but not before the backs of his knees hit the couch. His arms spun out of control with the momentum and his legs flew up in the air, toppling him over once again, but saving him from his attacker's next swipe.

For a second, the madman lifted the blade high overhead and I thought he was going to finish Connor off, so

I shouted unintelligibly. It sounded ridiculous, but it did the trick and the robed figure paused and turned from the couch. I pulled my retractable bat from inside my coat and extended it, daring him to come after me.

Instead of attacking, however, the cultist flicked his wrist, and with a barely audible click, the blade disappeared up one of his voluminous sleeves. Connor reached up from behind the couch and made a grab for him, but he kicked Connor's hand away, turned, and dashed out the apartment door.

Connor groaned as he lifted himself slowly up from behind the couch. His free hand rubbed the back of his head. He seemed on the verge of falling over again, but he grabbed the edge of the couch and steadied himself.

"After him," Connor said and stumbled across the room. I ran for the door and together we burst into the hallway outside the apartment . . . to emptiness. I looked up at the elevator indicator, but neither car was even remotely close to our floor. I caught movement in the corner of my eye, though, and turned to see the door to the stairwell slowly closing. I rushed through it and looked down into the opening between the stairs going down. Catching a glimpse of robe several floors below, I hesitated a moment to check on Connor.

"You up for it, boss?" I asked. I was worried. He was still rubbing the back of his head.

"Am I up for it? And let you have all the fun, kid?" Connor leapt past me, taking the steps four or five at a time. I followed at a slightly less breakneck pace, holding on to the railing as I went. Connor was the more experienced of us, after all, and I was more than happy to let him be the more reckless pursuer, but I didn't want to tumble to my death in my haste. And if my mentor got to collar the son of a bitch first, more power to him.

But as the chase continued downward flight after flight, it seemed like Connor was unlikely to catch up with the fugitive. The intruder kept an almost inhuman pace all the way to the ground floor. When I finally reached the bottom and caught up with Connor outside the Westmore, the robed figure had dashed into traffic on Central Park West, causing much screeching of brakes and honking. Connor and I looked at each other, registering our mutual exhaustion, and sprinted off after the cultist as he dashed into the woods at the edge of Central Park.

The rest of the chase was a blur. Trees with their low-hanging branches, pedestrians lounging on the Great Lawn, vendors . . . sometimes a combination of all of these got in my way, but I refused to let up on our prey. I had no idea why the stolen wooden fish was important or why it had been taken, but it was Irene's and I wanted it back. Forty blocks later, the chase ended when the figure jumped the security turnstile at the Fifth Avenue entrance to the Empire State Building. I watched as he shoved past the tourists waiting to get in and ran off into the building. When we attempted to follow suit, however, a well-built security guard blocked our way.

"That man stole something from us!" I pleaded. "We've got to stop him. He's getting away!"

A particularly nasty woman with yellow teeth thwacked me on the arm with a postcard book as she waited to get in, shouting, "There's people on line, mister!"

"Relax, lady," the guard said. Connor flashed his D.E.A. ID, which did count as official local government documentation, but I was still clutching my bat as I fished mine out. The guard checked them over carefully before gesturing us through the security gate one at a time.

"Don't worry," he said. "That guy's not going anywhere. Damned cultists are already giving this building a bad name."

I stood there, stopped reholstering the bat, and stared at the guard in amazement.

"Wait a second. You *know* he's a cultist?"

"Sure," the guard offered with a sour look on his face. "They've been stinking up the building for 'bout six months, ever since they started yammering to the Mayor's Office about equal rights. They're up on thirty-three, I think."

We thanked him and walked toward the elevators. Connor shook his head. "Unbelievable."

"I wonder if anyone has been informed back at the D.E.A.?" I asked. We stepped into the waiting elevator and I pushed 33.

"We'll find that out when we talk to the Inspectre. Right now I want to get that goddamn fish back."

The doors shut and I looked at Connor quizzically. "What's so important about that fish?"

"I'm not sure," Connor replied, "but if they wanted it bad enough to trash Irene's place, then maybe it was worth killing over, too. Somebody wanted it awfully bad. *That's* why I want it back."

"Ah."

I had hoped for a more concrete answer. Something like, "It's the sacred fish of the Mondoogamor tribe," or "It mystically cures young teens of acne," but just wanting it back because it was stolen worked, too.

When the elevator reached the thirty-third floor and the doors opened, we braced ourselves for an attack. After all, the man we were pursuing had tried to fillet us, so it seemed wise to make sure the coast was clear. Connor stuck his head out quickly to the left, and I did the same on the right side, finding nothing.

"Clear?" he asked.

I nodded.

"Great," he said.

"Where do you think he went? I'm not even sure what offices we're looking for."

Connor pointed to the directory on the wall straight across from the elevator, and from the listings, there was really only one choice.

Most of them were pretty standard, ending in "LLC" or "& Associates." Only one of the listings truly stuck out. It was three simple letters done up in a Gothic bloodred font. The clincher, of course, was the fact that they had been laid out on the directory to look as if they were actually dripping blood.

S.D.L., they read cryptically. An arrow pointed down the hall to our left.

"Not much for subtlety, are they?" I asked.

"If they were subtle, they wouldn't be cultists, would they?" Connor said, and started down the hall cautiously. "I suspect we'll find out soon enough what they stand for. You might want to have your negotiating tool ready."

I pulled my bat free and hid it under my coat once it was extended. "Should be lethal enough if it comes to it, I think."

"Just follow my lead, kid. Don't be overhasty to use it, all right? If things get hairy in there, I'll give you a signal."

"Right," I said.

My body was cold from the accumulated sweat of the downtown chase, but it was also a reaction to my discomfort with the situation. The idea of pulling my bat in defense against a group of humans, regardless of their fanaticism, didn't sit well with me. Beating a bookcase to death was one thing. Attacking humans was another. I tried not to overanalyze the situation, wanting to take things as they came.

The frosted glass doors at the end of the hall gave no hint as to what went on behind them, but the letters "S.D.L."— this time over a foot high—marked the entrance. Connor crouched and pressed his ear to the door, listening carefully while I tried to center myself with several deep breaths.

"I can't hear anything," he said. "They must be sound-proofed, or else it's a lot quieter in there than we're expecting."

"Maybe we should pull ourselves together before going in," I said, tucking my shirt in. "It's an office building, after all."

"Fine, Mr. Blackwell," Connor said.

He stood up, straightened his tie, and ran his fingers through his sandy mop of white-striped hair, which did nothing to change the frantic-looking muss. I checked my grip on the bat as I smoothed down my coat for lack of a tie to straighten. *Appearance is everything,* Quimbley had told me in one of the early seminars. If you looked calm and composed upon entering the unknown, it went a long way toward controlling whatever situation might arise.

"You ready?" Connor asked.

I shook my head.

"We're never ready," I said. "Doesn't mean I'm not going through that door, though."

"Good," Connor said, clapping me on the shoulder. "And remember, no caving anyone's skull in unless I tell you to."

I paled at his suggestion, hoping it wouldn't come to that.

I was prepared for a lot of things when it came to cultists and the dark arts, but what we saw when Connor threw open the doors took me totally by surprise.

12

Connor and I stepped into the spacious waiting area of a normal-looking office space. The furniture in the main reception area was sleek, silver, and modern. The walls were covered almost completely by inspirational posters showing kittens clinging to tree branches begging the workers to HANG ON, BABY! Other posters thanked God it was Friday. Motivational quotes were written across posters of dazzling sunsets and peaceful oceans. Hundreds of memos were plastered on a large bulletin board, many of which carried official-looking seals from the state of New York. Dozens of workers toiled away at desks, and each desk had its own pile of paperwork that threatened to topple over and bury the person working there. It was a little comforting that their office looked as overburdened as ours.

I recognized the mark of it all.

"Government work."

Connor tapped me on the shoulder and pointed at the wall directly behind the reception desk. "They've got to be kidding."

The letters on the wall were the same style as the ones listed out on the directory and the ones on the glass doors, except this time they spelled out the full name of the operation.

The Sectarian Defense League.

The receptionist sitting just below them at the desk was a heavyset woman with welcoming eyes and straight black hair pulled back so hard it stretched her face. She looked up from her magazine and noticed us for the first time. She smiled pleasantly . . . for a cultist.

"Can I help you?" she asked with the hushed tone of a librarian.

There seemed to be no need for the hysteria or theatrics that I was prepared to engage in, and I relaxed momentarily—even though I was still confused by what purpose this office served. These were businesspeople, reasonable office folk who could be dealt with in a civil manner. Things could proceed calmly.

And things *would* have proceeded calmly had I given Connor a chance to speak, but the cultist who had been swinging the kukri at us was too fresh in my mind and I snapped. This was where he had come. We were dealing with practitioners of the occult here and I rushed toward the desk.

"You're damn right you can help us!" I said with menace. "We've come for the fish."

The woman stared back, perplexed. I could tell she had no idea what I was talking about, but she *had* to know something.

"Which fish is that exactly?" she asked nervously. Her smile faltered.

"You know what fish!" I said, and threw my jacket open, freeing the bat. I whacked it hard against the reception desk. The woman jumped back, startled, and nearly toppled over in her chair.

"Simon," Connor said, reaching for my arm, "calm down."

It was already far too late for calm. Every last person who had been working at the desks had leapt up and surrounded us. At first glance this assortment of temps and assistants had looked like any other group of office workers, but now I could see the raving fanaticism in their eyes. These were a determined-looking bunch of extremists that hid behind a thin veil of office pleasantries and seventy-dollar ties. We had to do something to gain control of the situation I had so hastily created . . . and fast. The mob of angry workers had us boxed in.

"Sorry about that little outburst," Connor said, making direct eye contact with the receptionist. His grip on my arm became viselike. He pushed down until my arm and the bat slipped out of view below the counter. "My friend here's a little . . . overtired. You see . . . we're here on behalf of the D.E.A."

"But we're environmentally friendly!" the woman pleaded, still eyeing me with nervous fear. "We recycle. We don't dump any contaminants. Honestly!"

In general the Inspectre didn't like us throwing around the name of the Department, but we were still recognized by the city government and allowed to invoke that status if we thought it might have some sway.

"Not the Department of Environmental Affairs or the Drug Enforcement Agency," I said bitterly. "The Department of Extraordinary Affairs."

As soon as the words left my lips, the crowd around us snarled and began chanting in ever-increasing volume, drowning out Connor's further attempts at reasonable negotiation. I moved back to back with Connor and surveyed the room for any signs of escape. With a bout of hopefulness, I noticed the mob of workers thinning in one particular direction and I thought this might be our chance to make a quick exit. Before I could grab Connor and drag him toward it, however, I saw the reason for the crowd's dispersal.

A tall, shapely blonde plowed her way toward us with a clipboard in her hands. Her attractiveness and my chivalry aside, I wanted to smack the *I know something you don't know* look right off her pretty blond head.

"I'm afraid you two will have to leave . . ." she shouted over the noise of the crowd. "Now."

A clearing formed around the three of us, and the workers backed off slowly. They feared this woman. It wasn't apparent why, but I surmised that it would be wise for Connor and me to fear her as well. She looked fresh faced, and definitely not any older than me, yet she commanded the respect of everyone around her.

Connor stepped forward.

"We're not leaving until we get what we came here for," he shouted over the snarling crowd. "One of your people took something that doesn't belong to him. We want it back."

She checked the pages on her clipboard. "I'm afraid that's impossible. You see, we were merely recovering what was already ours."

"That artifact belongs to Irene Blatt!" I shouted.

"I assure you it did not," the woman said, staring at us with beautiful but cold eyes. "Now, you can leave here the hard way or the easy way."

The fanatics howled like caged animals all around us, waiting for any sign of resistance on our part as an excuse to tear us into bite-sized pieces.

"What's all the commotion out here?" a cheery male voice boomed out from behind the crowd. Every office worker's head turned, but none of them broke from their positions. At first I refused to chance a look, afraid to turn away from the menacing crowd even with the bat in my hands. After a moment, though, curiosity got the better of me and I snuck a peek toward the movement off to my right. I searched the crowd and locked on to a dark-haired European gentleman who appeared to be drifting through the throng toward us.

"Jane!" he called out to the woman with the clipboard. His voice held a hint of an accent, and at my best guess it sounded Slavic. "This is what I pay you for, isn't it? To tell me what's going on? So tell me . . . what *is* going on?"

Jane shifted uncomfortably, and I detected a bit of fear mixed with the anger in her eyes. "That's what I was trying to ascertain, sir, before our band of village idiots jumped up from their desks and decided to go all pit-bull."

The man glowered at the crowd and they all averted their eyes as they shuffled away apologetically. The circle around me, Connor, and Jane widened even further. *They're acting like a big, dumb collective puppy,* I thought, and I stifled the urge to laugh. I was watching an angry mob being scolded like a household pet and I wondered where Jane kept the rolled-up newspaper to bat them on the nose when they stepped out of line.

The man pushed past Jane, who was smiling smugly from behind her clipboard. Her boss stood an impressive six inches taller than any of us. He cast his eyes on me, smirking as he gave the bat in my hands a good look up and down, and then he turned his focus to Connor. "You seem like the rational one of this duo. Would you care to explain what he's doing brandishing a bat in our offices like Joe DiMaggio?"

"We've come for the fish," Connor said calmly. "And we're not leaving without it."

"Who the hell *are* you?" I asked sharply. I refused to be casually dismissed.

Jane stepped forward and poked me in the chest with a

corner of her clipboard. "Watch it, mister. You are addressing the chairman of the Sectarian Defense League, Faisal Bane, and you two are trespassing. This is a government office registered with the City of New York. Whatever misapprehension you may be operating under, I'm informing you that we're a legitimate organization in this town." She stared at me in silence for several seconds, then said, "You can put the bat away."

"Jane . . ." Faisal said sternly. "Never mind that. Bring me up to speed."

She turned to face him, and I saw a hint of fear in the woman's eyes. "Err, I'm not sure who these gentlemen are, Mr. Bane. The unarmed gentleman was arguing some claim for . . ." She scanned the clipboard with her index finger. "Item one-six-eight."

Faisal Bane snatched the clipboard from her without taking his eyes off us and she flinched. His eyes danced for a moment as he read the listing. "I see. So would either of you two gentlemen care to explain why you feel the need to act in such a barbaric manner in our office?"

Connor nodded and pulled out his ID.

"We're with the Department of Extraordinary Affairs, Bane. Property belonging to one of our clients was removed from her apartment earlier today by someone we tracked back to this office. The wooden fish."

Faisal Bane glanced at the clipboard again. "Ms. Blatt? She's with you, is she? Interesting. I thought she was . . ." He stopped himself and grinned. "Well, let's just say I thought she was elsewhere."

Faisal Bane and his minions knew something about Irene's death, and I had trouble holding back my anger.

"What do you know about her disappearance?" I asked.

Faisal smiled at me with false politeness and handed the clipboard back to Jane. "Nothing whatsoever."

"If you're responsible for what's happened to her—" I started, but Connor put his hand on my shoulder and interrupted.

"What is this place?" he demanded.

"Perhaps I can answer that," a familiar voice offered from somewhere by the main entrance. A man stood at the doors. Just yesterday, I had watched him talking on the television in the front corner of the Lovecraft. It was none other than the D.E.A.'s strongest protector and the Mayor's Office's talking head, David Davidson. In person, the gray at his temples was more pronounced, and although he wore the smiling face of a politician in his midforties, his eyes looked much older.

"Davidson!" Connor said. "Thank God! What the hell's going on here? Who are these people?"

"Easy now," Davidson replied in that even way of his. Like magic weaving its spell, I could hear the soothing quality of his voice—it was no wonder he was a natural political liaison. The Mayor had relied on him for years to smooth over problem after problem that came through City Hall. I didn't know if his abilities came from any sort of special power, but the fact remained that Davidson had a natural calming effect. "First, I think we need everybody here to take one giant step back from everyone else."

As if on cue, everyone but me, Connor, and Faisal Bane moved back in unison. Davidson's words had worked on the crowd and I was suitably impressed. I had never actually watched him work up close, outside of a TV screen. Although I hadn't stepped back when he instructed us to, I did find myself lowering the bat until it once again hung harmlessly at my side.

"Good," Davidson continued. "Look, Connor, I know the D.E.A.'s not really up to speed on what's been going on here. There's been a lot of red tape over this whole project back at City Hall, and the Mayor's Office felt it was better to keep you folks in the dark until certain goals and initiatives had been fully set up."

"Why don't *you* bring us up to speed?" I demanded. What the hell was the Mayor's Office playing at?

Davidson sighed. For a second I thought he looked almost as worn down as his eyes did. Then he was back to his regular self in a flicker. "We're talking about the cultists' rights movement. The city has pushed through legislation legalizing and acknowledging the status of cults as part of the equal rights movement's regulated standards and fair practices."

I stared at Davidson in disbelief. "You're kidding, right?" I said. "Please tell me that you're kidding!"

"Unbelievable," Connor added. "We're talking about people who perform ritualistic sacrifices on the living, for heaven's sake! They're bloody cultists!"

"Actually," Faisal said, raising a finger to interject, "we don't go by that term. It's archaic. The politically acknowledged term is 'Sectarian.' Didn't you notice the sign on your way in?"

"Oh, I'm sorry," Connor said with as much bite to his words as he could muster. "Did I offend you?"

Faisal's eyed flared with contempt. "It's just this kind of blanket mentality—this stereotyping—that the Sectarian Defense League has been put in place to prevent!"

He turned his dark gaze fully on us and pointed accusingly.

"The world is changing," he continued, "whether your high-and-mighty Enchancellors choose to deal with it or not, and we *are* the future of the new world order, gentlemen. Not you and your kind. You are dinosaurs, and like those pea-brained giants, you are headed down the same road."

Connor pushed through the crowd toward Davidson, and I followed. I blocked the doors to stop Davidson in case he tried to leave, but he made no move. Connor drilled into him. "Is this how the Office of Plausible Deniability is handling things nowadays? For God's sake, David, fighting people like these is part of the reason the D.E.A. was founded!"

"Listen," Davidson said, throwing an arm over Connor's shoulder. "These are complex times, Connor. You and Babe Ruth there can't simply run around threatening everyone you meet with a Louisville Slugger."

Davidson was trying to smooth things over, but it was too late. Whatever calming spell his voice had woven over us was now gone.

"I can't believe you're standing up for these guys!" I said. I reached for Davidson's lapels to shake some sense into him, but my hands found no purchase. Dave Davidson moved with a speed I hadn't thought possible, almost inhuman, and he was now standing a foot farther away.

"You don't want to do that," Davidson said with a cold stare. He adjusted his tie, all the while splitting his gaze between the two of us.

"You think *these* are complex times, eh?" Connor started. "Wait until Inspectre Quimbley tells the Enchancellors. Then you'll see complex."

Faisal Bane cleared his throat and the three of us turned.

"Gentlemen," he said. He waved at his employees dismissively and they returned to their desks. "I trust that your business is with each other and it need not concern me or my staff. We're terribly busy around here at the moment, much to do . . ."

"A shipment of sacrificial lambs coming in?" I scoffed.

Faisal ignored me and continued. "Mr. Davidson, I suggest that you and your two-man A-Team take your issues outside. Unless you'd like me to put in a call to the Mayor . . . ?"

"Hey," Davidson said, looking a little worried. He held up his hands in surrender. "Easy, easy."

A second later his composure was back.

"No need to bother His Honor," he said with a carefully balanced political chuckle. "I'm sure the D.E.A. and I can handle this back at their headquarters."

"And just where would that be?" Faisal asked a little too quickly. Greed sparked to life in his eyes, like a lawyer's at the scene of a fresh accident.

Davidson went to speak, but I beat him to it.

"That information is *not* part of the public record, Mr. Bane. Sorry to disappoint you."

"You're a government agency," Faisal said, "much like ours and far more secretive than us, it seems. You're required to be listed publicly. Just as we were."

"You're working under the assumption that we're set up like you," Connor replied. "Do you have any idea how long we've been around? Longer than the fat cats downtown and certainly much longer than any of these newly formed charters governing your institution. Don't try to tell me how things run. We work under special charter, designated on a 'need to know' basis by the borough of Manhattan. I find it highly doubtful that anyone, including Mr. Davidson here, considers you and your group as a member of those 'need to know' types. Isn't that true, Mr. D?"

"For the record," Davidson said, "I'm not sure." Connor's question had thrown him. For once, something worked to our advantage. I was sure that Faisal Bane would love to know all about us, but until Davidson figured out the boundaries, he wouldn't disclose anything further.

Davidson smoothed the lapels on his jacket and slowly backed toward the door, but I was still blocking the way. Connor nodded and so I reluctantly stepped aside.

"I'll be in touch with both of your organizations as soon as I've had a chance to confer with both parties separately,"

Davidson said, and slipped out of the doors before anyone could say another word.

A moment of silence followed in the reception area.

"So," I said, raising the bat again. "Is there anyone I should slug?"

Connor smiled appreciatively, but shook his head no. "That's all right, kid. Stand down. We'll be leaving here peaceably."

Relieved that I didn't have to smack anyone's bitch up, I waited for Connor to join me at the door. Not a single office employee attempted to bar our way. We were leaving in the nick of time as far as I was concerned. My nerves were shot. I had never been in a situation where I felt so outnumbered so quickly. I wondered if the bulk of D.E.A. operations went like this. With only a few months under my belt, it was hard to determine what was run of the mill and what was not.

"I'm going to make this easy on you, Bane," Connor said, turning around. "This is the moment when you insert your 'parting threat,' but let's just skip it, okay? I'll save you the trouble and we can just quake in our boots in the elevator."

Faisal stared at us for a moment and then held out his hand to his assistant.

"Jane," he said through clenched teeth, "clipboard."

The contempt was thick in his voice, and Jane handed it over as fast as she could. She flinched as he snatched it from her, raised it over his head, wound up, and threw it toward us. It flipped end over end before smashing into the glass of the door, sending a ripple of cracks out from its point of impact.

The clipboard and a small shower of frosted glass fell to the floor. Most of Bane's workers were doing a terrible job of pretending to work. None of them wanted to draw his attention.

Having held our ground (although I was actually quaking in my boots), Connor and I threw the doors open and left.

"Have that door replaced," I heard Faisal shout to Jane as he stalked off, "and bill it to the Mayor's Office."

13

We called in our incident at the Sectarian Defense League to the Inspectre, and after a quick rundown of what had happened, he dispensed a Shadower team to keep an eye on their Empire State Building offices. Connor and I headed back down to the D.E.A. but I wasn't happy about it. Filing the paperwork on our encounter was going to be a nightmare.

When we arrived back at the Lovecraft Café, I had hoped for the comfort of my office chair, but I had no such luck. There was already a buzz of activity concerning our discovery. Assistants were placing calls and scrambling hurriedly off into the bowels of the D.E.A. while the Enchancellors summoned the two of us to a private council. Once Connor and I stood before them, it was clear that I had misjudged the magnitude of our agency. The crowd consisted mostly of unfamiliar faces, faces that scrutinized Connor and me as we gave our account of our run-in with the Sectarian Defense League.

Afterward, we were dismissed from the assembly, but

told to wait. Eventually Inspectre Quimbley emerged from the room with a serious look on his face and whispered something to Connor that I couldn't hear. I had been on the verge of falling asleep with all that had happened already so I was surprised when, without any explanation, my partner grabbed my arm, led me out through the coffee shop, and hurried us toward the subway stop at Astor Place. That had been hours ago.

Connor was being tight lipped about just what we were doing, but if I were to guess, it had something to do with experimenting on how long it took my ass to fall asleep on the hard, orange plastic seats of the R train. While designed for commuting, they were clearly not meant for extended journeys. The blur of moonlit buildings and urban graffiti sped along outside the window as I stretched my back and shifted in my seat. We had covered the entire length of the R line several times over. The entire time, Connor had sat next to me, calmly doing crossword puzzles. Occasionally he would ask me for a three-letter word for "feline" or a twenty-letter word starting with "X" and having the clue "Ancient mythic cult from the Lower East Side." Other than that, he seemed quite content to sit in silence all along the rails of the subway.

"Are we supposed to ride this train all night or what?" I finally asked.

"We ride until we get what we came for," he said and erased one of his answers from the crossword.

"You sure we're on the right train?"

"Yeah, kid, I'm sure," Connor said, starting to sound annoyed. He folded the paper and set it down. "Look, Simon, consider this a lesson in patience. We're waiting for a sign. We're dealing with things on a cosmic and spiritual level. There is a whole subset of rules that we have to play by. Riding and waiting on the R train is just one of them."

I had experienced enough exercises in patience for one day.

The train was just heading back underground on its return trip from Queens when the door at the far end of the car slid open. The *click clack* of the tracks filled our ears, and an elderly gentleman shuffled into the car. He was dressed in a brown workman's jumpsuit and wore a tattered wool hat with earflaps, even though it was much too warm. His face was a mass of wrinkles, and I watched as his wild blue eyes darted around the empty car before settling on us. In his hand he carried a blue and gold paper coffee cup, and as he shook it, the sound of coins jingled rhythmically.

"Good afternoon, ladies and gentlemen," he said. I looked around, but there were only Connor and me. The man's voice was thick with an accent similar to Faisal Bane's, and once again, I couldn't quite place it. Serbian, Croatian, something that smacked of the former Soviet Republic.

"Please pardon the interruption of your commute to wherever your destination lies," he continued. "I'd like to perform a little number for you and if you can find it in your hearts to give . . . a nickel, a dime, whatever . . . it would be greatly appreciated."

Since the subway car was empty, it was obvious that his impromptu "number" was meant only for the two of us. With great enthusiasm, he shook his cup of change and it jingled in a faster rhythm as he hopped around the subway car with superhuman agility. He pranced across the empty seats one second and swung from the bars overhead the next. What he was, I didn't know. I threw open my coat and eased my hand toward my bat, but Connor's grip stopped me. I turned to him and he shook his head.

The old man's raspy voice belted out a song. I recognized the words as vaguely familiar, but couldn't place them.

"At first, I was afraid, I was petrified.

"Kept thinkin' I could never live without you by my side . . ."

"What the hell is he?" I whispered underneath the singing. The crazed man was now hanging upside down from the bars in the middle of the car. He flipped deftly down to the floor and swayed to his own rhythm. The sound of the coins went *clink clink clink* as his frantic pace increased, but not a single coin fell from the cup, no matter how fevered the rhythm or his dancing became.

I wasn't sure how to react. I wanted to smile at the clear enjoyment this man-creature was getting from singing, but at the same time, with Connor and me the sole objects of his focus, I began to feel intensely uncomfortable. The smell of garbage washed down the length of the car and I had to fight back the urge to cough. "Is *this* who we've been waiting for?"

I found myself slowly recalling the words of the song he was singing, mouthing them as the old man continued. I knew them from my childhood, from a music style I had hoped would never rear its ugly head again—disco. "I Will Survive."

The man finished the chorus and closed the distance between us by half. Now his scent was overpowering.

Connor shoved his crossword into the space between us while he dug deep into his pocket. He fished out his wallet and flipped it open as the man started to sing his next verse.

"Crap!" Connor muttered. He held up his wallet so I could see. Outside of a variety of credit cards and ATM receipts, it was empty. "Pay the man, kid."

I nodded and pulled out my own wallet. "I've only got twenties."

"So give him one!"

"Don't you think twenty is a bit much for an old seventies disco song?" I asked.

"Just do it!" Connor whispered urgently. "Trust me on

this; we need his help. Goes by the name of Gaynor. Or that's what he lets us call him anyway."

The man called Gaynor landed in front of us now. I coughed as a fresh wave of his stench rolled over me like a blanket. I held my nose and attempted to breathe through my mouth only, but still the strong scent remained. All the while, Gaynor's cup rang out *clink clink clink!* and the man did a little two-step shuffle, jumping maniacally back and forth from foot to foot.

I slipped the twenty into his cup, and immediately Gaynor stopped singing to let out a dry cackle. Up close, his features showed the signs of more years than one mortal lifetime could possibly know. Luckily, we rarely dealt with the possible. His eyes danced momentarily toward the cup and he thrust his fingers in and fished around until he pulled out the twenty.

"Oh ho-ho!" his dry voice cackled merrily. "Your little gentlemen's club must be wantin' to know something pretty bad there, eh?"

Connor looked at the weathered old man and smiled gently. "Good to see you, too, old friend."

"Eh!" said Gaynor, looking disgusted. "Enough with the 'old friend' crap. You in some kind of fucking comic book? Save your road-movie dialogue."

"Sorry," Connor said. I could hear the annoyance barely hiding itself behind his apology.

"And don't apologize!" Gaynor shouted. "It makes you sound weak . . ."

The belligerent way he handled Connor was something I shouldn't have found funny, but I couldn't help laughing, which switched his attention to me. Gaynor turned as fast as a striking snake and crouched down. His manic eyes locked with mine and his earthy smell overwhelmed me, causing the laughter to die on my lips.

"You find that funny, do you?" he asked. His eyes scurried

back and forth across my face. I felt the sudden urge to squirm out of my seat and dash as far away from the man as quickly as I could, but with the handrail to my left and Connor to my right, that was impossible.

"No," I replied, hating the sound of weakness in my own voice, "I don't find that funny . . . particularly."

I turned my head as far as I could to avoid his gaze. I couldn't explain it rationally, but I wanted nothing more than to make this creature go away.

Yes, creature. Although he looked human, no human moved like he did or could have caused this sensation in me unless it fell under the category of supernatural. It didn't matter how human it looked, it was still otherworldly—and that meant that it fell within my bailiwick in Other Division to deal with. I so didn't want to.

"The kid's new here," Connor offered. "Give him a break, will ya?"

Gaynor turned his attention back to Connor. I felt my intense discomfort fall away.

The subway train pulled into Lexington Avenue, and the doors slid open. The platform was full of people, but none of them stepped into the car. En masse, they faltered for a moment as if something was repelling them, and then quickly made their way to another car. As the doors slid shut with the familiar *bing bong*, our car was just as empty as it had been. The train lurched out of the station.

"Twenty won't buy you much time, ya know," Gaynor said, twisting the bill in his shriveled but powerful-looking hands. He stood up and tucked the twenty into one of the side pockets of his coverall. He pushed his hat back to an almost impossible angle and scratched at the mad tangle of gray curls covering the front of his head. "Better get crackin'!"

"We've come about a wooden fish," Connor said. He pulled out a pen and picked up the newspaper, sketching a rough image of the item stolen from Irene's. "It's about the size of a dinner plate and we think it's sacred or something. No one at the Department can make head or tail of it. We haven't come across any references to it in any of our research so far, but it was important enough for a group of cultists to nick it from under our noses."

"Ahhh," Gaynor said. He snatched the paper from Connor's hands. Was that recognition I saw in his eyes—or madness? "No idea what it is, eh?"

"None, I'm afraid."

Gaynor let out a sigh as he lowered himself to the floor of the train car and arranged himself cross-legged. He sat quietly as he gathered focus. Seconds later, his jaw fell open and his eyes rolled back into his head, reminding me disturbingly of my narcoleptic great-grandfather after Thanksgiving dinner.

The deeper Gaynor fell into a trance, the faster the train rocked and careened beneath Manhattan. The lights of the tunnel flicked by faster and faster outside. I had never been on a train shooting along so fast. I felt a little queasy and decided that if I were ever in Japan, I would avoid their bullet trains at all costs.

"Did we just go express?" I whispered to Connor, but he only shushed me.

The overhead lights flickered out, and the backups sprang to life, giving the car a ghostly glow. Gaynor's shadow rocked back and forth with the sway of the train, looking as if he might fall over any second. Then his voice exploded over the roar of the train.

"That which you seek," Gaynor boomed out, "is far more important than you know."

His voice was no longer his own. It spoke with a calmness and clarity that clashed with his mad beggar appearance. I waited for Gaynor to say more, but he offered nothing else. Several manic moments passed before I couldn't take it anymore.

"What is it?" I shouted over the din of the rocketing train. "Do you know what the fish is or what it does?"

The words sounded weird even to me, but believe it or not, I had said more foolish things in my time with the Department. I watched Gaynor for any sign of reaction, but he simply rocked back and forth. I assumed from the blank look on his face that the old man simply hadn't heard me. I leaned forward in the dimly lit car, hoping to catch a glimpse of some sort of reaction. I was inches from his face when his eyes sprang open and a faint blue glow radiated from deep within them.

"That which lies within is not for me to know," he said.

As the train car sped and shook, one of the ceiling vents came loose and clanged noisily to the floor beside us. Connor leaned toward Gaynor.

"What *can* you tell us?" he asked.

"That which you seek . . ." Gaynor's lifeless face said. "Its true purpose is known to only a few, but only one will lead you to it. Follow the Vegas trail and all will become clear."

The overhead fluorescents flickered to life, and the lightning speed of the car finally started to slow until it resumed its normal pace. The old man's head slumped forward onto his chest. He was drained from whatever force had been working through him. Connor looked bored, but I wasn't.

Consulting this type of wild oracle was new to me. It had been a lot more nerve-wracking and exciting than the pamphlet back at the office—*So You Want to Channel the Powers*—made it out to be.

Gaynor came to and adjusted his hat before scooping his coffee cup up off the floor. He leapt to his feet.

When he turned toward the door as the train pulled into the next station, I stood and barked, "Hey! What did you say about Vegas? What's that got to do with anything?"

Gaynor coughed his earthy cough and glanced over at Connor. "Did I say something about Vegas?"

Connor nodded.

Gaynor shrugged. "Beats me," he said before brushing aside my hands. "You might want to keep yer kid here in line. He might last longer."

With a final cackle, Gaynor turned toward the exit. As the doors slid open, he looked back over his shoulder and winked at me.

"Smile, kid, it won't mess up your hair."

The old man shuffled off the train and disappeared into the crowd. His earthy scent faded as people pushed and shoved to get on, stepping over the dislodged ventilation cover lying on the floor.

"What the *hell* was that all about?" I asked.

"I'm not sure," Connor said.

"I'm out twenty dollars!"

"Expense it," he said flatly.

"But—"

"Look," Connor said, using a hushed tone now that the car was jam-packed with people. "Stop griping about the money, kid. Do you realize what you just witnessed? The fact that we can even connect with something, some-*one*, like that is a miracle, in and of itself. Call it an act of God if it helps you sleep at night. All I *do* know is that he and his kind have been able to help us in the past."

"His *kind*?" I asked.

Connor shook his head. "Didn't you ever read the classics in school? All the way back to the Greeks, there have been those who had some kind of cable modem connection to a higher power. Seers, oracles, call them what you like . . . and every last one of them is as cryptic as the *Sunday Times* crossword puzzle." He looked down at the seat between us. "Actually, the son of a bitch stole my crossword puzzle . . ."

The doors dinged closed and the train took off beneath the city once again.

"So," I said, "it's up to us to figure out what the Vegas trail is. I really don't think the Department's going to okay an impromptu trip to Nevada for either of us. Not that I wouldn't welcome the change of scenery . . ."

"I'll ask Quimbley," Connor said, "but I suspect he'll be about as receptive to that as the Sectarians were to our request for the wooden fish."

14

"I really shouldn't be cavorting with the enemy," the Sectarian Defense League's Jane said with a vicious smile from across the table. "But that's what us cultists are all about, right? Embracing temptation and not always doing the right thing?"

I was as surprised as anyone to be sitting at Mesa Grill across the table from Faisal Bane's right-hand woman, but Dave Davidson had arranged a little reconciliatory pow-wow between the D.E.A. and the Sectarians. Since I had been the one who had rashly taken my bat to their reception desk, Connor thought it fitting that I had to lie in the bed I had made for myself.

Negotiation wasn't really my strong point (hence the bat incident), and in coming to this dinner, I hadn't known what to expect. Faisal Bane's personal-assistant-in-Darkness had negotiated that she at least get a decent dinner out of the meeting—courtesy of my rapidly dwindling expense account, of course. Mesa Grill didn't come cheap.

I relaxed after inspecting my third glass of wine in a

row for any obvious signs of poisoning before taking a sip. It worked its magic over me, the sound of craptastic light jazz mixed with the pretheater crowd around us. I found the idea of breaking bread with the enemy terribly uncomfortable. Especially when the enemy's tight black top left little to the imagination.

Jane's casual dinner outfit was far more appealing than the clipboard and business attire I had last seen her in. Even her face seemed less harsh with her blond cascade of hair no longer pulled back into a bun. It softened her features immeasurably.

Jane looked down at my hands. "Nice gloves."

I didn't want to really get into my psychometry with the enemy, so I quickly changed the subject.

"You don't strike me as the cultist type," I said. I attacked the chile releno before me. It was true. Cute, flirty, and sassy didn't really fit the cultist mold I had read about in the pamphlets circulating the office—and that's what Jane had proved to be over the appetizers.

"Is there a type?" she asked coyly as she poked around the greens and blue corn chips on her plate.

"Well, I don't want to sound like we stereotype," I said, "but we do a fair amount of profiling. There are plenty of telltale warning signs of cultism. Ritualistic tattoos or scarification, nocturnal goings-on, joining the church of Scientology. You just don't fit the bill."

Her smile widened as if she was relishing her evilness, but then her face crumbled. "It's that obvious, is it?"

I nodded.

"Look," I said openly. "I'm not here in any capacity except to smooth things over in the City Hall sense, but you're totally not what I had expected the Sectarians to send. How does someone like you even fall in with that crowd?"

"Same way I expect people fall in with yours," she said defensively. When I refused to take umbrage at her words, she softened and continued. "Actually, it all happened a bit oddly, really. Months before coming to work at the Sectarian Defense League, I had been temping, doing all kinds of meaningless jobs for a host of ridiculous companies. Answering phones for law firms, cutting fabric swatches in the Fashion District, hole punching countless binders, playing hours of Solitaire and Minesweeper."

It sounded wretched. "It sounds wretched," I said.

"It was okay, honestly. Being a temp is all about being an outsider. It gave me freedom. I never grew too attached to any one job, no matter how promising it might seem, because I knew full well that the next day I'd probably be working in an advertising office sorting headshots for a coffee commercial."

She stopped going a mile a minute, and averted her eyes back to her food, smiling apologetically.

"Maybe this is a bit more 'Dear Diary' than you'd like to hear over dinner," she said shyly.

"No," I encouraged her, "go on." Hopefully the wine and letting her guard down might lead to me finding out something useful.

"My whole life I've felt like an outsider," she said, leaning in and lowering her voice, "until the job with the Sectarians came along. Shandra, my handler—*handler*—geesh, I sound like I worked for the CIA! Anyway, she said there was a new client trying out our temp agency, a potential cash cow. So it was important for me to make a good first impression. 'A happy client is a repeat client,' she said. I wasn't even sure what a Sectarian was, but I knew it was important to Shandra and that was good enough for me. So here I am."

"Unbelievable," I said.

I found it ludicrous that a temp had risen so easily to become the right-hand woman to one of the most dangerous cultists in the Tri-State Area. I could be with my department for years and never come that close to the seat of power! It didn't seem fair that she had garnered such a lofty position by sheer chance. That type of job should have gone to someone like the old badass version of me. I used to have evil down pat.

"So they just jobbered you into a cultists' rights organization and threw you headlong into evil?"

Jane laughed, covering her mouth. "Oh, no! The first week was a bit boring actually. A lot of filing, transferring of calls, typical office stuff, and then there was the incident where Mr. Bane's original assistant director—a horror show of a woman—just disappeared. Not much of a loss if you ask me. I didn't care for her from the start, honestly."

"Why? Was she *too* evil?" I asked. I wondered if the forces of Darkness got all snippy with each other around the water cooler.

"No, Mr. Snarky," Jane said, "but as Mr. Bane's go-to girl, she knew she could be a condescending bitch and get away with it." She blushed. "Then one day, she was just . . . gone."

"Gone?"

Jane turned a bit more serious, and pushed her salad to the side. "Up and disappeared. Flew the coop or something . . ." She sipped at her wine then dabbed her lips with the napkin. "There's a ridiculous rumor circulating that one of the filing cabinets consumed her, body and soul, but that's just crazy talk. As if!"

She laughed, but I didn't. Having recently been the survivor of an assault by a rampaging, carnivorous bookcase, I thought the rumor was most likely true.

Dinner arrived and Jane fell quiet until the waiter stepped out of earshot. "At least it *seemed* crazy until the Big Boss requested a meeting with me. That's when I found out I worked for cultists." She dug into her chicken.

"And that doesn't bother you?!" I asked. I dropped my knife and fork as I tried to contain myself.

"Sure it did," Jane nodded. She cut another piece of chicken and held it up. "This is to die for, by the way. You want to try?" I shook my head, trying not to look too offended by what I was hearing. She popped the chicken in her mouth. "At first I was shaken by the idea, but you've never been a temp before, have you? Frankly, after whoring out my secretarial services for some of the shadier law firms in this town, the League seemed downright pleasant comparatively. Mr. Bane talked me through what it meant to be part of the cultist lifestyle. He assured me that cultists are just like anyone else, except possibly more ambitious than average and definitely more likely to own their home."

I gestured to the waiter for more wine. Though the conversation was getting to me, I reminded myself to keep my rising anger in check. The meeting was not just a political patch job; it was also an opportunity for some recon. I couldn't afford to blow my cool, and I needed the Department to get their money's worth out of our forced meeting.

Who cared if I felt uncomfortable dining with the enemy? Jane was a talker when it came to her life, and I prayed that she would be just as forthcoming with information about her boss. Still, I didn't know whether to laugh at the absurdity or be outraged at how easily she accepted working for the forces of Darkness.

"Finding out that I was working for a cultists' rights group actually came as a relief," she said. "It explained a lot of things I had noticed around the office. For one, outside of the front office, a lot of the employees look a little gray around the gills. I thought it might just be the fluorescents washing them out, but no. Zombies . . . some of the nicest zombies you'd ever have the pleasure of working with, but zombies nonetheless."

I pushed my food out of the way and leaned forward conspiratorially. "Jane, do you hear yourself? Do you hear what you're saying? When they made you the offer of becoming

Faisal Bane's personal imp, weren't you a bit hesitant? Sure, an important-sounding job and a title to go with it are flattering, but didn't some kind of alarm bells go off in your head? Like maybe 'Hmmm . . . I was sure I had heard or read somewhere that working for the forces of Darkness'—capital "D" there, Janey—'is somewhat questionable.' Didn't that occur to you?"

"Don't call me Janey," she snapped.

Her eyes narrowed and her face regained a little bit of the viciousness she had exhibited back at her offices.

"I told him that I'd have to think about it," she said. People around us were starting to stare at our heated exchange. Jane lowered her voice, but the hostility was still there. "I knew it went against many of the beliefs I had been brought up with back in Kansas and I needed time to think it through."

"I'm sure the Master of Darkness took that well," I fired back. Maybe it was the wine, but more likely it was my own stupidity for thinking a civil meeting of our agencies could yield anything other than grief.

When I looked up from my plate, Jane was on the verge of tears, which made me feel even more uncomfortable. Evil was hard enough to contend with without its appointed representative going all blubbery.

"I assessed my life that night," she said as the tears began to fall, "and found it came up lacking, okay? I had spent five years in New York City, and what did I have to show for it? Friends? None to speak of, really. How do you make any as *temporary* employment, Simon? The closest I came to friendship was this one likable guy I started talking to, and all it earned me was a week of phone calls going on and on about the troubles he and his wife were having with their sex life. I think you know where *that* was headed."

I could sympathize with some of what she was saying. I knew the role of the outsider well. While my loner status was more due to my unpredictable power, I had to admit that my own dance card of friends was just as empty as hers. But no matter how you sliced it, we were on the opposite sides of the same coin. Every day I made a choice to break my foot off in evil's ass, and technically she was on the receiving end of my boot.

Her composure returned and she wiped away the tears. "The more I thought about my life, the more I realized that I had been merely treading water, waiting for something to happen. What's that John Lennon quote? 'Life is what happens while we're making plans'? I was sick of waiting. If I had ever needed a sign, it was then. That's when my door buzzed."

"Oh, well, that's manna from Heaven!" Part of me hated the edge of moral superiority in my voice.

"Shut up," she said. "I know the doorbell ringing wasn't an actual sign! It was a courier from the S.D.L. delivering an envelope."

"What was in it?"

"The answer to all my doubts. *Benefits*—401K, incentive programs, stock options, a signing bonus, dental . . . you name it, it was in there. But the clincher was that my ob-gyn was already listed as In-Program."

I gestured for the check.

15

I left the restaurant and took three separate cabs back to the Lovecraft Café to make sure I wasn't being followed. Pounding out a report was the last thing I wanted to do at this late hour, but I wanted to get all the details of my conversation with Jane down before they faded. Surprisingly, the Inspectre was still in, and he sat me down in his office to go over my dinner conversation with the enemy. I recounted the details as best I could while the old man poured himself some tea and processed everything I had told him. I could have kissed him for the hours he saved me on paperwork.

"I think she could break, sir," I said with confidence. "She hasn't been with them for long, and I think she might be our best chance at getting some useful intel on Irene and the wooden fish."

"You really think so, my boy?" the Inspectre asked, sipping his tea.

I nodded.

"Hroomh," he said. "I already have several avenues being

pursued concerning this Sectarian Defense League, but if you think you have an angle . . . I say go for it."

"Me?" I said and caught myself before I broke out laughing. "I've got a mountain of paperwork waiting for me as it is, sir. Maybe we could get a Shadower team on it . . ."

"Nonsense," the Inspectre said. "You think I want Wesker's lackeys in on this? Besides, they're already overburdened. I've got faith in you, my boy."

"That's very kind of you, Inspectre," I said, hoping I was coming off as polite as possible, "but it's not really my jurisdiction. I really am swamped and Connor will kill me if—"

"Blast it, son!" he yelled, slamming his cup on the desk. Tea flew over the rim and soaked into the pile of papers beneath it. "Not your jurisdiction? What part of the *Other* in Other Division do you not understand?"

Quimbley wanted more intel, and that meant I would have to do my own surveillance work. I was looking forward to that in the same enthusiastic way I might look forward to a debilitating kick to the crotch. I didn't mind offering up my services to the Department as far as my psychic abilities were concerned, but the type of work Shadower teams did was far too invasive for my liking.

"I'm not really comfortable with the idea of spying on someone, sir."

"Well, then," he said, reaching into one of his drawers and pulling out a pad with *Fraternal Order of Goodness* written across the top in Gothic-looking script. "What better way to get acquainted with surveillance work than with diving in both feet first! That's a good lad."

He wrote on it briefly, tore off the sheet, and held it out to me.

"Here," he said. "Give this to whoever's on duty in the supply room. I've made a list of surveillance equipment you're going to need. Get some rest tonight, though. You look horrible. I want you out there skulking and stalking like the best of them tomorrow night, understand?"

I stood there, staring at the paper in his hand, but I didn't reach for it.

The Inspectre sighed and stroked his mustache with his free hand. "I appreciate your concern over being a Peeping Tom, Simon, my boy. I truly do. But blast it, man, buck up! That's an order."

I took the paper from him and turned toward the door.

"That's my boy!" he said, sounding like a dad at a father-son picnic. "Now go be lascivious!"

As high-tech as the spy gear in the black aluminum case was, the weight of it was almost more than I could contend with. Combined with the rest of the workload I brought home with me, it made an inconspicuous entrance into my apartment impossible.

Not that it would have mattered. When I opened the door, Irene was waiting expectantly on the couch and rose to greet me.

"Any luck?" she asked and the hope in her eyes just about killed me.

"The wheels of government-sponsored paranormal investigation turn slow," I said, paraphrasing something I had heard Dave Davidson say.

Her face fell. "Well, how was your day anyway? Did you do anything exciting?"

I was reluctant to bring up my dinner "date" with the enemy so I simply shook my head. "Nothing special."

"Well, I do hope you and Mr. Christos have better luck in the future," she said. She sat back on the couch, but she was still visibly upset.

"I'm sorry, Irene," I said, sitting on the couch next to her and throwing the aluminum case on the floor, "but on the plus side, I have this."

The weight of the case had shaken the floorboards when it hit.

"What in God's name is in that?" she said, eyeing it suspiciously.

"Technically, it's part of your case," I said. I flicked it open. The contents were a collection of gismos and gadgets that James Bond would have been in awe of. "I've got a little reconnaissance that needs doing."

"Oh my," she said. "I hope it's nothing too dangerous."

I slipped on my gloves. I picked up a pair of electronic eyes, fished out the instructions, and started reading up on how to calibrate them.

"Let's hope not," I said. "I signed on with the Department of Extraordinary Affairs, not the Department of Life-Threatening Affairs."

She smiled.

"Does it have to do with anyone I know?" she asked. "Or anyone I would know if I could remember anyone I know?"

She was trying to make light of the situation, but her body flickered in and out for a second, showing her frustration.

"No one I can discuss yet," I said, avoiding any talk of Jane for reasons both personal and professional.

"Well, what *can* you talk about then?" she snapped, and I looked up at her, taken aback. "Sorry."

I thought for a moment of something safer to talk about while I fiddled with the light sensitivity on the eyes. How the hell was anyone supposed to figure these things out even with the instructions?

"Do you know anything about a wooden fish?" I asked. It seemed harmless enough to bring up something that I knew had been her property.

"A wooden *fish*?" she said, laughing. "No, I think I'd remember that."

"Does the name 'the Westmore' mean anything to you?" I asked.

She shook her head. "Sounds like a hotel or an apartment complex. Did I die there?"

"I can't really tell you," I said, "but off the record? No. Not there."

Nothing I mentioned was triggering any memories of her past.

"Speaking of apartment complexes," she said, "I do believe you had a call from your building manager. He was going on about you falling behind on your maintenance . . ."

"Crap," I said. I selected a parabolic mike from the case and futzed about, trying to open the satellite-dish-shaped cone around it.

"I take it that's a bad thing?"

"Yes, it's bad," I said. "Unfortunately, working for the forces of Good isn't quite as profitable as . . . um . . . my old profession."

"Is there anything you can do?" she asked.

The concern in her voice was touching. I looked down at all the equipment spread out before me.

"Yeah," I said with resolution, "I can probably take care of it tomorrow during the day. I'll have to call in sick, though."

"Are you not feeling well?" Irene asked.

"Outside of being ashamed for falling behind on my maintenance fees?" I said. "No, I feel fine."

"Then what is it?"

"I need to play a psychometric round of *The Price Is Right*," I said and threw the equipment back into the case. By tomorrow night, I was sure I would have figured out how to use it . . .

16

I turned in early for the long day I suddenly had before me. Irene was still sleeping in my guest room when I quietly left the apartment. I felt bad blowing off work, but not bad enough to actually get off the train with my file box and head back south to the city. I was desperate for the cash, and besides, spying on Jane would require darkness so I had to wait until nightfall anyway.

In the meantime, I hoped to reunite one of the promising purchases cluttering up my apartment with its original owner. Kevin Matthews had been the name I had gotten off the Intellivision game system reading at the night market, and a Google search had led me to believe that he had most likely grown up to be a Kevin Matthews who managed a bookstore at the mall in White Plains—so that was my first stop. The four other items I had brought with me were good finds that I could sell off to a local antiques dealer I knew up there. If I didn't supplement my income unloading these goods, I doubted my building's management company would accept antiques as payment.

Twenty minutes into my trip, Connor called, and without thinking, I answered.

I debated putting on some form of sick voice, but decided against it.

"How ya feeling, pal?" Connor said. "You okay?"

"Yeah," I said, opting to sound not necessarily sick but not necessarily well either. "I'm okay. I've been better."

"Well, make sure you get lots of fluids." Why does everyone say that? You could be hit by a car or dive naked into a vat full of razorblades, but people were always suggesting that you get lots of fluids.

"Yeah, I'll make sure to do that," I said. The train slowed for its next stop, and before I even thought of covering the mouthpiece, the doors *bonged* open and a voice came over the loudspeaker.

"Ladies and gentlemen," the conductor said with all the enthusiasm of Droopy Dog. "The station stop is Crestwood. Crestwood station. Scarsdale will be next. Scarsdale will be next. Step in and stand clear of the closing doors, please."

I slammed my hand over the phone's mouthpiece.

"Ohhh," Connor said, "I see . . . you're *that* kind of 'sick' today."

Shit. Busted.

"Don't tell the Inspectre, okay?" I pleaded.

"I don't know, kid." Connor sounded dead serious. "You've already got a mountain of paperwork sitting here in your in-box. Then there are the open investigations you've yet to do any follow-up on. I really don't think it's fair to the rest of us in Other Division."

"How about if I promise to . . ." I couldn't come up with anything that might appease him. Connor outranked me. I couldn't bribe him by offering to do most of his tasks or reports that he needed to file. I also doubted he would take me being his coffee boy as payment for his silence.

"Don't sweat it, kid," he said with a laugh. "I'm just busting your chops. Everybody sneaks out every now and then. I'll talk to you when you get back to the office. And kid . . . ?"

"Yeah?"   •

"Next time, be a little faster on the mute button, will ya?"

After hanging up, I settled back and tried to enjoy the rest of the ride as the fall foliage whooshed past at breakneck speed. The foliage thinned as we pulled into the White Plains station, and I grabbed the legal-sized filing box I'd brought and got off.

A short cab ride through the White Plains business district of shiny modern buildings—tiny compared to the steel canyons of Manhattan—and I was at the Westchester Mall. I had never been there before, and my first thought was *Who the hell carpets a mall?* I made my way to the nearest directory, found the B. Dalton Bookseller, and headed off to it.

The scent of plastic, books, and fresh carpeting washed over me as I entered the store. After asking to see the manager, a matronly looking clerk named Yolanda showed me to their back room. It was stacked to the ceiling with boxes, and a lanky gentleman was unpacking one of them onto a sleek metal library cart. He would never win World's Hunkiest Librarian—midthirties, possibly older, with stringy brown hair that made him look all Six Degrees of Ichabod Crane.

"Kevin?" she said. "There's a gentleman here to see you."

"Thanks, Yolanda. I'll be with you in a second," he said, his face still buried in the contents of the box. "As you can see by the state of our store room, the holiday rush is upon us."

"Yeah," I said, looking up at the towering cartons. "Who knew the holidays could look so . . . dangerous."

"Please," he said with a gesture toward a small table with several chairs around it, "have a seat." He sat down, but looked distracted by the amount of work teetering behind him. "I assume you're here about the holiday help."

He pulled a yellow legal pad and a stack of blank applications from a nearby shelf, handing one to me. "You'll need to fill one of these out."

I placed my file box on the table and sat down opposite him. "No, I don't, Kev," I said, pushing the application back toward him.

"I'm sorry . . . do I know you?"

I shook my head. "Not really."

There was the tiniest hint of nervousness in his eyes and at the corners of his mouth. "Well, if you're not here for the job, what *are* you here for?" He gave a quick look toward my box.

"Don't worry," I said as reassuringly as I could, "it's nothing bad. I promise."

"Oh God," he said, with sudden revelation on his face. "Are you an author? Look, we have buyers at our home office who handle all that. I can give you their phone numbers but you have to go through the proper channels. We do very little direct buying of self-published work on the store level . . ."

"I'm not selling anything," I said, reassuring him. I was already losing patience. I still had the antiques dealer to see and I really didn't have time for Kevin's guessing game.

I went for the direct approach. I pulled the lid off the box and lifted out the Intellevision unit.

"This, I believe," I said, handing it to him, "is yours."

I reached back into the file box and began laying out game box after game box before him—twenty in all. There was a little water damage to some of the boxes from the puddle in the alley where I had helped Connor with the ghost, but other than that, they looked okay.

"My God. . . ." Kevin whispered and tears formed at the corners of his eyes, slowly rolling down his face. He ran his fingers over the individual boxes, pausing his thumb over tiny colored tabs that had been added to the upper-right-hand corners of each.

"What *are* those?" I said.

I always tried to maintain my emotional detachment when reuniting owners with their lost property, but I had to admit, I always loved seeing their reactions. They often cried, or had to do their damndest not to. The thing was that if an item had a strong enough emotional fingerprint on it that I could identify its past owner, it probably meant that the item was extremely important in the owner's life.

"I . . ." he started, and stopped. The words wouldn't come. Finally he grabbed hold of another one of the boxes. The words *Shark! Shark!* ran down the side of it, and he hugged the game to his body. "I'm sorry. I'm a little over-whelmed is all." He pointed to one of the tabs. "My friends—we were geeky as hell back then—and we used to color code the games by their genre. Sports games were green, for grass. Red was for fighting games, because, well, you know . . . blood and guts. Puzzle games were purple."

"Why purple?"

He shrugged and smiled. "We couldn't really think of a good color that stood for puzzles, really, so we went for alliteration. *Pu*rple *Pu*zzles. See?"

I nodded and checked my watch. I could make the next train upstate if I was out of here in the next five minutes.

"How on earth did you get your hands on these? And how did you find me?" he asked, drying his eyes on his sleeve. "I thought this stuff was gone *forever*. I know it must seem foolish that I'm crying over something like this, but there are a lot of memories packed in here."

"If you look on the bottom of the console, it has your name and old address on it," I said.

It was a lie, really. I had gone ahead and faked the signature because it seemed a much more plausible explanation than trying to convince him that I had tracked him down through a psychometric vision of his childhood. I hoped he assumed one of his parents had done it.

He picked up the machine, flipped it over, and looked at the signature. "Huh!" *Let's wrap it up, Kev.* Honestly, I wasn't insensitive to what he was going through. I loved giving someone that sense of connection to their past, but if I was to be straight with myself, my real motivation was the possibility of a cash reward. I checked my watch again. Four minutes left to get out of here and catch the next train up to see the antiques dealer in Poughkeepsie. It was time to close the deal. There were two approaches that usually worked. One was a simple "How much you willing to pay?" gambit, but I thought the subtle approach would catch Kevin hook, line, and sinker. He was weepy enough, for sure.

Step one. "I should probably be going," I said with the most sincere and sheepish look I could muster. "I just thought this stuff might be important to you."

"Wait," he said, getting up. "Please . . . let me give you something for your trouble."

Step two. Look surprised.

Step three. Refuse once. "No, that's okay," I continued. "Really."

"No, please. I insist."

Almost everyone says that. "I insist."

Step four. I reluctantly agreed, like I was doing him a favor by taking his money. "Well," I said with a kind smile. "If it will make you feel better . . ."

I walked out of the store with Kevin's gratitude and a check for just over three hundred dollars. He insisted I not take a dime less. It was amazing how high a price tag people put on healing their emotional scars. I sold memories. I sold a certain amount of healing and hope, too. It didn't mean that I didn't feel dirty about it sometimes.

17

When I got home from the sales trip, it was after dark, but not too late. I had been successful to the tune of two months' maintenance. I found Irene asleep in the guest room as I had left her earlier this morning and I didn't dare disturb her. Connor had talked about how her spirit might slowly start to degrade and turn into something like the one from the alley, but I figured the less I forced her to interact, the less energy she expended—and that might slow the degradation. I caught a few hours' sleep before waking up and sneaking the surveillance equipment I had calibrated the other night out of the apartment while Irene slept on, and I headed for Jane's address, which Connor had e-mailed to me.

Hours later, as I prowled the rooftops and set up a parabolic mike directly across from Jane's Chelsea apartment, I felt skeevy and voyeuristic. The Inspectre had assured me it was a necessary evil in the fight against, well, evil. But as I settled into an evening of spying on her, I found myself . . . liking it. Spying on Jane gave me a much better understanding of the woman. By the dull glow of my laptop's screen, I worked on my report for the Department, detailing every move that she made. Jane was a much more cheerful person when she was home alone, and I guessed that it was due to being free and clear of her responsibilities to the evil Mr. Faisal Bane. Well, not *quite* free and clear. Throughout the night, she bristled as she fielded several calls from her boss regarding his scheduling needs. I was impressed that the parabolic mike picked up his voice on the phone. The confused expressions that flitted across her face as she spoke on the phone made it clear that she didn't understand half of what her powerful boss was up to. Not that she was dumb, but I doubted she truly grasped the evil extent of what she had gotten herself into.

She didn't question any of his demands. As the S.D.L. had probably made clear to her, certain things—highly evil things, I had no doubt—were on a "need to know" basis. I bet the less you knew at the Sectarian Defense League, the longer your lifespan was.

It wasn't until nine that she made an outgoing call of her own. Take-out. When she asked for her sweet and sour sauce on the side, the same as I did, I smiled. Thirty minutes later her food arrived (she was a heavy tipper, I noted), but before she had a chance to put it down, her cell phone went off yet again. This time, as I positioned the mike, I caught her cursing under her breath.

I adjusted the mike and their voices came in loud and clear.

"What's up, boss?" she said.

"Good evening, Jane. I trust you're enjoying your time off tonight?"

Jane looked at the unopened bag of Chinese food in her hand.

"Oh yeah," she said with mock enthusiasm. "It's a regular party at my place, sir."

"I'm afraid your party will have to wait," he said. "I've got some errands I need done."

He really didn't get the whole sarcasm thing. Perhaps it had something to do with that dark, brooding European sensibility of his. Or maybe he just didn't get idioms.

I knew that a lot of people would be bothered if their time off was constantly interrupted, but after my dinner with Jane, I knew she was probably making the best of the situation in her head already. I bet she was thinking, *Doesn't Chinese reheat just fine?*

I watched through high-tech optical headgear as she walked over to the fridge and tossed the bag in next to four others. Thanks to the power of the electronic eyes, I could even make out the other packages in there: one Mexican, one Italian, and two other Chinese.

"Where do you need me, sir?" She slammed the refrigerator door shut.

"Do you have something black to wear?"

"Of course," she said as she crossed her kitchen.

Over dinner, she had actually said that day one of her Human Resources training, the Sectarians had sent her out with a corporate credit card to pick up a variety of outfits . . . all of them in black. The corporate equivalent of hairnets, paper hats, and smocks for the forces of Darkness, I guessed.

"Good, good," Faisal said. "Wear something you can be flexible in."

"Flexible, sir?" she said, puzzled. "Like a leotard?"

My mind wandered as the image of her in clingy clothing filled it. She was working for evil, but even evil could be hot, right?

Faisal chuckled on the other end of the line. "No no, my dear. Flexible as in the 'I'm going to be climbing, spying, and gee, I hope I don't get caught' kind of flexible."

"Oh, *that* kind."

"Yes, *that* kind."

"I'm sure I have something," Jane said, and headed out of her living room into the darkness of the next room over. I switched the goggles over to night vision and suddenly had a perfect view of her bedroom lit in a wash of monochromatic green. The goggles read body heat and I couldn't help but notice the red-blue swirls it picked up and the curves of her figure. Torn between gentlemanly respect and a sense of duty, I forced myself to keep watching. She headed straight to a chest of drawers. It was already open and clothes hung out of it in disarray. Jane started pawing through them. "May I inquire as to my mission?"

"You may indeed. I need you to check out those two men from the incident at our offices the other afternoon. I need you to tell me if one of them isn't talking to someone."

Jane's face scrunched up, confused, and I found I was making the same face underneath the goggles. *Isn't* talking to someone . . . ?

She continued to rummage through her chest of drawers. "I'm sorry?"

"I beg your pardon," corrected Faisal. "I need you to tell me if one of them is talking to someone who isn't."

Jane held up a shirt and stretched it across her body. Slimming, a bit tight, but if she was caught spying, she'd look dynamite in it. Perfect choice.

"I'm afraid I don't follow you, Mr. Bane."

"Then follow this!" he barked, causing me to reach for the volume on the headphones.

This was the Faisal I had expected. Jane nearly dropped the phone. She stopped fussing with the shirt and gave Faisal her full attention. "Thanks to that careless object retrieval you scheduled, one of my pet projects has been compromised, Jane. Some very important enemies are becoming all too aware of the Sectarian Defense League's goings-on and I'm blaming this wholly on you."

"Sir, the agent I sent to Ms. Blatt's on the retrieval—"

"Was *still* your agent, Jane. You *do* take responsibility for people under your command, I assume?"

Jane was getting nervous. She started pacing and fell silent.

What could she say? I knew she was way out of her league, probably had been from day one. Right that moment, though, she had to think fast to please her boss. Her newfound career with the S.D.L. was on the line. How she handled Faisal would affect whether she lived or died, even if she wasn't fully aware of the severity of her situation.

She seemed so small and insecure just then. I wanted to help her out, even if she was playing for Team Evil. I wished I could send thoughtwaves to her. *Keep in mind where your bread is buttered and you'll know to please him above all else to survive.*

As if in response, Jane's face calmed and she said, "Yes, of course I'm responsible for what my people do, sir."

"Good," he said, softening. Monochrome Jane relaxed even further. "That's what I like to hear. Now when I said 'I need you to find if one of them is talking to someone who *isn't*,' I meant just that. It is tragic that the Department of Extraordinary Affairs knows about our existence now, but their bursting into our offices was not a total waste of my precious time. There was something one of them said that made me think. They implied they were working with someone I personally know to be out of the picture. Do you follow?"

"I think so, sir."

"Excellent. You take care of this for me, Jane, and you'll make me a very happy man. And if you find that this *person who isn't* is still around, I expect you to *correct* the situation. Do you understand or should I use more monosyllabic words?"

Jane sighed and began to search through a sock drawer.

She pushed the socks aside and pulled a gun out from underneath them.

"I'll do my best, sir." She held it by two fingers like it was a dead fish and then checked the safety before sliding the gun neatly into the back of her belt.

"See that you do," Faisal said. "I'll expect a full report on my desk in the morning."

Jane threw the phone onto the bed and wrestled her way into the black top she had picked out. This time I watched unabashed. She pulled her blond hair back into a manageable ponytail, and I tried to figure out how a relatively sweet girl had come to toting a gun. She must have marveled at all the changes in her life over the past few months, the feeling of importance that came with newfound power and security. I was pretty sure that no temp job had ever let her have a gun before. She probably chalked up carrying a piece as part of her "benefits package."

She walked back into her living room and began looking through a stack of folders she had spread out on the coffee table earlier in the evening. I was startled when she picked one of them up and flipped it open to a photograph of me standing in the Sectarians' reception area. I was a little flattered that I was the one whom she meant to spy on. And obviously Irene was the "someone who *isn't*" that Faisal was looking for.

Jane wasn't a killer . . . was she? I knew she was after Irene, but would she kill me if I got in the way? I didn't know her well enough after our two encounters, but it had felt like there was a tiny bit of chemistry between us the other night during dinner. Would that prevent her from sending me to the big dirt nap in the sky? Asinine questions—especially those regarding my attraction to a cultist—would have to wait. I had to get back to my place before she did.

I hastily packed my equipment while watching Jane pack hers. I was thrilled to see that she wasn't in possession of a parabolic mike, which meant she wouldn't be able to listen in on my apartment the way I had on hers. That was some relief.

I took one last look. Jane was so sinisterly cute, and everything felt more confusing than ever.

I just prayed she wouldn't have to use her "benefits package" on me.

18

I raced back to my apartment in record time. I had to be there to keep Irene safe. I knew Jane would be watching the two of us in much the same way I had been watching her, and while I felt the whole procedure was just as invasive, I had to admit the prospect was strangely exciting. Knowing ahead of time that someone was going to be watching me all stalkerlike was a godsend. It meant I stood a better chance of controlling the situation.

Now Jane would be the voyeur and I would be the one on display. The possibility that she might attempt to shoot me or do something to Irene did take some of the intrigue out of the sitch, though. But I figured that if I could get the curtains drawn in the living room before Jane got to my apartment, Irene and I would be relatively safe.

On the way home I made the decision not to tell Irene about our possible surveillance. Irene had enough on her plate without needing the added burden of worrying over someone who probably couldn't do her harm anyway— and I needed Irene to be calm and relaxed. I couldn't have her flickering in and out with nerves if I was going to keep her safe.

When I got back home, Irene was in my living room marveling over the woodwork of a cabinet I had picked up in New Hampshire. Her gaze was so fixed on the piece that she barely registered I was in the room. She looked up as I shut the door behind me and locked it. I ran to the windows and hastily pulled the curtains over each of them. I started pushing crates and boxes out of the way and up against the bank of windows.

"Hello," said Irene. "Tough day at the office?"

I forced a laugh and was thrilled to see how calm and content she was. Her body looked solid as a rock, not a hint of transparency. "Why don't you have a seat?" I said, moving a stack of books from the couch to give her more room. "I'm just going to tidy up a bit."

"Now?" she said, with a giggle that gave way to uproarious laughter. The reaction was so cartoonish, so out of character, that I wondered if maybe she was beginning to degrade, as Connor had warned she would. "But it's so late!"

"Well, better late than never, right?" I said.

I threw myself down on the couch, checking to make sure my bat was still hanging from my belt. Jane had to be outside spying by now, and God only knew what she might do. If she made a move on the apartment, I wanted to be ready. Irene sat at the far end of the couch staring at me. She seemed to have settled back to her normal, refined self.

It was funny how small talk seemed hard to come by when I really needed it. There were so many topics I wanted to avoid right now to keep Irene in good spirits. The biggest elephant in the conversational room, of course, was her own case, which she naturally brought up.

"Dare I ask if there are any new developments?"

"Be patient," I said, looking over toward the windows.

I spun around and checked the door. "Something will come up. There's nothing new."

Unless I counted the fact that I knew Faisal Bane was interested in her, but I didn't think telling Irene that would be terribly calming. Instead, I did what I did best when I felt uncomfortable. I rambled.

We had antiques as a common ground after all. I told her about all the wonderful pieces I had seen back at her apartment, leaving out the fact that most of them were smashed to bits. The mere mention of so many of her things kept her fascinated, and did the trick of making her seem all the more alive. A strong part of me wanted to forget that she was no longer living.

The threat of Jane slowly faded from my thoughts as I became more and more immersed in my conversation with Irene. But just when I was lulled into a real sense of comfort, a commotion arose somewhere outside my wall of windows.

"Wesker, no!" a male voice shouted from the rooftop across the way.

The windows were shut, but the shout cut through them. The thunderous din of something or some*one* crashing full force into the alleyway below rang out. I threw the sash up on the window and chanced a look outside. Lights throughout the building were coming on, and several others people were already poking their heads out. It was too dark to make out anything distinct in the alley below, and I gave up trying to see anything when a rapid knocking sounded at the door.

"What's going on?" Irene said nervously. I looked over at her and her body flickered briefly due to her sudden emotional state.

"Keep it together, Irene," I said, running for the door.

When I opened it, two men stood there: Inspectre Argyle Quimbley and Thaddeus Wesker of Greater & Lesser Arcana. The old Brit looked positively winded, but Wesker just looked pissed off. He pushed his way into the apartment and Quimbley stumbled in behind him, clutching his side. I was stunned by their sudden appearance at my apartment, and in the middle of the night no less. No one from work had ever been here before. Well, unless you counted Irene. I shut the door and ran for the window, pulling the curtain down again now that Jane had *four* potential targets to choose from. Wesker was staring darkly at Irene.

"What's *she* doing here?" he spat out.

"Excuse me," Irene said, heading angrily toward Wesker at a fast float. "Am I not in the room?"

"What's going on?" I asked, quickly stepping between her and Wesker. Irene stopped in her tracks. "What the hell was that? Inspectre, was that you I heard calling out?"

Quimbley nodded in response, and gulped down a deep breath as he gathered his composure, starting with grooming his walruslike mustache.

"Wesker intercepted some intel from the Sectarians," the Inspectre said, "regarding both you and Connor showing up at their offices. He learned that even though they now have possession of the fish artifact, they were still particularly interested in Ms. Blatt. All we know is that someone was very keen on finding her and was sending someone after you. So rather than involving the Enchancellors at this point, I convinced Wesker to keep things quiet and we decided to investigate the situation ourselves. Neither of our divisions wanted the red tape and triplicate forms of openly declaring a joint venture. We tried getting you on your cell, but you didn't answer. We feared the worst."

"I turned it *off* because I was on a surveillance mission!" I said defensively. "One you sent me on!"

The Inspectre was wheezing now.

"Sir, are you okay?"

He nodded. "Ripping good rooftops in SoHo. Took me a bit of effort to climb up to the top of the building next to you, though. That's when we observed a woman in black moving into position near your apartment. Striking-looking young lady."

"That would be Jane," I muttered quietly. The two of them stared at me blankly. I kept my voice low, hoping Irene couldn't overhear. "Bane's errand girl? The one you sent me to watch tonight? Look, I *know* Jane was watching me. I had everything under control here."

Wesker perked up at the mention of her. "On a first-name basis now, are you?"

"No," I said, shaking my head perhaps just a bit too much. "She was just there when Connor and I first encountered the Sectarians. When I went a little bat happy in their reception area."

"You realize how bad that's going to look for your future at the Department, don't you?" Wesker said.

I smiled weakly. "Sorry," I added.

"Nonsense," Quimbley said, "happens to the best of us at times, my boy. Now, where was I?"

Wesker's face tightened and he looked like he wanted to strangle the Inspectre right there in my living room.

"I believe you were moving in on Jane . . ." I offered.

"Ah yes!" the Inspectre said, eyes lighting up. "Yes. Anyway, *Jane* had lowered herself over the edge of the building across from yours, and before I knew it, Wesker was sprinting across the rooftops like some damned fool superhero. Before I could catch up, he pulled a switchblade and flicked it through her tie-off line. I tried to call out, but alas, too late."

It was true that Jane was with the enemy here, had even brought a gun to deal with us if she had found Irene in my apartment. Still, it bothered me to think of her being harmed. That was a gut-wrencher I hadn't expected. I couldn't imagine Wesker killing her in cold blood. We had procedures and protocols in place for the handling of humans under the influence of dark forces. But then again, it was *Wesker* we were talking about.

"He didn't kill her, did he?" Irene asked suddenly.

Quimbley shook his head. "I don't think so. When I looked over the edge of the rooftop, I couldn't tell."

Wesker stepped forward.

"Enough of this concern for the enemy," he said and glared at Irene over my shoulder. "What is *she* doing here?"

I tried to look past Wesker, seeking guidance from Quimbley, but all the old man could do was look at me sympathetically.

"Don't look at him," Wesker shouted. "Answer me! What is she doing here?"

I tried to compose myself, keeping my anger over his tone in check, but the best I could do was sarcasm.

"I'm sorry, Director Wesker," I said. "I didn't realize that the Division of Greater and Lesser Arcana had generously provided accommodations for clients such as Miss Blatt. I suppose that's why no one *noticed* her or *helped* her all day when she arrived. When I stopped by the office on my way home the other night, I found her pushed aside just like another stack of paperwork. The woman was practically beside herself. So tell me, where do you propose we have Ms. Blatt stay while the investigation is ongoing?"

"We're not in the practice of running a boardinghouse for wayward ghosts," Wesker said testily.

"You're not in the practice of providing accommodations for *any* of the entities we deal with," I said, shouting. "Unless you count containment, of course, but Irene's not a prisoner."

"You want to watch your tone with me, Canderous," Wesker said.

"Or what?" I was losing what little patience I had. Connor had warned me several times before about my handling of superiors at the D.E.A., but Wesker was being openly hostile in the presence of the Inspectre, so I wasn't afraid. Sure, the man was dangerously ambitious and everyone knew he had it in for the Inspectre, but Quimbley was respected throughout the entire organization—and a lifetime member of the Fraternal Order of Goodness to boot! Thaddeus Wesker knew he would never be as well liked as the Inspectre and that frosted his biscuit. His general mistreatment of me was just ineffectual lashing out.

"What will you do to me?" I continued. "Last I checked, I answered directly to the Inspectre here, not to you. And since when does the Director of Greater and Lesser Arcana concern himself personally with the doings of a lesser spectral apparition like Ms. Blatt anyway?"

The words were out of my mouth before I had a chance to think of how Irene would take being called "a lesser spectral apparition." I felt like a heel for letting the words slip out. I turned to apologize, hoping she hadn't taken offense. But whether she had taken offense or not wasn't an issue.

Irene Blatt had disappeared.

Wesker finally backed off when he noticed Irene had vanished. The three of us took a quick look around my apartment (I handled the investigation of the White Room) but there was no sign of Irene. Quimbley suggested that he and Wesker leave, but not before giving me orders to report to his office first thing in the morning.

I was sick to my stomach over Irene's disappearance. I had taken her in when the rest of the Department couldn't be bothered, made her my charge, and now I had lost her. But I couldn't obsess over it now. There was someone else I had to check on. I headed down to the rear exit of my building and let myself out into the dark and trash bag–filled alley. The stink was powerful, but I fought back the urge to vomit and started picking my way through it.

It didn't take long to find Jane. All I had to do was follow the soft moans and grunts of pain from a pile of trash bags that had exploded when she had landed on them. She was completely out of it when I picked her up. Next to her on the ground was a small black notebook. I scooped it up and slid it into my jacket pocket with one of my gloved hands. The last thing I wanted was to be psychometrically sucked into her life. Right now, I needed to get Jane up to my apartment.

As I carried her on to the elevator, I thought about my options. First I'd assess how badly hurt she was. Finding Irene would have to wait.

As the elevator stopped on my floor, I slid the cast iron door aside. I hurried down the hall, hoping none of my neighbors would stick their noses out, and I was thrilled when we made it to my apartment safely. I laid Jane down on my couch. She was motionless except for the telltale signs of gentle respiration. The left arm of her spy gear top was peeled away, along with several layers of skin. A slow but steady trickle of blood dripped down the side of my couch and gathered in a small pool on the floor. Her face was bruised down the left side, but otherwise she looked peaceful.

Blood was a funny thing in real life. I had seen much more gruesome sights thanks to television and the movies, never once feeling woozy. But the smell of real blood mixed with garbage in my own apartment was something else. I was barely able to hold my stomach down.

"Jane?"

I tentatively touched her good arm, and she stirred, groaning in pain. Her eyes fluttered open, and after a moment, they focused and smiled.

"Hello, Simon," she said weakly. "Hope you don't mind me dropping in."

I brushed golden strands of hair away from her face as I inspected her for damage. Her left arm hung uselessly at her side. She looked like shit, but even so, she was still cute. I felt slimy for thinking it, but as I checked her over, I couldn't help noticing her body once again. It curved in all the right places, even battered like this.

"Jesus, Jane," I said. "Are you all right?"

She nodded slowly, wincing and looking a little loopy. "Ow. As all right as someone who just plummeted off a roof can be, I guess. I had some painkillers with me, but I don't know where they are anymore."

She raised her good arm and opened her hand. It was empty.

I looked at her glazed, unfocused eyes. "Um, I think you already took them. You think you can move?" I asked. Jane couldn't stay here. She was in danger for several reasons. I took a look around the apartment, and though I was worried sick about Irene, I was glad I saw no sign of her. It was odd, but I felt like I was somehow betraying Irene just by having Jane here. It was all in my head, I told myself. I didn't owe either of these women anything, and here I was feeling guilty. The dead girl and the enemy. Great taste, Simon.

My work was mixing terribly with the rest of my life, and I felt helplessly out of control. I had to take charge as best I could of this situation, though, not only for my sake but for Jane's.

"Is anything broken?" I asked.

Jane slowly assessed herself, flexing muscles wherever she could.

"My arm's pretty beat-up," she moaned, "and I don't think I can make my Pilates class tomorrow with my ankle like this, but I think I can move."

She smiled through all of it. It was probably the painkillers mixed with loss of blood making her delirious. I gently took hold of her right arm, the good one, and slowly helped her into a sitting position.

"Nice place you've got here," she said. Then she looked down and saw her blood pooling on my floor. A slow whine began in her throat and her breath hitched as she started crying in long deep sobs. "Oh, look at that. Simon, I'm so sorry."

I ran to the bathroom, and held a towel under the faucet. When I returned, I applied it to her arm and then wiped her tears away as best I could.

"There's no need to apologize, Jane. Listen, we need to get you out of here. If the Department finds out you're in my apartment, I'll be fired for sure." I wasn't sure if that was true or not, but it sure sounded true. "I have no idea what your own people will do to you. So don't worry about the blood. There's much less than if you had got a chance to shoot me, believe me."

She looked at me blankly, then squirmed her good arm behind her and produced the gun by its muzzle. She dropped it to the floor and sniffled through her tears. "I don't think I would have gone through with it, Simon. Honest."

She looked sincere, but just in case, I kicked the gun under the couch. "That's very reassuring, coming from a cultist."

She looked hurt, and I felt like an asshole. Clearly this was no time for me to get petty. Jane favored one leg as I got her into a standing position, and I grabbed a nearby jacket and threw it around her. It would cover up the majority of her injuries to the casual observer. I kissed her forehead the way my mom used to when I came in, all too often, with a scraped knee.

"You're doing great, Jane."

This brought a slight smile to her lips. She looked up at me gratefully. I resisted the inappropriate urge to kiss her on the mouth. I was pretty sure that snogging the enemy was frowned upon. The Department had given me a pamphlet entitled *Blind Date with Disaster* and an orientation lecture concerning intimate relations with the forces of Darkness. Strictly taboo, and spelled out in an ancient tale about a D.E.A. member named Edgar and his obsession with his lost love, Lenore.

The smile faded from Jane's face as her eyes rolled back into her head, leaving me only the whites to stare into. Her legs gave out and I balanced her on the armrest of the couch to keep her from falling. "Stay with me, Jane."

The blood loss had made her light-headed. I eased her back on to the couch and ran to the fridge to grab a carton of orange juice. My medical expertise might be lacking, but with my psychometry-induced hyperglycemia, I knew O.J. might be enough to bring Jane around.

I tipped her head back and placed the carton at her lips. Her eyes fluttered as the juice hit her tongue and she began drinking greedily.

"Easy," I told her. "What happened? What do you recall?"

She gasped for breath as I pulled the near empty carton away.

"Thank you soooo much," she said, the life returning to her.

Her face looked a thousand times better and her eyes were alive again, though still a little glassy from the painkillers. They bore into mine, and without warning, she kissed me. My first thought was of juice. Her tongue tasted like juice. After that, all other thoughts left me. The idea of this being taboo lurked somewhere at the back of my mind, but clearly my own eager urges had taboo pinned safely out of my brain's way.

My hand traced the back of her neck, my fingers running through her hair. Our bodies moved closer, toppling back onto the couch, and I felt the warmth of her body underneath mine. She jerked with a sudden convulsion.

"Owwww!" she hissed as she bit my tongue mid-probe. "My hip. I think it might be broken."

In that instant I recovered my senses and slid off her. She was half doped up, for God's sake. "Sorry, I shouldn't French with the forces of evil."

"Don't be," she said, not taking offense. I helped her sit back up. I glanced at her briefly, and this time, she was careful not to look too deep into my eyes. "Don't you want to know why I was here?"

"Later," I said. "I think we both have some 'splainin' to do, but first we need to get you to a hospital."

Immediately there was terror in her eyes. "You can't!"

"Jane, you've got to get medical attention . . . all I've got is juice."

"It's just . . ." she started, but couldn't speak. "I can't let Faisal or the Sectarians know I got hurt this bad. I'll never live it down. They'll fire me . . . or worse."

In all the madness, I hadn't considered what the Sectarians might do to someone who had failed. Especially someone as fresh-faced as her.

"Take me home," she said. Under other circumstances, I might have been thrilled to hear those words from her lips. Now was not one of those times.

"Right," I said, nodding. "Sure."

Now that I was coming to my senses, I wanted to get her out of here should Irene suddenly reappear. She had seemed . . . strange, and I didn't know how she would react to finding Jane in the apartment.

"My apartment is at—"

"I know where you live, Jane," I interrupted. She looked at me quizzically. "Like I said, I think we both have some 'splainin' to do."

I scooped one arm around her and started for the door. As an afterthought, I grabbed the Other Division emergency kit the Inspectre had given me months ago. I was pretty sure that escorting the enemy from your home before she died certainly counted as an emergency.

If I was lucky, I'd get her out of here without further incident. If I was unlucky, Faisal and his people would be waiting for us.

19

Although it was late, it was still New York and I found a cab fairly quickly. The cab driver didn't even blink while I arranged the battered and bloody Jane in the back of his cab. I got in beside her as she rattled off her Chelsea address and then she closed her eyes. I let her rest, riding in sleepy silence until we reached her apartment building. Because Jane had left a small pool of blood on the seat, I tipped the cabbie generously. I made sure the coast was clear of anyone looking particularly evil outside her building, then carried Jane across her lobby, into her elevator, and up to her apartment. I pushed aside the pile of clothes on her bed to lay her down properly. Finally she looked moderately comfortable, despite how banged up she was.

As I arranged her pillows behind her, her eyes fluttered open and she smiled.

"How you holding up?" I asked.

She reached out to me and squeezed my hand in reassurance. Her speech was slurred, but she said, "Right now, I'm just concentrating on the intense amount of pain I'm in. More importantly, I was wondering if you thought I was a decent kisser."

I pulled my hand away from hers. I should never have kissed her. She was the enemy.

"I don't get it on with evil," I said. "Remember?"

I decided to change the subject from snogging to something more constructive.

"Look," I said, softening. "I know I'm on the wrong side of your evil fence, Jane, but do you want to tell me how you got all battered like this?"

Thanks to Wesker and the Inspectre, I knew what had happened, but I wanted to see what she could recall or, more to the point, what she would truthfully tell me and how much I could trust her.

Jane smiled back at me and said, "When I was a kid, I used to love that stomach-dropping sensation you get from rides at an amusement park, you know? After that fall? Not so much. I should be dead."

Her damaged upper arm was matted with blood and bits of garbage from the alley. I tore the remaining bits of sleeve free from it. "What do you remember about the fall?"

She winced as I lifted her arm to clear away the cloth. "I remember skidding down the brick face and getting that scrape you're working on. I lost all sense of direction, but I made out the fire escape whirling by and reached for it. It caught me in the stomach and drove the wind right out of me. Then I was falling again and landed in your trash. Comfy trash, by the way. Smell pretty, don't I?"

I brushed her hair out of her face.

"I've smelled worse," I said.

"I knew whoever cut the line would come looking for me," she said, "but I couldn't even move. Then my instincts kicked in."

I opened the Other Division emergency kit. There were dozens of items in it, none of them familiar, but thankfully each of them was labeled meticulously and included full instructions. There were several rolls of what I thought were gauze, but looking closer, they appeared more like human fingers wrapped in funereal bandages.

Mummy Fingers, the label read. *In case of emergency, place against damaged surface and let them go to work. Warning: Do not use over nose and mouth. Consult an Arcana Specialist if misapplied.*

I placed one against Jane's arm and it started to writhe like a snake as the bandage uncoiled and rolled securely around her arm. Jane kept talking, seemingly unaware of what was happening to her arm, but I was seriously creeped out.

"Lights came on all along the alley," she said, "and I could make out the sounds of commotion up above. I couldn't call Mr. Bane for help. My cell phone had been crushed completely."

I pulled off one of her boots, but when I tried the other, it was swollen tight around her sprained ankle. I moved as gently as I could, but she yelped in pain when I finally forced it free. She started to cry.

"I'm so sorry," I said. "I tried to be as gentle as I could."

She shook her head and laughed through her tears. "It's not that. I was thinking about that rumor about my predecessor at the League, the one they fed to a man-eating filing cabinet for screwing up? The thought that I might be next in line doesn't really improve my morale. Look at me. I'm battered, bruised, I smell, and my mission is totally a failure in almost every possible respect."

I placed another of the Mummy Fingers against her, this time alongside her sprained foot. I cringed as it pushed her ankle back into proper position. There was no escaping the audible pop and this time Jane screamed.

A fresh wave of chilled sweat formed on her forehead and I stroked her hair back from it.

"If it will help set things straight at work," I said, "I can *let* you kill me."

She laughed through what remained of her pain. "Thanks, but no thanks."

"You really think you're in that much trouble?" I asked.

"Well," she said, "there's only one way to find out."

She reached for her bedside phone, but I handed her mine instead.

"It's untraceable. Is anyone going to be there this time of night, though?"

She nodded, dialed, and held it close between the two of us to listen. I tried to ignore the fact that I was literally lying in bed with the enemy.

"Sectarian Defense League," said the woman on the phone. The look on Jane's face told me she didn't recognize the voice. "How may I direct your call?"

I felt her hand twitch to hang up, but I steadied her and she stopped.

"Yes," Jane said, attempting to change her voice as best she could, "I'd like to speak to Mr. Bane's personal assistant, please."

There was a pause.

"Hello?" Jane said. There was the sound of muffled conversation from the other end of the line. The woman on the other end had put her hand over the mouthpiece.

"One moment, please," the voice said when it returned, and the phone clicked over to an orchestral version of some pop tune I vaguely recognized.

"What the hell is going on?" I whispered. Jane shrugged, but before I could ask anything further, the music went away and a male voice came on the line. "This is Mr. Bane's assistant."

"I'm sorry," she said. "Actually, I was looking for Jane."

Sounds familiar, she mouthed.

Silence. "She's out of the office indefinitely right now. Can I possibly help you?"

"Do you know where she is, please? It's urgent."

Another pause.

Faisal? I mouthed. Jane shook her head.

"If you can just hold on the line," the man said, "I'm sure I can put you through to someone who can be of assistance."

I covered the phone's mouthpiece. "He's stalling," I said.

Jane looked panicked. "I can try again later. Thanks!"

"Wait! Don't hang up." The man on the other end of the line chuckled. "Jane? Is that you? Where are you hiding, girl?"

What color that was left in Jane's face drained away and she hit END.

"Well?" I asked. "Jane?"

She turned to me, her face a mask of fright.

"I didn't know who the first person was," she said, "but the man . . . it took me a second to place him, but I know who he is. I even set him up with a freelancer position with the S.D.L. Did his preinterview and everything."

She was shaking so hard I took her hands in my gloved ones.

"Jane," I said, "calm down. Don't worry. I can take care of you. Just tell me who he is."

"The name he gave me back then," she said, failing to remain calm, "was Jason Charles, but everyone knew right off it was an alias. It's the specialty we hired him for that has me totally freaked out, Simon."

"What does he do?" I asked

She sat up, regardless of the pain she felt. "The Sectarians do a lot of their own dirty work when it comes to the occult. There are times, however, when certain special assignments come up that even they find unsavory, such as hunting their own. They tend to outsource that kind of work, especially when it's a corporate job. They like to use someone versed in the corporate world as well as wetwork."

"So they've put a contract out on you already?" I asked. "You've only been off the radar for what, an hour or two?"

Jane gulped. "That's long enough. Faisal knows I've failed.

"I never gave Jason Charles a second thought before now," Jane continued. "I wasn't on the receiving end of his business, so what did it matter to me? And recently there had been some talk about using him against the D.E.A. . . ."

"They were going to send him after us?" All the politicking Dave Davidson had done between our groups, keeping us civil toward one another, flew out the door. "Just what the hell is this Jason Charles anyway?"

Jane's eyes widened. "He's a corporate headhunter. And if he's watching my office and handling things for Faisal already, it means I'm on his shit list. So are you, since they'll send him to finish up what I couldn't back at your apartment. If we leave the country now, they just might leave us alone."

Corporate headhunters. I had heard of them, but until now I had thought they were just a rumor, like government funding. You didn't want to tangle with one of them.

"And if we don't leave?" I asked. "What then?"

Jane looked ready to pass out again.

"Prepare to be downsized."

20

I couldn't leave Jane there for their corporate headhunter to find so (in four separate cabs) I took her to a hotel over on the Upper East Side and checked her in. I headed home around 5 a.m. There was still no sign of Irene and I slept for a fitful three hours before heading up to the Lovecraft Café. I grabbed a coffee and went back to the offices to face the Inspectre. His door was shut and the muffled sound of arguing came from behind it. I sat down and waited.

I bet myself a new armoire from the ABC store on Eighteenth that it was Director Wesker getting yelled at. It was hard to imagine anyone more deserving of getting chewed out than him.

When the door to Inspectre Quimbley's office opened, it shook in its frame and revealed an extremely agitated-looking Thaddeus Wesker. He hadn't changed since last night—wearing the same suit, tie, and look of disdain. His disdain doubled when he noticed me sitting there waiting, and he stormed off down the stairs. I stood when I heard an exasperated sigh from within the office and walked in to find Quimbley sitting at his desk, his head in his hands. He, too, was wearing the same clothes from last night.

"Sir . . . ?" I shut the door behind me.

Quimbley jumped at the sound of my voice, but when he saw it was me, he relaxed. He picked up his glasses, fitted them on his face, and grabbed the folder lying before him. "Simon, please . . . have a seat."

I sat in the leather chair opposite him. "Is everything okay, Inspectre? Director Wesker seemed in a far fouler mood than usual."

The Inspectre peered over the top of his glasses at me and smiled. "You noticed that, too, eh?"

I smiled back cautiously. My limited encounters with my superior left me wary in his presence. Connor was much closer to our Other Division leader. I wasn't sure how political I should be in responding to any questions concerning my personal feelings about Director Wesker. I didn't want to step on any toes, so I chose to speak with caution and voice as few of my own opinions as possible.

"Wesker's mood on his way out was kind of hard to miss, sir."

Quimbley sat silently for a moment, possibly weighing his thoughts. "True." Another pause. "You don't like Director Wesker, I take it? Given last night's events, I mean . . ."

"Truth be told, Inspectre, I don't think I'm in a position to judge."

"No?" the Inspectre said. "And why not, dear boy? You must have an opinion one way or the other. Come, come!"

I shifted in my seat uncomfortably as I thought it over. "Well . . ."

Quimbley dropped the folder and softened as he looked at me, his wise old eyes without any gleam of judgment.

"I'd be hesitant, too, if I were you, Simon. Here you are, so new to the D.E.A. and already dealing with such bizarre and unusual circumstances. You're worried you might say the wrong thing or drop the wrong word in the wrong person's ear? Perhaps you're concerned that if you speak against another agent or director, you'll be seen as disloyal."

I nodded. "I guess that's part of it, sir."

"I want to assure you," he offered conspiratorially, "that nothing you say here will get back to Thaddeus Wesker. This is not a test of your honor or loyalty, boy. I would simply like to hear your take on the events of last night."

If the Inspectre only knew all of the events last night, I thought, he'd kick me out of the Department altogether. I shut those thoughts out of my mind and tried to relax a little, finding, much to my surprise, that I was able to.

"Very well then," I said. "No, sir, I don't particularly care for Director Wesker, not after last night. Coming into my apartment like that . . ."

"If you remember," he said, "*I* came into your apartment as well last night. A bit winded, to be sure, but I was there also. Yet you hold no ill will toward me, Simon."

"Yes," I countered, "but you didn't come in flinging accusations . . . acting like something illicit was going on, that somehow I was compromising the Department."

"And why do you think Director Wesker did that, boy?"

I pondered the question for a moment, but the answer seemed clear. "Because he knows I'm allied with you and Other Division."

Quimbley smirked, nodding slowly as he ran his thumb and forefinger through his mustache. "Yes," he said. "Yes, I can see that. But I think you're barking up the wrong tree, boy. It's no secret that Thaddeus Wesker has no love for me, but it's also no secret that there's nothing he can do about it . . . yet. Let him gather all the power that he can and then we'll see."

"But then it'll be too late!" I practically cried out. "And what will he do to you when he does? Connor is just as worried about this. Both of us have questioned his allegiance to the Department."

The mirth on his face from a second ago was gone, and had been replaced by a look of utter seriousness.

"My boy," he said, "what I'm about to tell you is strictly between the two of us, something only a few other people know around the Department. Director Thaddeus Wesker, head of Greater and Lesser Arcana, is a member of the Sectarian Defense League."

Thank God I was sitting, because I felt like my legs had just been knocked out from under me. The very idea that Wesker—like Jane—worked with the people that I held responsible at least in part for Irene's death made my head spin.

"I knew it!" I said, punching the air.

"It's not like you think," Quimbley said, waving his hands at me. "It's terribly complex, Simon, and there's much that I'm simply not allowed to tell you. But what I *can* tell you is this: A lot of people who have come to work for us over the years have come to us from . . . shall we say, suspect backgrounds. Involvement with the dark arts, telemarketing, and worse. Need I remind you of your own life as a petty criminal before coming into the fold?"

My embarrassed silence was enough of an answer.

"I have been assured," he continued, "by the Enchancellors themselves that Thaddeus Wesker is a loyal agent of the D.E.A. He was chosen as the perfect covert operative to send in. Standard black ops work . . . feeding their intelligence officers misinformation so that we may continue our work here uncompromised. Despite all the running around everyone is doing over your discovery of the Sectarian Defense League, the Enchancellors have known about them for a while, but we're stepping up our investigation into them now that it's public."

It slowly began to come together. "So being an evil,

abrasive prick is just a cover for around the office? A front he has to maintain so that when he reports back to Faisal Bane, he's convincing?"

"Oh no," the Inspectre said. "He really is a 'prick,' as you call him. I personally don't trust him as far as I can throw him, and given my sad showing of physical fitness last night, it wouldn't be very far. But someone higher up seems to believe he's trustworthy, and that is good enough for me. And it will be good enough for you, too, Simon."

He picked up the folder before him again as I sat in awkward silence, wondering if I had been dismissed or not. I knew the Inspectre disliked Thaddeus Wesker almost as much as I did, which made it all the more difficult to swallow my own feelings for the sake of such a delicate mission. But I would.

"Am I in any trouble for yelling at Wesker?" I asked.

"No," the Inspectre laughed. "If everyone who ever thought ill of Wesker was in trouble for it, we wouldn't even have enough people to run the coffee shop out front, let alone the Department."

A wave of relief washed over me.

"Now go home and get some rest, my boy," he said. "You look positively exhausted. I want you to come back later in the day, though. I need you to figure out three things: One, find out where Ms. Blatt disappeared to. As long as she's out there missing, she's still a target for Bane and his cultists and we need to know why."

"Okay," I said.

"Two, I need you to find out what happened to Jane after Wesker cut her safety line." At the mention of her, I held my face like stone, hoping that I wasn't giving away the fact that I knew exactly where she was. "Like you said, she's relatively new to the Sectarian Defense League, so we may be able to sway her."

"Okay," I said.

"And three, I'm still waiting on that report on the Oracle."

"Oracle?" I asked.

"Gaynor," the Inspectre said. "The train mystic."

With all the craziness in my life right now, I had totally forgotten Gaynor. Connor and I would have to sit down sometime relatively soon and hammer out the details so far on Irene's case. But first, there was the riddle Gaynor had left us with.

I nodded to the Inspectre, and headed for the door as thoughts of Irene—and now Jane—filled my head. They would have to wait until later in the day. Right now, the call of sleep was already weaving its comfy tapestry around me and I had a date back home with a pillow that I didn't want to miss.

21

It was just after two in the afternoon when I woke, and despite my growing concern for Irene's whereabouts and my sequestered cultist hottie's safety, I had experienced an intensely restful and immediate slumber thanks to the power of sheer exhaustion. As a bonus, there had been only four new calls on my answering machine from Tamara telling me how worthless I was and I had slept through them all. I considered myself doubly blessed on that count.

Freshly rested, I walked back through the Village to the Lovecraft Café, slowly feeling the worry of the past few days snowball itself upon me as my mind began to focus on my caseload again. When I walked in, Mrs. Teasley was at the rear of the coffee shop divining the location of a lost dental crown for a young couple. Normally I would have listened for a quick laugh and gotten fuel for a whole day's outrage as to why that old charlatan was still on staff. With everything else on my mind, however, I proceeded straight through the coffee shop and back into the darkened theater. The projector was showing *2001*—HAL was explaining to

Dave why he couldn't open the pod bay doors. I worked my way down the aisle to the heavy wooden door leading into our office.

As I headed for my desk, my mood became even darker. Connor and I were making little progress with Irene's case. Her disappearance from my apartment last night made it even harder.

If Irene were just another case, I might be coping better or thinking straighter. But Irene had been more than that. I had enjoyed her presence in my apartment more and more. Then there was the strange kiss I had shared with Sectarian-in-exile Jane.

Jane.

I was worried about that sitch also. Maybe I'd gain some insight by reading the little black book of hers I'd found, but I hadn't dared look at it yet. I was pretty sure it was a diary. I was both afraid and unprepared to violate her private thoughts. Having spied on her was one thing, but oddly enough, reading her diary was a level I wasn't ready for yet. Everything about Jane threw me. The darkness in her was juxtaposed with a pleasant, earnest personality and what seemed like a desire to please others, and I couldn't help but admit that I found her damn attractive despite her alliances.

As I approached my desk, I spied Connor sitting across at his, flipping intently through some books.

"Hey," I said in greeting. I looked at my desk in disgust. It looked like a filing cabinet had thrown up all over it.

Connor smiled. "How ya feeling, kid?"

He didn't seem to mind me strolling in midafternoon so I assumed that the Inspectre must have talked to him.

"I'm better," I said, not wanting to get into all the dark details of the past twenty-four hours. "Long night."

"So I heard," Connor said, closing the book before him. "Don't worry. I won't make you recount the whole thing to me. I'm sure you've gone over the good, the bad, and the ugly of it with the Inspectre. Unless you want talk about it . . . ?"

I appreciated the buddy-buddy effort Connor was extending, but I hadn't told the Inspectre everything that had happened last night, and I wasn't going to share it with Connor either.

Acting all touchy-feely wasn't something Connor did too often. Usually, he'd give a lecture on objectivity or professionalism, about staying detached from my coworkers and our clients. He took a while to warm up to people. He didn't talk much about his previous partners in the Department, and he had given me enough of a cold shoulder on the subject that I was smart enough never to bring them up. But suddenly he was being a regular Chatty Cathy. I wondered what exactly the Inspectre had told Connor about last night.

"Thanks," I said, "but nah, I don't need to talk about it. I'd rather we got down to business."

"Fine by me," Connor said. He grabbed up another book and buried his nose in it. After a few minutes, he gestured for me to join him, so I scooted my chair around. He had been a busy little researcher during my slumber this morning, and his desk was cluttered with travel brochures for Las Vegas, printouts of topographic maps, gambling guides, and a plentiful array of playing cards. Anything that might give us a clue to make sense of what we had heard from Gaynor.

"Any progress?" I asked. "What was it Gaynor said on the train again?"

" 'Follow the Vegas trail and all will become clear,' " Connor repeated, trying to sound like the mystic, but failing completely. "As you can see, I ransacked the resource room to find out everything I could about Vegas. Even brought in several decks of playing cards my grandmother brought back from a trip there several years ago. I called down to Lesser Arcana, hoping for some help tarot-ing up the cards. All they could spare was a lousy intern and she wasn't very much use. She was able to tell me some secrets about where my grandmother hid our Christmas presents, but she didn't give me anything useful about Irene."

"Think the Department would spring for two plane tickets?" I asked hopefully. A little investigative work mixed with sun, spectacle, and the gaudy neon paradise of the Strip might be just what the doctor ordered to clear my head.

"Have you seen the revised budget the Mayor's Office sent to us?" Connor said. "Davidson dropped off the newest cuts this morning."

"Davidson was here?" I asked. "Today? You've got to be kidding. The man practically betrayed us at the Sectarian Defense League and now he has the unmitigated gall to show his face here?"

Connor shook his head. "Look, kid, I need you to keep an open mind . . . the verdict's still out on Davidson. He's been a good friend to the Department in the past. You weren't here last October, but he cleared up this huge fiasco when the Chrysler Building was overrun by a legion of undead from a pet cemetery down by the East River. Things That Go Bump in the Night Division had us all working overtime on the cleanup, but it was Davidson who took the heat for us back at Town Hall. He did his politiciany magic and plausibly denied the whole thing when the media came sniffing around. He's done well by us in the past."

I rose and wheeled my chair back over to my desk.

"But he's working with the Sectarians!" I shouted.

"Easy, kid, easy!" Connor said. "You're gonna blow a gasket. Look, don't be such a purist. Okay?"

"Meaning what exactly?"

"Meaning that *obviously* Davidson isn't a saint," Connor said. "You wanna know the first clue? He's a cog in the political machine! That means he's already tainted. Working as the Mayor's liaison means working both sides of the fence. He's probably seen things that would make a hard case like Wesker weak in the knees. Government work is a dirty game, Simon. If we want to stay in it, we gotta step up to the air-hockey table, you know?"

I nodded resolutely, acquiescing to Connor's take on the bigger picture. What looked black-and-white to my eyes looked different through his. I had trusted him these past months with my life, and I supposed I would have to trust him on this, too. For now, at any rate.

Connor picked up one of the Las Vegas guidebooks and thumbed through it. "Care to get back to business?"

"Any leads popping up with any of the guides?" I asked, settling in at my desk. I opened the left-hand drawer and readied a roll of Life Savers.

Connor shook his head. "Let me give it a try," I said.

I took off a glove, popped half a roll in my mouth, and then reached across the desk for a colorful-looking guide that sported a neon cowboy hitchhiking on its cover. *Weller's Guide to Losing Your Shirt in Las Vegas*, the cover read.

Focusing my will on the book, I felt the electric spark of divination kick in.

My mind flashed through a series of disconnected images that I had trouble focusing on—book binderies, typesetting machines, paper mills—all images to do with making the book itself but nothing else. As those images threw themselves at me, I let them fall away. Finally one forced itself forward and I had no other choice except to embrace it.

The vision put me in a mom-and-pop bookstore. Several fixtures of well-thumbed paperbacks sat askew in a metal spinner rack along one of the aisles. Suddenly a figure carrying a tall stack of books blocked my view. I pulled my focus to the details of the figure and he came into resolution. The face was that of a young man, awkward looking with a bad spot of acne across his forehead. He was absolutely unfamiliar to me.

What else was noticeable? There had to be something useful.

I soaked in everything around the teen. The details. The clerk's clothes, for instance. Parachute pants, skinny leather tie, and a FRANKIE SAYS RELAX button just above his nametag. The Weller book sat at the top of his pile and he slipped it off to shelve it. I double-checked his face, noticing the telltale mullet flaring out from behind his head, and I had all the information I needed to know I had hit a dead end.

I shook myself free from the vision. Connor had given up his book and was watching me instead.

"Anything?" he asked.

"Nothing linking to the case directly, no," I said, "but maybe indirectly. I think I might have found an error in our approach."

I felt the hypoglycemia kick in and helped myself to the other half of the Life Savers roll. I replaced my glove and picked my way gingerly through the rest of the pile of books, confirming my suspicions.

"All I got off the Weller book was some image from the mideighties of the book itself being shelved. Most of these books you pulled are seriously outdated. They're useless to us."

Connor flipped through several of them, checking their copyrights. "Hadn't really thought of that, kid. Nice catch. A lot of what we end up with in the Resource Room is through donation or leftover from church sales. Not a lot of first-run material. Again, those goddamn budgetary concerns."

"I don't think these books are going to help us," I said. "They only cover the old Strip of Vegas. There's the whole new Strip that's been building up over the past twenty years that isn't even mentioned in these books."

Connor stared at me. "And you know this how, New England boy?"

"Jesus. Don't any of you bookworms have cable? I saw it on the Discovery Channel," I said. "It was a special on building roller coasters. One of them runs right through one of the newer hotels in Vegas. New York, New York, I think."

Connor rolled his eyes and reached for his mouse. "I'll bring up a link to their tourist bureau."

The Internet was rarely our first line of investigation, owing to protocol. Between the speculative fiction, blogs, and porn, we simply didn't have the manpower to sift out legitimate sources from the bullshit ones. Plus a lot of the wisdom of the ancients that resided in the arcane tomes we used had yet to be scanned in. Digital investigation might be the tool of the future, but not until the funding kicked in.

Within a minute, we had an interactive map covering the modern Vegas Strip. Starting at the Stratosphere, Connor systematically passed the mouse over icons for each of the venues. A window full of stats popped up for each of the hotels, each with the intent of bringing fat-walleted tourists into their oasis in the desert. I started reading the names out loud as Connor scrolled.

"Stratosphere, Sahara, Slots-A-Fun, Stardust, Frontier, Treasure Island, The Venetian, Mirage, Royale, Harrahs, Paris, Aladdin, Excalibur . . . I never knew there were so many different places to lose money at."

I continued scrolling until the screen revealed one final

casino at the farthest end of the Strip, hiding just past the obsidian pyramid of the opalescent Luxor. One final hotel.

"Mandalay Bay," I read out loud.

"Mandalay?" Connor asked, slowly narrowing his eyes.

"Mandalay," I agreed. "You don't think—?"

Connor interrupted me, finishing my developing thought. "—that Gaynor's riddle about the wooden fish and 'following the Vegas trail' is about *Cyrus* Mandalay? How many Mandalays do *you* know?"

Possibly having solved the riddle felt satisfying, but the dawning realization that Cyrus might be involved in this whole stolen fish business gnawed at my stomach. If so, how? And had we given anything away when we'd walked right into his shop?

Connor was excited, though. "This is a great lead."

"You see?" I said encouragingly. "We don't have to invoke a power to do every little bit of investigation. *Perhaps when a man has special knowledge and special powers like my own, it rather encourages him to seek a complex explanation when a simpler one is at hand.*"

Connor looked impressed. "You come up with that on your own, kid?"

I shook my head. "Sherlock Holmes," I said. "Never read it, but one of the books I accidentally triggered off in my past belonged to some guy who really liked the line. It stuck."

"Oh," Connor said, rolling his eyes. "Well, speaking of books, I think it's time we head back to Tome, Sweet Tome and find out what Cyrus has to say for himself." The reality of what it would mean if Cyrus was really involved was clearly sinking in. Connor's face grew angrier by the second. Cyrus had been acting a little shady the last time we had been to the Black Stacks, but wasn't he someone Connor relied on, after all?

Sure . . . for a price. Now it seemed as if all signs were

pointing to his involvement in something far more sinister than simply overcharging his customers.

Connor stood up and headed toward the door without another word, full of purpose. I had never seen this type of silent anger building up inside him. He was going condition critical. As I stood to follow, he called out.

"Don't forget your bat."

22

Connor was silent the entire cab ride up to Tome, Sweet Tome, and I sensed the tension in him building. Hell, I felt it myself.

All because of Cyrus Mandalay.

Despite the tattoo down the entire left side of his face, his dreads, his sharklike teeth, and imposing figure, Cyrus had always portrayed himself as a good guy—an advocate of reading and responsible arcane usage—and we had believed him. He was *supposed* to be on our side. If Cyrus was somehow tied to Irene's death or had dealings with the Sectarians without telling us . . .

It sat like a bad taste in my mouth.

We stopped in front of the bookshop, and I spied Cyrus through the front window. I was surprised to see that rather than wandering casually into the store and then cornering Cyrus, Connor leapt from the cab and sprinted toward the door. Clearly Connor didn't like playing the fool, and Cyrus's deception had gotten to him more than I thought.

He had thrown caution to the wind. If I was suddenly the rational one, we were probably in trouble.

I saw Cyrus's eyes widen through the main window at the sight of a charging Connor, and he took off toward the back of the store. I quickly paid the driver, but by the time I was done, Connor had already flung the doors to Tome, Sweet Tome open and stomped in. I raced in after him, pulling my bat free from my belt as I ran.

A crowd of kids stood in the teen-friendly section across from the registers, but they were pointing toward the back of the store down an aisle where a stack of books had recently been knocked over. Unheard of at Tome, Sweet Tome.

Connor dodged some of the still falling books and sped down the same aisle at a full run. He hadn't even hesitated for a moment to look back and see what I was doing. That was either a sign that his trust in me was growing or that he was too angry to care. Probably a little of both.

"Cyrus!" he shouted as he ran through the Stacks. "Don't make me chase you! I really don't need this exercise, and when I catch you, I'm only going to be more pissed off!"

I paused by the confused-looking teens and smiled. "Stay here. Don't come any farther into the store." Another thunderous cascade of books rang out and several of the kids jumped. One of them looked like he was about to throw up. "On second thought, it might be safer if you just cleared out all together. Catch a movie or something. Go start a gang."

Slinging my bat over one shoulder, I started down the aisle, slowing occasionally to make my way past several of the literary avalanches. My progress slowed even further as I stopped to check out two stunned customers I came across that had been knocked over in the chase. The first was a dazed older woman who had been shoved face first into the Horticultural Necromancy section, but was otherwise all right. The second was a man clasping his wrist. I stopped for a quick glance at his injury, but possessing no medical knowledge whatsoever, I could only pat him compassionately on the shoulder and point him toward the front of the store.

"Good luck with that," I offered, and sped off.

"Simon!" Connor yelled out from somewhere nearby. "A little help here!"

As I rounded the corner of the next bookcase, I could see why. Cyrus stood just inside the gate of the Black Stacks with Connor's head *wedged* between the gateway and the iron bars of the gate itself.

Cyrus slammed the gate hard against Connor's throat and his face turned purple. Cyrus Mandalay would kill him in a matter of seconds if I didn't intervene, and fast.

I closed the distance with five bounding steps and swung the bat, aiming for Cyrus on the other side of the gate. I got lucky on the downswing and the bat passed effortlessly between the bars, catching Cyrus on his right shoulder. He stumbled back, and Connor pulled himself free of the bars.

With Connor's head no longer in the way, all three of us grabbed for the open gate, but Cyrus was quickest and snatched it closed. The clang echoed back into the Black Stacks.

"It's not what you think, gents," he said.

There was panic in his eyes, and it felt good to see it. I flicked the bat at his exposed knuckles where he held the gate closed and he flinched.

"I bet it's exactly what we think," I shouted.

I flicked the bat again, and this time it cracked fully against Cyrus's right hand, causing him to let his grip on the gate go entirely. He grabbed another section of it, but he looked scared.

Connor tried to pry the gate away from him, but to no avail. I slammed my bat against the iron bars, rattling them.

"Relax, kid," Connor said, grabbing my shoulder to stop my next swing. "We just chain this shut and wait until the D.E.A. shows up. I'm sure Cyrus here will be thrilled to have the Enchancellors upgrade him to a Class 3 Paranormal Fugitive!"

Cyrus laughed as he slowly backed away. "Do you really think I built the Stacks with only *one* means of exit?"

"Crap on toast!" Connor said as he reached through the gate toward Cyrus. He got a handful of Cyrus's shirt for his effort. Cyrus struggled, but Connor impressively held him fast. "Don't just stand there, kid. Get him!"

It was near impossible to open the gate as they struggled through the bars of it. They twisted and pulled at each other through the bars, each of them jockeying for an advantage. With neither man willing to relent, it was the cloth of Cyrus's shirt that ended up giving way first. There was a tearing sound and both men stumbled back from the gate, finally giving me an opportunity. I threw open the gate, nearly smacking Connor on the head in the process.

As I closed in on him, Cyrus stumbled farther back into the Stacks. He grinned, showing off his vicious-looking rows of teeth.

"Black Stacks . . . *attack!*" he shouted and turned, running down the next aisle, his dreads bouncing side to side.

Before I had a chance to take another step, the bookshelves erupted. They shook as books flew recklessly through the air across the aisles. I couldn't even inch forward, could only watch as Cyrus disappeared down the aisle. Connor finally entered the section and stopped next to me. We looked at the tornado of malevolent literature before us.

"We've got to keep after him," Connor said, rubbing his throat where the gate had pressed against it. It already resembled the world's largest hickey.

"How?" I shouted over the growing flutter of pages and

heavily thumping tomes. "We'll never make it through all this."

"We have to try," he said, and then grinned. "Besides, I got you a present."

Connor held up the torn edge of Cyrus's shirt and dangled it in front of my face.

"Let's see what you can do," he said. "Fetch, kid."

I shook my head. "I don't think so. I don't think I can divine anything off this."

Connor shoved the piece into my hand, then closed his own around mine.

I didn't get a chance to argue further. Before I could say that it was probably a useless exercise, Connor pulled his jacket protectively over his head, and dashed off down the aisle into the storm of books. Not one to leave my partner to face danger alone, I wrapped my hands tightly around the bat with the piece of cloth firmly in hand and batted my way after him.

Between the piles of scattered twitching books on the floor and the occasional ones targeting me as they leapt from the shelves, it was slow going. Several volumes gnawed at my ankles, biting like a pack of rabid Chihuahuas, but with only paper teeth, they were more a nuisance than any real threat.

I caught up to Connor, my arms already sore from swinging. He was standing at an intersection looking confused. He looked at me.

"Try," he said.

"I can't," I said. "Clothing is a hard thing for me to get a reading from."

"Don't give me that," he shouted, knocking away several flying books. "Remember when I hit you at the Antiques Annex? Tap into that raw emotion you felt, the kind that sparked your power. There's a science to this!"

He wasn't taking no for an answer so I threw my

concentration into the strip of cloth and prayed that a book didn't catch me in the temple while I attempted to pull a vision from it.

I thought of how Connor had hit me, the pain and shock of it causing my blood to rise. Then I thought of the events of the last few days—Irene's tearful eyes and her trashed apartment, Jane's fall through the air and her mangled arm. It could all be Cyrus's fault. Anger mixed in to the swirl of emotion and I felt the sudden spark of connection to the piece of shirt in my hand. My psychometry kicked in.

I wasn't sure how far back in time my mind's eye was taking me, but I could see Cyrus sometime back in his past carrying a bucket full of building supplies and tools through the Black Stacks. It was hard to tell what aisle he was walking in, but I hoped it would give me some clue as to where he was going now. I needed some kind of visual clue to orient myself. I caught a small sign along one of the rows of books.

M.

I snapped myself out of the vision. "Head toward the *M*'s!" I shouted and dashed off to the right. I plowed my way through fallen books, made two lefts, and then another right before I led Connor into the *M* section. Cyrus was nowhere to be seen, but the books were even wilder here, harder to push through. I stumbled blindly forward as I attempted to get another reading from the strip of cloth. It took considerably more effort this time to read the item, and when the image came, it was not as strong as the previous one had been.

"It's losing its charge," I said. I pushed Connor out of the way as a particularly nasty copy of *Crime & Severe Punishment* flew toward the bridge of his nose. Unfortunately, my selfless act meant that I caught the full force of the book's corner against my cheek, and immediately tasted blood. But I was still clutching the cloth, and before

I could control it, the pain flipped me back into my vision. I saw Cyrus with his tool bucket once again. I pushed back the pain and flipped back out. "Back to the *B*'s."

We must have been on the right track, because as we continued forward, the intensity with which books were throwing themselves at us increased dramatically. I fended off books with such ferocity that I had to make sure I wasn't in danger of cracking Connor's skull open. By now, the books were piled knee-deep and our pace grew slower, both from weariness and from plowing the books aside. When we reached the *B* section, however, there was no sign of Cyrus.

"Again," Connor said. He continued to dig away at the books around him.

I dropped my bat and gathered the piece of cloth in both hands. Concentrating like a kid taking the SATs, I felt weariness set in as I went for my third use of my powers. I hadn't eaten anything coming into this to boost my blood sugar, and adrenaline was the only thing keeping me going. There was a tiny tingle of connection, but it was so faint I could only make out a quick psychic flash—Cyrus adjusting the hinges on a hidden doorway built into one of the bookcases. Behind the *H*'s, maybe for *hidden*, I thought.

Abandoning the image, I came back to reality, popped a roll of Life Savers out, and quickly began downing them one by one as we pelted toward the *H*'s. I immediately started to feel less shaky. It still took five minutes to clear our way to the bookcase I had seen. My arms felt like they had been digging for hours.

We cleared out a space in front of the bookcase. Once there was room to move, I pulled it away from the wall. Behind it was a hallway that led down a short dark corridor and dead-ended at a door. I pulled out my lock picks, but Connor barged ahead of me and kicked it open instead.

"Sorry, kid," he said. "Time is of the essence."

I prepared to swing at any sign of Cyrus, but when the door fell open, the sight before us caused me to forget all pursuit. We had been prepared for a secret escape route. We were not prepared for a pile of bodies. My arms went weak and the bat fell from my hands.

Cyrus was nowhere to be found. My first impression was that Connor and I had entered some kind of mass tomb, except it struck me (morbidly so) that there was no stench of rot or decay. The dark room smelled only of the unwashed, some of whom stirred lethargically in response to the thin column of light pouring in behind us. At a quick count, there were close to twenty people lying on the ground—and they all looked like utter crap, but I was relieved that they all looked alive. There were men and women, some old and some young, but they all had one thing in common: their hair was completely white.

"What in God's name is going on in here?" Connor said softly.

I stooped over a girl in her midtwenties and moved her head from side to side gently, looking for bite marks. Despite the lack of vampires in a city like New York, I had no idea what else it could be. The girl seemed barely aware I was in the room. She looked quite gaunt, though physically unharmed. Connor bent over, scooped something up, and turned to face me. In his hand was a small clay pot, roughly the size of a tennis ball.

"Look familiar?" he said. "All those broken shards of pottery in the alley that night . . ."

"They looked strung out," I said.

Connor handed me the pot. It was empty, but whatever had been in it had left a sickeningly sweet smell, like overripe fruit. A drop of opaque residue clung to the container's lip. "What is it?" I handed the pot back to Connor, who slipped it into his coat pocket.

"It's a residue left by the plasmic energy generated

from the electrical impulses of a spirit when it's been confined to a tiny area for too long."

"Spirits are tangible?" In my dealings with Irene, I hadn't been able to touch her, but it made sense that there must be some level of corporeality. As Connor had pointed out, she could sit on a chair or walk across a floor without constantly drifting through it.

Connor nodded. "Some spirits more so than others. Depends on their after-death strength. Like your Irene, for example. There's not really an exact science to it, although I hear that Haunts-General is doing some fantastic phantasmagoric research in that area."

"If these jars are here and the residue is here," I said, "where the hell are the spirits?"

One of the bodies near my feet stirred, rolled over, and resettled on my shoes. I stepped back gingerly, careful not to disturb anyone in the process.

"That's what I'm getting at," Connor said. He looked sadder than I had ever seen him. "This is some serious stuff going on here, Simon. These spirits have been entirely destroyed by this group of junkies. They're Ghost-sniffers."

I stared blankly at Connor.

Connor simply looked at me and continued. "The Fraternal Order of Goodness basically put a stop to this type of activity over thirty years ago, kid. Certain cultists and spiritualists became addicted to the momentary high experienced when a spirit passes through a living person. When an uncontained spirit passes through someone, no harm really comes to either party, unless you count the hair damage. Thing is, the spirits that were in these jars have been purposefully packed tight into containment. These addicts have been mainlining concentrated plasmic energy straight into their systems."

"Sounds ghastly," I said.

"Ghastly?" Connor said. "Christ, that's an understatement. Just look at them! Even for Ghostsniffers, they look bad. Something's amplifying the effect on these people like some kind of supercrack. Normally they'd have streaks in their hair, like mine, but they've gone totally white. Whatever is juicing things up is shocking out the pigment entirely."

"Maybe the fish has something to do with this," I suggested. "I mean, we asked Gaynor to point us toward the fish and this is what we find."

"Maybe," Connor agreed, "but we still don't know the why of it all."

I looked down at all the people lying around us. These had to be some of the sickliest-looking people I had ever seen. Not only were their eyes sunk deep into their sockets, it seemed like their very souls were sunken as well.

"This is bad juju, Simon. It's a taboo practice even among the more hardcore cultists. It wouldn't be so bad if the spirits survived the process, but it absolutely destroys them when they've been forcibly concentrated like this. We've got to figure out who's been processing these spirits. Containing them, distributing them . . . it's not an easy task."

"You mean this isn't just Cyrus's doing?" I asked.

Connor shook his head.

"I don't think so," Connor said. "It's too large a project. Look around. This is just a flophouse. There's no equipment set up for this type of operation here. At the worst, it looks like he was running a Ghostsniffing lair, like one of those old opium dens."

"I'm still going to hold Cyrus accountable when we catch up to him," I said. "This is not cool. Not cool *at all*."

I wished I knew what to do to help these pathetic souls, but this wasn't my area of expertise at all. I pulled out my phone, but there was no signal. "Once we're outside, I'll call it in."

"We need to get these people help," Connor said. "Have them send a Shadower team to watch the store in case Cyrus comes back. Make sure they put someone on Cyrus's apartment, too."

I nodded.

"I'm sure Greater and Lesser Arcana would like to get their hands on some of these books," Connor continued. "They'll probably want to get one of their agents in here to run the store until the Enchancellors figure out exactly what to do with Tome, Sweet Tome."

I looked down at the pile of near lifeless users on the floor. They were our first priority. Catching Cyrus would have to wait.

23

As expected, the Inspectre was disturbed by our find at Tome, Sweet Tome, but both he and Director Wesker seemed quite pleased to add the Black Stacks to their list of departmental acquisitions. Representatives from every division showed up, especially a large contingent of archivists from the Gauntlet. I spied one of their rank-and-file members, Godfrey Candella, grinning from ear to ear, despite the abominations that had happened there. He and several other agents chased a few eager-to-escape books around, scooping them into fishing nets.

At that point, there wasn't much for me to do. Using my psychic ability over and over to track Cyrus had exhausted me, and I no longer felt of any use. I'd offered to try to use my power on one of the clay pots once it came back, but Connor's face had gone white. "I would not recommend that, kid," he said, stricken. "You might not come back." Since there was no update from Shadower on Cyrus's whereabouts and I had little expertise in dealing with a roomful of ecto-plasmic nose-candy junkies, I quietly dismissed myself from the store and let those better equipped to do so work the scene.

I made my way back to the Lovecraft, but stopped by my desk only long enough to grab Jane's journal. I didn't want to do this, but the stakes were getting higher and higher. Maybe the journal would give me some insight into the Sectarian involvement in all this. I walked out to the coffee shop after deciding to forgo the office environment entirely for the comfort of an enormous puffy chair. The steaming hiss of the espresso machine did little to relax me while I waited for a coffee. I stared at the unopened book. Its cover was gilded with astrological signs. Tension mounted thick across my shoulders.

Hadn't this exact sinister act, reading someone else's journal, been the very thing Tamara had accused me of? The guilt was consuming. Was I really going to learn enough about Jane from what she might have written to help the investigation? Was I in a state of mind to deal with what I read? And why was I reading it here? Was I hiding away from the office environment as well as avoiding my apartment now?

I knew why I brought Jane's notebook to the office, though. If Irene suddenly reappeared in my apartment, I feared how she would react to seeing me nose deep in another woman's personal thoughts in her newly unstable state. I told myself I was doing the heroic thing.

I took a tentative sip of my newly arrived drink, and opened the book. I flipped through it, starting at the back and watching the blank pages slip on by until I caught the first sign of words, and I sought out her entry from last night.

Dear Diary,
Subject: Simon Canderous—Surveillance

Next time, definitely no thong on a stakeout. Stakeouts require prolonged periods of squatting. Had Faisal not sent me out in such haste, I totally would have worn something more sensible . . . or at least something that didn't feel like it was trying to cut me in half lengthwise!

It is a lonely dance I do here among the secrecy of the rooftops.

Manhattan is simply breathtaking at night, the sparkle of a million lights flicking on and off across the cityscape like the fireflies back home.

Fireflies? Did I just compare Manhattan to fireflies??? Geesh. A bit of the smalltown girl coming through, I suppose. Up here, I can see the individual lives carrying on around me. Here are all the stories of the city, tucked snugly into skyscraper-shaped containers. Through one window I can see a man playing joyfully with a child who can't be any more than three years old. I can't make out if it is a boy or a girl, just that the child seemed to be giggling madly as the father bounces him or her up and down . . .

Incoming call vibrating away. BRB, Dear Diary!!

Faisal AGAIN! I'm a little tired of his grumpiness. I hope that I didn't come off sounding too eager to please. I've been working on my professional tone lately, aiming for what the Sectarians call "sinister amiability." Don't think I've got it down yet. Practice, practice, practice!

He sounded agitated, especially when I told him I just got here. What can I say? I got a little lost! Up here, everything looks the same without storefronts or street numbers. Thanks to resourceful me, Dear Diary, I used the lit-up spire of the Empire State Building as a guide to get back on track. Yay me!

I am now settled in across from Simon Canderous's place to write to you, my Dearest Diary.

The curtains are drawn but I can see in through the cracks here and there. It's two stories down and only allows for a partial view into Simon's apartment. I looked over the edge just now, and a slight bout of vertigo hit me. Ick! A sudden gust of wind and I could imagine myself going over. Bad news, Dear Diary!

OMG! From what little I can see, Simon's place is absolutely GORGEOUS. It looks totally swank and fabulous in an old-world way. It sure beats my tiny Chelsea place. Does the Department of Extraordinary Affairs pay their underlings well enough to live like this? Maybe I need to trade up!

Diary, what am I to make of this Simon fellow? He was a defensive meanie the other night over the departmental dinner we had.

I know I mustn't rush to judgment on assessing him or this situation, even though Faisal and the Sectarians have convinced me how dangerous these D.E.A. members are. But how can someone that cute be dangerous? I can make up my own mind. I'm a City Girl now. Girl Power!

I hope first impressions don't mean anything. When we first met, I think I came off as a bitch, but he was the one brandishing a bat at me! Back to work . . . BRB, Dear Diary!

I checked the safety on my gun just now and released it. Push aside the feelings, Janey. Don't think. That's not what the Sectarians pay you for. Just obedience.

I sure hope I don't have to shoot anyone. I'd feel bad about that. Just like I feel bad about you—my truest of friends—that I'm already going to have to edit you down for Faisal's report. Sorry!

Dear Diary, damn this thong! Something this invasive usually buys me a drink first!

Be right back . . .

I closed the book. I knew what happened next, of course. Director Wesker would answer for cutting her lifeline.

This was not the journal of someone committed to evil and the dark arts. A wave of optimism washed over me. This was the journal of a small-town girl transported to the Big City, a girl who seemed to be crushing on me. She could be turned to our side, a hot, perky version of Darth Vader.

I felt more ashamed than ever for having read the diary, but at least I hadn't taken off my gloves and "read" it. I suddenly realized that I wouldn't have been able to bring myself to do that—and that *meant* something. Maybe I didn't want to know Jane on a psychometric level because . . . she was someone I was actually interested in, and I didn't want to fuck things up preemptively.

I didn't recall my walk home from the Lovecraft Café that night. I was far too wrapped up in what I had read to think of much else. But why was that old nervous feeling at the pit of my stomach working its way to the top again?

24

When I got home, there was no sign of Irene. It seemed odd not to have her there, but I couldn't imagine where to look. Connor hadn't given me any ideas either. I hit the White Room to center myself and it seemed to do the trick. I thought about calling Jane at her hotel to see how she was doing, but decided against it. I could be under surveillance if Jason Charles was really out to get me. Just after midnight I had decided that my only possible course of action was sleep when my cell went off. It was Connor.

"You awake?"

"Does it really matter?" I muttered sleepily.

"Good point," Connor conceded. "Can you get out to Williamsburg?"

"Now?" The other night, when Connor called me to help him with that feral spirit in the alley, I had been looking for a distraction, but tonight I was exhausted.

"Trust me, kid, you'll wanna be here. I've tracked Cyrus down."

I sat up and started dressing immediately, sliding on jeans and a tee. "What? How?"

"Well, interrogating those junkies was no use. They're all still totally out of it. But you know how there have been more and more of those disoriented spirits showing up? I did a few therapy sessions with some of them. One of them knew of Cyrus, even had an address where he said Cyrus hangs out a lot. Make sure you bring your bat. He's got a lot to account for. Plus, it's payback for making us look like assholes in the paranormal community."

Connor gave me the address and I took a car service over the Williamsburg Bridge to River Street and North Sixth. River Street, aptly named for its location by the East River, had a spectacular nighttime view of the New York skyline. I stood marveling at it when I stepped out of the car until Connor *psst*ed at me from the shadows nearby. I walked across the deserted stretch of Sixth and joined him. He pressed a finger to his lips and pointed to an old wooden industrial warehouse at the water's edge.

"You think maybe we should have brought a task force or something?" I whispered.

Connor shook his head. "The Department already blew their budget using emergency funds just to get all those people out of Cyrus's bookstore and take it over. Besides, I think the two of us can easily exact a little vengeance on a book nerd, even an occult one. Hope you brought your lock picks."

I nodded. We crossed the street in silence, headed for the building. When we got to the door, there were three locks to work my way through. My biggest concern was busting one of the thin metal slides I was using, but after ten minutes I had successfully opened all the locks. Connor gave me a silent golf clap and I felt a swell of pride. It was disgraceful how much I craved his approval at times.

"The place has been dark for hours," Connor whispered, "so either Cyrus goes to bed superearly or else he's not here."

After I gave my eyes a moment to adjust to the low light pouring in from the city skyline, Connor and I headed up a flight of stairs set straight across from the front door. The upper floor opened up to a large loft space with floor-to-ceiling windows and the same spectacular view. The room itself was a mishmash of boxes, crates, and stands, all with one common theme—there were fish everywhere.

"One fish, two fish, evil fish, good fish," I said with a low whistle. Every square inch of space was occupied by fish statues or artwork relating to fish. Most of them had been carelessly thrown around, but some of the pieces were hung on the wall with care. It looked like Cyrus was either a collector or else he had been searching in vain for a while for a very specific fish . . . the one from Irene's apartment, I would bet.

I would never have guessed that there were so many potential forms of fish art out there. The most striking piece was a large silvery metallic fish that hung on display as a clear centerpiece for the room. "Ooh, shiny," I said and headed for it. I pulled off one of my gloves to read it. Clearly something that ornate had a story to tell.

"Simon, don't," Connor said, when he spied where I was heading, but it was too late. I attempted to trigger my power, but instead felt a swell of magical energy building from the fish and knocking me back. Instantly the shiny fish started glowing and arcane runes I didn't recognize traced themselves out in fiery lines along its body, and then out along the warehouse's floor and walls. Glowing lines began to crawl across the wall from one mounted fish to the next, until the flame patterns actually ignited the wood of the old warehouse. A building as old as this was built to burn, and already the heat was intense.

"Everything in here's been warded," Connor said, looking around. "It's a trap."

"Gah!" I shouted, disappointed in myself. "Can't believe I fell for the old shiny object ploy. We deserve to be incinerated."

"Speak for yourself, kid," Connor said and ran back toward the stairs. As he tried to head down them, he slammed into an invisible barrier at the top of the stairs and bounced back. "It's impassable. I bet this place is riddled with magic meant to mess with us."

Smoke rapidly filled the room and I breathed in a big lungful of it. I looked to see if Connor was okay, but . . . inexplicably . . . he had turned into a zombie—skin gray, flesh hanging in messy strips from his face, dead sunken eye sockets, and a slack jaw that seemed to be hanging on his face by a thread. His clothes were in ruins also, his Bogey trench torn, tattered, and covered in blood.

"Meant to mess with us," I repeated. I was sincerely hoping that Connor's sudden transformation was simply a glamour caused by the nefarious, hallucinogenic smoke. *Oh God, unless he'd been bitten the other night during the zombie extermination.* "You don't say?"

Zombie Connor tilted his head at me, his slack jaw falling off onto the floor. "You okay, kid?" it said, slowly shambling toward me. "Did you breathe in some of that smoke? You know you gotta avoid that stuff. Breathe through your shirt."

I nodded, but pulled my retractable bat out just in case. If I had stopped, dropped, and rolled in the first place, maybe I wouldn't be wondering if I might have to take a bat to my mentor. But he was a zombie now. I choked the bat up like I was in the World Series.

"You having any strange cravings?" I asked, backing away.

"What?!" the zombie said, shuffling closer. "Like chocolate?"

"Or brains," I suggested. "Or chocolate-covered brains . . . whatever."

Zombie Connor looked at the bat nervously. "Why don't you put that down?"

It was hard to see through the smoke, and I stumbled back as I tried to think of a plan. Nothing came to mind other than beating Zombie Connor down, but I was reluctant to do that. I stopped when I backed into the wall of windows. I glanced over my shoulder in an effort to find one of the handles, but when my hand found one, the handle bit me. Luckily it was my one gloved hand, but it still hurt. I screamed in pain and Zombie Connor rushed me.

"Give me the bat," the rotting corpse said, and started prying it from me.

"No!" I shouted. "I'm too young to have my brains eaten!"

"Just give me the bat!"

I held on as tight as I could, but it was no use. Connor's two hands were stronger than my single one that held the bat. He was strong for a zombie. He tore it away from me and raised it over his head to strike me. Of all the ways I had imagined my death, getting beaten by my zombified mentor while trapped by a cannibalistic window handle wasn't one of them.

Zombie Connor's blow never came. He swung the bat down in a fluid arc, but he went wide and smashed through a section of the window. The tiny metal fangs I felt biting into my glove let go, and I pulled my hand away, nursing it while the zombie went to town on the rest of the window. When the one section of the frame was clear of glass, he tossed me my bat, his hand still attached to it as it flew through the air at me.

Zombie Connor looked out the window, then back at me before his eyes melted away.

"Hope you can swim, kid," he said. He ran for the gaping

hole in the window and leapt out. Seconds later, I heard a splash. I could burn to death up here or I could take my chances leaping into zombie-infested waters. I opted for the water when the sleeve of my coat started to smolder. I took one last look at the warehouse full of burning fish and leapt out the window, hoping I could at least use the rotting zombie as a flotation device.

25

Once I hit the water, whatever glamour was being caused by the traps in Cyrus's warehouse flew away. Connor was already swimming for the shore and I was relieved to see that his flesh wasn't rotting and his hand was still attached. I could only imagine the amount of paperwork I would have had to fill out if I'd clubbed my partner to death.

Not finding Cyrus here meant that he was still at large, which made me increasingly nervous—especially for Jane. He and whoever he was working with had trapped me so easily. I realized that I really needed to step up my game of Jane and Go Seek before he or the Sectarians found her.

The next morning, Connor and I had the Inspectre send Greater & Lesser Arcana to check out the remains of the warehouse while the two of us filled out mountains of forms regarding the incident. When the investigators returned, the best they had come up with were a few burned pieces that might have been vaguely fish shaped, but could just as easily have been vaguely blob shaped, too. With no leads on that front, I snuck out of the office and headed out to deal with Jane.

I made sure I wasn't followed to the Upper East Side. When Jane opened the door to her hotel room, I was glad to see she had used the chain across the door as a precautionary measure. It meant she was starting to be cautious, rather than being the slightly naïve girl I had dined with at Davidson's insistence. When Jane saw it was me, she looked relieved and let me in.

"Why do you smell like smoke?"

"Long story," I said. "Let's just get you moved again. I'll tell you on the way."

We quickly packed her things and rode silently in a cab to a new hotel, far west in Chelsea, finally giving me the opportunity to slip her journal into the bottom of one of her bags as I helped her unpack. The relief of giving up that guilty burden was tangible, and despite my near death last night, and the danger of Jane's current situation, I found that helping her was actually a small oasis of fun. Once we were done unpacking, I sat down and told her about my brush with death at the hands of Cyrus's fire trap.

"My God," she said with genuine concern. The look on her face was far more sincere that I'd expected from a recently exiled cultist. "Are you okay?"

I nodded, then remembered all the fish art that had been on display at the warehouse, not to mention the stolen fish from Irene's that we had chased all the way back to Jane's old employers.

"Do you recall anything from your time with the Sectarians about a fish?" I asked, hoping for something useful.

Jane thought it over a moment and then shook her head. "For a while, we had a lot of fish coming in. I remember the one you were after, but I'm afraid they kept me in the dark as to what they do. I only received and processed the shipments. Sorry."

I was disappointed, and she saw it on my face.

"We kept pretty accurate records, though," she added encouragingly. "You'd be surprised what OCD sticklers Sectarians can be about keeping track of things. They're like the Felix Ungers of the cultist world."

Maybe there was something useful in that, and I wrinkled my brow while I thought about it.

After I had been silent for several minutes, Jane spoke up again. "You okay?"

I snapped out of my thoughts, none the wiser about what to do. Jane's concern for me was touching, but it was me who should have been concerned about her.

"How's your recovery coming?" I asked.

Jane struck a superheroic pose, hands on hips. "Nothing short of miraculous, thanks to that bag of mystical healing thingies you left with me. I'm running out, though."

I doubted I could easily get access to another emergency kit in a hurry. I still hadn't told anyone in the Department that I was secretly nursing Jane back to health.

When I said nothing, she said, "Don't get me wrong. I'm not asking for anything more. You've done more than enough already . . . it's just that I'm kinda dwindling my savings here . . ."

I still wasn't sure how to help Jane other than hiding her, but maybe if I got her out and about, we'd hatch some kind of plan.

"Let's get you out of here," I said, "go for a little walk, see how well you're healed up. I've got a couple of errands to run anyway."

Jane looked a little frightened by the prospect. She hadn't really stepped foot from the hotels I had been moving her to. "You sure it's okay?"

I nodded. I doubted anyone from the Department would run into us, and none of the Sectarians would probably do anything during daylight hours if they saw us either.

Plus, I had made sure that no one had followed us down-town.

"C'mon," I said. "It'll be fun. We can try to one-up each other over who's been more damaged lately—you for falling off of the roof or me from smoke inhalation."

The metallic blue-checkered framework of Manhattan Super-Storage took up the entire northeast corner of Twenty-Third Street and Tenth Avenue. The sun shone off the boxy building, casting streaks of light from its many windows down onto the sizable crowd gathered out front. I led Jane into the throng as she looked around warily but with a growing good humor in her eyes.

"What is all this?" she asked.

Storage places were never this busy normally, but this was no normal day. The sidewalk was awash with an al-most street-fair-like atmosphere—full of food carts, per-formers, and people pressed together tight like books on a shelf. The scent of grilled meat and roasted corn rose off the food vendors and filled the air with mouthwatering goodness, but I pushed aside all thoughts of getting a bite. Eating could wait.

"These things keep getting trendier and trendier." I sighed.

A small table was set up by the entrance to three of the loading bays, and I walked over, found my name, and signed in. The bays themselves had been closed off and turned into a common feeder line that wove around a variety of tables. Each was covered in plentiful piles of other people's belong-ings. The rest of the crowd, those who hadn't signed up in ad-vance, lurked near the line in the hopes of getting a chance to browse as well.

"Lot of people don't ever come to claim their storage items once they default on payment," I explained. "The crap that accumulates is auctioned off to make room for actual *paying* customers. Ever since *Time Out* wrote it up as a kitsch thing to do, it's like the Ringling Brothers took over. All these assholes come here hoping to avoid Ikea, but to me, anything I luck into here just goes into supporting my apartment. Hey, maybe I can score you something to help you out with your money sitch until things smooth over."

"Maybe I should just head back to Kansas," Jane said, sounding defeated.

"Are you really ready to throw in the towel on the Big Apple already?" I asked, even though, if you'd asked me a couple days ago, I would have said that the city could definitely use one less Sectarian. Like many people who were transported New Yorkers, I felt Jane had something to prove to herself here, and was reluctant to leave. She would probably be safer if she left town, but that stubborn part of her that I could totally identify with was still holding out.

I checked my watch and realized we had a little time to kill. My stomach growled and I led Jane off in the direction of the food vendors. I was hungry enough to eat whatever rat on a stick or cockroach knish they might be selling.

My God, I realized. *This feels more and more like a date, doesn't it?* I found that despite Jane's previous alignment with the forces of Darkness, the idea didn't scare me as much as I thought it might. Maybe if I approached this like it was a date, Jane might be more likely to give herself over to the forces of Good. In a moment of spontaneity, I approached a guy standing nearby making balloon animals. The twist of green and red he was working on looked vaguely like a wiener dog, and he handed it to a kid with a big grin on his face, who then ran off in the direction of his mother.

"Hey, pal," I said, fishing out my wallet. "I'll take one of those. Can you make a flower or something like that?"

The balloon guy was shorter than me, chunky, and wore a fanny pack to store his balloons in. He looked at me and shook his head—his black, shoulder-length mullet swaying back and forth like seaweed in the ocean. "Sorry, pal. I wouldn't want to send any of the little kids home sad or crying because I ran out of balloons giving something away to an adult."

I looked around the crowd. There were only a handful of children scattered here and there, most of them already with balloons. "It's for the lady," I said insistently. I gave him my most sincere c'mon-be-a-pal-don't-fuck-this-up-for-me smile.

He shook his head again and I could feel myself going a little Hulkish around the edges.

"C'mon," I said, lowering my voice. "Not even for the young at heart?"

This time he simply rolled his eyes and began to turn away, but I wouldn't be deterred. I couldn't control myself. I grabbed him by the shoulder and spun him around.

"Dude," I shouted. "You're a guy whose only freaking job seems to be—and correct me if I'm wrong here—blowing and twisting. It's not that hard. I think you can take two minutes out of your busy schedule here to whip one up for us big kids who are more likely to tip your sorry ass for the trouble than little Billy or Suzy here. Let's not be a Balloon Nazi about this, okay?"

Jane beamed like a kid on Christmas Day as she attempted to keep hold of the barely manageable variety of balloon-made items in her hands. Streaming along with her were a flower, a wiener dog, a pirate sword, a musketeer hat with a balloon plume, a poodle, a sleeping cat, an airplane, a goldfish, and something the balloon maker had feverishly assured us was a flying mouse.

"Oh my God," Jane said. The wiener dog suddenly made a spirited break for it, but I grabbed it by its snout and handed it back to her. "You are the man! You are totally a rock star in the world of balloon animal negotiations! I bow to your superior scare tactics!"

"It's my gift," I said with a flourish of my arm and a deep bow. She laughed and hugged her balloons. One of them exploded with a loud pop and she screamed. It was a moment of fright that should have passed quickly, but suddenly tears were running down her face. I moved to put my arm on her shoulder.

"Hey," I said, "Jane . . . what's wrong? What is it?"

People had turned to stare now, including several children, but I figured that was probably just balloon envy. I moved us away from the crowd toward the edge of the street and next to a cotton candy machine.

"God," she said. I could hear the self-loathing in her voice. "I *hate* when I get all small-town spooked."

"Don't worry about it. Just try to relax."

"*You* try to relax!" she snapped. The tears were still coming, but suddenly she was getting angry. "A couple of days ago my life was going fine. Now I'm essentially unemployed, I've lost my dental plan, and I flinch at every loud sound because I think it's a corporate headhunter trying to put a bullet in my brain!"

I was getting upset as well. I wasn't really a fan of getting yelled at, and especially not when I was just trying to help.

"Look," I said after counting to ten to calm myself, "I can't imagine how much this sucks for you, Jane, so I'm not even going to pretend. We'll figure something out, I swear. I just need time to investigate things the proper way. I hate every moment that you're at risk. In the meantime, though, I need you to let me do what I came here for. That doesn't mean I'm going to neglect you. I'm going to do everything I can to help keep you safe."

I looked her in the eyes, and she nodded.

"Not that you need to be kept safe," I added awkwardly. "I mean, I'm sure you can take care of yourself, but, well . . . I'm in the Good business, so keeping people safe is part of what I do. It's not a chauvinist thing, I swear."

I felt like a social retard, so I shut up.

Jane softened and said, "I'm sorry. I'm one of the bad guys. I know you're doing your best. You've already gone above and beyond with all this."

"Gee, thanks," I said. *Gee, thanks?!?* Did I actually say that? Why couldn't I just shut up and take a compliment?

"You're welcome," she said, wiping away the tears. "Besides, you probably thought I was all kinds of crazy reacting so emotionally."

"No, it's fine," I lied.

"It's not fine," she said gravely. "I haven't been totally up-front with you. You don't know the whole story. But I like you and I think you have a right to know."

"Know what?" I asked.

Jane took a deep breath, exhaled the last of her hysterics, and looked me in the eye. "Their headhunter—Jason Charles, the one I spoke to on the phone the day I was injured—may be a bit more aggressive about finding me than I might have led you to believe."

"And why's that?" I asked warily.

"We sorta dated," she said, her voice trailing off. Her nose crinkled as she braced herself for my response.

"Sorta?!" I asked. I could feel myself turning fifty shades of horrified. I had just started thinking I might be turning the corner with Jane, making some progress with her, but how could I begin to trust someone who *dated* a professional assassin? "Sorta dated? Or *did* date?"

She was fighting to explain it—I could see it in her face—but that didn't change the feeling of frustration building up inside me.

"I went out with him three times, but that was months ago!" she said as if somehow that excused it. "He seemed nice enough. Well-groomed, business suits every day . . . but once I realized the type of mentally unstable individual it took to be a hired gun in that creepy little business world of theirs, I broke it off."

"So how did he take it?"

I wanted to grab her and shake her for her own good. She was a nice girl, but it was becoming increasingly likely that she was going to get both of us killed.

"Well," she said, "since I worked for the big boss, there was nothing Jason could do to me. So rather than giving me any trouble, he just became inordinately professional in the office and we stopped talking."

I sighed and rubbed my eyes. "But now you're fair game. In fact, you're a target requested by paying customers. Great. Any other little gems I should know about?"

Jane shook her head, but couldn't raise her eyes to meet mine.

I looked over at the tables full of storage unit leftovers. It was pointless being here. I wasn't going to be able to concentrate on reading anything. "I have to go," I said.

Jane looked up. "Where?"

"I don't know," I said. "Just away for now."

"But why?"

"Because I need to think," I snapped suddenly. "I keep forgetting you're tied into hardcore evil, Jane. It's beyond me how you could have dated someone who kills people for a living. Connor would freak out if he knew I was helping you, and I just need to sort things out for myself."

I couldn't think of anything more to say so I turned away. Was I just upset about her withholding information about the Sectarians, or was I experiencing some kind of odd jealous reaction? I didn't know.

I walked off feeling angry and confused, but I restrained myself from running back and childishly popping every last balloon Jane was carrying.

26

On the way back to my apartment, I started to cool down. Looking back, I knew that Jane wasn't the only one who had ever made the wrong choices in life. I knew Jane had been displaced from her apartment, *her life*. Sure, she'd held a little information back, but she'd come clean and it was no reason for me to have gone off on her. I planned on calling her once I got back home, but all that flew out the door when I stepped off the elevator and headed down the hallway to my apartment.

The lock on my door was busted.

I reached inside my coat, pulled the retractable bat out, and pressed the button. It extended to its full length, and I held it at the ready as I eased my front door open with my foot. My living room was trashed. It had been messy before with all the crates in it, but now everything had been displaced and everything that had been on my shelves had been thrown to the ground. A lot of it looked broken. It was like being in Irene's apartment all over again and my heart sank.

Knowing my apartment as well as I did, I crept soundlessly across the floor toward the hall, hoping I could sneak up on anyone who might still be here. My plan for silence fell apart when I noticed the door to the White Room was also smashed in.

"No no no no no," I said as I rushed to it. Everything in the room was overturned or broken, which meant the worst had happened—my inner sanctum had been contaminated by someone else's memories, corrupting the one place in the world I could turn to as my safety zone. My heart raced and my head swam. I used the bat as a walking stick to steady myself rather than touch anything in the room for balance.

I had never felt so violated, but then I realized that I could find out exactly who had done this. All I had to do was touch anything in the room, use my psychometry, and I would know. I stepped slowly toward the chair on its side in the center of the room and moved my hand to grab it.

"Simon," a woman said, stopping me. I looked around the room, but there was no one there.

"Irene?" I asked hesitantly.

The plain white of the wall right in front of me crackled with a blue flash of electricity and Irene phased out of it. She was dressed the same as always—the curse of the dead—but her face was a mask of worry.

"Are you all right?" I said. "Where have you been? What the hell happened here?"

Irene flickered. "I don't know where I've been! Some force keeps pulling me away from here. All I remember was those men from your office coming in here and being upset . . . the kindly older one and the creepy one. Then there was nothing except flashes of that wooden fish you talked about, and a hazy mist, like the one your friend used on me that first time we met in the café. It's all so unclear."

"Nothing else?" I asked. She shook her head and started to flicker again. "Stay with me, Irene . . . calm down or you'll disappear again. I just have to do something. I'll be gone, well, mentally gone, for a minute or so. I have to know who did this." I reached toward one of the shards of the Tiffany Lamp.

"You don't have to do that!" she shouted, her humanity stretched to its limit with that cartoonish exaggeration I had seen her exhibit before. In a flash, she was back to herself, but the burst seemed to take a lot out of her and she started to fade. "I know who it was," she said. "I heard him say his name. He was on the phone . . ."

"Who?" I said.

Irene's voice faded as her body did, but I heard part of what she said before she blinked out completely.

"Jason . . ." she whispered, and was gone.

Charles, my mind completed. Faisal Bane's corporate headhunter. It made sense. He must have come here looking for Jane when he couldn't find her anywhere else. Bane must have set him on the trail to my apartment, the one Jane herself had originally been following. And now it was trashed.

The phone rang in the living room and I worked my way toward it through the mess. I couldn't find it in the chaos of the room. Why wasn't the machine picking up?

I found the phone cord sticking out of a stack of books and traced along to the phone, dug it out, and answered it.

"Canderous," I said.

There was laughter on the other end. "I was wondering when you might pick up," Jason Charles said. "I've been trying all day."

"What the hell have you done?" I asked.

"You don't like the way I redecorated?"

"Fuck you," I said.

"Just tell me where Jane is, and I'll leave you alone."

"I have no idea," I said.

"Fine, don't cooperate," he said. "I'll find her on my own."

"Good luck with that," I said. "Good-bye."

As I went to hang up, Faisal's corporate headhunter shouted into the phone. "Wait. One more thing . . ."

"What?" I said. "I really need to be assessing the damage to my property. I'll be billing the Sectarians."

"I sent you a little present at work," he said. "I suggest you check it out."

The line fell dead.

What the hell was he up to? As I returned the phone to its cradle, it hit me. The reason the answering machine hadn't picked up was because it was no longer connected to the phone. I dug around where I had found the phone in the first place, but the machine wasn't there. After several more minutes of searching, I found the answering machine sitting neatly on the kitchen counter. Jason Charles had definitely been listening to it, checking my old messages. I plugged it back in and flipped back through several of the calls. If he had checked the caller ID on any of the last fifty or so messages, there was going to be trouble. They were all from Tamara's number.

I threw down the phone and ran for the door, heading for the Department of Extraordinary Affairs, but not before dialing Tamara's number for the first time since our breakup.

By the time I reached the Lovecraft Café, I still hadn't been able to get Tamara on the phone. I raced through the coffee shop, down the aisle of the theater, and back into the offices. Connor was at his desk, making a tiny dent in his paperwork. He stood as he saw me running toward him.

"Kid, what's wrong?" he said.

"Did we get any packages from a messenger?" I asked, breathless. I started picking my way through my in-box.

"Yeah," he said. "One came earlier. Why?"

"I just got a call from Faisal's corporate headhunter," I

said, throwing aside two boxes on which I recognized the return addresses. "He said there's something here."

"Faisal's *what*?" Connor said. I forgot I hadn't mentioned any part of this to him.

"I'll explain later," I said, still frantically searching.

"Try that one," Connor said, pointing toward a box about the size of a watch case. I grabbed it and pulled it free, knocking over the rest of the pile.

There was no return address on the box and I cautiously slit open the tape across the top of it with a letter opener. I used the tip of the opener to flip open the sides of the box and looked inside. A letter was folded neatly across the top of whatever was in the box and I pulled it out to read it.

To Whom It May Concern,

In lieu of delivery of the Sectarian Jane Clayton-Forrester, please accept this token as to the seriousness of my intent to reclaim her as part of my contract. She will be downsized whether you like it or not.

Sincerely,
The Management

I looked down into the box and my face went white.

"What's in it, kid?" Connor said.

"It's a clay pot," I said. "Like the ones we found in the back of Cyrus's shop. It's got Tamara's name on it."

There was a prolonged moment of silence as we stood there.

"You okay, kid?" Connor said finally.

"He killed her," I said, stunned. "*They* killed her."

"Yeah," Connor said, trying to comfort me. "Well, they wouldn't be evil if they did nice things, would they?"

27

Connor said he'd have Haunts-General and Greater & Lesser Arcana see if they could do anything to free Tamara's spirit from the tiny clay pot, but I didn't think anything would come of it. No spirit had ever been successfully recovered from a Ghostsniffing operation. The Inspectre even went so far as to dispatch a Shadower team to check out Tamara's apartment, but as I feared, there was no trace of her. The Inspectre let me leave early to regroup, as well as look through my trashed apartment for any clues. I was useless at the office and racked with guilt that my cowardly avoidance therapy with Tamara had gotten an innocent woman killed. I returned home, hoping that at least Irene had reappeared, but she was still missing. I busied myself as best I could changing the locks and cleaning the living room—gloves on, of course. Actually experiencing my apartment's destruction would be even more painful than throwing out the fragments of some of my most beloved possessions. Around midnight, I had only managed to deal with half the clutter but I was tired to my soul and barely stumbled to my bed before passing out.

Sleep, however, didn't last long, as the sounds of a woman shrieking at the top of her lungs filled the room.

"WHO IS SHE, SIMON?" I heard Irene yelling.

Not the way I would choose to be woken up. I was more of a nuzzling sort as far as rousing goes, but as I rose to consciousness, I was met with the sight of Irene silhouetted by the moonlight in the center of my bedroom. It was more eerie a reappearance than I had hoped for.

"Irene?" The sleep was thick in my voice. "Irene, what's wrong? You disappeared again. Do you remember what was pulling you away from here?"

"Who is she, Simon?" Irene hissed. There was rage in her words, pure and full of venom. Was this the degradation of the spirit Connor had been talking about? This reaction was so out of place, so over the top, that I almost laughed.

"I know there's another woman. Who is she?" Irene's anger caused her to phase in and out and I could see through her to the far wall.

"Calm down. What are you talking about?"

"On your answering machine," she said. "JUST NOW. Who is she?"

The alarm showed that it was just shy of 3 a.m. I hadn't heard the phone ring, not even once. But if someone had called, it was either a wrong number . . . or else Jane calling from wherever she was staying. It certainly wasn't Tamara anymore. I jumped out of bed and made my way to the answering machine. One message. I pressed play. It was Jane, all right, and from her tone I could tell she had been drinking. I had totally forgotten to call her back and make up with her after I'd left her in such a huff earlier today.

"I keep going over it again and again in my head, Simon,"

she said. "So that was it back at the storage place? You just leave me with an armful of balloon animals to fend for myself? I thought you were helping to protect me! You're not a real man. A real man would have stayed. A real man would have had the guts . . ."

I didn't need to hear the rest of it and hit the erase button. The words hurt, even though I discounted them given the drunken slur of her voice. I turned to Irene. "That's just this girl . . . she's part of this project for work."

"WHO IS SHE?" Irene screeched, causing me to step back. Her reactions were pure over-the-top emotion, with none of the checks or balances that humanity normally provides. She wasn't making sense. It was true that I had found a lot to like in Irene from our talks. I had even found myself attracted to her, but . . . she was a ghost. Where could that possibly go for either of us? True, my mixed feelings about both her and Jane were strong enough that I'd been keeping information from Irene. And there was guilt stemming from my attraction to both of them, but even so, this reaction to one tiny answering machine message was way out of proportion. There was no reason for her to behave this way.

"I told you she's a work thing," I said. "Not that it should matter. What's the problem?"

"You have got to be kidding!" Irene said. "You expect me to believe that?"

I was starting to lose patience. "I fail to see how that's any of your concern."

Irene's eyes flared with anger and a cold mysterious force wrapped around me. It lifted me up and flung me across the room. These old buildings were built with endurance in mind and my impact with the solid plaster knocked the wind right out of me. People talk about seeing stars when they suffer trauma to the head. I saw constellations, maybe even a few planets.

My knees buckled when I tried to stand. Dizziness had me and I teetered back against the wall, using what remaining strength and determination I had to keep standing. Irene's anger was manifesting itself as an unseen physical force, and for the first time, I felt scared.

Still, the fear wasn't enough to stop me from getting angry myself. Everything was getting to me. I was sick of it. Tamara was dead. Jane's life was in jeopardy, and right now in the darkness of my bedroom, there was a miniature tornado forming with Irene going all Glenn Close in the middle of it. I had to get control of the situation, and fast.

"May I remind you that you're a guest in my home?" I said civilly.

"And you're off running after other women," she spat out from the center of the room. The bed sheets had blown free and were swirling around her figure hauntingly.

"So what if I am?" I yelled. I didn't want to, but I was feeling cornered, hurt, and pissed at the same time. I pushed away from the wall, using one hand to steady myself. "So what, Irene? You're a guest here because of *my* generosity. You're not my girlfriend, not my wife, not anything. You're dead! The only thing I owe you is my hospitality, and barely that."

In the darkness, something the size of my storage bench at the end of the bed—possibly the bench itself—flew within inches of my face and hit the wall with an explosive crash. I squinted my eyes shut as shards of wood flicked across my face, and I felt the tiny sting of several pieces biting into my skin. If I didn't do something proactive, this was how I would die.

I covered my face and moved for the bedside table. I groped in the darkness until I found my cell phone while I tried to assess the room. Irene was between me and the door, blocking it completely. But before I could decide what to do, a book hit me squarely on the side of my head and another white-hot flash of starlight welled up behind my eyes. Not wanting to endure any further damage, I dashed across the room and into my closet, slamming the door behind me. The heavy clumping of my belongings rained down hard against the closed door. I looked down and was relieved to see that I would be able to hold the door shut by the knob on the inside of it.

I flipped open my phone, grateful for the little bit of light it gave off. Connor had earned the honorable position on my speed dial as number one and I dialed him up.

Although it was nearly 3 a.m., he answered almost immediately.

"This call may be recorded to assure *excellent* customer service," he said. "Please state the nature of your emergency, kid." It was a joke, but thankfully it was also to the point.

I talked as loudly as I could as the thumping against the door and the howling of the wind in the bedroom grew louder. Connor listened intently as I explained the situation.

When I was done, the doorknob was slick with sweat, but I held on tight.

"Where are you now?" he asked.

"In my closet," I said.

Irene's voice assumed a high-pitched wail on the other side of the door and I pressed my head against some of my clothes to drown her out.

"Perfect," he said. "Get dressed and get the hell out of there, kid. You're not going to be able to rationalize with her spirit."

Just like Tamara, I thought, and look what had happened to her. Dammit, I had to get her out of my mind. There would be time for being racked with guilt later.

"You get out of there and meet me down at the Odessa on Avenue A, all right?"

I fumbled in the dark for a pair of pants, using the keypad lights on my phone to help. I grabbed a pair but lost my balance attempting to put them on. My head thumped solidly against the wall and this time I felt the world fall out from under me.

"Kid? Kid?" Connor called out when I didn't respond. "You there? The Odessa, okay?"

"Ow. Yeah. I'll meet you there."

"I can't stress how careful you should be getting out of there, Simon. You know the expression 'Hell hath no fury like a woman scorned'?"

"Yeah."

"Times that by ten," he said. "Ghosts start to degrade in personality over time, and become more like raw emotion. You're now dealing with an entirely irrational creature, a degraded spirit experiencing rampant mood swings. The logic of regular human conversation is beyond her right now, so don't think you can talk her down or reason with her. Course, it doesn't help that she has that telekinetic ability to throw stuff at you."

"You're telling me," I said. "She's gone totally *Twister* over here."

Tiny blasts of wind began shooting through cracks in my rapidly deteriorating closet door.

"Trust me," Connor said, "you'll wish you were only dealing with a scornful woman if she gets ahold of you."

"Don't worry," I said, grabbing a shirt as I prepared to make my escape. "I'm a pretty fast runner when panic sets in."

"Time to come out of the closet," Connor said. I could hear him laughing as he said it.

"So *not* the time to make with the funny, boss."

I threw open what remained of the door just as it ripped

away from its hinges and blew right out of my hand. The sound of it tearing to pieces as it smashed against the opposite wall sent me running. I had no desire to be the next thing torn apart.

28

When I breathlessly entered the Odessa Diner, I noticed a flurry of movement coming toward me and my first panicked thought was *My God, I'm about to get swarmed by ghouls*. After the night I had been through, anything was possible, and I did a double take. Upon closer examination, it was merely a group of Greek waiters eager to seat me. They were simply enthusiastic, not the walking dead. I spotted Connor next to a table of plaid-clad punks at the rear of the restaurant and headed back.

Even though it was now 4 a.m., the diner was packed with Alphabet City residents and NYU students trying to take the edge off their binge drinking with a late-night infusion of food. That meant it was loud, but I didn't mind. Right now, I felt safer in a crowd.

I sat down across from Connor as a waiter clunked down a four-inch-thick binder that I assumed was the menu. I ignored it for the moment and looked Connor over. He was far more composed than I was. To be fair, I *had* dressed in a dark closet while attempting to flee for my life, so the lemon yellow pants and purple shirt should be forgiven. Hell, I didn't even know I owned lemon yellow pants! I looked to the next table and the punk rockers gave my outfit a thumbs-up.

"Were you followed?" he said. I shook my head. "How ya holding up, kid?"

"Well, Tamara's still dead," I said frankly, "and now another room of my apartment is getting trashed just after I put the place back together."

"At least you got out of there alive," Connor said encouragingly, "if not with your dignity."

"With all due respect, Connor, shut up."

"Oh, and don't forget Cyrus," he added. "He might be missing and his warehouse burned down, but several more Ghostsniffing junkies were brought in after you took off. It's going epidemic. It's all the rage."

Someone cleared his throat nearby and I turned to see the curly haired waiter looking down at me. He tugged at the edge of his black polyester vest and flipped open a pad. "You ready?"

Connor was already eating some sort of sampler platter that had one of everything in the diner on it, all of it battered and deep-fried. I looked at my yet unopened menu, felt deterred by its girth, and shrugged.

"You're not gonna eat?" the waiter asked. He sounded like I had just disgraced his whole family or slept with his wife. All shock, with a little disgust mixed in for good measure.

"I'm not hungry," I said.

"You've got to sit at the counter then." The waiter sighed and stared off at the far wall as he spoke. "That's the rules. If you're not going to eat anything, you have to sit at the counter. Tables are for our customers who are eating."

I shook my thumb at Connor. "He's sitting at a table. I'm sitting with him."

"He's eating," the waiter said as if he had been having

this argument since the dawn of time. "You're not. Those are the rules."

I looked to Connor, incredulous, but he merely shrugged. He popped something deep-fried but unidentifiable into his mouth.

I flipped the menu open. "Fine," I said. "I'll have a grilled cheese and a bowl of matzoh ball soup. Oh, and a chocolate milkshake . . . and a coffee."

The waiter snapped my menu shut before I had a chance to say anything else and scurried away.

"I can't believe that."

"You know what I can't believe?" He popped another deep-fried unidentifiable into his mouth. "I can't believe they charge eight bucks for a grilled cheese! That's without tomato or bacon even!"

"Do you mind if we talk about something more pertinent?" I asked testily. "How about, say, Irene going all Amityville on me?"

Connor looked at me seriously for a second, and then laughed. "Simon, listen, I'm sure whatever happened was bad. But the Inspectre taught me that any situation where you make it out alive and have the opportunity to sit down and bitch about it is, comparatively, a good situation."

I mulled that one over until my milk shake arrived. A long sip and a bit of brain freeze later, I was noticeably calmer.

"I don't want to beat an old departmental horse," Connor said, "but there's a reason why Other Division doesn't shelter any of our clients, kid. They're simply too unstable for us to deal with. Besides, we really don't have any good way to contain them even if we wanted to. This isn't like *Ghostbusters*."

"What about the way you were able to bind Irene?" I asked. "Or something similar to those jars in the secret room at Mandalay's shop but bigger?"

Connor shook his head. "Binding Irene with a potion was an extremely temporary measure. As far as those jars the Ghostsniffers use, I wouldn't wish that fate on any spirit. Any containment like that means absolute destruction of the soul, kid. Never forget it."

My food arrived with a side order of mild disdain (courtesy of our waiter), and I dug in, determined to get at least eight dollars' worth of enjoyment out of this grilled cheese. As I ate, I told Connor how I awoke to Irene screaming at the top of her lungs, how she seemed upset over the idea that I was chasing another woman.

"Well, that's a little unexpected," he said. "Spirits are known to be emotional over things, sure, but usually there's some basis in truth with what's upsetting them. I mean even though we know Irene's got a thing for you, it's not like she had anything to be jealous of . . . right?"

I pretended to find something at the bottom of my soup bowl and avoided eye contact.

"Simon . . . ? There's not something you want to tell me, is there, kid?"

"No," I said. "There's nothing I *want* to tell you."

"Oh God." He sighed. He pushed his plate away, gripped the edge of the table, and leaned across to me. "You're not involved with that Jane, are you? You realize this is the type of thing I'm supposed to report to the Enchancellors, don't you? Crushing on the forces of Darkness's secretary isn't just frowned upon; there's a pamphlet expressly forbidding it!"

"I'm pretty sure that wasn't in my orientation packet," I offered.

"That's hardly the point," he spat out. "The point isn't about you at all. You've put *me* in a shit situation, kid."

"I'm sorry," I said. And I meant it. My private entanglements were just that, private. I didn't want to drag Connor into this.

Connor's face softened a bit, but he still sounded angry.

"I suppose it's my fault, really. I should have seen it coming. I'm the mentor, after all."

"Nothing's happened," I said and thought about it. "Okay, well, that's not entirely true. We kissed, but that was only after I pulled her out of the garbage in my alley."

Connor simply stared at me. "Oh. Well, if that's all it was!"

"The Sectarians are probably going to kill her for failing!" I said, my voice rising. The table of punk rockers stared over at us now. I lowered my voice. "Look, feelings aside, I think we have a real opportunity here. She's scared now. I think we can turn her."

I watched Connor think it over before he spoke. "I want you to listen very carefully, kid. I'm not going to the Inspectre or the Enchancellors with this . . . yet. See what you can get out of the situation. I think this whole thing's a mess, but it's your mess, and because I'm a generous guy, I'm going to give you a chance to clean it up."

"Thank you," I said, relaxing a bit.

"Don't thank me yet," he said, hardening. "I'm doing this for myself as well. You know how bad it will look if I report this while they're rating my mentoring this quarter? I *need* to give you a chance to fix this if I'm ever going to save face in the Department. Understand?"

I nodded.

"As far as the rest goes, let me give you some mentorly advice? May I?"

I nodded once again.

"You are familiar with the works of Dante?"

"*Divine Comedy* Dante?" I asked.

Connor rolled his eyes. "No, Frank Dante over in Things That Go Bump in the Night. Of course *Divine Comedy* Dante!"

I had a passing familiarity with his books, but if his

name came up on *Final Jeopardy*, I probably wouldn't bet all my money.

"Dante wrote a lot about Divine Love," Connor said. "Beautiful stuff. Anyway, he goes on and on about chivalry and, most importantly, forbidden love. That which is labeled wrong or unattainable."

He stopped to flag down the waiter and made the internationally accepted check mark symbol in the air to get our bill.

"Anyway, when Dante descends into the Inferno, one of the first places he's taken is to the level of least sin—the lustful. Giving in to the wrong *kind* of love is the least offensive of sins to him, see? While he's there, he sees the spirits of famous ill-fated lovers—Paris and Helen, Cleopatra and Antony. Real tear-jerker material. Condemned to the Big BBQ Pit simply for choosing the wrong kind of love, the kind that led them astray from the path of love that leads to the divine, to God. A simple sin, really, easy to make."

The waiter stopped by the table with the check, and lingered as Connor spoke. Even the punk rockers were listening now.

"It's not *loving* that's the sin," Connor continued, "but more the act of choosing the incorrect *kind*. A slippery slope, if I ever read of one. So, you'll want to think carefully before you make your next move."

"But what should that be?" I asked. I was exhausted, fearing to return home. Ever since Irene had disappeared— or was pulled away by whatever mysterious force was out there—I had been wishing for her return. Now for my own safety, I hoped that she had disappeared again.

Connor threw down a few bills.

I felt for my wallet. "Can you cover me?" I asked. "I left my wallet back at the apartment when I was running for my life."

Connor threw down a few more bills. Then he reached in his pocket and pulled out a vial of the viscous, patchouli-like fluid he had used on that spirit back in the alley. He slid it across to me. "Use this if she gives you any more trouble, kid. And then call me." I picked it up and slid it in my pocket, feeling relieved.

"You wanna get your head together and figure out what you should do?" Connor asked. "Let me jump ahead several hundred years to answer that one, if you don't mind. I've come to use it as my personal mantra. 'Dead is dead and life is for the living.' Helps me get through the day in our line of work."

Connor stood. I rose. "Who came up with that?"

"The Master himself," Connor said as he threw up the collar on his trench coat and stuck a cigarette in the corner of his mouth. "Humphrey Bogart." He lit the cigarette, and then with the worst Bogey impression I had ever heard, he said, "Here's lookin' at you, kid."

I stood there, shaking my head as he left. Connor walked toward the door, the waiters swarming him angrily for lighting the cigarette in the diner. He parted them like the Red Sea and was gone, leaving me with much to wonder about. One thing I knew for sure. I certainly wouldn't be renting *Casablanca* in the near future.

29

I didn't go home that night, but sat at the diner, milking free refills of coffee until the owner threw me out. The sun had been up for an hour, and I walked the streets of the Lower East Side, watching the city slowly coming to life. I couldn't face going home if Irene's spirit was still trashing the place, and I wasn't in any shape to head back to the Department, so I let fate be my guide as I wandered, nervously looking over my shoulder for any signs of being followed the whole time. I spent hours thinking about the case and how I could help Irene, but that in turn only led to wondering about Jane. I had walked out on her, and God only knew if she was okay. I was failing everyone right now, and I decided I had to do something to change all that, starting by dealing with Jane. I returned to the last hotel I had moved Jane into, hoping she was still staying there. I also prayed that my abandoning her on the street hadn't caused her to revert to evil just yet.

When Jane opened the door to her room and saw me

standing there, she left it open and walked back into the room without waiting.

"Lookitme," she said sarcastically. "Not dead yet . . . survived a *whole night* by myself!"

Evil I could handle with the retractable bat hanging from my belt. Sarcasm took a gentler hand than that.

"Jane, please . . ." I said.

"Please what?" she said. "I think I'm in pretty good spirits, all things considered. Do you walk out on all your cases like that, or just me?"

My gentle approach flew out the window, and I couldn't help but feel a little incredulous.

"I don't know what you want me to say, Jane," I said. "You seem like a good person here, but you're not giving me a whole lot of faith in that. You want my help, right? You seem to want me to blindly trust you, but then I find out you're holding information out on me . . ."

"What's it going to take to get you on my side?" she said. "The Sectarians, *my own people*, want me dead, and that's not good enough?"

"It's not just me," I said. "Eventually my Department's going to figure out that I'm helping you, hiding you. It's just a matter of time and what I'd love out of you is some . . . I don't know . . . grandiose gesture that's going to put you in good not only with me but with them as well."

I knew I was being manipulative—partly because I needed answers about Tamara and Irene, but also on a personal level. I liked Jane more that I felt was right, and I would love to feel like it was justified.

Jane fell quiet so I pressed on. I needed something that could help me gain the upper hand in our fight against Bane and the corporate headhunter he had sent after her.

"Give me something, Jane," I said. "Help out an underpaid psychometrist with bills to pay. Prove you're on my side. I need a break if I'm going to help you or make any headway on the case I'm working on. Didn't you tell me that the Sectarians were obsessive about their record keeping? Get me inside the Sectarian Defense League."

Jane looked at me like I was crazy. "You want me to go back there?" she said. She looked like she was going to argue, but she stopped herself. "Fine. If that's what it's going to take. I can probably find something on that fish you asked about in my old records."

"I don't think they're going to let us just walk right in, Jane," I said.

"You don't have some brilliant plan?" she said, smiling for once.

"No," I said, "but clearly you do. Why don't you tell me what *your* plan is?"

"We'll need to get past building security first, so we'll wear all brown," she suggested, perking up. "Jumpsuits maybe. With matching baseball caps."

The twinkle in her eye made Jane look like she was Wile E. Coyote, Supergenius, hard at work at the drawing board. "Or blue. Doesn't matter."

I looked at her skeptically. "And this will help how . . . ?"

"Delivery people," she said. "Does anyone *really* pay attention to delivery people? No. It's always someone dressed in a jumpsuit or some kind of generic-looking outfit. You never remember the person. All you see is a blur of ho-hum colors and a hat."

Jane was right. I couldn't remember what any delivery guy I had ever encountered looked like.

"Won't they route us to a mailroom or something?" I asked.

Jane shook her head.

"No," she said. "One of the great things about being cultists is that trust is always an issue with them. They route everything straight through to their office. They're so not going to risk the chance of the Mask of Yojeeti or the Basket of Sepiroth going missing at the hands of a mail-room clerk. As if!"

Several hours (and one trip to K-Mart) later, we breezed past check-in at the Fifth Avenue entrance to the Empire State Building. Security barely gave us a glance as we signed the building register. My bat was hidden discreetly in a flower delivery box, underneath an all-too-pricy cover of roses. I fully intended to give them to Jane if we made it out alive. I also intended to expense them.

We made our way up to the thirty-third floor. It was af-ter normal business hours, but to be safe, Jane kept the brim of her hat pulled down low in case we ran into anyone she knew. Luck, however, was on our side, and we arrived at the door without a single run-in.

"Most girls get dinner and a movie," Jane said as we stood outside the now familiar glass doors of the Sectarian Defense League. "I get breaking and entering."

I adjusted my gloves as I looked at the dripping red let-ters on the door and then at Jane.

"Complain much?" I said.

Jane smiled sweetly and shook her head. Her blond ponytail bounced from side to side, and for a second I did feel like we were out on a date instead of hell-bent on infil-trating her old workplace. I eyed the keypad at the side of the double doors.

"What are the chances that your old pass code still works?" I said.

I had come prepared to try my hand at lock picking, but an electronic lock was beyond my abilities. I supposed there was always the bat, though that might not be the sub-tlest entrance.

"Worth a shot." Jane shrugged and punched her old

number in. The red lights turned to green and the unit chirped a happy signal of approval. I gave her delivery hat a playful push down onto her head and she giggled. Connor would never have let me do that to him.

However, Connor *would* kill me if he knew what Jane and I were up to, but hopefully it wouldn't matter if the two of us actually succeeded.

I pushed at the door and it gave way. "That was easy enough. Makes me a bit nervous, though."

"Getting past the door really wasn't my concern, Simon. It's what might be on the other side of it that worries me."

We moved quietly through the door and into the darkened lobby of the Sectarian Defense League. I hoped my eyes would adjust quickly to the half-light. As I edged forward, I was relieved to see that the room was silent and there was no hint of motion. I felt Jane's arm press against mine, and though for a second I thought she was trying to take my hand, I realized quickly that she was trying to stop me.

"Wait," she said with a squeeze. "Look."

I came to a halt in the middle of the lobby, and as my eyes finally grew accustomed to the darkness, I realized we weren't alone. The desks around the outer rim of the reception area were filled with dark figures. I slowly crept forward to examine one, and was relieved to see that they did not react to my presence.

Zombies. After work hours, they were almost motionless as they clacked softly away at the keyboards before them, no longer working at the pace I had seen them filing and typing on my first visit here. It made perfect sense that they were still here. At the end of the workday, where did these corporate zombies have to go, really? They didn't have homes, and without a single working brain among them, they would sit there silently until their masters returned in the morning. Their faces reminded me of so many I saw among the commuters here in New York—lifeless and slack-jawed. Even though I'd been known to take my bat to rotting zombie flesh from time to time, I felt sorry for the restless souls that remained trapped in these rotting corpses. I reminded myself to talk to Davidson about zombie rights if Jane and I made it out of here alive.

I moved back to Jane.

"Won't they start craving the taste of our yummy, yummy human flesh?" I whispered.

Jane covered her mouth to stifle a laugh. When she regained her composure, she said, "I'm pretty sure they've been fed for the evening. Last thing Mr. Bane wants is for them to start wandering the building in search of . . . snacks."

I shuddered at the thought. I wondered *what* exactly they had been fed earlier, but Jane cut me off before I could ask.

"Relax, Simon. They don't normally feed them on human flesh anyway. The building would be empty in a week! It's mostly cow brains and entrails. They also seem partial to hot dogs from street vendors."

"Well, that's of some comfort," I said.

"Besides, human flesh is an occasional treat . . . like catnip for cats," she said with a wink.

I wasn't sure if she was pulling my leg or not, but now was not the time for a lengthy discussion of the culinary habits of the undead. I pushed it all out of my mind and smiled. "Lead on, milady."

I kept close behind as Jane led, none too curious about what might happen if I should stray. We made our way out of reception and down a short hall that opened into a large bullpen. I was relieved to see that there were only two zombies in sight. Jane stopped at a door bearing her name and swiped a card at it. It clicked open and we stole inside quickly, shutting the door behind us.

She flicked the overhead light on and I stood there

momentarily in awe. Her office was *huge*. It was littered
with ultramodern Norwegian furniture that was so nice it
made me want to burn down the next Ikea I saw. It sure beat
the shitty secondhand desk I had been assigned back at the
D.E.A. Jane's hand brushed against my cheek and I mistook
it for affection until I felt her lift my jaw back into place.

"Look," she said. "I'm sorry that evil pays better. Isn't
that part of its appeal, after all?"

She turned away and went straight to work searching
her old desk and pulling out anything personal she came
across. She laid a framed picture of some very corn-fed-
looking parents of the Kansas variety on top of the pile.

"Do your parents know?" I asked. "About you working
here . . ."

She pulled out a sheaf of papers and began sorting
through them. "No, and they never will. They think I'm
working for an animal rights group."

"I suppose you could spin it that way. Some sort of
'Save the Zombies' angle . . ."

"Fudge!" she said, throwing down the papers. "It's not
here."

"What isn't?"

"The manifest on item one-six-eight," she said as if I
knew what the hell she was talking about.

I looked at her with the kind of blank stare usually reserved for the zombies themselves.

"Better known to you as 'that wooden fish thingie'? I
should have all the details here on where it's being stored,
but they're missing."

"Keep looking," I said. I placed my flower box on her
desk to help out with the search.

Since it was Jane's office, I really didn't know exactly
what I was looking for. I left her to go through the rest of
her drawers while I packed her personal effects into my
bag. Jane had made the choice never to return here after

this, so whatever I could do to help her get out of here quicker, I would.

Her desk was cluttered with stuff. Pictures, a squishy little stress-management toy, a collection of breakfast cereal action figures. The Trix Rabbit, Count Chocula, Booberry, the Lucky Charms leprechaun, even the Cookie Crisp bandit! I was in love. Good thing I was wearing the gloves or the nostalgia of all these items might have put my powers into overload, leaving me flopping on the floor like a fish.

A small collection of plants occupied one corner of the desk, but they would have to stay behind.

I hadn't told Jane why I was looking for information on the fish or that it had been Irene's. All she knew was what she had seen the first time I came into the League swinging my bat. Just because her days with the Sectarians seemed over didn't mean she was getting full disclosure about my assignments at Other Division.

If Jane chose to be taken into the fold of the Department later, which I hoped she would, she might find out everything concerning my mission to reacquire the fish so we could discern what happened to Irene's soul. For now I was quite content to keep it a mystery. My dealings with my favorite ghost girl were complex enough as they stood. My department's line of "on a need to know" basis came in handy once in a while, and just then it was helping to alleviate some of the guilt I felt for keeping Jane in the dark.

She checked the same drawer she had just taken the papers from again. "It should be here!"

"Looking for this?" said a familiar European voice from behind us.

I spun around. Faisal Bane was standing in the middle of the room, smugly holding up the missing manifest—the one that listed the wooden fish. Behind him, a section of the wall that had been there a moment ago had now slid back to reveal a hidden alcove. Tricky! "Or perhaps you're looking for your Hello Kitty coffee mug?"

He produced said object in his other hand, examined it slowly, then threw it as hard as he could toward the opposite wall. It smashed against a picture of the Manhattan skyline and shattered, pieces of mug and picture frame showering the carpet. Jane gasped.

"No! Kitty!"

I grabbed the box of flowers, and pulled the bat free from it, sending flowers flying in every direction. Another figure stepped from the darkness behind Faisal and into the light. My stomach sank as I recognized the man's face. I had seen it every day back at the Department of Extraordinary Affairs. It was Thaddeus Wesker. The Inspectre had confided that Wesker was an undercover agent here, but right now he looked every bit on the side of evil.

"Un-uh," the Director of Greater & Lesser Arcana said. He flicked his arm in my direction and I felt the bat pull free from my hands. It twirled end over end toward Wesker and he plucked it from the air.

"How did you do that?"

"Hello to you, too, Simon," Wesker said. "I am the head of Greater and Lesser *Arcana*, after all, or did you forget?" He turned to Faisal with a grin on his face. "I told you if we waited they'd eventually come sniffing around for it."

Faisal turned his head. "Is this the one you mentioned?"

"Yes," Wesker sneered. "He's one of their precious little Other Division."

"So young!" Faisal said as he looked me over. "Apparently, they're desperate to replenish their fading numbers, eh?"

It was bad enough that Bane was here, but now there was Wesker to contend with, too. Maybe this had been a setup. Maybe Jane was in on it, too, playing me all this time while secretly helping the Sectarians . . .

"Leave him alone," Jane said and surprised me by moving between me and the two of them.

Bane waved her away with a dismissive gesture. "Save your theatrics, Jane, and put aside any misguided thoughts of heroics, would you?"

Despite the growing fear in my chest, my male ego went "Doh!" *I* should have been the one to step forward. Stupid gestures were *my* bailiwick, not hers.

"Bully," I heard her mutter. Fast as a shot, Faisal closed the distance to her and drove his fist into her gut. Jane crumpled to the floor without a sound. There went the idea that she was secretly on their side.

"I don't let my subordinates talk to me like that," he said as he stared down at her, "and I certainly won't let a traitorous whore like you either."

Wesker moved to stand by Faisal's side, but his attention was all on me. I glared at him and said, "I see only one traitor here and that's Wesker."

Faisal continued to ignore me, but Wesker took a step in my direction, my bat held over his shoulder loosely in one hand. "Well, Mr. Bane, what do you recommend I do with him?"

Faisal grinned as he turned, his eyes menacing me. "Well, he *did* bring his own bat. Cave his skull in with it."

30

An overactive imagination can be both a blessing and a curse. For instance, when I think of supermodels, I consider what my mind can conjure up a great benefit—wildly imagined slow-motion pillow fights, for instance. But conversely, when I had just been told that my skull was going to be caved in, I would have rathered that my mind couldn't conceive—down to the last detail—what that might look like. Cracked shards of bone digging into my brain, my gray matter poking through, clumps of bloody hair . . . but then again, it was enough to snap me out of my useless stupor and into action.

Jane was down—but hopefully not out—for the count, so it was up to me. With Wesker in possession of my bat, I reached behind me toward the desk and grabbed whatever my hand fell upon. A green-domed banker's lamp. Just great.

I didn't figure my training in Unorthodox Fighting Techniques would be coming into play so soon, and I was untested in a real-life dangerous situation, but I had little choice. Giving a tug, I tore the cord free from wherever it was plugged into and started swinging the lamp in wild circles over my head. Wesker backed closer to Faisal and there was a genuine look of concern on his face that hadn't been there a second ago. I pressed what I thought was my advantage and let the lamp fly.

When people replay a moment in their head, there is a clarity that the actual moment itself never seemed to have. That's how it was with me anyway. In the playback in my head, I now understand what happened as I let loose the lamps of war, although the moment itself passed in a heart-beat.

Evidently, my training had paid off more than I thought. I had worried about timing the release of the cord so that the lamp would head in the right direction, but my aim proved perfect. The lamp snaked out from my hands, the cord feeding through my fist as it flew and the glass dome exploded against the *back* of Wesker's head. I had been aiming for Wesker's face, but what I hadn't counted on was that he would turn away from me to clock Faisal with my own bat. Wesker wobbled, but didn't drop as he whacked the leader of the Sectarians across the shoulders. Faisal dropped faster than a one-hit wonder from the pop music charts, but Wesker remained standing.

"Son of a bitch!" Wesker shouted. He cautiously felt the back of his head and examined his fingers for blood as he stumbled around the room. "What is wrong with you?!?"

Surprisingly, he threw my bat back to me, and I caught it midair.

"Can't you see that I'm trying to help here?" he hissed as he crossed to me and got in my face. "Or didn't they teach you that anyone attacking your enemy is an *ally*?"

I looked at Faisal spread out on the floor. His eyes were closed and he wasn't moving. I picked up the manifest from where it lay next to him.

"You knocked him out cold!" I said.

Wesker glowered at me. He moved to Faisal, squatted down, and examined him. "Could you stop stating the obvious and do something useful? It's only a matter of time until he comes around. And we'll need to be out of here when he does. Check your woman there, would you? I need to secure our prisoner."

I had forgotten Jane in the heat of the moment, but I did as Wesker instructed and checked on her. She was unresponsive as I scooped her up, and I stopped for a second as something dawned on me. I turned back to Wesker.

"Wait a minute," I said. "*Prisoner?* We're taking Faisal with us?"

Wesker sighed. "You don't miss a word, do you? Yes. Look, I honestly don't know *what* we should do with him, but I know I don't want to just leave him here. We're not sure if he saw me hitting him with the bat from behind or not, so we take him in until we find out what he recalls. We've got nothing we can technically detain him for, but at least if we take him in to the D.E.A. like we are arresting him, maybe we can find out if my cover's been blown. Now wake her up."

"Did you see what he did?" I shouted. "He punched her!"

Wesker jumped up from where he knelt and crossed to us. "You act as if that matters, Simon."

"Are you telling me that hitting a woman doesn't matter?"

He squatted down next to Jane and produced a tube from his own pocket. He removed the stopper and waved it under Jane's nose. She began to groan and sputter as she turned her head away from it.

Wesker gave me a look of contempt as he stood. "I'm telling you to see the bigger picture here, newbie. Ideas like 'a man shouldn't hit a woman' don't ultimately matter in the fight between good and evil. You hold on to these archaic

notions and these cultists will kill you while you're still processing which chivalrous deed to act on first. I'm as sorry
she got punched as I would be for *anyone* being punched,
equal rights amendment aside, but you want to know what
I'm most sorry about? That this woman here is actually re-
lying on you to save her."

I looked at him, and all I wanted was to smash his face
in. "Why are you helping me if you hate me so much?"

"It's not about you, newbie. Again, *think* of the big picture! You think I'm going to let my personal dislike of a
snot-nosed upstart like you distract me from my purpose
here? Think again."

I pushed him away from Jane as her eyes fluttered open
and I helped her to her feet. "You okay there, Janey?"

"Owie," Jane said. She was trying to play off the pain.
She winced as I stood her upright. "You sure we're not
dead yet? It sure feels like I'm dead."

"I'm afraid that's just wishful thinking on your part," I
said.

She smiled, but it faded as she caught sight of Faisal
Bane lying on the floor. "My God, did you do that?"

Before I could answer, Wesker snorted. "Him? Please!
He couldn't fight his way out of a fifth grade choir practice!"

"Who's he?" Jane asked, eyeing Wesker suspiciously.

"Wait," I said. "You both worked for the Sectarians and
you don't know each other?" Of course, their paths had
crossed the night Wesker cut Jane's line—but with a rare
show of discretion, I decided not to bring that up right now.
We had some pressing things to accomplish right now.

"It's a big organization," Jane said. "There's a lot of
skulking that goes on. There was even an official Lunch
and Learn: Skulking 101, but no, I haven't had the displeasure of meeting him."

"Oh, believe me," Wesker said snidely. "The displeasure
is all mine."

"Well, you're awfully unpleasant," Jane said with a look.

"Yes," he said. "I know. It's part of my mystique. Look, I'd love to stand around and chat all night with you and Prince Harming here, but I do believe we have more pressing matters to attend to."

"Such as getting out of here alive?" Jane asked. She must have been feeling better because she seemed to be back to her feisty self. Wesker ran to the door, peered out, and then shut it. He turned to Jane.

"Faisal's been talking about you," Wesker said. "Do you know that the Sectarians set that corporate headhunter—Jason Charles—after you? We don't want to make it easy for him to find you now, do we? I don't think it helps that we're hanging around in your old office. We need to get out of here."

My guilt rose up at the mention of Jason Charles, and thoughts of vengeance over Tamara filled my head.

"I already know he's looking for me. I've been evading him for days," Jane said proudly. Score one for Team Petty Victory!

It didn't last long, though. Wesker snapped out of whatever state he was in and looked the two of us up and down. "Why the hell are you wearing matching outfits?"

"It's how we got in," I explained. "Delivery people."

"Classic," he said with a roll of his eyes.

"Hey! It worked, didn't it?" I fired back.

"Ahem . . . guys?" Jane said. She ran back to her desk and began to pack the last of her things. "I really hate to get in between the two of you verbally assaulting each other. It's very macho and all—thanks for the effort—but we really need to come up with a plan and quick. I don't see how we're going to get Faisal out of here."

Jane was right. We were falling apart here. Connor would have been disappointed. Lock picking our way into Irene's apartment was one thing, but I knew he wouldn't have approved of us breaking into the Sectarians' office. And the petty way I was losing focus of our objectives by letting my emotions over Tamara and my dislike of Wesker rule the situation went against everything Connor had trained me for.

"Look," I said. "I'm sorry. For everything. Thank you for saving us."

"Finally!" he said with exasperation. "A little gratitude!"

"You know," I said, "you're really not making this easy."

He shrugged and said, "Why don't I make things real easy for all of us then? I think I know how we're going to get our large European friend out of here without drawing too much attention on ourselves."

Thaddeus Wesker smiled with the perverse pleasure of one who relished the role of leadership. "You two dress-up playmates should be tickled pink about it. I'm promoting you."

I had a sneaking suspicion that I wouldn't like what he was about to suggest.

"Welcome to the world of professional carpet cleaning," Wesker said.

31

The plan was this: Jane and I would roll the unconscious Faisal Bane into a carpet, essentially making a human burrito, and sneak him out of the building. The foolishness of the plan was further complicated by the fact that as we rolled Faisal Bane into an oriental carpet, it looked exactly like a carpet with a body rolled into it.

My gut reaction to Wesker's plan was alarm bells going off in my head, screaming STUPID STUPID STUPID. But since I had nothing better to offer in the way of cohesive escape, we were stuck with it.

Wesker and I hefted one end of the Faisal carpet burrito onto my shoulder.

"Won't the zombies try to stop us?" I asked. "I mean we've essentially made a giant joint with their master inside of it. Won't that set their zombie senses tingling?"

It was Jane who put my fears to rest as Wesker moved to help Jane lift her end of the carpet roll.

"Zombie sense?" Jane said, shaking her head at me.

"What are they teaching you at the D.E.A.? There's no such thing, Simon."

"You sure?" I asked.

Jane nodded. "I don't think they'll even notice us leaving. I've worked with that lot of undead word processors, and without their zombified brains being directly controlled on a project, they have the functionality of a small child. A regular person might look at us and be able to figure out we've got a body in here, but a zombie, like a child, couldn't figure it out. It's like if you cover something up with a cloth, a baby will forget it's there. Object permanence, it's called."

I tested the weight at my end of the bundle and it was much heavier than I thought.

"It's the same for the zombies," Jane continued. "Unless they're ordered directly by their master or they see him in jeopardy specifically, they're not likely to attack."

"Good enough for me," I said. "That sounded very professorial of you."

Wesker cleared his throat pointedly. "If you two don't mind . . ."

For once, I was glad to hear him chime in because our carpety coffin was not getting any lighter. Wesker opened the door for us and waved us out.

"Aren't you coming with us?" I asked.

"I'll meet you outside," he said. "I'm going to go a separate way so as to not draw attention to our secret partnership. I'm worried that my cover might be blown, remember?"

"I doubt it," said. "The way you clocked him, he probably won't even remember who *he* is."

"You'd be surprised," Wesker said, shutting the door behind him. "These Sectarians are a hardy sort. Still, there might have been enough confusion in the fight."

Without another word, Wesker headed off in the opposite direction as Jane and I headed for the lobby.

Surprisingly, our trip went smoothly. Jane's arm—still tender after healing from the fall into my alley—began to act up, but she was a trooper and didn't bring it up until we hit street level along Thirty-Third. Wesker pulled up in a van—God knows where he'd purloined it from—and we loaded Bane clumsily into it, thankful to have his weight off our shoulders. Wesker gave the two of us a few sneers in the rearview mirror but otherwise fell silent for the rest of the ride down, which was fine by me.

Because of Wesker's deep-cover operation, he decided to make himself scarce just in case he hadn't blindsided Faisal as well as he thought. That meant that he wouldn't be able to claim this capture as a victory for his precious Greater & Lesser Arcana department. I knew that would kill him, and I did an inner happy dance over the thought. We were hauling in one big evil fish and I would most likely get all the credit. Maybe Jane would win some points toward convincing the D.E.A. she was much less evil than they'd thought.

I wasn't sure how long we'd be able to detain Faisal, but we'd see how far we could take it. It wasn't until we unloaded the van on East Eleventh Street that I began to feel an unexpected excitement from it all. There was a buzz in the crowd as we entered, even in the rich-smelling confines of the coffee shop. Operatives from the graveyard shift perked up at our arrival, and they parted as we hefted our load from the van and headed back toward the office. As we worked our way through the storefront and down the main aisle of the theater, the D.E.A. crowd surged around us and lifted the rolled-up villain out of our hands and continued forward. I didn't mind, though. I was riding the wave of our high, too busy accepting the congratulations, handshakes, and pats on the back from my peers to care. Most of the other agents probably didn't even know why they were cheering or what was going on, but they figured anytime someone walked in with a body wrapped up in a carpet roll, it was most likely in the plus column for the good guys. As I continued forward through the throng, my free hand held tight to Jane's.

Connor stood by the entrance to the offices and I met his eyes as we approached. If he was there to reprimand me, I wanted to face it head on while I was still full of congratulatory empowerment.

"When I told you to take some kind of action at the Odessa last night," he started grimly, "I didn't expect you to bring down the enemy single-handedly. You could have gotten yourself killed, kid."

"And me," chimed in Jane cheerfully. "Don't forget he could have gotten me killed as well!"

"Word has it you're M.I.A.," he said to Jane with a sour look.

Connor looked down at our intertwined hands and I faltered for a second, feeling my grip loosen.

"Listen, Connor, I don't know what to say." I paused for a moment, unsure of what I wanted to say to justify myself. "I'm a man of action, see . . ."

"And I'm not?" Connor fired back. "I'm a man of action, too, Simon. Thing is, I don't go charging into a situation unless I know the score first."

"Problem here, gentlemen?" the Inspectre said, appearing as if out of nowhere. He looked at Jane. "Well, this should be an interesting story. Last I saw, you were plummeting off a rooftop wearing a black unitard."

Connor cooled in the Inspectre's presence, and I relaxed.

Connor regained his composure in front of our boss.

"Just giving the kid here a piece of friendly advice. Hoping to prolong his life, that's all."

Quimbley stroked his mustache for a moment, looked at me, and clapped Connor on the shoulder. "Well, carry on, Connor, but don't be too hard on the boy, eh? He is in Other Division, after all, and it's almost impossible to run wholly by the book around here, isn't it?"

Connor looked on the verge of saying something pointed. Instead he simply said, "Right, sir. I'll keep that in mind."

"That's a good chap," the Inspectre said. "Now if you'll excuse me, I have some interrogation to get to."

The Inspectre nodded to all of us and was off with a look of excitement in his eyes that I had never seen before.

"We'll be going as well," I said and moved toward the doorway.

"About that," Connor said, blocking my way again. "I'm afraid she's not allowed in the offices."

The crowd was surging around us now and I was having trouble focusing.

"I'm sorry," I said. "What?"

Connor sighed, but made no attempt to move out of our way. "Standard procedure, Simon, you know that. We can't just let the forces of Darkness into our inner sanctum."

His words hit me as hard as an actual blow. "Didn't you see her helping me carry Bane in here? Does that sound like a cultish thing to you?"

"Not necessarily," Connor said. "But subterfuge comes in many forms and I wouldn't put it past her to be part of something more nefarious."

"You have no idea what we just went through," I said. "He practically killed her!"

"You're right, I *don't* know what you went through," Connor said bitterly. "*That's* part of the problem, isn't it? You're working with the enemy and not with your partner."

"I see," I said. "This isn't just about me then. This is about me getting the collar, isn't it?"

"It's not about anything," he said, "except the facts. Until Jane's been debriefed, I'm not letting her anywhere near our operations center. Understood?"

"Ask Wesker," I offered. "He can tell you exactly what happened."

"Oh! Wesker's in on this, too?" Connor laughed. "There's a name I run to for trust and legitimacy!"

"Go ahead and quote policy to me some more, Connor . . ."

I felt a tender hand on my shoulder and turned to see Jane, who had stayed silent through all of this. "Go on, Simon. It's okay, really . . ."

It didn't feel okay. What should have been my finest hour was turning south and there seemed to be little I could do to control it.

"Simon," she started, and turned to my partner. "And Connor, is it? You're the other one from the lobby at the S.D.L., right? I think you were going to be next on my list."

Connor nodded.

"Sorry 'bout that," she said with sincerity. "Look, I don't expect anyone to buy that I've changed overnight. I'm not sure I believe it myself. But, Simon, I do know that I've got the patience to go through whatever it's going to take for you and your friend to believe me. So go."

Her composure in all this floored me. In the face of all of Connor's insults, she was holding herself together far better than either Connor or I was.

"You're sure?" I said, and she nodded.

"Absolutely." She took off her delivery hat, leaned in, and kissed me gently on the cheek. "Now get in there and enjoy your moment in the sun."

Had the shoe been on the other foot, I'm not sure how

I would have handled all this, but here she was taking everything in stride.

"Are you going to be okay?" I asked. Jason Charles, our friendly neighborhood corporate headhunter, was still out there. Looking, waiting . . . I didn't want to abandon her again.

"I'll be fine," she said, squeezing my hand. Then she turned to Connor. "And as for you, Mister Man, I look forward to you questioning me someday. I can't wait to see what you're like when you're not treating me like a crazed cultist. Simon speaks quite highly of you, you know."

It was Connor's turn to smile, but it was mixed with a look of suspicion.

"Yeah," he said. "Well, the kid's got talent, that's for sure. I'd hate to discover that someone was using him for it."

"So would I," she said with conviction, and with a final look at me, she headed through the crowd and toward the door.

32

I went to change back into my street clothes, and after I finished shaking hands and pushing my way through the crowd to the office, Faisal had been unceremoniously dislodged from his carpety burrito. Seeing his face as they secured him to a sturdy metal chair further diminished my good vibe.

The feeling had faded pretty darn fast ever since Connor had turned Jane away at the door. Oddly, all the well-wishing didn't seem nearly as important without her present. A gold star on my permanent record here at the Department was still a gold star, so I tried to keep my spirits up.

Seeing Faisal sitting stoically in the chair made it hard, though. The urge to smack him around like a piñata on Cinco de Mayo was overwhelming, and I stayed to the back of the room to keep myself in check. Besides, I was pretty sure that if I took a swipe at Faisal with my bat, he wouldn't be filled with candies or little plastic toys. What would be the fun in that?

We had taken over one of the lesser used conference rooms even though it was already doing double duty as a storage area. Space was at a premium at the D.E.A. and the mounting clutter of paranormal research—spell components, cursed items, and boxes containing the unknown—piled up faster than the crates of antiques in my living room.

Luckily, this meant that due to our space confines, most of the departmental looky-loos had to be shooed out. Only a handful of divisional leaders (excluding Wesker, of course) were present along with Connor and me.

"Hroom!" the Inspectre sounded. Everyone settled quietly into their seats. "What's say we get this unpleasantness out of the way, shall we? Why don't you start, Mr. Bane, by telling us why you stole that wooden fish from Irene Blatt and what is it used for?"

I was surprised by the impressive figure Inspectre Quimbley cut. I admired the old man, but there had been many times when he appeared almost comically grandfatherly. Seeing this side of him when it came down to hardcore occultism reminded me that the Inspectre could really pull out all the badass stops.

This, however, did not mean that Bane would actually give up any information under Argyle Quimbley's interrogation. In fact, Bane looked more composed than ever. He was devilishly handsome, and not a single strand of hair looked out of place, even though he had been wrapped in a carpet for the past half hour. Most people would have looked a little rough around the edges, but Faisal looked ready to pose for the cover of *Occultist's Quarterly*. The only thing that looked out of place was the thick coil of rope lashing him to the chair. It held him tightly in place, not that he was making any effort to strain against it. This surprised me.

I'd expected him, as the villainous head of fanatical cultists, to be full of wrath and rage in the face of his capture.

Instead, he sat calmly, passively, and worst of all, unansweringly.

The Inspectre looked exasperated by Faisal's silence as well. He paced back and forth, stroking his mustache. Every so often he would drop down in front of Faisal as if he had heard the cultist say something, but if he had, I couldn't hear it. This slow process dragged on for another twenty minutes, each moment of silence seeming longer that the last.

Again the Inspectre got in Faisal's face.

"What's that?" he asked. "Eh?"

Silence.

"I've got all night," the Inspectre said. "Or would you rather I start asking you more about *this*?"

Like an old vaudevillian stage magician, the Inspectre rolled up his tweed sleeve and waved his hand through the air with a flourish. The manifest that Jane and I had taken from Faisal earlier appeared at the Inspectre's fingertips. Faisal's eyes moved to it and flickered with interest for the first time since we had brought him in.

"Ah yes," Faisal said with a grin. His eyes left the manifest and turned toward me at the far side of the room. "The item retrieved from Ms. Blatt . . . I do wonder, though, is she still around?"

I didn't like hearing her name on his lips, but I honestly didn't have a clue as to where Irene had disappeared to since last night. I kept quiet.

With faux innocence in his tone, Faisal asked, "I wonder, Simon, does our precious little Janey know about her?"

His eyes actually twinkled and a wicked grin sprang upon his face, a grin that ran clear down to his dark soul. I felt the hair on the back of my neck bristle, but I held my ground. I could give silence as good as we had been getting it from him.

"Now, now," the Inspectre said as he stepped directly

between us. "You leave the boy alone. I'm asking the questions here."

"Yes," hissed Faisal. "And I see how well that's working out for you . . ."

"Well, at least we've got you talking now, haven't we?" the Inspectre fired back caustically.

Faisal fell silent again, then cast his eyes toward the door. "Not for long apparently."

I turned to see mayoral liaison David Davidson standing in the doorway. As usual, he was impeccably dressed. Even the knot of his tie was perfect, and he looked every bit as composed and unruffled as Faisal had when we captured him. Davidson's eyes scanned the room briefly before coming to rest on Faisal and the Inspectre.

"Sorry to do this, gentlemen," he said with that friendly *I'm-about-to-screw-you-so-bend-over* tone of his. "I'm afraid I can't allow you to continue with this line of questioning."

"Coming to the rescue of cultists again?" I snorted.

"Sectarians," Davidson reminded me with a waggle of his finger. "They're officially referred to as 'Sectarians.'"

"Your timing is impeccable as usual," I said. "Do the Sectarians have you on their payroll as well?"

Davidson shook his head and resumed his politician's smile. "The Mayor is *trying* to look after *all* his constituents and their needs, Simon. He doesn't play sides."

Perhaps the Department had a mole or a leak that had alerted Davidson. Perhaps it was Wesker who was really playing both sides and he had called Davidson in. That mystery would have to wait, though. Right now I was too busy having trouble just moving.

Davidson's words had an immobilizing and calming effect, the same one that I had experienced during our initial encounter at the Sectarian Defense League. Davidson made his way to Faisal and started undoing the rope, and although I wanted to stop him, I could barely move. The best I could muster was a leisurely stroll down the aisle toward them.

The Inspectre seemed to be the only one unaffected. "Seems to me that no matter how you dress it up, Mr. Davidson, evil is still evil."

I think his understanding of the politics of it all was the only thing that kept the Inspectre from laying a hand on Davidson as he released our prisoner.

"Everything okay, Mr. Bane?" Davidson asked as the last coil of the rope fell to the floor. "Are you hurt?"

Faisal stood, brushing the creases out of his suit. "Only my pride, Mr. Davidson. Only my pride. Somehow this young man here got the drop on me in my offices and gave me a bit of a wallop. Not sure how he pulled it off really, but perhaps I'll press charges."

Although I didn't like the idea of having charges pressed against me, I was somewhat relieved that we hadn't blown Wesker's cover.

"You'll have to take that up with the police," Davidson said. This seemed to disappoint Faisal, and he frowned.

"Took your time getting here, didn't you?" Faisal said with a sneer.

Davidson's smile faltered for a second. "The wheels of justice are ever turning, Mr. Bane, if not always briskly."

By the time the effects of whatever Davidson had done wore off, I found myself standing next to Inspectre Quimbley. His eyes were fixed on Connor. Something unspoken was happening, but I didn't know what. The Inspectre put his hand lightly on my shoulder.

"Simon," he said, "be a dear boy and hand me that clipboard over there, would you?"

I slipped on one of my gloves. I had no idea if I would get a reading from the clipboard but I grabbed it and handed it over. The Inspectre casually slipped the manifest page onto it and slowly began to creep the whole thing behind his back.

Faisal paused from sneering at David Davidson and cocked his head in our direction. He tsked-tsked us. "I'll be taking that back, thank you."

"What?" the Inspectre said with feigned ignorance. "Oh . . . this? Yes, of course you will . . ."

He pulled the manifest free of the clipboard and held it out to the head Sectarian. Faisal raised one of his thick, black eyebrows. "It's good to see such obedience." He turned to me. "You could learn a thing or two from him, lapdog."

"I've learned plenty," I said, feeling totally ineffectual. "And I'll learn what you did to Irene, too."

"Perhaps," he said with a smile, "but if you could only prove it . . . or anything for that matter."

Davidson stepped in at this moment. "You don't have to say anything more, Mr. Bane. We're leaving."

"No," Faisal said almost cheerfully as he narrowed in on me. "I don't mind. Tell me, Mr. Canderous, you seem quite taken by Ms. Blatt, don't you? Every time I run into you, I seem to be subjected to one of your little fits of misguided bravado over her."

I felt embarrassed and angry at the same time, my face turning bright red. I did care for Irene, but I didn't want all of it coming out right here in front of my own Department—especially in front of Connor. I didn't even want to think of what the Inspectre would make of my involvement in all this.

"Your obsession with Irene," Faisal continued, "seems to be clouding your judgment, I suspect, and corollary to that, it causes you to meddle in my affairs far too often. Maybe what I have to say now will make you back off my people once and for all."

"Are you going to threaten to kill me?" I said.

"Yes, you'd like me to say something like that, wouldn't you?" he said. "Here in a room full of witnesses. No such luck, I'm afraid, but I want to give you something to think about." His eyes fell to the manifest and he tapped his finger at the page. "You're terribly concerned about this wooden fish. So intent on getting it back. Did you ever give a thought for a single second that maybe the fish wasn't Irene Blatt's in the first place?"

"What the hell are you talking about?" I made a sudden lunge for the manifest but he easily avoided me and held it out of reach.

"The day you accosted one of my fellow Sectarians in Ms. Blatt's apartment . . . did you take a good look at her place? Anything strike you odd? Single woman . . . living all alone in a veritable paradise of antiquities . . . ?"

I recalled her apartment, trashed as it was. Her tastes and collecting habits were so similar to things I had or would love to own. It was one of the first things that had intrigued me about her. I lived in the same type of antique-freaque way, and maybe I needed to start looking at our similarities for clues instead. Maybe she was more like me than I thought.

"She's a psychic?"

Faisal scrunched his face at me, looking like one of those Chinese dogs with all the wrinkles. "What?! No, you nitwit!"

"Then I don't know," I said. "I don't know why she owned all that stuff. Maybe she had a rich family or something."

Part of hunting down who Irene Blatt truly was had fallen to me, and the truth was I hadn't been able to come up with much on her in the real world. Over the past week, it had fallen farther down the list of priorities, especially with Tamara's death and Jane's appearance in my life.

"Irene had a bit of a habit," he said. "A real pro with the

sticky fingers. A little something that you can see she turned into quite a profitable career."

"She's no thief," I said defensively. There was only one ex-thief around here, and that was me. I moved for Faisal, but the Inspectre held me back.

"Wasn't she?" Faisal said. He folded the manifest and slipped it in his pocket. "Then answer me this: What was she doing freelancing for a filthy cultist like me then? I suppose the fact that she whored out her skills in high-class, high-stakes thievery to us was just a coincidence. And when she got a little greedy over one of my commissions and decided to hold out for more money . . ."

"Hold on," Davidson interjected. "Hold on for a second. Are you implying you had someone murdered? The Mayor's Office does not condone that sort of conflict resolution . . ."

"Just giving Mr. Canderous here some hypothetical food for thought," Faisal said. "Of course we would have *never* harmed her."

As he turned away from Davidson, Faisal winked at me and I snapped. I couldn't help myself. I dove forward, intent on killing him if I could just, God willing, wrap my hands around his neck. He was begging for the eternal dirt nap, and I was more than happy to be the one to give it to him.

The Inspectre had me by the arm and was trying to pull me back, but I didn't take notice until I felt a second set of arms wrap around my waist. Connor had joined our little circle of friends.

"Don't," he whispered in my ear as I struggled to break free. "That's what he wants, kid. Davidson will be witness to it, report it back to Town Hall, and they'll shut us down faster than you'd believe."

"We're just going to let him walk out of here?" I asked. Inspectre Quimbley nodded.

Davidson cleared his throat and I turned my attention to find him looking sternly at me. "Mr. Canderous, I really think us leaving here is the least of your concerns right now. I've got several bones I could start picking with your Department if you'd like. I understand that Mr. Bane here was kidnapped from his place of work, rolled into a carpet no less, and I highly suspect that you had something to do with that. Frankly, I hate to think what charges he might bring against the D.E.A. should you *not* let us walk out that door right now."

Connor and the Inspectre let go of me. I turned silently, feeling utterly helpless. Any heroism I had felt earlier was squashed now, and my ego had practically shriveled up, crawled under a rock, and died. I stood mute.

"Fine," I said, making an unexpected dive for Faisal now that no one was holding on to me. "Go, but not before I give our friend here a hug good-bye!"

Faisal didn't have a chance to react. I pulled my gloves off as I went and then did something I had never done before—I grabbed Faisal's face in both hands and tapped directly into him. I concentrated on my raw emotions the way Connor had taught me to, and flipped into a psychometric vision with one thought on my mind. *Irene*.

The room around me fell away. An image resolved in my mind's eye—Faisal in his office talking to Irene, only in this vision she was alive. In life, she was more radiant than I had ever seen her. She was quoting him a price, a price Faisal would have to pay if she was going to steal the wooden fish for him. Faisal knew it was in a private collection on the Upper West Side, its owner unaware of its value to the Sectarians, but he desperately needed it. I tried to guide Faisal's thoughts in the vision, but they wouldn't tell me why he wanted it so badly.

Time slipped forward in the vision and this time Faisal was on the phone with Irene and they were yelling at each other. Irene had stolen the artifact as asked, but kept repeating over and over into the phone that she'd never sell it to Faisal, now that she knew what he was planning on doing with it. All I had to do was wait long enough and I was sure I'd hear the specifics of what Faisal had been planning . . .

Except I was suddenly torn out of the vision and back into the real world with the sickening sensation of having the wind knocked out of me. I was doubled over kneeling on the floor, clutching my stomach. Faisal stood over me, his fist still clenched from the blow.

"Stay," he panted, "out."

His face looked as drained as I felt, except he was able to stand, while all I could do was flounder on the floor, flopping like a fish. Forcing myself into another person's mind was a violation like no other and it tore at my nerves as if I had run into an electric fence. It wasn't something I ever wanted to repeat. It had weakened me more than psychometry usually did. Maybe tapping into another living creature used up more energy, on top of the pronounced unpleasantness of it all? I didn't know. I started fishing in my pocket for my Life Savers. Faisal and Davidson turned away.

"We'll be in touch," Davidson said as they started for the door.

"I say, so shall we," the Inspectre said, stopping them in their tracks by the door. "It's awfully brave of you to intimidate my young initiate here, old boy, but you'll find me a different story. Rest assured, I will get to the bottom of all this."

Faisal glanced back as he reached for the handle. "The only thing you're bound to reach the bottom of is a bag of chips, old man . . . or the East River."

As soon as he and Davidson walked out, the divisional managers scrambled out of their chairs and followed, leaving just Connor, the Inspectre, and me. Connor helped me up in the immediate and heavy silence that hung in the air as the door closed. None of us dared looked at the other.

"Well, that was certainly different," I said.

"You look like hell, kid," Connor said.

"Good. I *feel* like hell."

"Hope it was worth it. Did you get anything?"

"Most of what he said about Irene *was* true," I said. "She was a thief, like a freelancer to them, but she wasn't holding out for more money. She refused to help him when she found out what the Sectarians were going to use the wooden fish for."

"And what were they planning?" the Inspectre asked.

I shrugged. "I don't know, sir. That's when Faisal went all Cassius Clay on me."

"Well, that's a start," the Inspectre said encouragingly. "That's more than we knew before. And we do have an avenue or two more to explore . . ."

Connor and the Inspectre exchanged that look again. I was too wiped to say anything more. Connor took the empty clipboard and slid it in his satchel.

"I could use a stiff drink after that," Connor continued as he ran his hand through the white streak in his hair. "Shall we?"

"Hrooom!" the Inspectre blasted as he headed for the door. "That may indeed be the best idea I've heard all night, boys. Tonight the drinks are on Other Division."

33

Eccentric Circles was the ancient dive that catered to a clientele of the mysterious and the strange. Naturally, it was a departmental favorite. As usual, the place was packed with secretive folk who wanted little in the way of small talk or questions, but it was a safe bet that just about all of its patrons dabbled in something arcane, other-worldly, or just plain fucked up. We fit in perfectly.

The first few drinks helped rebuild my sugar depletion, but the trade-off was that I was slowly getting drunk. Three rounds into it, I started feeling bad. There was a growing mountain of things I should be dealing with and I was sick of not dealing with things—it had gotten Tamara killed. Also, I had essentially abandoned Jane right after she had helped me bring in Faisal, and now she was somewhere out there alone in the city, unsure of her own fate. Irene had yet to manifest again, and I didn't know if she'd be hostile or not when she did. I attempted to leave at one point to check my messages, but the Inspectre stopped me and confided that our drinking and bonding were every bit departmental job functions as time in the office was. I wasn't sure I believed him, but after my third pint I was willing to give it a shot. Other Division was buying, and after the downward spiral my day had taken, I found it a meager but welcome reward. Three cheers for job-sanctioned drinking!

Connor returned from the bar, pushing his way through the buzzing crowd. He was carrying several pints, which he slammed down on the table. Having matched the Inspectre and me drink for drink, he was in a jovial mood.

"Sorry it took so long," he said. "Some of the guys from Greater and Lesser Arcana were up at the bar and pulled me into the old argument."

"What argument?" I asked, grabbing one of the glasses.

"Historically," Connor said, "drinking is a common pastime among agents. There's a lot of stress on everyone and the biggest in-Department pissing contest is over who suffers the most. Those guys always think that they're the ones."

"They could be right," the Inspectre said. "They do carry the additional burden of answering to Thaddeus Wesker."

I liked hearing the Inspectre be a little cheeky, and knowing Director Wesker as I did, I thought the old man made a pretty convincing argument.

"I don't think they do," Connor said. "Shadower has the largest group of heavy drinkers. I think their world of infiltration, subterfuge, and constant surveillance might take the prize."

I stared at my pint as the foam slowly settled, and I felt the weight of the past day pressing down on me.

"You okay, kid?" Connor asked.

"None of today happened the way I imagined," I said with a sigh. I took a sip, relishing the oaty thickness of the brew.

"Anything particular?" Connor asked.

I sipped at the dark pint again, having no recollection of what I had ordered but happy with it nonetheless. "Everything! The entire evening. The whole epic struggle between good and evil. We've dead-ended on tracking down Cyrus even."

The Inspectre laughed as he took a swig. His mustache was covered with foam as he pulled the pint glass away. "Not quite the theatrics you were expecting, eh?"

"I guess not," I said with a shrug. My moment of triumph had turned into two separate games, one that ended in a stalemate during the questioning of Faisal Bane and the second of departmental politics that generated so much red tape that I was sure I could patch the *Titanic* with it.

Connor shook his head at me, and started speaking with that lecturing attitude he had been taking all too frequently lately. "You can keep your ideology when it comes to the battle between good and evil, kid. The somewhat romantic notion of the clear-cut struggle doesn't exist. None of the fight has ever been black-and-white, or if it has, I sure as hell ain't ever seen it."

He put his pint down, leaned across the table, and gave me a serious look that was undercut by the amount he had been drinking.

"There's more to be seen in the shades of gray," he added.

"Then how the hell do we fight it if we can't make heads or tails of where the line is?" I asked.

The Inspectre looked at me with a mixture of kindness and inebriation. "My boy, you are talking about evil as a concept. You can't fight a concept!"

I slammed my glass down on the table a bit too hard, and its contents sloshed onto my hand. "But I expected *something* to come out of tonight! Conflict, fighting, something, anything!"

"Evil is damned peculiar that way," the Inspectre said.

He picked up a napkin and wiped the foam from his mustache with it. "It takes many forms, as you might well expect, but evil is at its most devious—at its worst, actually—when it makes us lazy, when we cease to take action against it. Evil is slow, crafty, and even slothful at times."

"You speak of it like it's a person, not an idea," I said.

The Inspectre leaned closer. "Isn't it like a person? What makes up the essence of a person but the totality of their actions, Simon? Every person has the chance at any moment to choose their own path, their actions coming down to simple good or bad intent. Conceptually, evil itself is not half as frightening as the actions of those who follow its path."

"That's comforting," I muttered.

Connor grabbed my arm across the table. "Don't discount what the Inspectre has to say, kid. It has a lot of bearing on what you're going through. If what Faisal said is true—that Irene was a freelancing thief for the Sectarians in life—that part of her is gone now. Those actions are dead and the evil gone on with them. It's not a part of who she is anymore, and you have to judge her soul based on the person you've come to know."

It was a blow to find out that someone I held affection for—my dark-haired beauty gone wild—was in league with the Sectarians. I wasn't sure if I was ready to believe it even though I had seen it. Had my powers failed me, distorted what I was seeing? The woman I knew was not an agent of Darkness.

In truth, I was no better than her, was I? I had once been a criminal in the not so far away past, yet I had always felt that at my core I remained a good person. That was long behind me anyway. I had given up those actions, my petty crimes, and turned away from that path.

It made my relationship to Jane seem even more important than ever. She was choosing the right path now, and I wanted to be there for her.

"Fat lot of good all this talk does us," I said. "The only lead we had—the manifest on that wooden fish and who it was going to—is back in Bane's hands. We had it in our possession, and thanks to Davidson, we lost it again."

"Yes," the Inspectre said. "About that . . ."

"We kinda brought you here to get you away from the Department so you could recharge a bit, kid," Connor said. He rummaged around in his satchel and pulled out the clipboard from the interrogation. "Remember this?"

He tossed it across the table and it slid to rest in front of me. I looked at the empty clipboard.

"Yep," I said. "Looks great without the manifest on it, too."

Connor pulled a notebook and a pen from his satchel and slid them over to me.

"I don't know how it looks with the manifest on it," he said. "You tell me."

"Stop tormenting me, all right?" I said. "Just let me drink in peace."

"I'm not tormenting you," Connor said. "I'm telling you to read the clipboard . . . psychometrically."

It was a brilliant idea on his part, and I wondered why I hadn't thought of it. "With my luck, I'll probably get stuck in a mental documentary on the exciting world of clipboard making."

"Just try," Connor said.

I avoided the pen and paper for now. I didn't want it conflicting with anything I might get off the clipboard. I laid my hands on it like it was a Ouija board and envisioned the Inspectre as I had seen him before, placing the copy of the manifest on it. I flipped into the vision and threw my concentration into that exact moment, freeze framing my mind like pressing a pause button. I could actually make out the words on the form. A delivery address.

I felt the pull of hypoglycemia when I came out of the

vision but not as badly as I'd expected. Somehow I had managed not to throw too much of my energy into the reading. Maybe it was the booze . . . I quickly wrote down the address on the piece of paper.

"Why didn't you tell me about this back at the office?" I said.

The Inspectre laughed with all the force that his size held and clapped his arm around me. "What? And have you miss out on the departmental tradition of drowning your sorrows?"

"We've got to move on this," I said as I stumbled my way out from behind the table and attempted to stand. I was drunker than I thought, and I reached for my chair to steady myself, missing it completely. Connor and the Inspectre caught me and eased me back into my seat.

"Haven't you listened to your Inspectre?" Connor said with a laugh. "Evil is lazy. It likes to sleep in, kid. I think this can wait until morning. Besides, we need to strategize."

I wasn't sure if strategize was a euphemism for drink till I couldn't see straight, but with my mood improved, I was willing to give it a try. I had the feeling that the next few days were going to be a bitch, and I hoped I could store up my liquid courage like a camel getting ready to head out into the desert.

34

I found Jane waiting for me at the Lovecraft Café the next morning, and I felt instant relief. The smell of coffee mingled with the sandalwood scent that came off her. After proving herself with last night's kidnapping of her old boss, my wariness of her was worn down, and I could embrace the idea of liking her more than I should. Sitting in the coffee shop in the crushed velvet splendor of a wing chair with her knees curled under her, Jane looked so comfortable, so *right* in my environment. Still, there was the old maxim *Once a cultist, always a cultist* to think about.

Across from Jane was Mrs. Teasley, cat in lap, doing what she did best—swirling her fingers in gentle circles through a pile of soggy coffee grounds. Jane's eyes sparkled like the chandeliers in the Lovecraft's theater as she watched the old seer in action. Jane was in a tight-fitting powder blue T-shirt that read I CAN'T WAIT FOR TOMORROW CUZ I GET BETTER LOOKING EVERDAY.

"Nice shirt," I said, rolling my eyes. Jane looked up, startled.

"I'm shopping at dollar stores now," she said sheepishly. "I take what I can get." Then she surprised me by
standing up and throwing her arms around my neck. Being
this close to my day job, I felt a little awkward and was
about to pull away, but it felt like such a sincere gesture I
stopped myself.

Through the hazy remnants of my hangover, I felt less
than chivalrous for running out to Eccentric Circles with the
Inspectre and Connor under the guise of business/drinking
rather than finding out where she'd got to and protecting
her.

"I'm sorry, Jane," I said. "I didn't mean to leave you in
the lurch like that, especially with Jason Charles headhunt-
ing you . . ."

"Don't worry," she said, surprisingly optimistic. "I survived my first twenty-six years without you to watch over
me. The concern's cute, though." Having gotten out of the
Sectarian Defense League's offices alive had put her in a
good mood. She ruffled my hair like I was her dog.

"Well, sorry anyway," I repeated lamely.

"You *never* have to apologize for being too kind, Simon," she said and hugged me again.

I was on the verge of apologizing for my apology, but
just then Mrs. Teasley cleared her throat. I turned, but as
usual she wasn't even looking up from her table.

"Janey, dearie," she said with a flourish through the wet
coffee grounds.

Janey, dearie? Since when had they become best pals?
While I might still be wary of Jane, it was clear that she
had already gotten Mrs. Teasley's seal of approval in the
Department. "I see you getting kissed by a dark-haired
young man in the near future."

"You mean like this?" she said and grabbed me, once
again taking me by surprise.

Jane wrapped her hands into my hair and kissed me out

of nowhere. Nothing like this had happened since the time I dragged her back to my apartment after finding her in the alley, and this time I took a moment to actually enjoy the non-painkiller-induced oddity of it all. But then I pulled away gently, embarrassed to see that this time Mrs. Teasley was staring up at us, smiling.

"Yes," the old woman said as she plopped her hands deep into the coffee. "*Exactly* like that!"

Her cat swished its bushy gray tail in approval. Or what I imagined was catlike approval anyway.

I turned to Jane and looked at her with as much seriousness as I could. "Jane—" I started, but she cut me off.

"Yes, I *know*," she said. "*You don't tongue kiss with evil.* I get it. You're like a broken record. What's it going to take for you to believe I'm on your side now?"

"There's more to it than that," I said.

I stood there awkwardly, the hiss of the espresso machine filling the silence like a low-flying plane. I wasn't sure what to say to correct the situation, but it was Mrs. Teasley who jumped in with a different awkward matter altogether.

"Not having any of your usual troubles with this one?" she asked me sweetly.

I cocked my head at her.

"Well, Simon," she said. I could see the matter-of-factness in her eyes. She dabbed her fingers in the wet pile on her table. "The coffee grounds never lie. They've told me that your trysting has never met with much success." She looked unexpectedly tired just then. "I suspect it's the same story for all of us with such talents."

She fell silent and scritched at her cat.

I gave what she said a moment to sink in: Was I having my usual trouble with Jane? Maybe Mrs. Teasley was on to something with her question. Perhaps it was time to cut her some slack. She was proving far more observant and asking the right kinds of questions. I *hadn't* picked up a single vibe from Jane or anything I had touched of hers.

I didn't know why she was exempt from my powers. Maybe I was actually learning to control them. If so, I had Connor to thank for that.

As if just the mere thought of Connor was enough to summon him, he appeared from between the curtains that separated the coffeehouse from the movie theater. He stiffened at the sight of Jane sitting with Mrs. Teasley, but I shot him a look that said *Don't start.* I felt a moment of triumph as he softened, even if ever so slightly, and then he focused on me once again.

"How's your head today?" he asked. By the time we had left Eccentric Circles, we were both experiencing trouble walking.

"You don't need to shout!" I said as I grabbed my head and pretended to reel. Any hints of tension seemed to dissipate as he laughed.

"Sorry," he said in a mock whisper. "You want to go over what I've discovered out back or you want me to hit it with you right here?"

I self-consciously put a hand on Jane's shoulder and squeezed it. "Right here is fine. If it's got anything to do with her former employer, I think she needs to be in on it. They're practically hunting her anyway."

"Fine," he said, but his tension from yesterday came back immediately. I knew he wasn't happy to have Jane involved, but I think he also knew I wasn't going to back down this time.

"Lay it on us," I said, and sat down next to Jane.

Connor threw himself on the sofa sitting kitty-corner to us. "You know, having the delivery address for that wooden fish certainly came in handy when I talked to some of the recently living this morning."

"Was it Irene? Did you talk to her?" I asked, tensing at

the thought. At the mention of Irene's name, Connor looked briefly at Jane and sighed before turning back to me.

"I have cases on my plate other than your little . . . client," he said. "Anyway, no, I didn't have contact with Irene. I've been communing with a few other spirits crossing over the past few days and I was able to glean a little other side info from it all."

He reached in his coat and brought out his Palm Pilot.

"Fancy," I said. "We in a new budget cycle or did you get a raise?"

"I wish," he said, looking up. "It's a loaner."

He stylused down the screen until he found what he was looking for. "Here we go! We've been noticing a lot more restless souls than usual processing through the Department lately, and most of them are familiar with the address on the manifest. Thing is, kid, they're all experiencing the same type of memory loss and displacement. They're either like that ghost in the alley or like Irene."

Connor scrolled farther along. I would have bet money he was feeling all Six Degrees of Lieutenant Columbo right now.

"So what's the address for?" I asked

"Hold your damn horses, kid." He slowed his pace, scrolled back a few screens, and stopped. "Ah, here it is! I had to piece it together from what several of the spirits said, but they thought it belonged to a group called the Salvador Breton Foundation although none of them could remember anything clearer than that. That name mean anything to either of you?"

Jane shook her head. Mrs. Teasley did so as well, even though she wasn't really a part of our conversation.

"Don't ask me," she chimed in. "Heavens, it's rare that I ever deal in specifics anyway, isn't it, boys?"

"You, Simon?" Connor asked, ignoring her.

"The only foundations I'm familiar with are antique

houses and artists' trusts, but this group does sound vaguely familiar."

Connor grabbed my by the shoulder and sat me down. "Close your eyes, kid. We're gonna figure this out my way."

"Is this gonna hurt?" I asked, only half joking.

"Only if you make me slap you," he said, and covered my eyes with his right hand cupped over them. "I want you to relax. Now listen to the words again. The Salvador Breton Foundation. I want you to visualize them, twirling and spinning, trying to fit into place like jigsaw pieces . . ."

I felt silly letting myself be guided through a creative visualization, but if it somehow tied into Irene's death and our pursuit of her killers, I would give it my best shot.

"Think about the details so far, kid. The oracle on the subway, Cyrus Mandalay's shop, the Ghostsniffing operation . . ."

"Nothing," I said, moving to push Connor's hand away from my eyes, but he held it there still.

"Now think larger, kid, like the wheels of the cosmos are just churning away, things clicking into place for reasons that are becoming increasingly clear."

"This isn't going to work," I said. "I've tried to fit myself into this puzzle. Why me? Why am I in the midst of it all?"

"You don't need to know why," Connor said, "just accept that you are."

I gave in to Connor's demand, stopped questioning, and gave over to simply thinking free form. I never used to take into account such concepts as "the grand scheme of things." Working in my current environment and having this power, however, it had become more and more obvious that the grander scheme was something I needed to figure into both my own life and my work.

A grand scheme meant some sort of planner and that brought to mind the larger question of theology. Was I experiencing, through my power, a direct relation to God or several gods for that matter? Did the divine even factor into it? Was I predestined to be a lowly thief and con artist all those years to put me on the road toward fighting for Good? My criminal past didn't seem to jibe with living the life of the righteous and good.

My mind was going off on tangents piecing details together, but I needed to get back to basics in my head, and my thoughts drifted to Irene. I contemplated all the points where our lives intersected, the commonality between us, and like a divine spark, it hit me.

"I have it!" I said. The three of them turned to me expectantly. "Well, at least I think I know the significance of the name 'Salvador Breton' anyway."

"Please," said Connor as he poised his stylus over his Palm. "Enlighten us."

"This may not have to do with anything," I said, "but if any of the finer points of this case are connected, I think that foundation has something to do with the Surrealist movement."

Blank stares from all around. Finally, Connor said, "Go on."

"You know I have a somewhat shady background in art history so bear with me for a moment if I get all lecturey. When you have my ability, you take an interest in the art world. But Surrealism wasn't just an art movement; it was a serious way of life for people. To that point, there was a huge blowup, in the thirties I believe, between two of the leading fathers of the movement, Salvador Dalí and André Breton."

"I've heard of Dalí," Jane said. "He did all those creepy stilt-legged animals and melting watches, right? I think I've seen them at MOMA, but I don't think I've ever heard of this André Breton character."

"Not surprising," I said, feeling quite juiced now that I was in my element. "Outside of the Surrealists, few people knew him, but he's a poet who was regarded as the 'pope,' as it were, of the movement. Eventually he kicked Dalí out of the elite inner circle of Surrealists because he was considered too far right-wing, and if you can believe it, even too extreme for them."

"*That is* saying something," Connor said.

"I know," I said, nodding. "There was a huge falling-out in their circle, and it upset Dalí greatly. His pissy response to it all was, 'The only difference between me and the Surrealists is that I am a Surrealist.' The whole movement started as a very literary thing, but eventually their philosophy snowballed until it became more like a religion."

"I'm not sure how all this fits into what's going on here," Connor said. "It sounds like the foundation may take its name from them, but to what end?"

"I'll tell you," I said, excited by my sudden epiphany. "As an artistic movement, the Surrealists are big on the symbology of the fish. In the twentieth century, it's a reoccurring motive in their artwork. It we extend that artistic use of it in form and theme into the lifestyle and not just the art, the fish takes on a totemistic nature. Meaning—"

"There's a power in that wooden fish," Connor finished. "Good work, kid. Of all fish that Cyrus hunted out, this was the one that eluded him, probably the only one he really wanted. Why else would he let all the others go up in smoke?"

I stood up. "I'm not sure, but maybe the F.O.G.ies will have some insight now that we have an idea about the fish. They must have been around when the whole Surrealist movement was going on. I'll ask the Inspectre."

I looked to Jane. "You going to be okay?"

Jane smiled. "As fine as an ex-cultist hiding from a contract killer can be."

"Play nice with the other kids," I said, "and have Connor get you an iced mochaccino. They're to die for."

I ran back toward the movie theater section, leaving

Connor and Jane to themselves. I'd find a way for those two to bond or die trying. I continued farther back to the offices and through the desks and cubicles before hitting the stairs leading up to the Inspectre's office. Once again, I walked in on Argyle Quimbley just as he was settling down behind his desk with a cup of tea. He looked up when he saw me coming through his door and his face fell. He set his cup down.

"Easy, son," he said. "Nothing too loud. The spirit—or should I say spirits—of Eccentric Circles still pervades me . . ."

Trying to contain my excitement, I quietly described what Jane, Connor, and I had been discussing. When I was done, the Inspectre remained silent.

"I thought maybe the Fraternal Order of Goodness might have some insight?"

"Ah, yes," the Inspectre finally said. He seemed to be struggling with what to say. "I will certainly pass that information along to the other F.O.G.ies, but I'm afraid I can't comment on it myself."

I looked at him, puzzled. "Sir . . . ?"

"Until I'm actually in council with the other members of the Fraternal Order, I'm afraid I can't discuss our take on the situation just yet."

"But you're part of the D.E.A.!" I said, confused.

"The Order works outside the confines of the D.E.A.," he said. Why was the Inspectre stonewalling me?

"What's the blasted difference anyway?" I said out of frustration.

"Ah, well, that *is* something I can tell you," the Inspectre said, warming. "Being part of the Department of Extraordinary Affairs is a *job*—a worthwhile and important job, but a job nonetheless. The Fraternal Order, however, is a way of life, reaching far beyond the confines of what this office can do. Unfortunately that means we keep our own counsel. I'm sorry."

The Inspectre seemed sincere and a little sad, but right now I wasn't having it. People I had come to care about were at stake.

"Fine," I said, heading for the door. "I'll be sure to send a funeral wreath to your next meeting if Jane gets killed in the meantime."

"Simon," the Inspectre said, trying to stop me, but I kept walking. There was work to do, people to protect.

35

Apparently, what I said had more of an effect on the Inspectre than I thought. Minutes after I returned to Connor
and Jane, rumors of the Inspectre calling the Fraternal Order into secret session were flying. An hour later, those rumors were confirmed when the office erupted in a flurry of
activity. After using my information as a springboard, the
F.O.G.ies finally agreed to merge their information with
the rest of the Department, and since I had pegged the Salvador Breton Foundation as the group we were looking
for, piecing together a plan became remarkably easy.

We overheard from the Enchancellors that F.O.G. had
even called Director Wesker into their secret session to find
out what he had gathered in his covert ops at the Sectarian
Defense League. Luckily, his cover had proven to still be
safe. Wesker had learned of an upcoming gala cosponsored
by the Sectarian Defense League and the Salvador Breton
Foundation. The one thing that both the D.E.A. and F.O.G.
agreed on was that something big was up, and with Wesker's
help, invitations were secured.

None of us were quite sure what to expect, but the decision was made to crash the gala—the smaller the team, the more unnoticed we would be. The Inspectre hand selected me, Connor, and several members of Shadower team for the mission. Since Jane wasn't part of the D.E.A., she hadn't been invited to our little party crash.

Apparently, the location always changed for these events, but this time the bad guys had done things up in style by obtaining the Metropolitan Museum of Art as their venue. Never slaves to convention, the Surrealists had chosen to host the event as a "Come As Your Favorite Dead Celebrity" affair, and while we waited on line to enter, I immediately noticed several people sporting the curly-cue mustache of Salvador Dalí himself in their not-so-creative costumes.

For my own costume, I had gone with one of my childhood idols. There had been two potential costumes, both from shows I had watched as repeats. First, there was the man who made the *William Tell Overture* popular among generations of kids, the Lone Ranger. The second was a folk hero from the old Mickey Mouse Club serials, none other than Zorro. Figuring they wouldn't let me in with holsters and guns, I opted for Zorro. He had always struck me as more interesting anyway, less of a Goody Two-shoes than Tonto's kemosabe. The fact that I didn't really know how to use the plastic sword hanging from my belt didn't make it seem any less cool to me.

Most importantly, I had opted for the traditional black gloves of the Zorro outfit. Museums were full of potential danger where my powers were concerned, and although I was exhibiting some newfound control over my powers, touching any of these artifacts was likely to overload my powers and cripple my mind in a heartbeat. The energy off these ancient pieces—psychic imprints from people who handled the installations, the actual artists and crafters of the items, millions of tourists—I didn't even want to think what could potentially happen to me.

The man at the door checked my invitation and inspected my plastic sword before handing it back to me and waving us into the museum. There was something about being in a museum at night that was eerily intimidating. The absence of thousands of tourists had settled like a blanket over the Met, the quiet echoes of footfalls drove home its enormity. It reminded me of wandering the halls of my high school while waiting after hours on parent-teacher night. It almost held the same sense of doom, too.

We found the bulk of the crowd gathered near the Temple of Dendur in the Egyptian part of the Sackler Wing. The members of Shadower did what they did best and immediately disappeared into the sea of people. Mood was everything to the Surrealists, it seemed. The room was lit with a haunting blue haze that hung over the temple like a faux Egyptian night sky would have. I thought for sure the event would have been set up where the work of the actual Surrealists was kept, in the Modern Art section of the museum, but the Egyptian wing trumped it in oddness and seemed as surreal a venue for tonight's soirée as any.

"Well, we certainly ain't in Casablanca, kid," Connor said, loving every moment of playing dress up as Humphrey Bogart. The clothes were pretty close to what Connor normally wore, and his impression, as usual, was painful to listen to.

The rest of our team had also come with the entertainment motif in mind. The Inspectre had taken the daring route and come as Isadora Duncan, the deceased dancer who had passed away tragically when one of her trademark scarves got caught in the wheels of her car, snapping her neck. He was dressed in a long white gown with fake blood caked down the front, a womanly wig (made even more ridiculous given his bushy mustache), and a long tattered scarf with a hubcap hanging from the end of it. Even I was impressed at the lengths he had gone to.

We split up and each of us set off in our own direction. For a "Dead Celeb" party, there was a suspicious lack of Elvis Presleys in the crowd, a fact that I blurted out to the nearest passerby. She was a woman in her twenties, possibly pretty but it was hard to tell because she was done up as a traditional Napoleon, complete with his famous hat and her hand tucked firmly into her vest.

"Excuse me, but where's the King?" I asked.

"Wheech keeeng?" she asked with an outrageous French accent. She waved her free hand around the room. "Zere arrr two Hen-ree zee Eighths over zhere, a couple of Tuts up by zee temple . . ."

"No, no," I corrected her. "*The* King. Presley!"

Napoleon laughed and slapped me on the shoulder.

"Silly!" she said. "Zhees is a *dead* celebrity party!"

Before I could further argue the point, she walked off to join a group who had come as the painting *A Sunday Afternoon on the Island of La Grande Jatte*.

A Marilyn Monroe holding a carnival mask on a stick sidled up to me, laughing.

I turned and there was Jane dressed as a most impressive and stunningly attractive Marilyn Monroe, right down to the billowy white dress that had danced over an air grate to the delight of millions of men (and a few women, too, I suspected). Between the wig and the mask, I had hardly recognized her.

"What are you doing here?" I whispered, pulling her close so no one could hear.

"Good to see you, too," she said with just a touch of bitterness. She lowered the mask a tiny bit. "Jesus. You think because your precious Department didn't invite me, I couldn't get in here? I'm not wrapped up in this whole evil thing anymore. I came here looking for answers and to prove myself to you, Connor, and the Inspectre . . . hell, the whole damn Department."

I was going to argue, but I stopped myself. The truth was I was glad she was there. Jane had been getting screwed over by the Sectarians this whole time and she had every right to be here.

She nodded toward the female Napoleon who had just walked away.

"Flirting, are we?"

"Yes," I said, brandishing false pride. "And I *do* think the Emperor of France was quite taken by me."

"Oh really?" she said with a playful squeeze of my arm. "And what makes you think that?"

"Well, I haven't been thrown into exile yet, have I?"

She groaned. "I'm going to check the crowd for any of the hardcore S.D.L. folk. I mean, everyone here is working for Darkness pretty much, but I want to make sure all the key players are present and accounted for. Try not to get exiled or married while I'm gone, okay?"

She raised her mask back to her face. I watched the sway of her dress as she moved off into the crowd, and I pushed any thoughts of desire from my mind as I scoped out the room. There was a curious lack of museum staff present in the wing, but I guessed that the funds from the Sectarian Defense League and the Surrealist Underground combined had bought them a significant blind eye to tonight's proceedings. I felt sick to my stomach. The D.E.A. could have never been able to swing an event like this financially. Hell, we probably couldn't afford anything in the gift shop.

After a quick circuit of the room, I spied Faisal by the temple entrance. He was talking to a group of men and women, every one of them dressed as Dalí. Faisal himself was dressed as Don Corleone (minus the added bulk) with his hair slicked back and colored gray.

I made my way toward them, hoping to catch a part of their conversation if I could. Were this the movies, I would have arrived just in time to hear, *"And now, gentlemen, allow me to reveal my secret plan, my evil scheme that will unleash my wrath upon the world."* Instead, when I got closer, I spent several minutes not understanding a damned thing Faisal was saying. He was doing a dead-on Godfather impression, mumbling his way through the conversation unintelligibly. His cronies nodded and laughed as if they understood every word, but I was pretty sure it was just a lot of ass kissing. I was frustrated, but I had to admit he was really quite good at Brando. Connor would be jealous.

Eventually he excused himself and broke from the pack. As he stepped to the podium before the temple entrance and adjusted the microphone, the room quickly settled down. The costumed crowd made a strange montage awash in azure light and I wished someone would capture it in paint and add it to the museum's collection. I could imagine it selling next to copies of dogs playing poker and velvet Elvises.

As the head of the Sectarians gazed out over the sea of people, he looked pleased.

"Mmmdies nn' gnnndlmn," he started, then stopped. He reached in his mouth, produced two wads of cotton, and dropped them behind the podium. "Ahh, much better!"

A light chuckle rose from the crowd. I looked around for the rest of my team but none of them were in sight. Faisal adjusted the mike once more and continued.

"Ladies, and gentlemen," he repeated, cotton free this time. "I'd like to thank you all for coming out tonight. I realize a lot of you would prefer to be sitting comfortably at home watching ritual sacrifices on HBO9, but I promise you . . . this will all be worth it. Tonight, *la famiglia, I'm gonna make you an offer you can't refuse."*

Another round of laughter for Faisal and another round

of not seeing my people in the crowd for me. Maybe costuming ourselves had been a bad idea. Shadower Division had disappeared entirely, which wasn't a surprise given their specialty. It was just them doing their job well. *Too* well.

I worked my way across the room, careful not to move too fast and thus attract attention. I stole a glance toward the temple. Faisal was clutching the sides of the podium and his face looked solemn as the last of the crowd's laughter died.

"Seriously, my brothers and sisters," he said, "this has been a good year for Evil. We've achieved legitimacy through legislation, the Sectarian Defense League! A voice for the weary, downtrodden cultist to be heard in our government, and all it took was some hard work, the generous funding of our beloved hosts, the Salvador Breton Foundation, and a little spilt blood."

The applause was deafening.

"Well, maybe more than a *little* spilt blood," he continued. "But hey, you can't make an omelet without slitting a few throats. Am I right?"

The crowd erupted in laughter and once again I felt sick to my stomach. These were people who, despite the charm and charisma of their leader, relished the idea of sacrificing life in the name of their cause. Were I not terribly outnumbered, I would have done something stupid like rushing the podium.

"Your funding," Faisal said, "has made it possible to finally have a voice in the real world. No longer will we have to meet in secret, hiding our identities. The Mayor of this Big Rotten Apple—an apple ripe for picking—will soon be under our control."

This time there was an appreciative silence throughout the crowd as the weight of Faisal Bane's words washed over them.

"I know what you're thinking," he continued, tapping his forehead. "How can we advance our cause, our most damnable work, now that we've got our foot in city hall's door? Doesn't overtaking the government cost money? Well, yes, quite frankly, it does. And tonight you will see what the fruits of your financial help, your seed money if you will, have bought us."

Faisal paused for dramatic effect and then grabbed something off the top of the podium. All eyes followed his hand as he slowly raised it overhead. The object was instantly familiar to me. I had seen hundreds of them in the hidden room at the back of Tome, Sweet Tome. In his hand was one of the clay pots—the same kind Tamara's spirit had been delivered to the office in.

"Ghostsniffing," he said. There were triumph and pleasure in his voice. "This is our financial future, my friends. This is ectoplasmic gold, pure and simple. Sales from this substance will ensure not only our legislative future, but a substantial piece of the profit pie for all of you. For all of you investors, we've set up a mobile processing plant in the next room so you can see how the process works, and what your money's going toward. There's no sample like a fresh sample, and if you're daring enough to try one—in moderation, of course—you'll find they pack a certain . . . surreal . . . extra punch thanks to the very heightening power of your fish totem."

Applause exploded and I watched as Faisal smugly rode the wave of it. After the crowd had gone on for far too long, he gestured for them to settle down. "My fellow workers . . . let's just call a spade a spade, shall we? My *minions* are busy in the next wing preparing those choice samples, but before we get to that, I'd like to bring up your leader, the head of the Salvador Breton Foundation himself. Here's the man who made all of this possible. Get on up here!"

The costume party was the perfect way to keep most of the Sectarians and members of the Surrealist Underground anonymous. But even dressed as a swashbuckling pirate— maybe Captain Jack Sparrow—there was no mistaking the imposing figure of Cyrus Mandalay as he swaggered on stage toward the podium. He shook Faisal's hand vigorously.

"Great to see so many of you in attendance," he boomed out. "I've spoken to a lot of you individually tonight. I heard a lot of your concerns, and I know you haven't seen me around much since the 'incident' at my bookstore, but rest assured things are going according to schedule. Thank you, Sectarian Defense League, for that. I'm sure I speak for us all when I say we're looking forward more than ever to a lasting partnership with our Sectarian brethren . . . and sistren."

Sistren? I couldn't listen to any more of this. Just seeing him made me livid. Somewhere in the crowd I knew Connor was beside himself with rage, probably being restrained by some of the Shadower guys. I needed to get out of this room, and I also needed to confirm the worst of my fears. There were only two exits from the room, and I pressed through the crowd toward the nearest one. I had a feeling that out of the "choice samples" of spirits that Faisal had picked for the demonstration, I knew at least one personally. Irene's disappearance had been because she had felt something pulling at her spirit. I could only imagine it had been because of some arcane dog whistle tuned to a frequency that drew spirits into this trap. It was only a gut feeling that she was here, but it was a strong, nasty one. God help me if I was too late to do anything to help her or any of the other spirits selected for tonight's Ghostsniffing demo.

The kicking of much ass could wait until I found out if Irene was here. If I was right, they were trying to force her into a clay containment jar, and it would destroy her like it had Tamara. I couldn't let that happen again. I wondered for a second where Jane was, but I wasn't too worried for her. She could hold her own, what with having been all evil and stuff. It was Irene that was most likely helpless if she had become caught up in these machinations. And as Zorro always knew, when in doubt, go for the girl in distress.

36

There were several S.D.L. guards throughout the room, and although they looked silly in their hokey Renaissance Faire garb, I took no chances, cutting a wide arc around them heading toward one of the doors.

As I closed on the doorway, the familiar scent of patchouli and cloves grew stronger in my nostrils. It was the same type of smell as the one Connor used to bind spirits with. My heart leapt in my chest, and by the time I actually stepped through the doorway itself, the air was sick with the smell. It was like being caught in a Dead Head's hair.

The room was mostly dark and its architecture was generic in style but classed up by Greek columns on either side of the door. In the half-light of the after-hours world, I could just make out the banners of heraldry hanging high overhead in tribute to the Met's permanent collection of arms and armor. Four mounted knights were on display as the centerpiece of the room, and the walls were lined with glass cases full of ancient armor, pole arms, lances, swords, and shields. Just thinking about the accumulated history surrounding me made my body quiver.

I was sure the majesty of such a display would have had even more of an impact on me if I wasn't distracted by what was out of place in the room. At the far end, past the horsemen, several workers were operating a bulky mechanical contraption of some sort. It looked liked a cross between a Rube Goldberg device and one of those astronaut training gyroscopes, except this one had several wooden circles that twisted and turned around each other.

Closer to me were dozens of quasicorporeal forms. They floated listlessly within a smoky haze rising out of an arrangement of evenly placed casks along the west wall. I crept toward the haze quietly and luckily went unnoticed by the men at the far end of the room. Score one for dressing all in black!

As I approached the casks, their purpose became readily apparent as the familiar smell of patchouli hit my nose— the casks were full of the same substance Connor had given me a vial of at the Odessa, the very material he used to contain and control ghosts. The fumes rising from them kept the spirits floating above them contained. The cloud twisted and swirled, and I caught glimpses of the translucent bodies contained within. A constant low chatter of weakened pleas of tortured souls tore at my ears. It didn't take long to pick out the distinctive lilt of Irene's voice as I listened carefully, but it broke my heart to hear it. I had been hoping beyond hope, and against my instincts, that Irene wouldn't be mixed up in this.

I stepped closer and suddenly Irene's voice rushed at me with all the force of a subway car. Out of the mist, her face formed in the smoke. It looked drawn and pained, like that of someone who hadn't slept for ages. Tears rolled down my face and soaked into the fabric of the Zorro mask.

"Irene?" I whispered. "Can you hear me?"

The form of her face nodded in response.

"How did you know it was me . . . ?" I asked. The lighting was poor, I was shrouded in black, and what little showed of my face was shadowed by the traditional Zorro hat.

Her image grew more distinct in the mist and somehow she forced a smile.

"I would always know you, Simon," she said, and there was kindness in her voice. The barest definition of fingers formed and the wisps of smoke brushed at my face. "You have an energy, an aura that's wholly yours. Everyone does."

This was a much different Irene than the one that had attacked me in my apartment. Connor wasn't kidding when he told me about the rampant mood swings a degrading spirit could go through.

I chanced another peek toward the far end of the room. My eyes had finally adjusted to the light, and I could see the technicians unpacking hundreds of tiny clay jars next to the contraption. I could only assume it was a processing machine. Just then I noticed the wooden fish sat on top of it in a giant frame. I don't know how I had missed it before—the damn thing was pulsing with a dull magical glow. There was no question that the totemic power of the Surrealist fish fueled the device. Faisal had made clear that it was the fish that gave the Ghostsniffing ectoplasm its extra kick. In the center of the processing contraption, a ghostly figure strained against invisible bonds that held him spread out across one of the wooden circles. I turned back to Irene.

"We can save our reunion for later," I whispered. "I've got to get you out of here now. You're on the menu tonight."

I had to free her, free *all* of them.

I set about the task of putting the lids back on the casks

beneath the swirl of spirits. As I moved down the row, I could hear Irene keening softly over the general wailing of the other spirits in the cloud.

"I'm sorry, Simon," she said, her voice rising. "You must think me a monster after our last encounter. I simply don't know what came over me."

"It's all right," I said. "Shh. You're just becoming more and more emotional due to your condition. It's not your fault. Connor explained it all to me. Now it all makes sense. You and the sudden rise of ghosts turning up with memory loss . . . all of you were being mystically rounded up before you could cross over, *harvested* to be used in their sick twisted scheme. Some of you were apparently harder for them to rein in than they planned for."

I was having trouble with the casks. The second of the wooden lids wouldn't fit. I stripped my gloves off for maximum dexterity and wrestled it into place. Eventually it slid in, but only after I thumped softly on the top. I looked at the workers, but there was no sign of reaction from the far end of the room.

"When Faisal's mediums captured me," Irene said, "they told me what sort of person I had been in life. All the horrible things I had done . . ."

"None of that matters anymore, Irene. None of it. Who you were before, that's all gone now, burned away. The spirit I first met, the person you are now, that's the best part of you. That's the part that needs to keep in control if I'm going to help you."

Phantom hands caressed me as some of the smoke cleared and the restless spirits broke free of their confinement. I tried not to flinch at their cold touch, but they were making it hard to focus on what I was doing. Once again, my hair was in mortal danger, but I didn't even care. There were at least ten more casks to cover, and it was only a matter of time until I was discovered. I wasn't sure if I'd have to take care of them all, but suddenly I had bigger problems to think about.

The answer was only one more cask away. As I fit the next lid into place, the booming chuckle of Cyrus Mandalay sounded from behind me.

"Avast, matey," he said in a mock pirate voice. He cautiously stepped toward me. "I should have expected some heroics tonight. Leave a roomful of ghostly victims, and just wait for someone to try something. The question is, Zorro, who are you and how did you get in?"

"Well, *Cyrus*," I said. I swung around with a flourish of my cape. "You can find out who I am if you can unmask me."

I pulled the sword from my belt and hoped to heaven that the darkness helped it appear less plastic.

"I see you know me by name," he said and smiled. Even in the half-light of the room, I could see the gleam of his sharklike teeth. That was a sight I didn't miss from before he had gone into hiding. Back then I had actually thought he was a decent, albeit intimidating, guy. He had even had that section of the store for kids! It flashed in my head momentarily and it hit me. One image had always stood out in that children's mural—the Daliesque turtle wizard melting a clock with his wand, an obvious sign of his allegiance to any Surrealist Undergrounders seeking him out—and I hadn't put it together until now . . .

There was no time to beat myself up for making the connection so late in the game. I had pulled my sword and now Cyrus pulled a sword of his own, a cutlass, and I could tell by the metallic sound of it unsheathing that it was real.

"Be careful," Irene whispered from behind me. I stepped forward in the hopes of keeping Cyrus the pirate away from the few casks I had sealed and he took the opportunity to rush me. He was unnaturally fast, and with one stroke he cleaved my pathetic plastic sword in half. I threw the remaining stump at him ineffectually, and in return Cyrus kicked me square in the chest. I felt something crack inside as I propelled backward, but I barely had time to register it. I spun myself to see where I was falling and braced for the impact.

Smashing through glass in the movies always looked effortless. The hero would run at it, leap in the air, and the glass would shatter on impact into a million pieces as he flew through it. I, however, stumbled forward toward an unavoidable collision with one of the museum's display cases. When I hit it, I felt another crunch inside my chest before the glass itself finally gave way.

I crumpled to the side of the case to avoid as much contact as I could. I was less concerned about getting lacerations, more about making contact with any of the antiques inside it. I was duly concerned for both their safety and the safety of my mind should anything so historically powerful come into contact with me.

The sound of the museum's alarm kicked in. I rolled over just in time to see Cyrus standing directly over me with his sword in readiness, and I had only a split second to make a decision. I could either sit there preparing for the cool sensation of air hitting the center of my brain as Cyrus cleaved me in two, or I could risk contact with one of the artifacts to defend myself.

I chose the latter, even though my brain and blood sugar would hate me in the morning. It was the one option that would allow me to even *have* a next morning. I reached blindly into the broken case to my right, and grabbed the first object my hand landed on. Fortune was on my side, it seemed, and I was thankful as I pulled a large shield from it. That was the best object I could hope for, really, but its historical significance was too powerful and my mind slipped into a series of visions as I struggled to control my powers.

It was 1934 and a handsome philanthropist was handing the shield over to the museum's collection. The shield was shaped like a reverse tear-drop and was damascened in gold and silver. The director of antiquities thanked him for his most generous contribution. Time bent further into the shield's past.

Now it was the fifteen hundreds, and I was a man working diligently on the shield between fits of coughing. He was slowly dying from the large quantities of silver dust than had accumulated in his lungs over his short lifetime. The images carved into this shield would be the culmination of his life's work. Time bent again.

This time I was another man, a French king no less, suiting up to do battle against the threat across the English Channel. I felt pure awe when I realized I was Henry the Second, and watched as he strapped the shield to his arm as the final touch. I felt the weight of his people, of his kingdom, and felt his conviction that with God on his side, Henry would prove victorious.

Disoriented, but feeling somehow strengthened by my last psychometric episode, I came out of the vision and found myself curled under the shield, weary from the transference of power, but somehow fending off Cyrus's wild swings. Chaos had broken out all around us. Much of the crowd from the temple area had pushed their way into the makeshift Ghostsniffing production area, and I could see members of Shadower making a dash for the casks while Connor barked instructions at them. The Inspectre, despite being surrounded, was holding his own and swinging the hubcap on the end of his scarf in a circle around him in an effort to keep the crowd at bay. We were seriously outnumbered. In my weakened condition, the shield I was turtled under was getting heavier and heavier.

I scrabbled to my knees and then my feet. I was quite

impressed that I had continued to keep Cyrus at bay even though he had gone wild-eyed in pirate mode.

"Simon!" Jane cried. I turned my head toward the sound of her voice. She had ditched the mask and was struggling with a mob of her own at the far end of the room. She pushed them away and balled one of her hands inside the other and swung with all her might at one of the display cases, causing glass to fly everywhere. I winced in sympathy pains as she did it. I was surprised how quickly everything had escalated and even more surprised when I saw Jane grab a sword from the case and toss it toward me. I moved the shield firmly between me and Cyrus and grabbed for the sword, no longer caring what touching it might do. I had just been Henry the Second, for God's sake. What did I have to fear?

I caught the sword at the same time Cyrus rushed me. His sizable frame drove me back across the floor, but before anything else could happen, I shifted into another psychometric vision. Already I could tell things were different—having been King for even a brief moment and bearing the weight of an entire kingdom on my shoulders somehow made the drain on my powers feel like less of a burden.

In my vision it was the sixteen hundreds. There were letters on a desk before me, all addressed to a Juan Martinez, renowned for his working of Toledo steel. All of Spain, all of Europe, demanded his craftsmanship. But he had merely been the blade master on this sword.

Time slipped and I became the sword's hilt maker, a crafter of bronze-gilt, paste jewels, and pearls. None of these visions felt particularly helpful, although the kingly burden I had felt seconds earlier lingered. Before I could give it another thought, I was pushed forward through time once again.

The next vision came on stronger, and was far more recent. I was one of the night watchmen for this wing of the museum. The case Jane had just smashed was whole in the vision, and the watchman took a quick peek around to make sure no one was looking before removing the sword. He had handled this sword before. He moonlighted as a stage actor. But most importantly, he had stage combat training. As him, my limbs were full of the physical memory of that training. I realized as I came out of the vision that my body had retained it.

When I came out of the vision, I felt strangely, miserably drained. Then I noticed warmth running down the right side of my chest. Cyrus's cutlass was digging against the exposed whiteness of my ribs. Maybe it was the shock of seeing that, or the adrenaline, or simply the fact that I might die, but the watchman's training kicked in. I pushed Cyrus's blade away using an effortless enveloping technique and then assumed a defensive posture.

A thought occurred to me. I didn't have to fight Cyrus to beat him. I was only fighting to keep him from killing me, and with that in mind, I started to back my way toward Jane. I chanced a look toward the swirl of spirits and was relieved to see that they were dispersing in greater numbers as Shadower team finished covering the last of the casks.

"Hello, Marilyn," I said to Jane. Her Monroe dress was a mess from the struggle and covered in spattered blood, but it still worked on her.

"*Hola, Señor Zorro,*" she said. The costumed fray was still in full swing around us.

I pushed away one of the many Dalís attacking her while keeping Cyrus at bay, but more baddies pressed into the room. They didn't seem deterred by the continuing sound of the alarm going off. It would be only a matter of time before we were overtaken. Despite our valiant efforts, things had gotten more extraordinary than the Department of Extraordinary Affairs was capable of handling.

Several cultists had finally disarmed the Inspectre and were shoving him around the room. Some of the Shadowers were still holding their own, and Connor was standing in the remaining swirls of mist, shouting. The deceased and crossing over were his domain, and I imagined he was working overtime in that department right now. Despite Connor's efforts, though, three cultists grabbed him and wrestled him to the ground.

Feeling helpless, hopeless, I did my best to parry the incoming attacks. With one arm I countered every strike and with the other I kept Jane safely behind the shield. It was really only a matter of time before Cyrus wore me down, though. If it weren't for the adrenaline rush, my body would have already collapsed from the energy expenditure of the visions, not to mention my blood loss. With the repeated blows of Cyrus's sword, however, that rush was waning and the odds seemed insurmountable. Jane was doing her best to help hold our shield in place, but she looked exhausted.

My eyes caught a whirl of activity from within the spirits. They rose in a column above the casks, breaking free from the last of their restraints. They now rose wraithlike, swirling high overhead.

The sound of exploding glass rang out as every display case in the room shattered simultaneously, shards of glass flying everywhere. Luckily, the shield kept most of it from harming us. Then I watched in awe as the contents of every case sprang to life.

The released spirits began manifesting themselves in the same way Irene had done when she turned my bedroom into a whirlwind of emotional destruction. Full suits of armor broke free of their supports inside the cases. Each of them lurched off menacingly into the crowd, grabbing for the nearest weapon they could, and started singling out the Surrealists and cultists.

Even with all the danger around me, and my exposed ribs, I couldn't help but be amused. Suits of armor lurched past me, some with the perkiest codpieces I had ever seen, intent on clearing a path through our enemies with mace, sword, or pole arm in hand.

Most majestic were the four horsemen in the center of the room, whose steeds charged off into the costumed crowd. Their lances knocked Dalí after Dalí aside and I felt sudden hope that there might be a chance for us to get out of this alive after all.

One of the swirling spirits spun with breakneck speed around Cyrus like an ethereal twister and suddenly shot itself straight into him. He convulsed as a spasm wracked his whole body, and he struggled for control.

"Simon," Cyrus said, but it was Irene's voice. She sounded strained as she fought him in the effort for possession. "Go . . . while I can control him."

I could tell Cyrus was struggling hard, fighting her for control of his own body, but it was no use. Irene was full of fury from her captivity and was far stronger than him . . . for now. She forced his hand to open and the cutlass clattered harmlessly to the ground.

"Go," she said, "and take her with you."

"Irene," I said, feeling a bit uncomfortable staring into Cyrus's eyes as I spoke to her. "This is Jane. She's . . . well . . ."

"I know," Irene said, softening Cyrus's face. "You don't need to explain. I can see her energy . . . intertwined with yours. It's okay. Life is for the living."

The softness disappeared from Cyrus's face, and as he began to win control of his body once more, he bent to retrieve his cutlass, his face contorted with the effort. Before he could grab ahold of it, Irene forced his body back to a standing position.

"Go!" she screamed. "He's pushing me out."

"Connor and I will find you after this, I swear."

Irene smiled, but Cyrus's sharklike teeth made it unpleasant.

"I don't think you'll need to," she said. "Something feels terribly right about all this." Irene turned to face Jane. "Take care of him. He's a terrible amount of trouble."

"You're telling me," Jane said with a faint laugh. Then with absolute sincerity, she said, "Thank you. I'll try."

Cyrus came to the surface again and I watched his arm as he balled up his fist. His face strained with the effort, the veins in his neck popping out like suspension cables.

"If you're going to do anything," Irene said weakly, "now would be the time . . ."

As Irene gave one final push for control over him, Cyrus's face went slack and his arms dropped lifelessly to his side. Seizing the moment Irene had provided for us, Jane and I swung the shield, rushing forward. The shield smacked into Cyrus's head, and it rang out like a gong. He fell to the floor. Jane stared at him for a second, and then we stepped over him, heading for the south end of the room. I think Jane gave him a parting kick on the way out, but I didn't look back to see where. I don't think I wanted to know.

Jane pulled ahead and took the lead. It wasn't hard to do, considering I was holding my ribs as I limped after her, while also trying to remove the shield from my arm. She effectively dodged the galloping horsemen and avoided the retreating cultists, who were clearly spooked by the sudden turn of events. I found myself crying and laughing at the same time. These folks wanted Surrealism; they certainly were getting it. I doubt anyone had expected a night like this.

Connor frantically waved us over and we plowed through the crowd, using the shield to reach him. Two of the suits of armor had responded to his commands like he was the sorcerer's apprentice, and stretched between their arms were Faisal "Don Corleone" Bane himself.

"Well, kid," Connor shouted over the noise. "What should we do with him?"

I looked around the room. So much of what was happening tonight rested on this madman's machinations. He was responsible for Irene and Tamara's deaths, and who knew how many more? Even Jane had been at his mercy. Given that we had yet to put a stop to Faisal's corporate headhunter, she still was. Though I had never killed anyone, in that moment I wanted to. Knowing the Department frowned on such behavior, I restrained myself, and yet I had to do something.

"We've got to get out of here," I yelled over the sound of combat. "There's no way all these evil folk are escaping scot-free with all the alarms going off, but there's a chance that we'll be able to."

Connor nodded. His hair whipped around wildly and his Bogart trench coat fluttered out behind him like a cape. "That still doesn't tell me what we should do with Faisal," he said. "I think the spirits want to rip him limb from limb, and I'm having a hard time coming up with reasons for them not to."

"All we have to do is detain him until the authorities arrive," I said.

"But you said it yourself, kid . . . we can't stick around for that. We've got to get out of here."

Faisal smiled as he hung midair between the two horsemen. Once we left, he surely would break free. There had to be a better way to keep the smug bastard in line.

"Jane?" I said as I turned. I presented the hilt of the sword to her. "Would you care to do the honors?"

She smiled nervously, reluctant.

"I don't want you to *kill* him!" I said. "We just need

to . . . detain him. I thought you might want a little pay-back. Don't forget, he *is* trying to have you killed."

"Might I remind you," she said, "that he tried to kill you as well? That's what he sent me after you for."

"Then I suggest we do it together. Drastic times call for, you know—"

"Do *something*!" Connor shouted.

Faisal looked pained from the tugging and pulling, and I took a dark pleasure in that. Jane and I hefted the sword together and thrust it forward through his shoulder, driving him against the wall. We forced the sword as deep as we could into the wall, nearly to the hilt, and Faisal was effectively pinned. He hissed in pain, but he definitely looked incapable of moving.

"Let's see our little butterfly wriggle free from this specimen board before the authorities get here now," I said.

"Guess you don't believe in handcuffs, huh?" Jane said.

"Don't really carry them," I said. "Most of the things I deal with can't be held by them anyway."

Connor clapped me on the shoulder. "Let's get the hell out of Dodge, kid," he said. "I'll go back and grab the In-spectre. You two kids make a break for it."

I surveyed the destruction as Jane and I started off, and the art enthusiast in me winced at the thought of all the property damage. The Museum would certainly have its work cut out for it, including the task of figuring out just what the hell the now toppled Ghostsniffing machine was. We passed it on our way out, and I was happy to see all the clay pots were empty or broken.

The wooden fish stuck out of the debris, the glow of its power fading from it, and I stretched down painfully to grab it. I tucked it under my shirt, careful not to put it against the open hole along my ribs. It was a bit of thiev-ery, but it didn't belong to the museum's collection any-way, and they would have enough to deal with tomorrow.

I gave one final look back as Jane and I raced out of the hall, but there was no trace of Irene anywhere now. Jane squeezed my hand sympathetically. The sound of rapidly approaching footsteps from the other direction snapped me out of it, and we headed off to find quiet and escape, arm in arm, thanks to the support of our army of the dead.

37

Most of Other Division was crowded around the television at the front of the Lovecraft Café. Jane was at my side, her hand openly around my shoulder, but I didn't mind it in public anymore. People could think what they wanted to think. Bruises, slings, and more than one set of crutches were signs that last night had not been a dream—that and the wooden fish now hanging on the wall of my apartment.

David Davidson was on the screen live from Town Hall, where he was looking nervous for the first time since I had known him. In the past he had been able to disavow much of the paranormal and occult activities in the city. But there was no way he could cover up the events of last night. You simply couldn't get away with destroying the Metropolitan Museum of Art. You especially didn't get away with it considering we had left an occultist ringleader pinned to the wall. Davidson floundered for words when the questions started coming. Claiming an emergency had come up he ran away from the podium, and I knew we had rattled him.

Godfrey Candella from the Gauntlet patted me on the

shoulder before asking me to stop by later so he could transcribe my oral account of what happened at the Met for their archives. On the television screen, the news cut away from the empty podium.

"Satisfied?" Jane said in my ear. I leaned into her.

"I guess so," I said. "Was kinda hoping the Mayor might fire him, though."

"Good heavens, no!" the Inspectre chimed in next to us. "And make us break in a new liaison? Why would you want that? You know how devilishly long it would take to get someone new jumping through the right hoops? We've got Davidson right where we want him now."

"I'd hardly call what Davidson does for us jumping through the hoops, sir."

He patted me on the shoulder and leaned closer. "He's no saint, m'boy, *that* is for sure. But he's certainly better than many men we could be dealing with."

Connor walked over to us. He was carrying iced coffees, one for himself and one as a peace offering for Jane, who seemed to have taken up his addiction.

"The Devil you know is better than the Devil you don't, kid," he said, "and Davidson's no devil. Not by a long shot. Imp, maybe, but he ain't no devil."

"Well," I said, "he sure as hell went out of his way to help Faisal and Cyrus and everyone in their big, bad clubhouse of evil there."

The Inspectre chuckled. The assembled crowd slowly split up and returned to the offices. There was a jovial camaraderie among the departments today, and even the White Stripes were high-fiving people who weren't part of their hair club for men.

"Enough, Simon, enough!" the Inspectre said. "You're not due to study *Cynicism and the Road to Ruin* until the Other Division conference in mid-December. I'm sure they'll expect one corker of a speech about last night out of you. I believe they've also nominated you for Most Battered in the Line of Duty, my boy."

I wasn't sure if he was being serious or not, but I laughed anyway. I instantly regretted it as I felt the tape binding my ribs pull tight. Jane's arm tightened around my shoulder in response.

"I'm okay," I said with all the believability of a politician. "I'm sure the internal bleeding will be just fine."

"No time for jokes," Jane said. "With your sense of humor, you're bound to puncture a lung before you realize it. Let's get you back to work. Up and at 'em. I can help you through the theater at the very least."

Though Jane still wasn't allowed back in the Department proper, there was serious talk about pushing through the paperwork because of the way she had proven herself in the line of duty. But the wheels of red tape were ever slow. I wasn't holding my breath that it would be anytime soon.

"I can take him from there," Connor said in the spirit of cooperation as he gathered our drinks.

When we neared Mrs. Teasley at the back of the café, her cat almost fell off the table as it leaned over to rub its head against my hand.

"I don't mean to alarm you two," the old seer said with her hands knuckle deep in coffee grounds, "but you should expect a visitation in the near future."

I scritched the cat under his chin and he purred happily. "Another one of your psychic readings, eh, Mrs. T?"

"No," she said. "Silly boy. It's just that Director Wesker seems to be waiting behind you."

Jane slowly turned us around, and sure enough, Wesker was standing there, his eyes hidden behind sunglasses as usual. I tensed immediately, never quite sure what his whole role in the Sectarian fiasco had been.

"Are either of you two familiar with a Mr. Jason Charles?" Wesker said smugly.

Just the mention of the corporate headhunter was enough to put me on guard and Jane followed my lead. She took her arm from around me in search of something to defend herself with. I wobbled tentatively as she abandoned me, but managed to stagger toward the counter for support. I braced one hand against it. Sadly, my bat was sitting on my desk out back so I scooped up the nearest object I could to defend myself—a pair of muffin tongs. Not terribly intimidating, mind you, but I had worked with worse during Unorthodox Fighting Techniques.

"Easy now, easy!" Wesker said, raising both hands high in the air. "So you are familiar with the name. Good. I thought you might be."

"Is he here?" I said, snapping the tongs as viciously as I could. The Inspectre and Connor stopped by the curtained doorway of the theater.

"No. And in case you forgot, Simon, I *work* here," Wesker said, then sneered at Jane. "Unlike some people. Now put down those tongs before you damage someone's muffin."

The Inspectre moved defensively toward Jane. He looked Wesker up and down. "What the devil is he talking about, dear?"

"Jason Charles was the man the Sectarians assigned to kill me, sir," Jane said, speaking up, "but he was about as effective at that as he was being a boyfriend. His solution to most of life's problems was to shoot them, especially for money. Hell, I bet when he found out I was the target, he offered to cap me for free."

Wesker stepped forward like he was going to push his way past all of us, but I clicked my tongs, *SNIKT SNIKT SNIKT*, and his eyes darted to me nervously.

"Jane," I said calmly. "This might not be the best time to squabble over who was shooting who and for how much . . ."

"Nobody is shooting anybody anymore!" Wesker said, exasperated. "Thanks to the deal I cut, naturally."

Jane and I shared a WTF glance.

"What deal?" I asked.

"The point I was trying to make if you would have shut up for a minute," Wesker said, "is that Mr. Charles will no longer be bothering you. Either of you."

"Oh," I said, hopping toward Wesker. "Just like that?"

"The Sectarians were footing the bill on you two, and since they seem to be under some hard times financially, they really couldn't afford his services any longer."

"So do I get a rebate for what he did to Tamara?" I spat out. "Is Jane supposed to just sit around waiting for the Sectarians to scrape up enough cash so they can pay Jason Charles to kill her at a later date!?"

Wesker shook his head and then I saw something I had never witnessed before—his face softened. "The contract's off, Jane. It's been bought out. You're free and clear. You don't have to worry about him coming after you anymore. No more looking over your shoulder, at least for him anyway."

Jane and I stood there, not truly believing what we had just heard.

"It's that simple?" I said. "Someone pays the corporate headhunter off and that's it? Who'd be that generous? Inspectre?"

The Inspectre shook his head. "I'm sorry, Simon, but I'm afraid our budget simply wouldn't allow for that."

"Well," interrupted Wesker with a smug smile, "that's only partly true. If you shared the expense with, say, another director, you could help ensure this young woman's safety. A small price to pay, wouldn't you say?"

"*You* bought out the contract on Jane?" I asked. This seemed all too kindly a gesture for Thaddeus Wesker. Sure, he had helped us escape the Sectarians when we were at risk, but that had been to selfishly maintain his own cover. I couldn't see his angle on helping us. "What's the catch?"

Wesker sighed and adjusted his mirrored frames. "My God, don't you ever tire with the questions?"

"The boy is merely cautious," the Inspectre said. "How does the saying go? 'He is most free from danger, who, even when safe, is on his guard.' "

"Nice one," Connor chimed in.

" 'Curiosity killed the cat,' " Wesker offered flatly. "I can offer up pithy sayings, too. The point, Simon, is this. For all that your Other Division has to offer you, just remember that there are shades of gray out there as well as your black-and-white world of good and evil. *I* embrace the Darkness to better serve the light. You'd do best to remember that. What you see as my coldness and ambition, I see as a practicality in an unending war with the forces of Darkness. But I do know a good soul when I see one, Simon, and I could hardly let Jane be lost to that fool now, could I? Besides, from what I heard said about her at the Sectarian Defense League, she could prove a useful asset to Greater and Lesser Arcana."

"You want to offer me a job?" Jane said. She seemed excited at the prospect, but it was still a position answering to Wesker. She looked to me warily.

For once, I was dumbstruck. As much as I found his motives suspect, at least Jane might be able to keep an eye on him if she was in his Greater & Lesser Arcana Division. I nodded subtly.

"I . . . I don't know what to say."

The Inspectre haroomed loudly. "You say thank you."

"Yes," Wesker said. "You say thank you. *To me*. Even if it kills you . . . and I know it will."

Wesker had taken Jane into his division because he'd heard what a professional she was, but I knew it couldn't hurt that he knew I would hate the idea. And now he was forcing me to thank him. Whatever his motives, though, I did have him to thank for Jane's safety from Jason Charles. It stung that Wesker was the one who had remedied the situation and not me, but that was probably his point in doing it in the first place.

I looked Wesker in the eye. "Thank you," I said.

Wesker looked like the cat that had eaten the canary.

Jane put her arm around me, spun me around, and started hobbling me back toward the office.

"One last thing," Wesker called out. All tolerance was gone from his voice this time. "If I hear about a lick of this getting out to the other staffers, I may have to put a contract out on you myself. I *do* have a reputation for evil to uphold around here, and frankly, I find fear a much better motivator for my division than your Inspectre's precious nurturing technique."

Inspectre Quimbley snorted in response.

I stared blankly back at Wesker. "You're kidding, right?"

"Wouldn't you like to know?" he said with the Grinchiest of grins and stormed off toward the offices before I could get another word in.

38

Jane went off after Wesker to Greater & Lesser Arcana to fill out a mountain of paperwork. The day wore on, and I filled out my own mountain until it was time to head home. It was marvelous to experience my first night of downtime in what felt like forever. As I settled into the chaotic comfort of my apartment all alone, I took stock of the past few days. I had grown to care for and respect almost all the people I worked with more than I thought possible, and I had even fallen for a cultist. In light of recent events, the apartment seemed eerily quiet. I was surprised to find that now that I did have some time alone, I wasn't really comfortable with it.

The answering machine I had been ignoring since Tamara's death stared at me, its little red light flickering like a spastic heart monitor. I was almost positive that most of the messages had been Tamara's usual tirades. I reached for the play button then thought better of it and simply unplugged the phone. What good would listening to them do now? Torturing myself for the inaction that had gotten her killed?

Enough was enough. I had a pretty good idea where I fell short now, how my powers had driven a wedge between myself and true happiness, but something had changed in me. I needed a fresh start for a fresh life. God, I felt like a Dr. Phil show just for thinking like that and I threw up in my mouth a little.

In celebration of my shift in attitude, I unpacked the remaining contents of my broken and overturned crates from the headhunter's break-in while wondering what role Jane might play in my life. Jane gave me hope that people *could* change for the better, and that reassured me about the change I had made. She had been at my side in the museum that fateful night. I had been in the mind of Henry the Second of France.

Looking back now, being in the mind of Henry the Second of France had probably helped effect a shift in my psychometric power. Recalling the mental weight of his responsibility for his country seemed to let me tap into reserves of calm and self-control, and made the problems I usually had seem bearable. Ever since that night, I had found it easier to control my psychometry. It was amazing what a brief stint as a historical legend did to give you a new sense of perspective.

Still, even with someone as wonderful as Jane in my life, Irene's passing and Tamara's destruction had left me with several mental truckloads of thoughts. Faith, for instance, had become the foremost nag of them all. Dealing with the extraordinary was hard enough without bringing up the question of a God or, possibly, gods. So much of what I had seen in my formative time with the Department just didn't jibe with any one particular branch of theology.

One particular thought weighed heavily on my mind: Every case I worked was its own brand of jigsaw puzzle.

Some of those puzzles had only a hundred pieces and were recommended for ages seven to ten, while others were designed for a full-time staff of Mensa brainiacs. I suspected that I fell to the lower end of that scale, but one of the biggest pieces of Irene's puzzle was why she was lingering around after death in the first place. Why hadn't she passed on?

Last night at the museum, Irene had spoke of how right everything felt in doing one final self-sacrificing deed that ultimately saved Jane and me. She was content that once the battle was over, she would be free. She seemed sure of it. If that was true, then she had remained earthbound for just such a specific reason—to be there for me. And if I was going to believe that she had been put there for a reason, then that spoke of predestination, didn't it? If I was a cog in someone's great machine, it put a considerable deal of pressure on me. Was I doing the right things—the Good things—in the face of some scheme far grander? It was both terrifying and glorious a thought at the same time. Of course, Irene may simply have been earthbound by some scientific coincidence involving energy, math, and Schrödinger's Cat.

That was the tricky part. Which was it? I wasn't sure, but I knew one thing: Some force was at work. Be it of logical explanation or a more spiritual one, I could feel its presence in my life nonetheless.

Thinking about all of it made my brain hurt. The greater mystery of what lies beyond life eluded me. Hopefully they would cover that in one of the pamphlets or a seminar.

Until then, I would drive myself mad if I thought about the totality of it all. The only way to comfort myself over it was to remember Irene's words in passing. Life was, as she said, for the living.

I tidied up my living room, stuffing the last of the packing materials into one of the empty boxes, and I started to visualize how all the unwrapped bits of furniture and antiques would fit into my setup. I was ever the puzzle solver. The place was finally starting to feel like a home. Only one piece remained missing.

I pulled out my cell and dialed Jane.

EPILOGUE

This offer is contingent upon successful completion of any and/or all pending casework/enchantments/removal of curses and please bear in mind that while we are affiliated with the Department of Extraordinary Affairs, we predate their organization by several centuries. You must also make arrangements for filling out our questionnaire in the presence of your sponsor. We, therefore, encourage an early response. Please set aside the appropriate five-hour block for this at your discretion.

Enclosed please find an enrollment contract, along with instructions for accepting our offer and completing the enrollment process. On behalf of the entire Fraternal Order of Goodness, we extend a warm welcome and best wishes for your success. We appreciate your interest in fighting evil and staying alive, and we hope you share our enthusiasm about your future with F.O.G.

THE ULTIMATE IN FANTASY!

From magical tales of distant worlds to stories of those with abilities beyond the ordinary, Ace and Roc have everything you need to stretch your imagination to its limits.

Marion Zimmer Bradley/Diana L. Paxson

Guy Gavriel Kay

Dennis L. McKiernan

Patricia A. McKillip

Robin McKinley

Sharon Shinn

Katherine Kurtz

Barb and J. C. Hendee

Elizabeth Bear

T. A. Barron

Brian Jacques

Robert Asprin

penguin.com

M12G1107

ABOUT THE AUTHOR

ANTON STROUT was born in the Berkshire Hills mere miles from writing heavyweights Nathaniel Hawthorne and Herman Melville. He currently lives in historic Jackson Heights, New York (where nothing paranormal ever really happens, he assures you).

His short story "The Lady in Red" can be found in the DAW Books anthology *Pandora's Closet*, and a tie-in story to *Dead to Me* entitled "The Fourteenth Virtue" can be found in DAW's *The Dimension Next Door* in July 2008.

He is the cocreator of the faux folk musical *Sneezin' Jeff & Blue Raccoon: The Loose Gravel Tour*, winner of the Best Storytelling Award at the first annual New York International Fringe Festival.

In his scant spare time, he is an always writer, sometimes actor, sometimes musician, occasional RPGer, and the world's most casual and controller-smashing video gamer. He now works in the exciting world of publishing, and yes, it is as glamorous as it sounds.

He is currently hard at work on the next book featuring Simon Canderous and can be found lurking the darkened hallways of www.antonstrout.com.